A BOUND

THE
NIGHT
MARKET

JESIKAH SUNDIN

FOREST TALES
PUBLISHING
Dystopian Fantasy and Faerie Tales

Forest Tales Publishing, LLC
PO Box 84
Monroe, WA 98272
foresttalespublishing@gmail.com

Cover design by MoorBooks Design
Character Potraits by Chicklen.doodle
Tree art scene by Alexandra Curte
Animal sketches + interior cover art by Lauren Richelieu
Interior design by Forest Tales Publishing, LLC

To Foxes...

You may be thieves and tricksters in folklore and mythology, but you'll always be Robin Hood to me.

And...

To males of all species who dance to attract a mate.

Ladies and Gents ...

... welcome to the Night Market

Irish Pronunciations

Filena — fill-en-nuh

Cian — key-ahn

Rhylen — Rye-lyn

Glenna — Glen-uh

Lonan — Low-nun

Bryok — Bree-yock

Fiachna — Fee-yah-ck-nah

Fáiléanna — fail-een-ah

Cillian — kill-ee-ahn

Fáidhbhean — foy-van (Irish: wise woman / seer)

Cailleach — kaul-yawk (Irish: witch / crone)

Torc Triath — tork tree-at (Irish: boar of Arthurian Legend)

Áine — Awn-ya (Irish: Anne, the faerie of love and light)

A stór — ah-store (Irish: "treasure")

A stór mo chroí — ah-store muh-cree (Irish: "treasure of my heart")

Mo shíorghrá — muh-heer-grawh (Irish: "my eternal love")

FOR MORE DETAILS on the magic systems (being Bound by Ravens, Fae Marked, and more) as well as what each name means in ancient Gaelic and Irish, skip to the back of the book to THE GLOSSARY OF ALL THINGS.

Seren

PRIMRY GREE

STELLAR
WIND
CASINO

CRESCENT
STREET
MARKET

BEGGAR'S
HOLE

FERRY
DOCK

FERRY

TRAIN

RIVER BELESAMA

Kingdom of Carran

FENNEL
MARSH

MINERAL
SPRING

FIDDLING
DUCK

DEN
MERROW

WITCH'S
COTTAGE

RIVER BELESAMA

edona Woo

TO THE EASTERN CITIES

KS

THE
AUTUMN
MARKET

THE
WILD
HUNT

Chapter One

FILENA MERRICK

A dangling bead fell into my eye. That shiny black bead *always* fell into my eye. By now, I should take this fated adornment fail as an omen.

Filena, the ancestors would say, *you will only see in part unless you change the view.*

The ancestors were full of ancient wisdom. Especially about headdresses. Their knowledge of costuming was, thankfully, infinite.

And, thus, with all the grace and patience I rarely bothered to possess, I pressed my lips into an irritated line and anger-pinned that ridiculous faceted piece of glass back into the fiery Underworld realms of my auburn, manufactured curls.

Ah. I could now *see* my future with both eyes, the ones stinging from all the smoke. I was destined to spend the night in a small, overheated, red- and purple-striped tent for strangers to seek answers on love, riches, and health. All the while, I plastered a mysterious, flirty smile on my sweaty face as I slowly baked to death in layers and layers of thinning, stained satins, threadbare lace, and with corset boning breathing its final death rattle by poking free from the frayed seams to dig into my side.

I rubbed at the raven bond mark on my wrist—marking me as the property of the family who owned me in West Tribe.

This night was the same future as last night's. The night before last. Last month when the full moon rose. All nights and all phases of the moon since I was fourteen, when the Caravan fae who owned me discovered my family secret.

My nan was a seer.

My mam was a seer too.

All the women in my family gained the Sight soon after their first moon cycles. It was a magic we couldn't control or master, I was told by a respected village green witch a few years back. And, so far, that has proved true.

Barry, my red fox familiar, lifted his head. "It's all your fault, darlin'," I teased with a wrinkle of my nose. He chuffed a disgruntled sigh, then curled away from me with a tail flick. "Muffin Moo," I cooed in my placating way. "You know I adore you, my fluffy red rain cloud. And you adore me." Barry yawned and closed his eyes in dismissal.

The monster.

I suppose all the sweets will be mine tonight. Poor Barry. How he will pine and I will laugh. Affectionately, of course.

It was true, though. Had he not arrived at my wagon's doorstep, my wee secret would have remained just that . . . a secret. But the gods gifted us Sighted women a faerie animal when our rare mortal magic manifested, one to complement our personality and to guard and amplify our gift.

With Barry, no faerie could coerce me or use my magic against me or others. But he was a grumpy sort who rivaled my insatiable craving for desserts. I wasn't sure exactly how he understood me and I him. But we always knew what the other was thinking and feeling.

My life could be infinitely worse, though.

Far, far worse. A true nightmare.

There was a reason my brother, Cian, and I ran away from home at ten and thirteen to join the Raven Folk Travelers—the Kingdom of Carran's Caravan fae.

Our foster family believed, to this day, that we were orphans. We still have never told them the truth, or our real names—Cillian and Fáiléanna MacCullough. Instead, we go by the alternate names our mam told us to use.

By law, the fae couldn't own a mortal who was owned by another mortal—enforceable now that mortals were the larger population in Carran. And, thus, if I were not owned by the fae, I would be owned by my oldest male kin. Backwood mortal villages were not kind to women either.

And to give me back to *him*? . . . I would rather die at my own hands.

If Cian and I remained on the move, it would be harder for our da to find me. Our da and the old, graying-haired man I was sold to in marriage at the age of ten and contractually required to go to at fifteen when he could legally collect me—per the terms of the arrangement.

Child brides were common among the more secluded villages of Caledona Wood. But no one, regardless of sex or gender, should be sold into marriage. And certainly not children. But Da was a cruel man given to drunken rages and only cared about coin for more drink and tavern women.

Our mam was forced into marriage with our da at fifteen—sold to him by her own da. She did her best to protect us. And, after *seeing* a vision, packed my and my brother's belongings with a small ration of food and sent us from our rotting cottage into the early morning darkness to find safety.

And here I was, now the tender age of twenty, owned by Raven Folk and forced to tell fortunes for profit with a never-can-please-but-face-squishably-adorable fox at my side. There were times I could retch before opening night, though, in fear that my da or that disgusting pig of a man he sold me to would walk into my tent.

I flopped back into my chair and lifted the hundreds of layers of petticoats up past my black stockinged knees, grateful the black tablecloth hid my indecency.

Where was my fan?

I twisted a button on my low-cut bodice, a terrible, nervous habit of mine. This week alone, I lost two painted rose stamped brass buttons. Two buttons I couldn't afford to replace. Sweat dripped down my back and I squirmed in my seat. Stars above, I was ready to send the remaining buttons flying across the tent in a mad dash to strip. What I would give to unlace the corset cinched tight around my waist and ribs right now too. Perhaps the ancestors could send a cool breeze my way and snuff out the pot belly stove while they were at it.

As soon as the thought ended, the tent flap opened and the night rushed in. I could moan. But I had a customer. I quickly righted my position and shoved my skirts back to my booted ankles while biting back a smile. The market didn't open for another candlemark.

This customer, however, a regular of mine, held a girthy slice of cake in his hands. Spice cake topped with fresh autumn berries.

I never refused cake. Or berries.

Or handsome, dangerous lads with boyish smiles sweeter than honeyed icing.

And he . . . he was the most beautiful faerie I had ever seen in all my years of drifting from village to village.

"You seek your fortune, Traveler?"

"Aye." He removed his tattered top hat and walked in.

I pretended to ready my oracle cards but, beneath lowered lashes, I couldn't drink him in fast enough. I never could, even after ten years on the road growing up together. He grew finer with age too.

A frayed black and gray pinstriped vest fit snug against his tall, muscled frame. The sleeves of his old linen undershirt were clasped just below his bicep with garters, the cuffs rolled up to his elbows, revealing a tattooed pattern of knots and swirls on his forearms. Long, silky black hair was braided in small rows above a pointy ear pierced with three gold hoops near the top and a black stud in his lobe. The kind of black that reflected a blue cast at certain angles. The uncorded strands and the tiny braids—braids woven with beads and charms, one boasting a silver feather pendant—fell past his shoulder blades in soft waves.

Dark purple eyes, lined with ash, flicked to the pot belly stove. A slight scowl appeared between his black brows.

"I have no coin, *fáidhbhean*."

Fáidhbhean—Raven Folk for seer, wise woman.

The same greeting he spoke each time we played this game.

He added extra emphasis on the last part of the word as a tease. *Fáidhbhean* was pronounced "foy van," a constant source of confusion for mainlanders from the eastern cities who heard "fae ban." Everything confused that money-heavy lot of mortals, though. No, I wasn't banned by the fae—clearly.

I'll take your coin now, thank you very much.

I sighed.

My "customer's" otherworldly gaze drifted back to me at the sound of my wistful tolerance and I was spellbound. Those eyes were the color of crushed elderberries limned in candlelight—deliciously rich and endless.

Berries were my weakness.

Barry quirked open an eye with a persevering sigh. He knew I meant berries but wanted to make sure I knew he was still ignoring me by not ignoring me.

"I can offer you a slice of cake infused with a bite of happiness. My sister's magic."

"Sit, pet." I gestured to the chair and reached for my divination cards. I adored this game we played before each opening night to ease my anxiety and had to work extra hard to remain in character when he set the cake before me with a devilish wink.

Barry eyed the cake with piquing interest and I mock-glared at him.

"I also offer you this, *fáidhbhean*." He slid an intricately carved button across the table. A rose stamp design coated in black, chipping paint.

My mouth parted. "Where did you find this?"

A pleased grin curved his lips. "The *fáidhbhean* is missing a button, aye?"

Our eyes locked. For a moment, I forgot the mechanics of breathing. "Two cards, pet. One for the slice of cake and another for the button."

"I will trade you a secret for a third card."

I leaned in.

Gossip was my other weakness. The fae couldn't resist a well-bargained secret or tale, either.

"I will trade," I said. This, too, was part of our game. My diet consisted of sweets and delectable morsels of dark humor and scandal.

That knowing grin widened. "Rhylen Lonan, have you heard of him?"

"The Raven Folk?"

"The very lad."

I shook my head. "Alas, I have not had the misfortune or pleasure, Traveler."

"Shame." His lips twisted in barely suppressed humor. "A fine looker, he is."

That he was, silver moons above . . .

"Your secret, pet?"

He paused a dramatic beat. "Rhylen's best friend was found passed out in a large, bustled gown, a fake mustache glued to his upper lip, rouge kiss marks on his face and neck, and"—he leaned in close and dropped his voice to a whisper—"cuddling a raccoon he called George."

Barry groaned a low, grimacing growl. He didn't like raccoons. Or most forest animals. They were, apparently, too uncivilized for his refined taste in company.

I broke from character and burst into a howling, unladylike cackle. "And Rhylen allowed his best friend to drink himself into a wardrobe change?"

"And domesticate a wild animal through the power of cuddling."

A loud snort left me and I clapped a hand over my mouth. My brother, Cian, was an eejit. The lad could never resist a revel.

I attempted to school my face while shuffling my mam's divination cards, ones she had packed into my runaway sack. But I could barely suppress my humor and sputtered another laugh while asking, "Three cards, pet. What answer do you seek?"

Rhylen slouched back into the chair and crossed his arms over his chest. "Does my mate love me back?"

The soft sound of his melodic voice sent warm shivers of pleasure down my arms despite the flushing heat. It was the same question he asked me at each Night Market opening—for at least three years. And the answer writhed and anguished in every besotted beat of my heart.

Slowly, melodramatically, I slipped the first card from the top of my oracle deck and flipped it over before him.

Fearn, the ogham rune for Alder. The tree that easily combusted into flame and wept blood for sap. The Tree of Ravens, strength, and shields.

My brows creased.

Chapter Two

FILENA MERRICK

Fire hisses and crackles in a light sprinkling of rain. People scream for help and weep in horrified grief. Wagons and tents blaze to smoldering ash. Rhylen frantically looks around, shouting a name. I can't make out the name. But creeping dread pools in my belly. I don't know if the fire is real or metaphorical. But I know the flames of passion dance right beside the loss of possession. To love will cost him—and greatly. A loss that will forge him into a solid shield of protection, like the Raven God, Bran. Rhylen will also find his mate, soon, and he will burn for her, spill blood for her. Not only burn but set fire to anyone or anything that comes between them.

I snapped out of the vision. It was only a couple of seconds. Even so, I had mastered the art of appearing present. The vision gripped me, though. I almost forgot his question. The one he had asked for a couple of years now.

Does my mate love me back?

"She will tolerate your collection of tiny acorn hats"—he had no such thing—"and loathe your obsession with feather boas made from the plucked wings of your enemies." He arched a single, black brow. "But she will love the way you belch in Bryok's annoying, princely face."

"Honestly, who doesn't love belching in Bryok's face?"

The chieftain's son was an entitled arse.

"Next question?"

"Does she think me handsome?"

I pulled the next card from the deck and flipped it over.

Úr, the heather ogham rune.

> Firelight kisses the skin and corded lines of Rhylen's tattooed bare chest and arms. His long hair is pulled up into an ornate fashion and decorated with black feathers. He wears a skirted wrap around his trim waist, showing off the muscles of his thighs and calves. Ash lines his eyes and paints mark his body. He had performed the Fire Dance at the Autumn Night Market, the mating ritual. Desire softens his mouth and eyes and flushes his cheeks as he approaches a girl. Her. His mate. The one he danced for. I can't see the girl's face but I am peering through her eyes and can feel her earth-shattering longings. Rhylen walks her up against a tree and kisses her with more heat than the towering bonfire behind them.

> "I am desperately in love with you," he whispers in her ear. "True Mate."

My heart cracked and nausea churned in my gut. Heather was the soft bed where lovers laid, the symbol for a happy, long-lasting partnership in marriage . . . and never-ending passion. Blossomed sprigs were commonly placed into bridal flower crowns and bouquets and tucked beneath pillows.

Pulling a heather oracle card could also signify a romance that would overcome dark shadows.

True Mate.

Rhylen watched me carefully, his forehead slightly wrinkled.

Barry was studying me too. He was acutely attuned to my emotions. But his yellow eyes slid to the cake in the next blink, the traitor.

Forcing an air of mystery to my practiced smile, I casually tossed out, "She thinks you're passable. Unfortunately, she is hideous. More so at night when she shifts into a feral swine. Though, you are smitten with her cloven hooves and named them Will, Bill, Swill, and Phill."

Rhylen grinned. "Feral swine?"

"Yes, a descendant of Torc Triath."

He appreciatively laughed at my riddled insult. Walked right into that one, he did.

All fae enjoyed riddles. It was their second language. Ravens especially enjoyed riddles woven into nonsensical tales of monstrous animals, like Torc Triath, the Boar King. A terrible, angry prince who was turned into a wild pig with the misfortune of having a comb and a pair of scissors nestled between his ears. Overhearing this tale, a giant hired hunters across the three kingdoms to bring back the magical artifacts so he could groom his beard—a wedding gift to his daughter.

What every lass desired on her most romantical of days, a properly groomed male in her life.

Torc Triath was still celebrated every Samhain in The Wild Hunt. A wedding game, hosted by the Caravan fae, where non-Raven fae males could pay to hunt for a woman in Caledona Wood from the slaves the tribes no longer wanted—to fae mark as their slave or bride.

Grooms, as the joke went, who lacked the grooming skills

Torc Triath

necessary to properly woo a bride. According to Raven Folk males, that was, who were known throughout the three kingdoms for their dark, meticulously groomed masculine beauty and primal courting magic.

It was a profitable mockery. One I would playfully continue to capitalize on at Rhylen's expense. Because of course she'd think him handsome—and he knew it.

"A feral swine, buuuut . . ." I dramatically dragged out the word, "you're keen on her girls." I winked suggestively at him. "Though they *are* hairy. Not a picky lad, are you?"

Rhylen winked back. "Hairy breasts make me weak in the knees, they do."

"Why is that?"

"Extra soft."

"Aye, they are," I replied with a serious, knowing nod of my head. "Alas, she will *boar* you."

Barry peered at me as if he were considering a proper shunning despite Rhylen's grin.

"It was funny," I hissed at Barry.

I swore the fox rolled his eyes at me.

Grabbing the plate, I cut into the cake and took a long, ecstasy-infused, moaning bite. Betrayal glittered in Barry's eyes. I cackled. Happiness magic, indeed. But dear moonless clouds, this cake was delicious. I popped a juicy berry into my mouth and returned to my oracle cards.

"Last card, pet," I said, trying—and failing—to slip back into character.

The other two questions I knew were sincere. Much to my bruised heart, the cards and visions had revealed hundreds of scenarios to me of Rhylen in love, Rhylen kissing, Rhylen happy. To-night, however, was the first time Fate had shown me he would meet his True Mate and while at the Autumn Night Market.

Clearing my throat, I asked, "What is the final answer you seek?"

"Will we have children?"

He always asked this question too, but another question brewed in his heart. One he never spoke aloud. But the gods heard his longings. I dreaded flipping this card, afraid of what I might *see* next.

Straif, the ogham rune for Blackthorn.

I sucked in a quiet breath.

No.

The faerie tree of pain, wounds, thorn-wrought damage, death, and . . . fate.

> *Rhylen is running through a dark wood. Trees and brush whip by him. Sweat beads on his face. He is truly stricken and appears on the verge of retching. Once more, he shouts a name. Once more, I can't make out what name he shouts. Wings appear at his back and he leaps into the air, furiously soaring through the trees instead of running. Then he spots her. His mate. The perspective shifts to her view. Rhylen lands and possessively pulls her into his arms. She is shaking with terror and sobbing. Not even two heartbeats later, he sinks his small canines into her neck and marks her as his.*

> *"You are mine," he growls. "No one will harm you*

again. No one will ever separate us. I promise you this, mo shíorghrá."

I swallowed back the bile burning my throat.

Mo shíorghrá, my eternal love.

True Mate.

"Your children will be hairy, too," I forced out.

What happened to his mate?

Who harmed her?

How were they separated?

"A thick, wiry coat of fur from head to toe," I continued. "They are fated to roam the darkest parts of Caledona Wood while singing bawdy pub songs. Any who hears them immediately drops dead. Villagers fear the Hairy Squeals of Death."

Rhylen threw his head back and barked a laugh so loud, Barry jumped to his feet. From a songbird line of Raven Folk, everything about Rhylen was musical too. His voice, the way he moved . . . his laugh.

"Filena!" The tent flap opened and Glenna, my best friend and Rhylen's younger sister, hurried in. Then abruptly halted. "Shoo!" she said to her brother. "I have very important business to discuss with the *fáidhbhean*."

Rhylen eased from the chair with a lazy stretch. Walking around the small table between us, he offered Barry a stale chunk of bread, who snatched it greedily.

"If you need anything, *a stór* . . ."

A stór, my treasure.

An endearment between friends. Ravens liked to collect pretty objects. Friends were a treasure they collected. But how I wished it meant more than friendship. How I wished we could be more than friends and that he loved me the way I loved him. But he was not mine to have. He was destined for another—his True Mate.

Regardless, Travelers were forbidden from marrying outside of their kind. To marry a mortal slave was one of the worst offenses they could commit outside of murder—and resulted in banishment. From *all* tribes. The Traveler bloodlines must be pure for their magic to remain. Without magic, their Night Markets would cease to exist.

"Aye, I'll call for you if a village gent gets too handsy."

He playfully tugged on a strand of my hair, as he often did, a boyish smile curving his lips. Then he angled past his sister, sticking out his tongue. She stuck hers out too and they both softly laughed. At the tent opening, he peered over his shoulder and blindly pointed toward the pot belly stove. "Don't let anyone put another log on. If you pass out—"

"You'll peck someone's eyes out."

Rhylen placed his top hat back on, then tipped his head. "Aye, lass." Then he was gone.

Glenna practically hopped over to me, a conspiratorial grin on her face. Until her nearly-black eyes rested on the cake. "Only *one* bite?" She lifted her chin with a huff. "Unforgiveable."

I picked up the cake and made a show of comically shoving a giant bite into my mouth. While chewing, making sure the chunks of mushed up cake were visible—like a proper lady—I said, "To preserve our sisterhood and atone for my sins." Then I moaned, because dark skies, this cake. "Witchcraft," I murmured around another large bite.

She heaved a dramatic sigh. "I suppose I can forgive you."

"Darlin', no you don't," I said with a flutter of my hand. "You only want to tell me about a village boy you kissed."

"Lena," she admonished and took the plate from me before I finished. I reached for the cake and she moved it out of the way. "*Lena*. He was a dream."

"Then you broke his heart." I grabbed the plate from her with a triumphant grunt.

"Then I broke his heart."

I started laughing. "The poor male who finally tames your cruel, dark ways."

"Tames me? Ha!" Glenna tilted her head and eyed my headdress. Fidgeting with that errant black bead, she said, "The lad who dares try to tame me will not only have a broken heart but broken bones too."

I flicked a crumb from the plate at her with a wrinkled nose. "So he was a dream . . ."

"Aye, he was." She narrowed her eyes at me for wasting a precious crumb of her cake. "A tall, mountainside of muscle and—"

"Blond hair."

"The blond ones are my favorite," she sighed.

"And blue eyes."

"Bluer than the sky."

"Dumb enough to trust a Raven Folk temptress," I added, tipping my fork at her.

"Temptress," she cooed in approval.

"Did you make this one cry?"

Glenna grimaced. "That boy was ridiculous."

"You told him he kissed like a rabid horse who ate an entire field of fermenting garlic!"

"He really didn't, though." She flashed a delighted grin. "I would have taken him to my bed if he hadn't confessed his undying love after five minutes of kissing. Those desperate, clingy types . . ." she shuddered, as if being elf struck was a mortal choice.

"So you broke his heart."

"I broke his heart."

I lowered my plate to Barry. The cake was gone but, as a gesture of my unending affection, I left him one berry and a couple of crumbs. I could see the rude gesture in his yellow eyes, making me quietly cackle again. But he licked the plate clean.

"What did this lad do?" I asked while straightening.

"Nothing." Glenna slinked toward the exit and gave a little finger wave over her shoulder. "Until dawn, darlin'."

"Behave!" I hollered after her disappearing form. A command that was about as useless as telling fire not to burn.

Fire.

My thoughts ran backward to earlier and paused. The oracle cards were still face up from Rhylen's "fake" reading.

I pulled cards almost every night, for friends, tribe Folk, and market customers. Being at the whim of the gods, I couldn't force a vision or insight into a reading. Rarely did I have a true vision for another. And *never* did I *see* my own future, my one limitation as a seer. Most of the time, I cycled through generic stories I had crafted over the years. Pretend fates and card readings, not that I let West Tribe know this.

But Rhylen . . . his soul called to mine and stirred my magic—always.

The gods, apparently, enjoyed playing with my bruised heart.

Sliding the side of my hand across the table, I collected the cards and quickly shuffled the deck. The Night Market would open any minute and I would face desperate, hopeful souls until the rising sun.

Pining souls as desperate as me.

Chapter Three

RHYLEN LONAN

I stuck my hands into my pockets and angled through the crowds toward Gran's wagon, my top hat tipped low on my forehead. My pulse was alive, thrumming heavily in my chest, my skin too tight and my breath too loose.

Hairy Squeals of Death.

Besotted with my fake wife's cloven hooves and hairy breasts.

Obsessed with feather boas.

Where did she come up with these scenarios? Every week, a new Night Market. Every week, new horrifically humorous card readings. Every week, I stared into the beautiful slate gray eyes of my mate and asked if she would love me back.

And she *was* my mate.

The other half of magic.

I had known since we were fifteen and thirteen that the gods had chosen Filena Merrick for me. The bond between True Mates had violently pierced my soul and left me aching. A cruelty. Raven Folk were masters of illusion—tricksters. But the illusion that she could ever be mine tormented me night and day.

I was forbidden from marrying outside of my kind. The punishment was grave. Even if I weren't my gran's and sister's caregiver, I wouldn't ask Filena to endure the consequences with me.

So, I courted her under the guise of friendship and seized every opportunity to gift her pretty treasures I found and desserts infused with a bite of happiness.

For three years, I had visited her on opening night to ease her nerves after I found her retching into a bucket minutes before the night bells tolled. Cake eased the nausea, it seemed. But not her anxious habit with buttons.

A soft smile flitted across my lips. The lass went through more buttons than any female I knew. Fairly certain more than any dressmaker in one year too. It's why I collected them in secret. I had a jar of buttons hidden away just for Filena.

I paused to let a mortal mother and child cross the pathway.

Market visitors were thickening around the oddity booths, as they typically did. Bizarre faerie creatures, preserved in jars, lined display shelves. Some with two heads or five eyes that still blinked or twins conjoined at the stomach. Women stifled gasps at the grotesque and men moved in closer to study what was nothing more than broken pottery illusioned into curiosities.

The old mortal toothbrush glamoured into a witch's skunk ornament was my favorite. A trespassing mortal, the story went, who tried to steal a slice of bread and butter from an old crone. The skunk's eyes were wide with terror. But it was the long, curly blonde hair and peasant dress it still wore that always lifted a corner of my mouth.

"Two drops in your tea, pet," a potion maker hawked to an

older woman. "The tears of kelpies are rare and potent. Two drops will cure your dropsy."

I snorted under my breath. Kelpies and sirens didn't have tears.

Mortals believed anything for a quick cure.

I dipped my head at another tribe Folk as I ambled by. A felloe, called felly for short, just like me—the lowest class of our kind, named after the outer part of a wagon wheel the spokes fit into. Spokes were the symbol of people in a Caravan tribe. And, in a wheel, they perpetually stood over us fellys, who were just one step away from eating dirt on the road.

We were required to be submissive to the entire tribe, save our own rank. Fellys were given last choice in food, the lowest wages, and wore old hand-me-downs. Neither were we permitted to look our betters in the eyes, unless challenging them. Above fellys were the middle-rank. They were afforded the best selection of food and wages outside of govs, our tribe's royalty and elders.

Our chieftain, and his son Bryok were top-notch arseholes.

And Bryok found it amusing to push me around until I reacted just so he could posture. Fellys rarely owned indentures, like my family. And it pissed him off that we owned Filena Merrick, a money maker for the tribe with her seer gifts. A slave my clan had granted permission to earn a meager income.

Closing my eyes, I drew in a steadying breath, then focused on my surroundings instead of that tail feather.

The familiar bright, illuminated colors of tents, booths, and wagons, many that were converted into shops, dotted the woods around me. Oil lanterns, in a variety of shapes and sizes, hung from tree branches wherever the eye wandered. The illusion of glowing flowers bloomed along a selection of trees in curling vines. Some wagons also decorated their awning fronts with illusioned exotic flowers and lunar moths.

Mortal and fae locals, from two nearby villages, streamed into the Night Market to experience this very magic—the kind that beguiled the eyes as well as the senses. And there was plenty to see. West Tribe's market was fairly large, the size of a small village. We were the largest and wealthiest of the four tribes.

I cut through a pocket of unmarried girls by the Truth Telling Tree, a large, ancient oak we wove in handfasting ribbons and anointed with lover's magic. Ribbons also hung from the branches to dance in the breeze—a rainbow of colors for Beltane and simple white for Samhain. The girls watched me, hiding giggles behind their hands and whispering into one another's ears.

"Traveler," a girl called out after me.

I paused and looked back; my brow arched. "Aye, pet?"

"Show us your wings." The girls erupted into giggles again.

My lips curled into a flirty smile, as was ordered of us single males. Part of a Traveler's charm. Part of the market's attraction. Mortal girls were easily elf struck and we unattached males were prettier than our counterparts, with braids, threads, and beads in our hair, ash around our eyes, rings on our fingers and piercings up our ears. I didn't want to attract a wife, or a dalliance with a village girl, but I was expected to play the part.

"And ruin you for any other male?" I teased.

Widening my smile, I turned and resumed my walk.

A breeze skipped by and I tilted my ear up toward the night. The lanterns above me swayed and chimes the tribe had strategically placed into the trees tinkled. A storm was rolling in from the east. Already the wind was picking up. My body was buzzing too. But the incoming rain wasn't the only reason why electricity crackled along my skin.

Tonight, Filena's dark auburn tresses rippled down her back to her waist in soft curls. She wore my favorite headdress too. Two large black peonies, one that covered each ear, held together by a band that stretched across her head. A strand of black beads trailed across her forehead from peony to peony.

And her dress . . . my mouth went dry and blood rushed to my groin just thinking about the black satin bodice molded to her shapely waist and the corset beneath that pushed up the soft swells of her breasts. Necklaces of varying lengths draped down her creamy skin. That smooth, porcelain teacup complexion, sprinkled in tiny freckles, was offset even more by the black bobbin lace sleeves hugging her arms. The same lace that swooped and dipped down her black and purple skirts.

As a finishing touch, gold was painted across the lids of her gray eyes, along the lash line, and rouge darkened her lips to wine. I ached to drink from those lips. Longed to grow drunk on her kisses.

Stars help me, I was an absolute fool for the lass—

A child bumped into me and grabbed my arm, shoving me from my thoughts. Blue eyes peered up in a plea for help, his skin pale in the way of the wild fae water spirits. The boy's gaze darted behind him and back to me in a full panic.

"Morenn," I said quietly to the wild fae orphan my tribe owned. "What's wrong, lad—"

A hand grabbed the boy by his shirt and yanked him out of my hold. "Does this slave belong to you, tramp?"

Morenn covered the raven bond mark on his wrist and bunched his shoulders.

I turned to a mortal man of middle years in a sharp three-piece suit. Anger flushed his face and I cocked my head to return the challenge, though my smile was friendly. Tramp, carnie, drifter trash . . . there were many insulting names for us Caravan fae.

"Aye, he's mine." I removed the man's hand from Morenn's shirt and tucked the boy in close. "What can I do for you, sir?" The boy wasn't my indentured foster child, but that didn't matter.

"This guttersnipe stole a bracelet from the missus."

"You sure, pet?" His face reddened at the Traveler term for outsiders, usually used for one's opposite gender. Seemed only fair to return the insult, a double one at that. "I found a bracelet a few paces behind me, I did."

I made a show of fishing around in my pocket, directing the man's attention away from Morenn. Before pulling out an acorn, I slid a quick glance at the boy who opened his hand enough for me to glimpse the stolen catch. Magic drifted down my fingers in a cool rush, like a gentle breeze beneath my wings. Two beats later, I revealed the acorn in my palm, the seed now illusioned into an image of the bracelet. I kept odd-end things in my pockets for this very reason. All us Travelers did.

"This the one? A pretty piece, it is."

The man's face slackened and he awkwardly shifted on his feet. "That is indeed the one."

The friendly smile tilting my lips curved into a darker threat, my small canines bared as I called my coercion magic to the front. "You will keep your lady's bracelet on you and gift it to her three days from now, when the wagons are gone and no sooner. If you refer to my kind as anything other than Traveler, at any point, the bracelet will turn into a snake and bite you." I dropped the glam-oured seed into his waiting hand and released my hold on his mind, the friendly smile once more in place. "Enjoy the Night Market, sir."

He blinked his eyes. "Good evening, Traveler." He tipped his hat and I returned the gesture.

It was against the law in several villages in Caledona Wood for a faerie to use coercion magic on a mortal. But we did it anyway. Most mortals didn't remember being glamoured.

"Come, lad." I placed a hand on Morenn's small shoulder and directed him to a less crowded pocket by the elixir wagons. "Good catch," I said, dropping to one knee to be eye level, "but work on your sly footing a bit more before thieving jewelry from a wrist. Easier for the target to grab you. Stick to pockets and sleight of hand awhile longer, aye? And *always* wiggle free from a target's hold. Don't stand there and take the accusation. Some villages hang their thieves."

"Thank ye, Rhylen."

I tousled his dark blue hair. "Run along, lad."

He shook my hand then quickly melted into the thickening crowd of villagers. I stood and dusted the dirt from my trousers. Dizziness floated in my head from the magic use. If I performed any other illusions or glamoured another mind, I would need to fly to replenish my stores. I was from the songbird line of Ravens, not the tricksters. We all had illusion magic, but songbirds less so.

Another young indentured slave, like Morenn, slipped past me. A mortal boy around eight, a boy his mam gave to us—sadly, a common situation for those with too many mouths to feed. It was children like him that Folk within our tribe could purchase from the elders and use as they pleased. Most had their young slaves do grunt work, freeing up their ability to focus more on turning profits at the market.

Unlike this boy, Morenn was one of many who lost their family and home to the Kingdom of Carran's military. The government, for nearly three decades, had been slaughtering wild fae for their rivers and forests in the Greenwood—or The Wilds, as most now called the isolated, primeval lands of Caledona Wood.

As a result of the civil war, Traveler Folk were given an opportunity to take in the orphaned children for a one-time stipend. The tribe pocketed the money, appointed a foster family, who would receive extra portions of food, and turned those wee ones into thieves.

But the wild fae orphans were owned by the tribe, not the family.

Morenn was fostered by the Ó Brannons, a middle-rank clan with perennial gambling and drinking problems. They had lost several slaves to Seren over the years to pay off debts and to bargain their way out of jail.

I sometimes think about those wild fae, especially my former friend Finn Brannon. A smile tipped my lips at the memory of that rascally green-haired tree spirit.

Like Morenn, he had been fostered in West Tribe since a toddling bairn. But unlike the young water spirit, Finn grew up alongside me and my gang of lads. Finn and I were close to the same age. But he and Cian were closer, both being slaves *and* agents of chaos. Flaming suns, the trouble those two got into constantly. But then he was sold to a Thieves' Guild on Seren when thirteen to bail out one of his foster parents from jail.

The Brannons were cunning tricksters and experts at riddling bargains despite their problems. One of the best at teaching children how to thieve for the tribe too. Seren paid good money for orphans fostered by the Brannons—either in coin or in trades. So much so, any wild fae fostered by the Ó Brannons carried their surname.

Mortal slaves indentured as children, however, often stayed with us for life.

We fae did prefer owning mortal slaves most. So much so, fae laws declared mortals our property in marriage too.

Cian and Filena were mortal slaves my clan owned. But they had never been property to us. They were our friends. Our family.

My heart.

I peered over my shoulder toward Seren, the City of Stars, the floating luxury island above Caledona Wood.

The nest was run by the carrion crime syndicate, our trickster Raven Folk cousins. Mainlanders, mostly mortals from Carran's eastern cities, flocked to the island in the sky and dropped unholy amounts of money at the casinos and nightclubs, then were glamoured to remember little of their debauched and gambling behavior.

A stationary money trap . . . fecking brilliant.

Until three weeks ago, Ren Cormac ruled Seren—a secret we kept from slaves, per a Caravan bargain agreement with the carrion crime syndicate, who regularly bought our indentures. Ren's Caravan cousins from North Tribe had sent runners to West, East, and South tribe with news of how he was led into a trap by Finn Brannon and a mortal girl, set up by the legendary Sisters Three.

A shiver raced down my spine. The Mother, Maiden, and Crone were rarely in the more populated areas of Caledona Wood—especially near villages with more mortals than Fae Folk.

Thinking about Finn, though, pulled at the corners of my mouth again. It was no surprise the lad was involved, not to any of us who once knew him. Wherever he was now, I hoped he could finally be free. All the wild fae orphans deserved a life of their own making—

"Rhylen!"

Speaking of agents of chaos . . . Cian approached me, a local fae girl under one arm, a mortal boy under the other, and a large, rascally grin on his still-hungover face.

"What happened to George?" A corner of my mouth hooked up.

"He only wanted my company for warmth, the wee bastard. Absconded into the night with my favorite fingerless glove too."

"The left one?" I asked, even though I had no clue which one was his favorite.

"Aye, darlin'. The left one." Cian lowered his voice and dramatically croaked out, as if on the verge of tears, "I feel so used, Rhy-Rhy." His gray eyes, so much like Filena's, then widened in silent communication to rescue him.

Arsehole.

I studied the boy and girl, my lips twitching. "I know the feeling well, *pet*."

Cian fake gasped. "Is my little Raven jealous?"

"I believe your exact words were 'need both hands,'" I tossed back with a smirk. "And 'your *large* mallet is my favorite.'"

He did say those things, but while setting up the market yesterday. As a slave and a felly, we were both on the setup and break down crew.

The fae girl erupted into a screeching laugh and Cian grimaced. The mortal boy narrowed his eyes at me before territorially licking Cian's cheek, who then grimaced even more.

Oh to leave him to his heroic choices . . .

Cian's face tightened with payback promises if I walked away. Absolutely worth it. But he was my best friend. More like a brother.

"Come, lover," I commanded Cian, as if I were a gov rank. "Attend me."

"Mmm," Cian purred. "The feather this time?"

The feather? I had to keep from laughing, the fecking eejit. "You know I like the talons best."

Cian extracted himself from the two locals and flashed them the raven bond mark on his wrist—the one that matched mine since age twenty, when Gran transferred ownership to me. "My master needs me to serve him." Lowering his eyes, he placed a hand to his heart and whispered, "Darlins, don't forget the drunken banshee screaming hip thrust maneuver I taught you."

"Will we see you at the pub tomorrow night?" the girl asked.

Cian blew them both kisses and walked backward into the market. "Missing you already!"

I trailed after him, rolling my eyes. "The feather?" I slapped the backside of his head.

Cian laughed, catching his cap before it landed in the crowd. "You *do* like feathers." Pulling out his one glove, he stretched it over his left fingers. I guessed wrong. "Where is your broody arse off to?"

"Gran's."

Cian grinned. He loved Gran and Gran loved him. She raised us both. Most indentured children were not as lucky to have a doting foster parent. Slaves were a part of our trade and children were the easiest to come by. I hated it. I had always hated it. My voice was only a pitch higher than Cian's. A rank that practically made me a slave too.

But when the Night Market opened, for a few blessed hours, I was free. We both were.

Chapter Four

RHYLEN LONAN

Gran's wagon was a showy shade of dark red, detailed in colorful swirls and flowers. Bright even in the shadows of night. On the yellow door, an all-seeing eye, decorated with seven stars, was painted as a ward against bad luck. The night was quieter on the outskirts of the market where she, Filena, and Glenna had parked beside other fellys. Cian and I shared our own wheels, the wagon that once belonged to my parents. Behind both wagons, our horses lay hobbled beneath the trees in sleep.

I knocked on the door before pushing it in. "Evening, Gran."

"Lad," she called back. "My hollow bones feel a storm brewing."

"Aye." I ducked inside, Cian right behind, who shut the door. "From the east."

Gran was nested in her favorite chair, bundled with threadbare blankets and shivering. The stove flickered with cooling ashes from earlier in the day, but no fire.

Cian's face pinched with anger.

Once more, the younger lads assigned with delivering wood and kindling fires for the sick and elderly, while their family members worked, had skipped Gran's wagon. The first time, I thought it a mere accident. Twice in a row? My clan must be marked.

I opened the stove. "Did they even poke their head in?"

"Oh, lad," she said on a heavy sigh. "Don't go look'n fer trouble."

I twisted toward her, a scowl deepening between my brows. "Not trouble, Gran. Justice. The Fiachnas can push me around as their felly, but no fecking way will they bring their gov arses down on an ancient. It's cowardly."

"It is the way of things fer our rank," she said with a level of acceptance that shivered in my thundering pulse. "I'm over three hundred years old and a burden, as lowly as I am."

My muscles flexed hot, my jaw tight. If I saw Bryok, I would swing first.

"Cian," I gritted between clenched teeth.

"Aye, on it." Filena's brother grabbed a lit lantern and slipped out the door to gather wood from the forest behind us.

"Let me see ye, lad," Gran said softly.

I pushed out a slow breath, closed the stove's door, and moved to kneel at her feet.

Dark purple eyes, like mine, swept across my face. For fourteen years, she was my da and mam after both my parents died in a wagon accident—my mam the only child she could conceive throughout her long life. And despite Gran's struggle to keep up with my and Glenna's fledgling energy in her wisdom years, she raised us without complaint. Doted on us endlessly. She paid for the Merricks too, when they showed up at West Tribe. Took most of her nest egg, but she wanted me and my sister to have family for after she walked her last . . . and felt, deep in her soul, that these mortals were meant to be ours.

"My sweet boy," she said, and cupped my cheek with her cold fingers. I leaned into her touch and closed my eyes. "Ye have fire in yer heart, Rhylee Lo. Careful not to burn down the world around ye."

"At least you'd be warm," I said with a small smile. She chuckled and patted my cheek. Taking both her hands in mine, I gently rubbed her fingers. "Just because it has always been the way of things among us Raven Folk is not an excuse for unkindness. Three hundred years is a long service to our tribe. They can bring you firewood and light your stove. It is a small thing to ask."

"Yer look'n fer trouble again."

"Justice, Gran." I kissed her fingers. "Justice. You are worth fighting for, understand?"

"The girl who owns the fire heart of me Rhylee Lo is a lucky lass, she is."

My smile turned impish. "Aye, she is."

Gran chuckled again. She had a lovely smile and was no doubt a looker in her day. Filena and Glenna insisted on styling her knot of gray-black hair each day and painted rouge on her lips during festivals. We picked flowers for her hair during the spring too. She deserved to feel pretty and young until her last walk.

Cian returned with an armload of wood and quickly set to lighting the small stove. Rising to my feet, I reached into my pocket and pulled out a cloth with a generous slice of buttered rye bread and a palmful of berries. "I'll bring you cake tomorrow night."

"Ye'll fatten me up!" She playfully huffed.

"That's the plan," I said with a grin and a wink.

Gran tilted her head and studied Cian. "Where's yer other glove, lad?"

"An ungrateful bloody raccoon stole it from me."

"In fairness," I added, "wearing a fake mustache and a large, bustled gown, George probably didn't know it was you."

"In fairness," Cian repeated, "he met me while dressed as the Lady of Man. We bonded. Then he stole my glove." Cian lowered his voice to a stage whisper. "It was all a lie."

Gran wiped away tears and pressed another hand to her belly in laughter. "Ye boys are too rich."

Cian bent down and kissed her cheek. "You would have liked George, Gran."

She chuckled again. "Cian, darlin', keep me Rhylee Lo out of trouble tonight. He's spoiling fer a fight."

"Is she well?" Cian asked me. "I think she asked *me* to keep *you* out of trouble."

Gran playfully swatted Cian's leg. "Making friends with raccoons is not a sign of wellness, ye wee goat."

"Now that's just hurtful." Cian grinned and leaned down and kissed her on the other cheek.

I kissed her cheek next. "I'll check in on you in an hour, Gran."

"Go, lad," she said with a shooing motion. "Enjoy the night."

I replied with a grim smile. There was only one way I would enjoy the remaining hours of this night.

I walked ahead of Cian and marched down the steps. I wanted blood. I wanted revenge. The boiling in my veins demanded I challenge Bryok for the gov position, too. I paced before the wagon as Cian shut the door. Gray eyes flitted to mine and I nodded with

George

my head to follow, then I strode toward the market.

I didn't hear the building wind in the trees or the tinkling
chimes. Nor did I hear the crowds or the musicians. Only the

pounding war drums in my ears.

Lanterns swayed back and forth from limbs above our heads. If they were candles, like we used until three weeks ago, most would have sputtered out by now. The oil lamps weathered the storms better, we were told. And an emotion other than rage simmered just beneath my skin.

Fear.

I was grateful my crew wasn't responsible for hanging lamps. We built and tore down the tents each week.

Cian peered up and frowned. He didn't say anything, but I could tell he was thinking the same as me.

"Fellas," Corbin, a lad from our small gang, greeted us and walked in step with Cian.

Single males formed gangs, a tribe within a tribe. Mine comprised of boys from the felly and slave ranks, both fae and mortal. All of us were in the setup and break down crew too.

Corbin gestured with a thumb over his shoulder to the brewery wagon where his older brother worked. "To the market pub?"

"To kick a feathered arse," Cian said. "Though I was instructed to keep ol' Rhylee Lo here from rabble rousing." He tossed Corbin a sly grin. "I have no such plans. The fecker deserves whatever he gets."

"Sean! Owen!" Corbin hollered to more of our boys as we passed the brewery wagons. "Bets on Rhylen!" he added.

"Who's he fighting?" Sean asked, jogging up to us.

Cian hooked an arm around Sean's neck and pretended to punch his gut. "He's fighting your ugly mug."

"Ah," Sean said with a grin. "He's challenging Bryok."

"How did you get that from 'your ugly mug?'" Cian asked

with a laugh.

Sean rolled his eyes. "Who else? And Raven Folk aren't ugly, *mortal*."

"Fair," Cian said. "And also unfair."

Owen pointed. "There's the tail feather."

Bryok, the chieftain's son, leaned against a table, close to a village girl he was charming into his bed. The lad was to be married at the Autumn Night Market next week. But, as a prince, he was allowed to keep mortals and other fae as official mistresses as well as marry more than one Traveler, while the rest of us mated for life and *only* with another Caravan Raven Folk.

But not forced.

No one, not even slaves, could be ordered into another's bed or into a mate bond. We Raven Folk were many things, mortals had fair reason to fear us. Our natures were not kind or trustworthy. But we didn't force anyone into our beds or into marriage. A Raven's magic drove him to conquer by wooing, to attract another by displays of virility and beauty. Our courtships were taken seriously, to the point of primal rituals and ceremonies. It was against our very nature to be otherwise.

And why I could never be with anyone but Filena.

She was the other half of my magic.

Bryok laughed at something the mortal girl said, pulling me from my rambling thoughts.

I swept a calculating gaze around the area and spotted one of his boys. Most were working the booths or performing. The benefit of being on the crew: the Night Market was ours to enjoy while on call for repairs.

"Bets, lads," Corbin said. Everyone reached into their pockets and tossed beads, rocks, string, and . . . Cian, stars blasted Cian, plopped a tin of rouge onto Corbin's palm with a humored shrug. The boys erupted into laughter.

"The legendary Lady of Man, gents," Sean said with a dramatic sweep of his arms toward Cian, who took an even more dramatic bow.

Straightening, Cian smirked then grabbed my face with his hands. "Darlin'," he said and smooshed my cheeks. "Make me proud." The eejit kissed my forehead, snatched my top hat, then turned me around and kicked my arse. "For good luck!" he shouted. He turned to the boys. "Make note, lads, that I kicked his arse first."

I gestured with my head for the boys to follow. Their faces tightened into scowls and their bodies relaxed into challenging stances—though they lowered their eyes.

Tiny sprinkles hit my fevered skin as I approached the prince. Another gust of wind rolled through the market. The beads and charms in my hair clinked; black strands and tiny braids blew across my face. Bryok caught my approach and straightened. His dark gaze leveled onto mine, a smug tilt to his lips when I didn't lower my gaze in submission. My wings itched for release. Wings I often kept shifted away. That fecker would see who the bigger lad was soon enough, though. I might be low, but one thing boys like me knew how to do was brawl. Survival depended on it. Unlike this entitled, plucked pigeon.

"Felly," Bryok greeted. "Filena tell you, did she?"

My steps almost faltered. Filena? I almost asked what he was talking about, but I refused to take the bait. "Is my clan marked?"

Bryok's smile curled into delighted arrogance. "She didn't tell you, then."

The Fiachnas were from the trickster line of Travelers and he was baiting me. Filena either didn't tell me about a specific situation involving Bryok—or *anyone*. He didn't specify. I was sure there were many things Filena hadn't shared with me just like there were many things I hadn't shared with her. Still . . .

"Answer the damn question," I said in a low growl.

"You forget your place, felloe."

I darkly laughed. "Any Raven can challenge a prince or gov, regardless of rank."

"Are you challenging me, then?"

It was a trick question. I was challenging him, but not for his position. "Is my clan marked?"

Bryok leaned in close, until we were nose to nose. My wings were practically beating for release now.

"Filena *will* be my mistress," he said with a razor-sharp smile. Territorial fire poured into my veins and my muscles flexed. "I *will* court her. But to ensure the slave—"

I didn't let him finish.

My fist swung and connected with his jaw. Before he could recover, I slammed a punch to his lower stomach. A grunt ripped from his lungs. He stumbled a step. I grabbed his hair and yanked his head back, until his body arched at an uncomfortable angle, and pressed my lips to his ear.

"Touch her," I seethed, "and I'll take your place and cast your family to the wolves after clipping their wings. I'll wear your feathers and crow in victory."

Bryok pulled from my grip and roared with fury. His wings unfurled with a snap. Baring his bloodied teeth, he lifted his fists into a boxer's stance and began circling me.

"Fire!"

Screams echoed around us. The banging of pots and pans filled the market. Bryok slid to a stop when the crowd burgeoned around us in panic.

"Fire!"

"Oh shite!" Cian said. And it was the way he said it that pulled me from my rage-induced haze.

My heart stopped cold in my chest.

Several wagons and tents were ablaze in Filena's direction. Villagers and Raven Folk were running in all directions. A gust of wind ripped through the market and I watched, in horror, as an oil lantern fell from a branch, spilling fire onto a small tent. Flames whooshed up the side of the canvas.

We needed to take down the lanterns—

My head flung back. Stars flashed in my vision. Bryok had used the distraction to land a solid hit to my jaw. But I straightened quickly with a growl, new rage pumping in my veins.

"Your market is on fire and you waste time hitting a felly instead of taking lead, *gov*?" I shouted at him. "You fecking coward!"

I pivoted on my heel and grabbed Cian by the suspenders, dragging him a few steps away with me. "Get to Gran," I instructed. "I'll find the girls." Cian opened his mouth to protest, his eyes wide with panic as he looked in his sister's direction. "You know why."

He nodded. As a male slave, regardless of who owned him, he could be ordered, as a sacrifice, to rescue gear and food from the fire. And I wouldn't put it past Bryok to do just that. We held each other's gaze for a rapid fire of my pulse, then Cian handed me my top hat and darted off.

"Fellas!" I shouted to my gang. "Start moving wagons and breaking down tents close to the fire! Tell others in the crew to take down the lanterns!"

They ran into the panicking crowd.

I didn't turn back to see if Bryok was still posturing at me with wings wide as I cut through the stampede. I hoped he walked around like the entitled peacock he was and singed each of his primary wing feathers.

Another tent whooshed into flame and people screamed.

Filena.

My heart was shouting her name, over and over and over.

I was struggling to breathe.

I needed to find my sister too. But I wouldn't rest until I first found my mate and knew she was safe.

Chapter Five

FILENA MERRICK

The man kept staring at my breasts. They *were* lovely; I would stare too. But he was the type of man who viewed females as vermin. He didn't deserve a wee glimpse of my ladies. If the sight of my girls brightened the day of a kindly gent, though? . . . I would tip my hat at him, ensuring he had a better view, and stroll on.

"Pet," I said in a firm tone, a tight edge to the mysterious smile still gracing my lips. His eyes bounced back up to mine. "Ask your final question."

He first asked when his wife would die; the cantankerous nag, he called her. This wasn't a new one for me, alas. Naturally, I broke the sad news that she would live a long, long, really, truly, incredibly long life—a miracle, it was. The rune staves never lied. Which was true, they never did. Me, on the other hand?

Would his sow farrow again, he asked next. The oracle cards also never lied. But, on this one, both the cards and I agreed . . . only so that his wife could be well-fed and outlive the bastard. So, yes, his sow would farrow more piglets.

Desiring the death of another aside, good fortunes equaled happy profits. Happy profits meant both Cian and I would live happier lives among the Folk. If I lied and this man came back the next time we rolled into his village, I would simply say, "You didn't specify which sow or when, current sow or a sow in the future."

Living with the fae taught me many things, being clever and riddling my words being a first and foremost lesson. *Especially* in this business.

"Will the ingrown hair on my back finally heal, *fáidhbhean*?"

I resisted the urge to wrinkle my nose. *Dear gods, I won't use a fake fate to get out of doing the dishes again if you spare me this vision.* My fingers began sliding the top card when shouts rang out, followed by the raucous banging of pots and pans.

"Fire!" a voice screamed near my tent. "Fire!"

I shot up from my chair. Fires happened on occasion—a villager accidentally knocked over a candle, pot belly stoves placed too close to the canvas walls. We were usually pretty good at dousing flames. Each tent had buckets of sand for emergencies. But I could see the orange glow through my striped canvas.

The man grabbed my arm. "My final card."

"Do *not* touch me." I yanked myself out of his grip. "Get out. *Now.*"

He circled on me. "I paid you, *cailleach*. Read the last card."

Over an ingrown hair? *Moons and stars . . .*

How quickly men went from wise woman seer to *cailleach*—fae witch.

Barry growled and the man took a small step back, surprised. My familiar remained hidden behind the table until moments like these.

"If you do not leave, *mortal*, I will place a curse on you and your house," I hissed between clenched teeth. "A plague of hairy warts and a need for a bucket at your backside until you are buried six feet deep. Bluebirds will always follow you too, growing in number until they fill your vision of the sky."

His eyes rounded. He peddled back a few steps more. Then he turned and ran.

That usually did the trick. A true bluebird sky was a terrifying thought. And very clever of me, but sadly wasted on an unclever man who used a fortune to know the future of an ingrown hair. *See a healer, sir, not a seer.* I sighed. If only I had fae powers to actually curse, like a *cailleach*. I would abuse them, constantly. And howl in laughter each time. It's a wonder the gods allowed me magic at all.

"Muffin Moo," I cooed at Barry, who loathed that nickname. But how could one not think Muffin Moo when looking at that adorably grumpy face? "Thank you, darlin'."

I quickly swiped my mam's cards, runes, and money into a satchel, then scooped Barry into my arms and trotted toward the exit. We needed to flee. I could feel the heat of the fire from inside my tent. Barry licked my chin and I melted. He was a pretentious sort and scoffed at the company of most forest animals—absolutely ridiculous—but he did care about me and I him. If that man had grown more aggressive, Barry would have bit his leg before leaving to find my brother or Rhylen.

"I promise to share my next dessert with you." He licked my chin again.

Pushing back the flap, I stepped out and gasped. Flames crackled up into the stormy sky. Tiny sprinkles of rain pricked my skin. This wasn't just a single tent that caught flame. Multiple wagons and tents were ablaze.

Fire . . .

My vision. Dark suns, Rhylen's Alder card vision.

No, no, no!

Terror clawed up my spine. Clutching Barry closer to me, I dashed into the pandemonium. Where was my brother? Rhylen? Thankfully, Gran was on the opposite end of the market as was the magical confections wagon Glenna worked in.

Smoke billowed around me on a strong wind. Dear gods, the wind. Behind me, the flames bent and spread in the gust—to my tent! My heart jumped to my throat. If we had left a minute or two later . . .

Tremors shimmied down my arms and legs. My head was growing listless. Faces with rounded eyes and silent screams blurred around me. Was I slipping into another vision? Or going into shock? I couldn't tell.

I turned my head to scan the sea of people for a familiar face in the smoke and soot. Rhylen emerged from the fray and skidded to a stop before my tent and threw open the flap despite the flames licking up the side. His body went slack and he pivoted on his heel to peer into the mass of people.

"Rhylen!" I screamed, but he didn't hear me.

On the verge of tears, I pushed into the exiting crowd toward him and was swept into the stampede. Bodies jostled into me. A boot stepped on my skirts and yanked me back, the same body then pushing me forward with the crowd's momentum. I started to fall but grabbed onto a wagon's awning pole with one arm while holding fast to Barry with the other.

"Rhylen!" I screamed again.

He moved away from my tent, cupped his mouth and shouted. A name. My name. His gaze frantically darted from face to face until his eyes landed on mine. Rhylen practically shoved people down in a mad dash toward where I clung to the pole for safety.

"Filena," he said softly, as if saying my name might shatter me to ash and dust. Before I could reply, Rhylen awkwardly folded me against his chest and released a trembling, hiccuped breath. He kissed my hair, my forehead, then pressed me to his chest once more—as close as he could with Barry in my arms. "If you were injured or worse . . ." his words trailed off. But it was his voice—tender and full of melodic, unspoken emotions I didn't understand. He kissed my head again and I stilled.

He was *kissing* me.

He had never kissed me before. Not once. Not even my hand.

If I weren't so terrified, I would bury my face in his chest and slowly die in his arms to the sunrise skies and spiced wine scent of him.

But this was the Alder card vision, down to him calling a name. *My* name.

I was so confused.

"Go to Gran," he said into my hair. "Cian is there already."

"No," I replied quickly. "We need as many hands as possible to fetch water from the village."

"Lena—"

"I'll be safe, Rhy." I peered up from his chest and those eyes . . . stars help me, how those intense eyes ignited my pulse.

He blew out a tight breath. "If Bryok touches you—"

"Bryok?" I pushed away. And that's when I saw the bruising along his jaw and the split lip. "Did you challenge that preening arse?"

"A tale for later."

I nodded my head slowly, agreeing but also not quite agreeing. My mind was whirling faster than a tumbling leaf in an autumn wind.

He lowered his voice and swept a frantic gaze over the blaze and thinning crowd. "I need to break down tents and move wagons away from the fire, lass."

"Go," I said with a shaky smile. "I'll find Glenna before helping with the water run."

Rhylen's gaze caressed my hair, my face. A muscle ticked along his jaw. "Send Barry if you need anything, *a stór.*"

My treasure . . .

He affectionately tugged on a strand of my hair, an unreadable slant to his lips. Swallowing thickly, he stepped back and his beautiful wings appeared and stretched wide. Before I could reply, or blink, or draw in another shaky breath, he shifted into a raven and disappeared into the thick smoke.

My fingers touched my flushing cheeks.

He *kissed* me.

The feel of his lips on my skin tingled still.

Rhylen had always been physically affectionate with his gran and sister. We did grow up together, even shared the same wagon until Rhylen and Cian came of age. No, I was simply like a little sister to him and he was comforting my panic.

I peered into the flames for another beat, then shoved off in the direction of the confections wagon.

A living ache writhed inside my chest. A keening sob that wanted to be free. Better that I bury these confusing, agonizing heart flutters into the embered ashes behind me, though. Our tribe's loss meant he would meet his True Mate at the Autumn Night Market next week. The girl he would burn for. The girl he would set his entire world on fire for as her sword and shield.

And she wasn't me.

She could never be me.

Chapter Six

RHYLEN LONAN

I squinted against the mid-day sun. Gran sat beside me in a forest clearing where our tribe had parked, her fingers clasped firmly in mine.

Bram Fiachna, our chieftain, had summoned the tribe to a meeting after consulting with the elders—the Caravan fae of varying ages appointed by the gods to act as the tribe's advisors and judges. Chieftains were also elders and granted the same elemental protection magic by the gods too.

I bit back a sigh.

Ash still stained my hands and blackened beneath my nails. My clothing needed a proper washing to rinse away the smoke. I wasn't the only one still disheveled from the fire. Around us, people sat on picnic blankets or on stools, many still covered in soot too.

Two nights ago, the fires burned a third of our wagons and tents and, with them, food stores as well as other much-needed, harder to replace supplies. We spent all that night and most of yesterday breaking down the market, cleaning up the debris, and rolling on, traveling most of last night too. I drove Gran and the girls, wanting them to sleep, while Cian led our wagon. Exhaustion was weeping from the marrow of my bones.

None of our people had died, thankfully, or any Night Market visitors. But three Raven Folk suffered from burns.

A tight breath left my smoke-tinged lungs and I peered over my shoulder. Behind me, Filena sat with Glenna on an old, quilted blanket, Barry in her lap and her and Glennie's faces pressed close together in a whispered conversation. Filena gnawed a corner of her bottom lip and twisted a button on her bodice. Worry lines creased her forehead while my sister was all smiles. There was almost a dejected slope to Filena's shoulders, a sadness in the tilt of her head. I started to look away when slate gray eyes, framed in thick dark lashes, slid in my direction as she released her bottom lip.

Feck. Me.

Falling stars shot through my veins.

My wings nudged at my back to appear and unfurl.

Though covered in spots of ash, her auburn waves falling down her back in tangles, and an old, threadbare, stained gown hanging limply on her frame, she was utterly mesmerizing.

I forced my gaze away before I fell into my mate's endless beauty and lost myself completely. It was an easy thing to worship her with my gaze alone. It was the only way I was allowed to worship her.

Cian lay stretched out beside Glenna, both hands behind his head and one eye open as he tried to eavesdrop on the girls. Biting his lower lip in one of his trademark impish looks, he rolled to his side and cuddled with Glenna's leg, as if it were a doll. The lad didn't know what to do with himself when left to his own thoughts.

My sister playfully flicked his forehead and Cian threw her a pout. Rolling her eyes, she then combed her fingers through his ear-length, blond hair and he pretended to purr.

I cracked a smile.

But it faltered and quickly faded back into a pensive line.

Gran watched me carefully, a strange glint in her gaze. "Ye'll find a way, Rhylee Lo."

My brows pushed together. "A way for what, Gran?"

Instead of answering, she patted my hand and returned her attention toward where Bram stood beside the elders in conversation.

My family clan, and others of our rank, sat near the animals, behind most of our tribe. Still, I could feel Bryok's gaze bore into me from the front. I ignored him. If the bastard so much as laid a finger on Filena, I would rip his wings off. Right now, however, I would resist physically fighting while our tribe needed full cooperation. This time of year demanded more from us before winter set in without adding new jobs to recover what was lost.

The Autumn Night Market was in a few days, our annual gathering with other Travelers to celebrate the new year at Samhain. Before the full harvest moon, when the veil thinned between this mortal plane and the Otherworld, Ravens found their mates. It was rare for the fae to find their True Mate and why selecting a life partner was a ceremonious event over the span of eight days.

Matchmakers, mostly busy-body mams and nans, ensured the courting pairs were suitable too or introduced potential lovers if their charge hadn't found another to bond with yet.

Males began participating in the mating rituals around six-teen. I was now twenty-two and had yet to participate in a single one, nor did I plan on ever doing so. With Gran's growing needs, I was able to forgo tradition.

Glenna could care for Gran instead, I supposed. But she had the very real chance to marry up in rank, unlike me. Felly males rarely bonded with females in a higher class. Glennie shouldn't be burdened with giving up a chance at a mate who could provide her and their children with a more comfortable home.

My heart swelled at the forbidden image of standing beneath a Truth Telling Tree with Filena, exchanging vows. But to declare my love would result in our shunning. No tribe would take us in. We would be branded as unclean.

The elders might even issue a blinding curse, where the minds of Caravan folk in West Tribe would be glamoured to no longer see or hear us, nor us them. Faeries couldn't coerce other faeries, but the elders possessed the kind of god-appointed magic that could.

Villages didn't hire Raven Folk either—we weren't trusted. The only way we could survive was to relocate to Seren. As a felly and a Traveler, I would become an indentured slave to the carrion crime syndicate. Filena, Cian, and Glenna too. They would assur-edly separate us and I'd lose my ability to care for Gran—and I'd also lose Filena.

No.

I wouldn't force my family into those unthinkable conditions. Nor would Filena if she ever returned my feelings.

My jaw clenched.

Bryok would soon wed Doireann Brannagh, a chieftain's

daughter from South Tribe. That would distract him from attempting to claim Filena as his mistress for a while—I hoped.

Stars, the next two weeks would be tiresome and trying.

There were days, like today, when I resented my Folk and all our rules. Resented drifting from village to village too. We would need less resources if our tribe nested in one place for a spell. Since the fire, I couldn't shake the notion of a stationary Night Market as a solution to recover what we lost.

In my tribe, if I had one of my own, people would be allowed to marry whom they pleased too. Magic was celebrated, but so were the unmagical. There were enough jobs for everyone and stations of birth played no part—in anything. Slavery no longer existed as well. And children were paid a fair wage, same as any other worker.

But we were Travelers. Only Seren Raven Folk didn't live a migratory life.

Seren . . .

Over Gran's head, I studied the floating luxury island above Caledona Wood.

What if a permanent market was set up beneath Seren, beside the train and ferry docks? And operated similarly to an Autumn Night Market? Would it remain profitable enough to permanently rest our wagon wheels?

The Autumn Night Market was a spectacle that attracted visitors from all over Carran, even people from neighboring kingdoms. Mortals and other fae flocked to watch the mating rituals and stroll the sprawling markets and exhibits.

And attend The Wild Hunt.

Stars above, my heart was racing over the idea.

"Flock," Bram spoke over the quieting gathering, redirecting my racing thoughts, "the loss is grave. Aye, without certain supplies, it will be impossible to recover on our own before the first snows. We will need to hire Travelers from other tribes to help build new wagons if there are none to purchase. Supply runs for food and canvas will be necessary too."

People murmured to one another and I swallowed against the growing knot in my throat.

"This will plunge our tribe into debt."

The voices around me grew louder.

"To recover, we will trade older indentures to Seren and other tribes."

As expected.

It's what most tribes did when treasuries were low. Or foster parents when debts, often gambling debts, couldn't be paid—especially since those running bets had magic in place to ensure money wasn't glamoured. If a family member found themselves in trouble with the law, a slave could be traded to pay the bail.

Indentures belonged to individuals or families. In emergency situations though, like this one, those slaves *also* belonged to the whole tribe. Better to sacrifice a slave to save a Caravan than a Raven Folk.

I turned my head to peer at Cian from the corner of my eye. If he was chosen, I would challenge the Fiachnas. Filena was too high an asset as a fortune teller to be sold. But my best friend, my brother, would catch a pretty price.

Bram continued and I faced forward once more.

"And . . ." he overly punctuated the word and the gathering quieted. "All unattached males have been placed into a lottery. If your name is called, you *will* find a mate at the Autumn Night Market and give the entirety of her dowry to the tribe. It is required of you. The alternative is banishment for refusing to care for your flock."

The muscles down my body stiffened. The intensity of Bryok's stare burned into me. *Oh gods . . .*

"Females from West Tribe are not permitted to marry this year. No doweries will leave West Tribe."

A few girls started crying and their mams joined the rising shouts of protest.

"Prince." Bram, ignoring the reactions, ordered his son to the front with a beckoning gesture. Bryok sidled up beside his father, his dark, laughing eyes locked onto mine. Bruises dotted around his jaw. His bottom lip was still slightly swollen. The chieftain accepted a top hat from an elder and lifted it up into the air. "Choose the first name, lad."

Bryok reached into the hat and pulled out a piece of paper and leisurely unfolded the slip. "Kev Brannon."

All eyes turned toward the middle-rank male, horror and outrage in their gazes. The chosen lifted his chin, his face giving nothing away. The ticking muscle in his jaw, however, said it all.

"How is this allowable?" I spoke aloud to no one.

Gran considered me a long moment. "Arranged marriages are nothing new among our Folk, lad."

My mouth fell open. "We have courting magic for a reason."

"When I was a lass, males courted, like ye do now. But it was the mams and nans who chose their daughter's mate. It was our way."

Fury bloomed in my tightening chest. "You were . . . *forced* to wed Granda?"

The corners of Gran's mouth dipped. "Aye, lad. But he was good to me, to yer mam too. I grew to love him and he me."

My teeth were grinding so hard, my jaw ached.

The prince reached in and unfolded the next slip. Nausea rolled in my tightening gut. His eyes flitted to mine and held them. "Aidan Broin."

He continued to call names. Fourteen lads sold into marriage. Fourteen lads who were required to put their tribe before their brides, their families, or be lost to them.

"One last name," Bram said to his son.

Bryok's lips tilted into smug delight. I knew the name he would call. He waited, wanting me to suffer to the very end. It didn't matter what name was truly on the paper. He could illusion it to be mine and no one would question his authority.

"Rhylen Lonan."

Glenna audibly gasped behind me, followed by the slapping sound of her hand covering her mouth. Gran squeezed my fingers.

The edge of my vision was fading.

My lungs were tight, too tight.

Blood pounded loudly in my ears.

The world slowed as the meeting ended and I blinked.

All around me, people stood and shook out blankets. As if we had just enjoyed a picnic beneath a lazy, golden summer afternoon. The atmosphere, however, was anything but. Bodies were stiff, eyes lowered. The hushed sounds of crying and angry murmurs rippled around me.

Daughters would not marry. Sons were forced to mate against their will. Not even slaves could be forced into a Raven Folk's bed. Nor did we practice arranged marriages—or so I thought. We mated for life and our lives were long. Choice of a partner, I was led to believe all my life, was the entire reason for our mating rituals. For our very primal magic.

I didn't move to leave. Couldn't move. The knife carving out the organ in my chest paralyzed me in crippling, shattering pain.

"Rhylen," a voice said softly. Hands cupped my cheeks. A blurred face swam before me. "Rhylen," Cian repeated. I blinked back hot, furious tears. "Rhylen," he said again and I flinched. "What can I do for you?"

"Rhy," another voice joined Cian's—Sean—and a hand touched my back. Crouched behind Sean were Corbin and Owen.

My vision was moving in and out of focus.

I couldn't breathe.

My stomach rolled. I blinked back a violent wave of nausea.

"Rhylen, say something, lad," Cian urged.

"What dowry could I possibly bring the tribe?" I choked out with a hiccuped breath. I already knew the answer. I knew he would call my name. But the stabbing pain ripping through my heart was too relentless to think straight.

All so Bryok could bed Filena.

He robbed the tribe of a dowry to dominate me. This was *all* to dominate me into obedient submission. To punish me for owning what no other tribe had for their markets or would ever allow him to possess.

She was *mine*.

In every way.

Fire, unlike any other, ignited in my veins. A protective rush of heat that flexed down my muscles.

I would destroy. I would consume.

Pushing away from Cian and Sean, I shoved to my feet. My wings snapped free.

I turned to catch Filena's eyes and . . . the knife dug in deeper and twisted. Tears glimmered on her cheeks and yet, strangely, there was a knowing look in her grief-stricken gaze. A churning sorrow, a furious acceptance. A searing pain that mirrored my own. Had she *seen* something? Was this why she was nervous and withdrawn earlier?

"Rhylee Lo . . ." Gran warned quietly.

I faced where Bryok still stood with his da, elders, and boys from his gang. A breeze swirled around me and I inhaled the smoke still clinging to my clothes. My soot-dusted feathers fluttered in the dancing air.

The first step forward vibrated up my body. I swore the ground shook beneath me. Folk stepped out of the way. Some even bowed their heads. I registered each daggered breath and my uncharacteristic commanding presence with a warbled disconnection. As if I were seeing everything from underwater.

Bryok's dark eyes slid to mine and a corner of his mouth hitched up.

"Felloe," his da greeted me as I slowed. I dipped my head to acknowledge my chieftain, keeping my eyes lowered. My fight wasn't with him . . . *yet*. "I know we are asking a lot, lad," he placated in a false kindness.

My eyes snapped to Bryok's. "Tell him."

"That you challenged me—"

"Tell him!" I shouted. The level of authority rippling from me stunned Bryok for a couple of seconds.

"You do not give me orders, felly," he sneered.

I bared my teeth. "Tell him."

"Prince," his da cut in. "What should you tell me?"

"You undermine my dominance?" Bryok's face contorted in rage.

"We would have lost more wagons and supplies if it wasn't for Lonan and his crew." The chieftain's words cut through some of the betrayal. "The lad," he continued, slowly, emphatically, "is two breaths away from challenging you for a gov position."

Bryok's wings stretched out wide and his glittering gaze invited me to try.

Preening arsehole. He looked ridiculous.

I lowered my eyes for my chieftain in a deference I refuse to show his son. "Prince Bryok marked my clan, sire, until I offer up my indentured and she agrees," I gritted out. "My gran freezes so your son can bed Filena Merrick."

The elders spoke in hushed, hurried voices while shooting me appraising looks. Were they weighing my measure? My gran may be poor and the lowest among us, but she was over three hundred years old and had given more to this tribe than most here, including our chieftain. It was considered an act against the gods to harm a fae in their wisdom years. They should be judging Bryok—not me.

Bram turned toward his son but remained quiet as the elders conversed.

But I was too angry to wait.

"Let's discuss a different option than selling our tribe into marriage, as if backwoods mortals, aye?" My voice was hot, clipped. "Let the flock contribute to solutions. We could set up a permanent market beneath Seren. Let the crowds come to us instead of traveling to them."

The chieftain arched a brow. "The elders voted and we are in a binding agreement."

Horror washed over me. They had sealed this decision in a bargain? The tribe could now curse me for refusing my magic-bound duty, unless . . .

"Then pull another name from the hat, sire," I demanded. "If the bargain is about money—"

The chieftain sighed, cutting me off. "Every chosen lad has a reason for a different name to be picked."

Another lick of fire curled down my limbs and I lifted my eyes to meet Bram's, the challenge clear. "What chieftain commands his unmated males to marry against their will or face banishment and *only* to secure money for his tribe? And then puts fellys in the lottery?" My wings stretched out and I shouted, "Girls of my class rarely have money! Draw another name!"

"Then," Bram replied, his voice tight, "do whatever is necessary for a girl with money to marry you, *felly*."

My mouth fell open. Was he suggesting depraved measures? Or trickery?

Voices behind me grew louder, but I barely registered them.

Bryok cocked his head. "Your duty, so other grandmothers don't freeze or go hungry."

I charged, fists ready.

Bram slammed a hand on my chest and pushed me back with a low gust of wind—elder magic, elemental powers the gods gifted to top govs to better protect their tribes.

"Go," Bram ordered. His gaze darted over my shoulder and swept across the clearing. The tribe was listening? Good. "Your grandmother is no longer marked, Lonan."

I narrowed my eyes. It was clear the man feared I would win a challenge against his son. Of course, I would. Bryok was shorter than me, leaner, neither did he work a physically laborious job day after day, nor did he carry elder magic since he wasn't a top gov. The peacock would feel the beating for weeks. And after I took the prince's place, Bram knew I would come for him next. Because I would. I wouldn't trust him to honor me as heir.

But I could wait.

Right now, I was in a position to bargain with the mighty Fiachnas. Our tribe would mutiny after his threat of banishment if I so much as issued a proper challenge. And, as much as I would give my left wing to pound those govs into the dirt, it wasn't what us fellys needed while heading into winter with so little already. If I lost against Bram, who had elder magic, my family could be banished, too, instead of just me for failing to marry a girl with money.

I couldn't take that risk yet. But I could still make demands.

"My clan is no longer marked now or in the future," I seethed. "You vow that Brenna Meadows and Glenna Lonan will not be physically harmed, starved, left to freeze, or banished regardless of what indentures of mine Bryok Fiachna or any other govs in West Tribe can or cannot have, for *any* reason."

The chieftain held my gaze steady. A muscle jumped along his jaw. His eyes peered over my shoulder again. "Aye, Rhylen Lonan." His voice was biting. "I agree to all you said."

"Say it back, in detail, *sire*," I commanded. "Loud enough for all to hear."

With the elders at his side, Bram repeated my words as an official proclamation, a fake smile on his face to trick our flock. Still, my shoulders relaxed a notch and I backed up two steps. My wings unfurled, my teeth grinding with the obliterating grief detonating in my chest. But at least I secured my gran's and sister's protection. I knew to secure Filena's was futile. She was a slave. But I would still fight for both her and Cian. For now, I won a battle before our entire tribe—and it wouldn't be my last.

Locking onto Bryok's furious gaze, I lifted a rude gesture right as I shifted into my raven form and flew off toward the nearby woods.

I couldn't bear to look at Filena right now.

Or anyone.

Chapter Seven

FILENA MERRICK

The forest was full of moving shadows this late in the day. As a mortal, wandering this side of Caledona Wood alone was a brave choice. But his breaking heart was calling to mine. I could hear the shattering melody in my pulse. His pain was falling around me like blackened, decaying stars.

I covered the slice of cake Glenna snuck me with my free hand as I ducked beneath a low-hanging branch. In my pocket was a pretty rock I found. I didn't have any buttons to spare, or beads. It was more about the gesture to Ravens than the object, anyway.

A stór.

My treasure.

The grip on my lungs tightened. This was the beginning of my nightmare and the beginning of his dream. Only, he didn't realize this yet. The grief tearing through him would soon fade into the deepest passion. He would love and love madly until it consumed him entirely.

I couldn't help but dislike her already, his True Mate. I bet she was breathtakingly beautiful with perfect, silken hair, the softest complexion, and the kindest soul. Being a songbird like Rhylen, forest animals adored her and begged for her to sing, annoying Barry endlessly. But he would forgive her because she was goodness itself, sunshine captured in a bottle. Probably a goddess who kept a perfectly clean home—I loathed cleaning—and made delicious food from the nothing we were allotted—I burned porridge. It was a true talent. And . . . she would be a solid reminder of how I was petty and that the gods were wise. I would be positively, delightfully terrible if I had the ability to curse another. I sighed wistfully. I really, really wanted to curse something at least once in my life.

I could never curse anyone or anything that Rhylen loved, though.

I *loved* him.

Had been in love with him since I was thirteen. Since we walked beneath the moonlight together after enjoying stories and games on a down night between markets. Cian was on his side and Glenna was on mine. Our fingers touched, then our pinkies curled around the other's. He didn't so much as look my direction. And, yet, I felt the beating wings of a thousand kisses in my wildly thrumming heart as if he were confessing love.

After that night, we were careful not to touch.

But I was a silly girl who had let silly thoughts tell her a silly story of a star-crossed faerie boy and mortal girl fated for one another, to feed my silly yearnings for a happily ever after that would never be. To keep those wings I felt at thirteen fluttering in my pulse until my soul took flight.

I should have properly buried those damn flutters in the burning ash like I had lamented two nights past. But the lad kissed me and I was . . . well . . . I needed to let go.

No matter what my future may be, I wanted his happiness, even if it wasn't with me. And why I insisted I find him in the woods, despite Cian's and Glenna's protests that it wasn't safe and to wait until he returned. I couldn't bear him suffering another heartbeat, though. I could feel it twisting inside of me.

I stepped over a fallen log, careful to balance the slice of cake and fork in one hand while lifting my skirts with the other. Holy Mother of Stars, the amount of petticoats I wore on a daily basis should be criminal.

Barry had hopped over the log first and sat ahead of me—waiting—his yellow eyes trained on the cake. Did he care if I fell to my death while the inhumane layers of cotton around my legs preserved my calves' modesty? No, the red furry lad would snatch the cake and leave me to my fate.

The monster.

Though, the gods knew I would probably do the same if I were a fox and probably why they gave me Barry. He was a mirror to my fae side, if I were fae. Still . . .

"Muffin Moo," I teased in a syrupy, cooing voice and his eyes snapped to mine and narrowed. "Be a good lad and scamper off to make a friend, darlin'."

His eyes narrowed farther and I cackled.

He really needed to get over his snobbery toward other forest animals. Were all foxes this ridiculous? Or just the faerie-touched ones?

Gnawing on my bottom lip, cake firmly in my grip, I passed by Barry and pretended I wasn't lost. For a girl who saw the future, I

Barry

had no idea where I was going. Or how I would know a raven, any raven, was him.

Not only did wood ravens and Raven Folk share the same forests, but Seren also had spy ravens trailing thieves who were assigned jobs on the mainland. They were more identifiable, though, with tags around their ankles.

Still . . .

Sometimes when Rhylen was in a mood, he'd remain in his raven form for hours and hours. He could be anywhere.

Filena, I could almost imagine the ancestors sighing my name— for the billionth time. *You will only see in part unless you change the view.*

I blew a strand of auburn hair from my eyes.

"Better?" I drawled. The lock of hair fell back in place and I snorted. Sorry, ancestors, I tried. Maybe if the forest would be willing to give this *fáidhbhean* a sign I could fix my view?

A caw sounded above my head.

Well, that was fast.

I slowed and peered up into a large oak tree. A beautiful raven, fluffing his wing feathers, sat on a branch not terribly high above the ground. I knew it was a male by his hackles, the extra fluffy feathers around his throat. They were so adorable. I had to resist tickling any male raven I encountered under their beak.

"Little blackbird from the rye fields, is that you?" That was the Raven Folk translation of Rhylen's name, who was born by a rye field, apparently.

"Caw!"

"Come down, Rhylee Lo," I said softly. My heart was thundering in my chest. What would I do if he shifted before me?

Do not cry, do not cry . . .

"Caw!"

I huffed a sigh to hide the storm of grief raging through me. "Rhy, please? I brought you cake infused with a bite of happiness."

The raven cocked its head and studied me but didn't move.

Fine, I guess I would fall to my untimely end while balancing cake and climbing a tree in these petticoats of death. What was so scandalous about calves, anyway? And why was cleavage perfectly acceptable? Whoever came up with these rules should be permanently denied desserts.

Stars, I really needed to curse something to get it out of my system.

I set the cake on a stump, glaring at Barry with warnings to remain still or suffer the same fate as the person who created fashion guides for proper ladies. Then, grabbing my skirts, I tucked them into my belt, revealing my stockinged legs and drawers. Satisfied, I grabbed the cake and began hoisting myself into the tree.

Up and up I went, much higher than anticipated, until I settled on a branch beside the raven.

"I won't ask you to shift, if this is what you need." I pinched off a crumb of cake and offered it to Rhylen, who hopped over and pecked it from my palm. "The pain you feel will ease, though. I have *seen* it." I pinched off another crumb and he took it with an appreciative ruffle of his wings. My pain, however?

I stared at the cake. If he insisted on remaining shifted, I might as well enjoy a bite of happiness too. Digging in, I met Barry's eyes, lifted the fork to my mouth—and froze. Was that a . . . hedgehog curled up against him?

A *hedgehog*.

Barry sniffed at the creature and lowered his head beside it.

Did he actually make a forest friend?

Huh.

"Caw!"

I turned back to Rhylen. "Impatient, aren't we?" I offered him another crumb, this one with a bit of cooked marionberry. "It's your fault I now prefer to drown my sorrows in confections and berries, you know. I blame you if this corset stabs me one day after eating my tears in desserts."

A heavy sigh left my chest and I swallowed back the building ache. I shoved a large bite of cake into my mouth.

"I promise you, Rhylen Lonan, you will be happy," I said while chewing. "And, when you shift, I'll share why. But I'm not going to discuss your love life while you're a bird—"

"What if the bird isn't me?"

I squeaked and twisted in the opposite direction. On a branch above me, on the other side of the trunk, was Rhylen. *In his elven form.* I slowly turned toward the raven on my skirts, the one inching closer to my plate of cake while I wasn't looking. The lad was just as bad as Barry.

"Who is this?" I demanded. "Sean, if that's you—"

Rhylen's laughter cut off my reprimand. "Just a wood raven, lass."

I sucked in a quiet, mock-outraged breath. "How dare you, sir," I said to the wood raven. "Tricking comfort cake from a distressed damsel. Poor form, it is." Then, before I could stop myself, I reached out and tickled him beneath the beak and cooed, "Darling, fluffy throat feathers." The raven flew to another branch and cawed at me and I grinned.

"Did you just patronize a male's hackles?"

My hand flew up to my chest and I whipped toward Rhylen with an embarrassing gasp and . . . met his beautiful eyes. He had shifted on a branch just below the one I was perched on, standing between my very exposed calves, his wings out. And still, he was taller than me.

Silver moons, I loved it when his wings were on display. Black feathers with a blue cast in certain lighting, just like his hair. I daydreamed about running my fingers down his feathers and wings, more than was proper.

Rhylen's gaze studied my face, lines wrinkling his forehead, his lips dipped in a pensive slant. Shadows lined his swollen eyes where there was normally ash, as if he had been crying. The silver feather pendant, woven into one of his braids, winked at me in the falling sunlight as the branch swayed. My fingers itched to fidget with the charm, with his long, wind-mussed hair. Instead, I continued my worried inspection.

The hem of his shirt was untucked from his pants and the sleeves shoved up to his elbows. Veins in his forearms throbbed as he gripped the branch on either side of my hiked-up skirts. I could see his fingers digging into the wood from my periphery. He softly blinked at me and . . . those flutters returned in a violent whoosh of wings.

"I brought you cake," I said, my voice awkwardly breathless, and lifted the mostly eaten dessert.

His lips twitched at the bite or two left. The humor faded quickly, however, replaced by a scowl between his black brows. "You walked through Caledona Wood *alone*, for cake?"

"And a pretty rock."

"Lena—"

"I couldn't bear for you to suffer alone," I blurted out. "Not when I can ease your pain some."

His chest rose and fell and he looked away, a muscle jumping along his jaw. I longed to caress the lines of his cheeks, his neck and soothe him.

"This pain I will carry for the rest of my life," he said quietly. "Bryok . . . he . . ." One of his hands curled into a fist and he gritted his teeth. "He gave me a fate worse than death, worse than banishment." Tears glossed his eyes, brightening their crushed wine hue. "But I will endure anything to protect what is mine. And I can't protect Gran, Glenna, Cian . . . *you*—" His voice caught and he swallowed. "I can't protect *you* if I'm banished, aye?"

"You *will* be happy," I offered weakly. Each word was a dagger to my heart. "I have *seen* it."

Dark purple eyes slid to mine and the scowl between his dark brows deepened. "How can I be happy in love with the one I tricked into mate bonding with me? She buys my continued place in my tribe! She buys my ability to stay with my family! And when she finds out that I was never attracted to her, that the mating rituals were all a lie . . ." He lowered his voice and his face grimaced in mild disgust. "I was told to do *anything* necessary for a girl with money to marry into my lower-class rank. It wasn't said, but I fear if I don't, I could still face banishment for failing to care for my flock."

Anything? My stomach sickened at the vile implications of that command.

"The elders bonded their decision in magic," he added on a cracking whisper. "My fate is sealed and so is the poor lass I take as my bride."

Swallowing back my fraying nerves, I rushed out, "For years, Rhylen, I have seen visions of you with your wife." A blush crept up my cheeks and I watched the ruffled hem of my petticoat ripple in the breeze. I couldn't look at him as I spoke the words that destroyed my happiness. "Of you with your *True Mate*. And . . . and you'll meet her at this coming Autumn Night Market. I haven't seen her face, not in any vision. Nor heard her name spoken. But I see through her eyes and I have never seen you smile so much."

"My True Mate?" he asked quietly, almost disbelieving. "I have a happy future with my *True Mate*?"

I nod my head.

"In these visions, we are free to love each other without fear?"

Why would they fear being in love? Did he worry his True Mate lacked a dowry?

"Aye, you do love freely and without consequence." I clutched the plate in my lap and began absently twisting a button on my bodice with my other fingers. Someone harmed her, though. I couldn't tell him that part. Not yet. Not while he was beginning to feel a glimmer of relief. Instead, I added, "You'll love her madly, obsessively, Rhylen. You'd be willing to burn your world to ash for her."

Chapter Eight

FILENA MERRICK

S ilence followed my confession. It *was* a lot to digest.

I drew in a ragged breath and tried not to squirm under his heated inspection. To distract myself, I reached into my secret pocket and retrieved the pretty rose quartz I found months ago while traveling along the eastern roads.

"For you," I said and held out the gift, my eyes still averted.

He took the rock from my hand and slowly turned it over in his fingers. I knew his eyes were bright in the way of Raven Folk when they happened upon a treasure that called to them. I could tell by the reverent way he touched my gift.

"I would offer you a button, but—"

"Does my mate love me back?"

The muscles of my stomach clenched.

He had humorously asked me this question at least thirty times a year for three years in the game we played. But never had his voice been this feather soft, nor the familiar words dusted in a pale hue of hope. What fae grieved over meeting their True Mate, though? It was a rare event and the ache gnawing at my churning gut grew stronger.

I lifted my eyes, despite the throbbing pain swelling inside of me, wanting him to see the truth of my confession, even if he believed it was about her.

"She loves you with every breath in her body," I whispered, my gaze lingering on his lips a heady beat before slowly meeting the intensity of his gaze. "She loves you more than every drop of water in the oceans, more than every leaf on every tree. She loves you endlessly, passionately."

Rhylen leaned in close and my pulse trilled. Wind danced through the leaves around us and played with the long, obsidian strands of his hair. The clink of charms and beads woven into his braids sang between us.

"Does she think me handsome?" His warm breath caressed my lips.

Visions of him from the Fire Dance filled my mind and I was growing dizzy with his nearness, imagining it was me he had pressed against a tree to kiss. It was my fingers trailing down the contoured lines of his body.

"You are the most beautiful male she has ever seen."

He continued to watch me closely, his breath quickened, a kind of hopeful desperation in the flushed part of his lips and molten gaze. "Will we have children?"

I could feel each word on my skin. Tears brimmed my lashes and my bottom lip trembled. I squeezed my eyes shut for a panging beat of my breaking heart. "She craves your touch day and night. Aye, your marriage will be full of passion, the kind that would lead to many children."

Rhylen cupped my cheek and brushed away a tear with the pad of his thumb. "You truly do not know, lass?"

At the feel of his skin sliding across mine, the intimacy of his voice caressing my lips, I closed my eyes in a long, shuddering blink. "No, I do not know," I answered, melting into his touch. "Fate hasn't shown me her face, only yours."

"Truly?"

"Truly." One word, but I was unable to hide the floating sensations tumbling inside of me as he cradled my face close to his. "If Fate reveals her to me, I'll tell you."

For a moment, he seemed conflicted, opening his mouth and shutting it again. The broody angle of his brows deepened into distressed, shadowed lines as fear darkened his gaze. I thought he would fly away to find solace in solitude once more. But then, to my surprise, he pressed his forehead to mine, his long fingers still holding my face. Our mouths were so close to touching. His thumb brushed the corner of my lower lip and I stopped breathing.

"Promise me, Filena Merrick," he murmured. "The very moment you know, you'll tell me."

The world around me faded and images flashed through my mind in rapid fire.

> Rhylen faces her in a bed, shirtless, tucking a strand of hair behind her ear, whispering, "I love you, mo shíorghrá." His eternal love. His True Mate.

> Rhylen laughs at something she says, a loud, happy laugh, then pulls her in for a kiss.

She is slow dancing with him beneath the moonlight, her head pressed to his chest, his arms wrapped around her waist as he hums a hauntingly romantic melody.

Rhylen is above her, his black wings curled around where they lie in the forest, his long hair cascading against her face. His lantern lit body moves in a sensual display of muscle as he worships her with every heaving breath. Pleasure heats in her core, a rippling intensity that rushes through her when his lips taste hers in a claiming so beautiful, so intimate she falls apart, hoping to never be remade.

I blinked and the visions left me.

Dark suns, I was dying inside.

Many kisses I have *seen*, but *seeing* him make love to her sliced my heart up into millions of tiny, bleeding pieces.

"Aye," I answered, my voice tight as I pushed back the sob tightening my throat. "I promise you, Rhylen Lonan. I won't let you bond with anyone unworthy of you."

"A *stór*," he whispered across my lips in reply and a blush warmed my pulse. I wanted him to press those words all over my body. "Thank you for giving me hope, lass."

I leaned back before I unraveled completely. His fingers softly trailed down my cheek, a whispered touch, before falling to the branch, and I plastered on a teasing smile to hide my flushed cheeks and too tight skin.

"Well, there's only two bites of cake left, darlin'," I quipped, "and I'm not keen on sharing my wee bites of happiness. I had to offer you something."

A black brow arched. "Imagine my relief that I'm not marrying a feral swine."

"You will miss her hairy girls, though, pet. Breaks your heart, it does."

He quietly laughed. "An inconsolable tragedy."

I nodded my head in pretend seriousness and stuffed the last two bites of cake into my mouth. But I didn't taste anything. It was mushy, like sawdust on my tongue. I pretended to swoon, though, complete with a sigh. His sister's baking really could bring entire armies to their knees, it was so divine.

Rhylen played with a strand of my hair as I lowered the fork to a now empty plate. A corner of his mouth lifted in a shy, boyish smile. Beautiful black wings stretched wide behind him and, with an affectionate tug on my hair, he pushed off the branch. For a couple wild beats of my tattered heart, he free-fell, his inky hair whipping around his face, his eyes locked onto mine, before shifting into a raven and flying off.

I knew he would follow me back home to ensure my safety. We couldn't be seen coming from the woods together, though, especially at dusk.

It didn't take long to climb down the tree and situate my skirts to, once more, protect my calves from wanton behavior unbefitting a proper lady. One could never trust a lady's calves.

I was about to call for Barry to follow when he approached and leaned up against my leg and affectionately rubbed his head on my now cottoned-up calf. I would laugh, but I understood. He felt my grief and wanted to comfort me. I crouched and pulled him into a hug, burying my face in his fur.

"Thank you," I whispered.

He pulled back and licked my chin.

He always licked my chin.

"We should go before the sun falls behind the trees." I drew in a deep breath and slowly pushed it out while standing.

Barry trotted back over to where he was laying and nosed the hedgehog with a gesture that suggested it should follow too. It was so adorable; I pressed two fingers to my lips in delight.

"Who is your friend?" I asked and approached the hedgehog. "Hello, darlin'."

The hedgehog lifted its tiny nose and sniffed, then waddled over to me.

"Do you have a home? A family?" I asked.

Barry nosed the hedgehog again, pushing the wee thing toward my hand.

"We can't take her with us," I said. I didn't know if it was a she, but it felt right.

Barry whined and nosed the hedgehog again.

My brow furrowed. This behavior was so unlike him, I had to take his request seriously.

Was it hungry?

A tiny drop of berry smeared the empty plate and I offered it to the hedgehog, who happily licked it up. Barry watched vigilantly and I couldn't resist a smile. It was too cute. When the hedgehog finished, I scooped her up and placed her into my pocket.

Barry trotted beside me as we trundled through Caledona Wood back toward camp, his eyes sliding between the empty plate and my pocket. What had gotten into the lad?

The shadow of a raven soared over the forest floor ahead of us and my heart clenched again.

Perhaps Barry knew I needed a distraction. Something tiny and adorable to dote on. Something he could tolerate sharing his desserts with which, let's be honest, was not an easy feat. My selfish arse didn't even offer Rhylen the last two bites of cake in my spiraling panic.

A candlemark later, I wandered back into camp and quietly slipped into the wagon I shared with Glenna and Gran. An empty wagon, thank the gods. Pain was tearing across my tightened chest. Masking my grief would be impossible right now. And I ached to tell Glenna everything. I wanted to pour my pain out to her and feel her arms wrap around me in comfort as we fell asleep. But sharing that I was heartsick in love with her brother changed nothing and . . . it was dangerous too.

Curling up on my bed, I finally let the tears flow and sobbed into my pillow. I wasn't sure for how long, but I eventually fell asleep with Barry and the hedgehog snuggled against me.

Chapter Nine

RHYLEN LONAN

My fingers quietly plucked the strings of my great-granda's lute. A cool morning chill settled on the skin of my face and forearms. I sat beneath a wild apple tree laden with tart, unpicked fruit, my eyes closed as I lost myself to a rolling melody. I could hear Cian rustle around inside our wagon, but I focused on the lyrical sway of my fingers gliding across the neck and over the soundhole.

Behind me, our horses nibbled on grass. I had brushed them down earlier and cleaned their hooves from yesterday's long hours of traveling on a muddy road. I cared for Gran's horses too. In a few minutes, Cian and I would leave to set up the Autumn Night Market. But first, I needed to enjoy a few moments to myself.

The notes flowing from my fingers danced and breathed through the air. I hummed a harmony, slowly opening my eyes to watch the sun rise over the snow-capped mountains in the distance. The urge to create music before dawn broke, to lift a song to the new day was a living melody inside of me.

It was the same for most songbird lines.

This was the first time since the fires I had indulged my true magic. And I felt like the sun was rising inside me too. A new beginning was birthing within my soul. A new future I never dared hope could exist.

Now I had to plan how to make Filena's visions a reality.

She *will* be my wife by Samhain, on the eve of our new year.

Every mating ritual I was forced to do would be entirely for her pleasure alone. I wanted her flushed for me, unable to catch her breath. Desperate for my touch, my kiss, my body. I ached for her to feel every singing beat of my heart. To freefall through a midnight sky that was made just for us and then know what it felt like to fly beneath the stars.

And it pained me, deeply, to not confess the truth to her a few days ago in the woods. I could feel her heartbreak just as she could feel mine—we had been tethered in this way to each other for seven years. But it wasn't safe. If another Raven overheard and shared with Bryok? If the mate bond grew too impassioned to control as a result? I could be banished or she could be sold to another tribe despite the money she brought into ours.

Or both.

If I lost her, if I could no longer protect her . . .

A soft, lilting voice trilled over the notes I played, pulling me from my heavy thoughts, and I turned my head to smile at Glenna. My sister lowered to the ground beside me and joined in with her harmony. I loved listening to her sing. It was earthy, sweet, and reminded me of Gran in many ways. Perhaps she sounded like our mam too. I hardly remembered our parents. Just bits and pieces, but I knew they were respected musicians.

Da was from a higher class. One that allowed him to play music as a regular performer at the markets. As Gran's ward, I was brought down to her rank. Occasionally, I was asked to join in for a revel or performance here and there. But I was mostly tasked with the lowliest work in our tribe. Honestly, I didn't mind. I enjoyed being free to wander the market once the gates opened. Especially since it allowed me to check on Gran while Glenna worked.

Cian trundled down the short steps of our wagon and leaned against the outer wall, a stolen lit cigarette in his fingers. He managed to pinch a handful of smokes every night, a bottle or two of wine too. His ear-length blond hair stuck out at odd angles; pillow creases marked the high sweep of his cheek.

"I would get owned by songbirds," he muttered. Pointing his smoke at me, he added, "You're too cheery in the morning for being a broody arse."

I snorted. "Or I'm too angry and this is my revenge, aye?"

Cian nodded his head in comical agreement and shrugged, lifting the cigarette to his lips. "Bloody Ravens."

Glenna stood and ambled over to Cian, her dark brow arched. "Darlin', your hair is a horror story."

"Not horror enough," he mumbled. "Rhylee Lo is still singing his little morning birdie heart out over there."

Just to piss him off, I strummed louder, a smug tilt to my lips.

He started to reply with a grumpy scowl, but reared back a half second later when Glennie attacked his hair with her fingers.

"Stand still," she huffed.

"What the feck are you doing?" he shot back.

My sister rolled her eyes. "Combing your hair, you eejit."

"Are you mad?"

84

Glennie snickered when Cian swatted her hand.

I slowed my playing and narrowed my eyes. Was my sister preening . . . Cian? She played with his hair a few days ago at the meeting too.

Filena walked out of Gran's wagon, a water bucket in her hand, and paused when taking in the scene. "Just let her fix your hair, you beardless oaf. She hasn't kissed a blond lad in days. Makes her twitchy, it does."

"My suffering *is* great. Not sure I'll make it to opening night."

Cian's brows shot up. "You only kiss blond lads?"

"Aye. Particularly fond of the blue-eyed ones." Glenna winked at Cian. "Then I break their hearts."

Cian stilled, blinked, then burst into laughter. "Glennie, darlin', you're touched in the head."

My sister plucked the smoke from Cian's fingers and cocked her head. "Tell me, *darlin'*, how you're not the same?"

"Well, for starters, *darlin'*," he said, "blond males are not really my type. I prefer them—" She flicked his forehead. "Ow!"

"Breaking hearts, Cian. You leave a trail in each village, same as me."

An impish, crooked grin curled the corners of Cian's mouth. "Are you suggesting we see who breaks the most hearts in each village? Because, if so, *darlin'*, bets."

Glennie placed the cigarette between Cian's lips and leaned in close. "Bets." Then she spun away and sauntered back into Gran's wagon without a single look back.

Cian watched her disappear then quietly laughed to himself. "Your sister is terrifying."

Filena walked by her brother and messed his hair back up

with a quick tousle followed by a wrinkled-nose, taunting grin. "Glennie!" she shouted with an evil laugh.

"That's not very relational, lass!" he called after her.

Filena ignored her brother—and me as I finger picked a tune—trailing by toward the river, bucket in hand. As she passed, a hedgehog poked its head out from a pocket in her skirts. Barry nosed the wee creature until it disappeared back into the fabric again, then trotted ahead.

My lips pressed back a laugh.

"Well, sunshine," Cian drawled, rubbing the butt of his cigarette out with his boot while eyeing Gran's wagon, "we better get moving."

"Glennie!" I shouted with a laugh.

Cian's mouth fell open. "You're worse than George, former best friend. At least *he* kept me warm at night *before* his plotted betrayal."

I smirked. "I'm too much of a looker for you to make me a former anything."

Cian's shoulders sagged with a dramatic sigh. "Bloody Ravens."

A few minutes later, with my lute tucked away and wagon locked up, Cian and I strode toward our market lot, toolboxes in hand.

The afternoon sun was merciless for late autumn. I wiped the sweat on my face with my bare forearm. An hour earlier, I pulled my hair from the tie at the nape of my neck into a knot atop my head. I could moan whenever a cool breeze kissed my skin. A few of the lads had already discarded their shirts, too, including Cian.

Feck it.

I only had one spare shirt, which still reeked of smoke and bore ash stains.

Balancing on a ladder, I lowered my mallet onto a rung then pulled my shirt off and tucked it through the strap and buckle on the back of my work pants. Most crew lads did this to ensure their articles of clothing weren't stolen—a common problem. We kept our cloths of food on us too, tied to a bag loop at the waist.

I scanned the sprawling market in various stages of construction. Each tribe had their own signature colors. Ours were dark red, purple, and various shades of gold.

"Ready your poles, lads!" Corbin shouted.

Cian, on a ladder beside me, pretended to grab his "pole" while swinging his hips in a thrusting dance. "Ready!" he hollered back, throwing me a wink. Sean and I huffed a laugh, shaking our heads. Fecking Cian. That mortal was filthy chaos, even when sober and overworked.

Owen rolled his eyes and tossed a sweaty rag at Cian. The grimy cloth hit him in the face, making us laugh again.

Cian narrowed his eyes. "Your knickers, Owen. Not your hankie. Show proper appreciation of my titilating performance."

"Fecking eejit," Owen replied with a grin.

"Top it off, boys!" a crew member said from the tent's center after inspection.

The wooden posts for the faerie animal menagerie we had anchored a foot into the ground—always a lovely time, that task—and the framed slats were fitted together with nails and joints. Unicorns, sirens, and other species would be put on display in this exhibit. A few of them real, most costumed or illusioned.

Below us, children combed the grass for fallen nails. Corbin had finally finished unfolding the canvas and tossed it over the frame. I grabbed my blunted pole hook, hanging on the side of my ladder, and eased the canvas toward me.

Sometimes, a Raven flew over the tent tops to yank the canvas toward the crew. Our wings were large, though, and created a decent wind, often making the task dangerous. Frames had collapsed, canvases blown away, knocking crew from their ladders.

We had one more tent to build after this: the mirror gallery. We'd frame and canvas the exhibit today and, tomorrow, we'd securely fasten the mirrors to the temporary walls. We would build the fencing and stalls for the faerie animal menagerie tomorrow too.

Normally we had two more medium-sized tents to build and five additional small ones, but they were lost in the fires. Including Filena's. For her, we had converted an older supply wagon into a divination room.

"Rhylen!" Cian said low, interrupting my thoughts, his eyes wide with warning.

Before I could even look behind me, the ladder was shoved and I lost my footing. My wings snapped out before I could hit the ground and I softly landed on the grass before Bryok. Around me, fellys lowered their heads and eyes. But I kept my glare steady.

"Missing something?" the arsehole asked.

A lad from his gang snatched my shirt.

I didn't move to retrieve it. A pointless effort, I knew. Instead, I kept a dead stare locked onto Bryok, my muscles flexing down my body.

"How old are you?" I asked in a bored tone. "Twenty-five, is it? Yet you behave like a fledgling." I swept a hand dramatically at Bryok and announced, "Ladies and gents, our heir."

"You continually forget your place, *felly*," he sneered. Bryok studied Cian and my stomach dropped. "Slave," he ordered. "Attend me."

Cian clenched his teeth and climbed down the ladder, his head and eyes lowered as he stood before Bryok. "Yes, sire?" he asked through gritted teeth.

"Your sister is the only reason we haven't traded you yet." Bryok slowly circled around Cian, inspecting him. "I bet she would do anything to keep you in West Tribe, too."

Territorial fire exploded in my veins.

Blood painted my vision.

That bastard wouldn't live beyond the next five minutes.

Before I could charge, Sean jumped in front of me and grabbed my arms.

"Control yourself," Sean warned in a heated whisper. "For Cian *and* Filena."

Even though I worried I wouldn't beat Bram in a challenge—putting the fate of everyone I loved in his hands if I lost—I wasn't sure I could control myself where Bryok was concerned. I completely understood his game now and I should have figured this out far sooner. It wasn't just to have a powerful slave as his own, one he could crow about over the other tribes. It was to ensure I never challenged him for the gov position. That disgusting arsehole knew Filena Merrick was my ultimate weakness.

"Cian Merrick," Bryok sang out with a delighted smile. "You are my property tonight."

"Yes, sire." Shame burned my best friend's cheeks.

I tensed and Sean gripped my arms tighter with a slight shake of his head. This wasn't done. Bryok couldn't claim a slave that wasn't his without the owner's permission unless it was for a tribe emergency, like the fires.

"The next time your master forgets his place," Bryok said, "it will be your sister instead of you and she'll kneel before me. I'll punish her any time he forgets his place and make you both watch, gagged and tied up. Now," the prince gloated, "get dressed."

"Yes, sire," Cian whispered between clenched teeth and threw his shirt on.

"Felly," Bryok said to me. "Remove your boots."

I closed my eyes for a furious second then began unlacing my boots. Cian would suffer if I didn't obey. Filena too. Sean stepped aside, but close enough to intervene if I saw red again.

"On your knees," Bryok commanded once I tossed my boots aside.

My blood was rapidly boiling, but I knelt before him, my eyes lowered.

Bryok pulled a switch knife from his pocket, yanked a braid free from my knotted hair, and cut it off. "A gift for Filena," he said.

I was going to be sick.

"If you weren't required to secure a dowry this week, I'd shave your head." To a lad in his gang, he said, "Take his shirt and boots. Cian will burn them."

Those were my only shoes—

A slap sounded across my face and my head whipped to the side with the momentum. The taste of copper pooled in my mouth and rage rippled down my muscles. A dark laugh began bubbling up from my chest, one I didn't set free. The lad had no idea he was fecking with a male who was protecting his True Mate, a different type of property. Our kind had rules for this and the prince breathed on borrowed time.

Though, I wasn't sure if the tribe would allow me to protect a mortal, a mortal slave no less.

Bryok spit on me and walked off. Cian slid me an apologetic frown beneath lowered eyes, then followed behind the prince's gang, his steps stiff, his back rigid. When they were far enough away, I lifted my head and stood. The crew eyed me, in fear, in embarrassment, in anger.

"Back to work, lads!" I shouted, as if nothing were amiss. "Our flock depends on us!"

Slowly, one by one, they returned to their tasks.

Righting my ladder, I climbed up and refused Bryok the satisfaction of my shame. He could burn my shirt, my only pair of shoes, use a mortal slave as a shield—a woman, no less—but he proved nothing other than he was a coward who would lose in a fair fight.

And that the size of my wings, as well as the rest of me, were far larger than him.

Chapter Ten

FILENA MERRICK

"Slow down," Glenna chastised me—again. "You'll cut off the peel."

I stopped the knife and glared at the apple in my hand. I couldn't peel an apple in one continuous curl on most occasions, let alone on the day it would reveal my one true love. The gods knew I would be useless in most feminine arts and, thus, gifted me with other skills.

Fine, *one* skill.

But it was a good one—just not on Áine's Day.

This was the worst day of the year.

The day before the Autumn Night Market opened.

A day I was required to endure matchmaking traditions with mortal and fae girls—from all four tribes—who desperately wanted a clue, *any clue*, as to who their future spouse would be. And, naturally, that meant I was a busy lass.

The amount of times I would shockingly pull the *Ceirt* oracle card today—the apple tree, symbol of the Otherworld and choice.

Often the choice of love. For Raven Folk, who mated for life, *Ceirt* represented the chosen Otherworldly romance the lovers hoped was fated by the gods.

Normally we celebrated Áine, the goddess of love, the goddess of faeries, on midsummer since she was also the goddess of summer and light. But Samhain wasn't just a time when the Otherworld's veil thinned, allowing us an opportunity to commune with our ancestors. It was a holiday steeped in romance.

Slaves who were granted permission to marry and Traveler girls hoping to mate bond before the new year played fortune telling games clear into the evening, even after the revel. And games they were, nothing more. Until me, it had been well over two centuries since a mortal seer belonged to a Night Market.

Unwed girls wove sprigs of herbs in their hair. Rosemary to show that she carried the love from her old home to her new one. Lavender for luck in love and marital passions. Catnip to make her more enticing to the eye. Before bed, the hopeful brides would light the herbs to smoke in front of a mirror and ask for a reflection of the lad they would marry.

Glenna was busy all last evening making Ring Cakes, which she and the other confectionists baked in complete silence, per tradition. Old rings were baked into tiny cupcakes. Whoever discovered one in theirs was guaranteed to find a husband. If she found a pea, however, she wouldn't wed that year. A stick meant she would have an unhappy marriage. I secretly laughed whenever a hopeful girl bit into a stick and believed her fate, the eejit. It proved that not all fae were clever.

A pity that males were not also influenced by cake sticks. There were a few I wished a very unhappy day *and* marriage.

95

But my favorite tradition? We had to climb stairs and pass through every doorway backward, all day long. For endangering our lives in our silly heeled shoes and mounds of petticoats would allow us to spot the handsome lad destined to be our husband.

Lucky him.

I tolerated Áine's Day. This year, however, it was a constant reminder of the shards of glass mercilessly, endlessly cutting into my heart. The only male who visited my dreams, the only one who haunted my visions, was a male I had to watch fall in love with another.

Regardless, my one limitation as a seer was that I couldn't *see* my own future. If I asked, "Who is the lad I'll marry?" he wouldn't appear to me. Not in smoke, not in pieces of cake, ripples of water, cooking hazelnuts, or discarded fruit.

Who found their lover by putting hazelnuts over a fire?

How did that even become a trusted form of matchmaking?

Hazelnuts were delicious, hard to come by, and deserved a better fate than charring to ash to see which lad would burn for his mate. I should create a vision of how the gods were no longer pleased by hazelnut sacrifices.

For the good of all, and hazelnuts, I would abuse this gift . . .

The girl next to me finished skinning her poor apple and tossed the ribboned peel over her shoulder with a delighted giggle. Gasps circled around me and I rolled my eyes. Glenna snickered with a gentle elbow-to-the-side reminder to behave.

"Fáidhbhean," a chorus of girls said. I paused the massacre of my love apple and glanced up. "What letter do you *see*?" the girl beside me asked.

I turned and studied the lump of peel sprawled across the

grass. Failed hopes and dreams? Frivolous traditions? Fake romance?

"F."

Giggles and squeals scraped the inside of my ears.

First, F is a difficult letter for any fruit to form. Second, all the best names begin with an F, naturally. Also, there was no letter. It was a browning peel tossed to the ground. No magic in it, just a holiday game. A peel they would tuck beneath their pillow this night so the fruit of love could reveal in their dreams the lad they would marry—one starting with the letter the peel formed on the ground when tossed.

Did they consider how many times they had tossed apple peels and, yet, their fruit-picked mate hadn't appeared to claim their heart?

Visions were not something I could control, either, despite Raven Folk beliefs that it was like any other magic. Not that I would let them believe otherwise. It's how Cian and I remained in happy positions as indentures.

"Fenry," a girl said.

"Fadam!" another squealed.

Fadam . . . poor lad.

And off they went, naming every single lad they knew beginning with the letter F. Barry made a grumbling sound and placed a paw over his ears.

"You're terrible," Glenna murmured, a wicked slant to her conspiratorial smile. She flicked the blue bow tying the side of my hair back—my mam's ribbon. "Not all of us see *gossip* visions like you do, darlin'."

"Tell me something utterly scandalous to cheer my soul." I

nicked a piece of the peel and offered it to wee Sheila in my pocket, the name I gave Barry's forest friend. "Dreadfully, horribly scandalous. I want to find joy in another's misery, I do."

"Kaela Branwen," Glenna began, leaning in close and lowering her voice, "dairy upsets her digestion and she had forbidden cheese—"

"So romantical."

"—Yes, well she ate romantical forbidden cheese before flight in her bird form and shited on Brenden Allan while shifted—"

My mouth dropped in horror. "No!"

"—many witnesses," Glenna whispered, her eyes wide with humor. "When Kaela realized what she had done, she panicked, started to shift back, and flew into a tree trunk"—I slapped a hand over my mouth to quiet my loud, unladylike cackle—"knocked herself out, she did. Guess who came to her rescue?"

I wiped away tears. "Brenden Allan."

"Did you *see* the answer?"

"Am I right?"

"Not if you cheated, darlin'."

I put a hand to my hip and arched a brow. "Finish the story before I curse your woo fruit to writhe with maggots. It will be known by all as the not-allowed-to-get-married-this-year death apple."

"That's dark," she replied with a sputtered laugh.

I gestured to the tables of apples and nuts and cabbages. "Why are we doing this—"

"*Fáidhbhean*," a giggling gaggle of girls called to me. I twisted to look at the peel they pointed at.

"F."

96

"Her lad's name begins with a F too?"

I arched a brow and drolled, "You dare question the *fáidhbhean*? Tell me, lass, what letter did the gods reveal to you?"

The gaggle tilted their heads in unison and studied the browning peel.

"I see it!" one of them shouted with an excited jump.

"Maybe you'll marry Fenry and she'll marry Fadam," I said to stir the pot. If I couldn't curse, I would create other forms of chaos. It truly was a wonderful, terrible burden, this magic.

I turned back to Glenna and drew in a deep breath and let it out slowly. "Now, darlin', was it Brenden Allan who rescued Kaela?"

Glenna leaned in close once more, her eyes bright and her grin large. "No, it was Cian. She landed on top of his lunch."

"WHAT?!" I howled. The sounds coming from me weren't human, I was laughing so hard. "Please tell me George helped him."

"Cian—"

"Aye?"

Both Glenna and I jumped to clutch the other.

My brother slowed before us. I would yell at him for sneaking up on us, but the dark circles under his eyes and grim curve to his frowning lips gave me pause. A travel sack rested over his shoulder, down his back, and . . . Rhylen's lute was gripped in his hands.

"Tell me he's not considering . . ." Glenna whispered, pressing a hand to her stomach. Blood visibly drained from her head and she blinked back an emotion I didn't understand.

What was going on?

"What choice does he have?" Cian replied in a voice so defeated, the hairs on my arms lifted. "We used our savings to repair a wheel last month and to re-shoe a horse. Nothing else we own would fetch a price."

"Fetch a price for what?" I asked, looking between them.

Glenna looked away and Cian's throat noticeably bobbed.

I grabbed Cian by the suspenders and dragged him away from the Áine's Day festivities, and Glenna trailed behind me. Once out of earshot, I hissed, "Start talking."

"Rhylen was stripped yesterday evening. By Bryok." Cian's gaze flit to Glenna's and back to me. Did they conspire to not tell me? I darted Glenna a look which she deliberately ignored. "Took his shirt and boots," Cian continued, "and I was forced to burn them as his hijacked slave for the evening."

He made my brother do *what*?! My heart dropped to my stomach. "Bryok would take out his crew lead when we have already lost so much?"

"You believe Bryok cares about anything?" The bitterness in Cian's words rumbled through me. "Anyway, I'm on my way to the nearest village to trade for a pair of used boots and, if enough is left over, a used shirt."

"Trade his great-granda's instrument . . ." I whispered. Stars, I wanted to retch.

"And his da's cuff links." Cian closed his eyes in a long blink. "He was asked to play at tonight's revel too."

But he needed work boots.

Being Raven Folk, the village wouldn't trust him to make a fair trade or trade with him at all. Bryok probably thought Cian was finishing setup tasks today and didn't think to busy him with anything else.

Fellys were typically punished by losing articles of clothing too, especially shoes. Besides their wagons and horses, it was often the only object of means the lower ranks possessed. A barefoot lad of his age would be a telltale sign to the gathered tribes. No one interfered with a gov's domination. Just like no one would interfere with a felly challenging a gov.

Tears glistened on Glenna's lashes. Her fingers slid down the front of her family's instrument.

My mind continued to spin. An intuitive feeling settled deep in my gut. Bryok hadn't busied Cian with other tasks, knowing Rhylen would need to trade his granda's lute, then asked for him to play at tonight's revel as a deeper dig.

Anger twisted inside of me. A roaring flame.

Bryok wouldn't destroy Rhylen, not while I drew breath.

Leaning in closer, I quietly shared, "I have a small nest egg. Enough for a used pair of men's boots."

Cian was quiet for a moment. "Rhylen would murder me if you spent your savings on him."

"Rhylee Lo isn't here to protest," I said with a shrug. "If his feathers get murderously ruffled, I'll just tell him I *saw* it in a vision. The gods' will." My hand fluttered in the air dismissively. "Ends every argument, it does."

"You . . . lie, *fáidhbhean*?" Cian asked in pretend horror. Pointing at a random girl in the crowd, he added, "Her ancestors are weeping in their graves. 'Shame!' They cry."

I studied my nails and heaved a bored sigh. "Are you done?"

"Shame . . ." he said in a dramatic whisper.

"Stay here with Glenna and I'll be back." I took a step, paused, and stepped back, leaning in close to my brother. "See the girls over there?" I gestured with my head.

"The ones with black hair and dark eyes or the ones with black hair and dark eyes? Or the group of girls by them with black hair and dark eyes?"

"Aye," I said in a mysteriously serious voice, making him snort. "Walk over there, look at the peel on the ground, all the peels, and say, 'they look like the letter F.'"

Cian barked a laugh. "You are a wicked mortal, lass."

"Or a clever trickster fae." I tapped his forehead with a wink. "If you really love me, truly love me, you'll also mention that Fenry and Fadam are lucky lads."

"Fenry Black?" He scrunched up his face in mild disgust.

"Terrible kisser," Glenna said with a similar expression.

"Aye," Cian agreed. "Too much spit."

"And the teeth. Why the teeth?"

Cian nodded his head in vigorous agreement. "He bit my tongue! Made me talk funny for days."

Glenna put a hand on Cian's shoulder. "But have you kissed, Marlene?"

"Pouty lips Marlene?"

"The very one."

Cian's smile was slow. "Oh aye. She's a looker. Knows how to use those pouty lips too."

My friend's replying smile was also slow. "That she does."

"Glennie Lo," Cian cooed, his smile turning impish, "who else have you kissed?"

Before Glenna answered him, I gently pulled the lute from Cian's hands. "I'll leave it with Gran."

Cian kissed my cheek and winked. "I adore your rebel ways,

sister dear."

"Keep Glenna out of trouble until I return."

"Encourage her to get into trouble?" he playfully asked, pretending he didn't quite hear me.

Glenna kissed my cheek next and squeezed my hand. She wouldn't say "thank you," but I could see it in her eyes.

"Love you," I whispered.

"Love you more," she whispered back with a teasing smile to hide her grateful tears.

Her hand slipped from mine as I ambled back to Gran's wagon, leaving Cian and Glenna to carry out my mischief.

Chapter Eleven

FILENA MERRICK

I angled through the hopeful girls crowding West Tribe's lot—involved in games, placing flowers and herbs in each other's hair, or watching boys while giggling behind hands. I took it all in and pressed Rhylen's instrument close to me.

"Pretty mortal."

Of course I couldn't escape unnoticed. I huffed a sigh. This pretty mortal was on a mission nor did I possess a shred of patience for tricks or bargains. Ignoring the male, I gripped the lute tighter in my hand and continued walking.

"Mortal, you *will* stop."

A wave of warm, tingling magic dewed my skin. But that was as far as his coercion magic touched me. Barry peered behind him and I swore he huffed, like I had, while rolling his eyes. I was an indentured in West Tribe and, thus, had some protections against coercion. But also . . . my fox familiar was a guardian against magic. No faerie could compel or curse me. With Muffin Moo, my magic also couldn't be enthralled to use on others.

"*Mortal—*"

I twirled toward the voice behind me and narrowed my eyes. A fae from a different kingdom regarded me curiously—a Púca more precisely, or what mainlanders from the eastern cities called a Puck. Small horns protruded from his silvery hair, like a pile of soot from the firepit, with pewter eyes to match. A friendly smile tempered the more angular features of his face.

I arched an impatient brow. I rarely had patience. But I *really* lacked patience for fae males who manipulated mortal women for their amusement.

Barry bared his teeth and growled.

"Do you know who I am, pet?" Before he could reply, I answered, "Try your magic on me again and I will curse you to see only hands for eyes. The reaching fingers of many will claw at your vision until you pluck your own eyes out from insanity."

The Puck's already pale complexion grew whiter than the waxing moon.

"Now shoo," I said, gesturing with my free hand. The male sprinted off, knocking down a Traveler lad in his panic, and I cackled at his retreat. Watching males run in terror of me was more beautiful than an entire confectioner's wagon filled with delectable, magical desserts.

A blissful sigh left me as I scratched behind Barry's ears. "Thank you, darlin'."

Normally Barry licked my chin, but he licked my fingers then began trotting forward again, knowing I would follow him. His tail wagged happily; his ears perked too. It wasn't often Barry used his protection wards anymore, but it always made him merrily skip afterward when he did.

A few minutes later, I cleared the festivities and leisurely strolled toward the felly wagons, weaving between trees, Barry close on my heels. A song lilted in my mind and I hummed the tune to myself. Late autumn wildflowers swayed and bobbed their heads in the light breeze and I closed my eyes as the sweet, floral scent swirled around me.

"Why do you have my lute?"

My eyes snapped open and I spun on my heel.

Rhylen leaned against a tree, barefoot, arms crossed over his chest, a deep scowl between his black brows as his swollen eyes sharpened on the instrument in my hands. A warm, delirious ache drizzled down my body at the sinful sight of him. Suns and moons, he was shirtless and I couldn't form a coherent thought. Tattooed knots and swirls decorated his defined chest, shoulders, and down the curves of his arms. The ridged muscles of his stomach disappeared into the pants hugging his trim waist. All the long, silky strands of his black hair were pulled up into a messy knot. A few flyaway strands fluttered around his face and I held back a sigh.

He was so beautiful I could weep.

The barest hint of a smile teased the corners of his mouth. "Lena," he said softly and I blinked back my daze.

My eyes darted around the meadow and up into the nearby trees. A few crows pecked the ground, a few perched up in the branches above. But no ravens—Folk or otherwise.

Swallowing thickly, I approached. My heart was thudding wildly in my chest. My breath was tight and awkward. I slowed before him and he arched a single brow. The skin around his eyes was red and I grit my teeth as anger twisted inside of me once more. Ravens like Bryok were the very reason some mortals called a gathering of Travelers an "unkindness" and I wouldn't stand for it.

"Why do you have my lute?" he asked again.

"You're not trading your great-granda's instrument," I whispered, in case a Raven I didn't see was nearby. "I won't allow it, Rhy."

A muscle ticked along his jaw. "It's not your choice to make."

"No," I said, stepping in closer. "But it's not the only choice either."

"Choice," he repeated with an ill-humored laugh, "is a privilege neither you nor I possess, lass."

"I choose you," I whispered and his gaze locked onto mine with a heated intensity that seared each beat of my racing pulse. "I would do anything to protect you, Rhylen, even protect you from yourself. That arsehole will not strip you of your magic too. Music is in your blood." I lifted the lute. "This belongs to your family. Shirts and shoes are replaceable."

He closed his eyes and leaned his head back onto the trunk. "Lena," he breathed on a long, heavy sigh. "Whatever you're planning—"

"I will do without your permission. I don't care that you own me."

Those mesmerizing dark purple eyes opened and narrowed on me.

"I have a nest egg—"

"No." His voice was a low growl.

I lifted my chin. "Yes."

"No," he repeated.

"And let Bryok win? You would aid him in robbing you of more? Why don't you throw in your wagon and horses while you're at it!" I huffed. "Don't put your pride before reason, darlin'. Or revenge."

Rhylen gritted his teeth. "Fecking Cian."

"You can't stop me." I skip-walked backward, a challenging tilt to my lips. "Unless you tie me to my bed—"

I cut myself off.

Flaming stars, why did I say bed instead of chair?

A sensual smile softened the harsh scowl brooding between his brows. "Tempting," he replied quietly.

Did he just *flirt* with me?

Boldness swept through me at the thought. "Maybe if you're a good boy and let me buy you a pair of shoes like the gods will."

Rhylen threw his head back and laughed. "Filena, what am I to do with you?"

"I thought we established what was to be done with me, pet."

My eyes widened. What in the midnight skies just left my mouth? A blush heated my stinging skin. Mortification didn't even come close to the riptide of embarrassment rushing through me right now. I needed to walk away before I suggested other scandalous ideas. I really couldn't think straight with his hair a mess from work and . . . and . . .

"Did Bryok burn your spare shirt too?" I blurted awkwardly.

His humored grin anchored my feet before I could flee. A rascally, boyish smile I felt in every heating corner of my body down to my curling toes. "I didn't give him the opportunity." He winked at me.

Then he strode toward me, his steps leisurely, almost flirtatious, his gaze locked onto mine. I was dying a thousand deaths right now. Each one blissfully slow and tortuous. Why did he have to be so perfect? Why couldn't he bring me liver and onions instead of cake and berries, and have significantly less muscles? Much, *much* less muscles. Sweet moons, every line and curve of his body called to mine.

I didn't know what to do with my face or my hands. Did I smile back? Casually flip my hair? Bat my eyelashes like a desperate girl on Áine's Day? Hold my hands prim and proper at my waist? Fist them onto my hips?

Dear goddess of love, help me. I would peel a hundred apples, sacrifice a thousand delicious hazelnuts to a fire, wear an entire lavender bush in my hair.

Oh stars . . .

Gently, he cupped my face and neck with one hand while taking his lute back with the other. Rhylen tilted my head up, our mouths dangerously close. The warmth of his body fevered through me. I wanted to place my hands on his chest, to feel his skin beneath my fingertips.

"Remember when I broke a bone in my wing?"

I blinked a few times, trying to calm my heart. He was fourteen and had tumbled in a play-fight with Sean in a game to see who the stronger lad was. They had hit an unsecured tent post and the frame crashed atop Rhylen.

"You mewled like a wet, hungry kitten," I said in a mock serious tone. He had silently sat scowling in a corner, angry to miss out on the older fledgling races the next day. "Kept us all up at night with your loud weeping, you did."

Rhylen's eyes were a warm smile as they swept across my face.

"Aye, the misery," he teased back. "But a redheaded lass brought me her favorite button. Her dress was threadbare, several buttons missing. An anxious habit, it is." His gaze trailed over my auburn waves and paused at the bow on the back of my head. "She wore an old blue ribbon in her long hair. One she only wore twice a year."

Beltane and Áine's Day, the two most romantic holidays for Travelers.

"It was August." He drew in a quickened breath. "She wore the ribbon for me."

I had and my skin warmed at his confession. He knew. All these years . . . the ribbon had reminded me of my mam and I knew he missed his too. But I also knew Ravens liked pretty objects—buttons, rocks, ribbons, jewelry—especially the sentimental kind. It brought them happiness. Seeing his disappointment, his pain, I did the only thing my twelve-year-old mind could think of without drawing attention to his embarrassment over the incident.

"She gave me one of the most expensive treasures she owned," he continued, "wore a piece of her heart in her beautiful hair for me . . ." his voice trailed off and he swallowed thickly as his gaze lingered on the old, stained blue satin strip tied into a bow behind my head. "Later that day, a village boy pulled her mam's ribbon from her hair."

"You brawled and knocked him out cold." And with a broken wing. All to protect one of the only things I had left of my family.

Tilting his mouth closer to his, he whispered across my lips, "I choose you, too, Filena Moira Merrick."

His breath fluttered, his chest rising and falling furiously.

Was he about to kiss *me*?

Why would he kiss *me*?

He shouldn't be kissing *me*.

But I was far too weak to push him away or refuse him—*anything*. And selfish. I was so, so selfish. He belonged to another and yet I craved every forbidden second we shared just now to care.

His beautiful berry wine eyes lingered on my lips for a drunken beat before drifting back up to hold my gaze. "You are mine." His voice was low, breathless. "Mine to protect. And . . . I am *always* yours, *a stór*."

My heart sank.

A stór, my treasure. My *friend*.

I caressed the raven mark on my wrist. Of course, I was his. He owned me. We were bound by ravens as master and slave, he and I.

Childhood *friends*.

There was no romance in his words. No confession of longing.

The fae didn't thank another. To do so was a bargain, indebting them in an unspecified favor owed, one their magic acknowledged. This story and physical affection were nothing more than his gratitude. Protecting his magic, his happiness was what moved him.

Not me.

Not in the way I wanted.

But what I wanted was dangerous.

"I better return to Cian, aye?" I stepped out of his touch. "Play each song tonight in Bryok's honor," I said with a trembling, conspiratorial smile—I didn't plan on attending the revel. "Make him suffer."

I didn't wait for him to reply. I picked up my skirts and dashed toward our wagons.

My breath was coming in quick. My legs were shaking. My

mind swelled with images of tasting Rhylen's lips, memorizing his body, confessing my love.

At the wagon, I slowed before Gran in her rocking chair. Barry licked her hand, like he usually did when greeting her, and I offered a small smile as I took a step.

"Backward, me Filly girl," she quickly admonished. "Don't anger the gods by being foolish on Áine's Day."

Gripping my skirts, I turned and felt for the first step and awkwardly climbed the next, blinking back the tears in my eyes. Perhaps it would be a small mercy to fall to my death right now. Barry would have all the desserts his wee fox heart desired. Glenna would feed him cake to comfort his inconsolable sorrows.

"Eyes forward," Gran said.

Gritting my teeth, I lifted my gaze and locked onto Rhylen as he leaned against a tree, plucking his lute. My chest heaved at the heady sight of him.

You are mine.

I am yours.

"Do ye see yer future husband?" she asked me quietly, a wink and smile in her voice.

I swallowed thickly. "I can't *see* my future, remember?"

"That's because yer not using yer eyes, Filly girl."

Oh how I wished it were that simple.

Chapter Twelve

RHYLEN LONAN

The vibrations from the bodhrán drum in my hand moved through me. The tempo had picked up and the tipper in my fingers flew across the goatskin. Magic soared in my veins, the wings of my pulse beating in rhythm to the lively reel. My fellow musicians seemed to fly in the same melodic sky, each lost to their instrument. I had played my lute for the first twelve songs. The lead asked me to take up the bodhrán the last three to give our other drummer a much-needed break.

On the dance floor, revelers clapped three times above their heads, then clasped their arms and spun in place with their partners while lifting a cheer. Glennie swirled by me with a wink and I snorted. An elf struck, blond-haired village lad was on her arm. Around her, girls had hiked up their skirts to step to the quick beat. The gents had tossed their coats and rolled up their sleeves.

Nothing compared to a faerie revel. Especially one among natives of Caledona Wood. And the Áine's Day celebration had been burning bright for a couple of hours now. Folk and mortals from the Caravan tribes, as well as our Autumn Night Market attendees, would continue to eat, drink, and make mischief until the sun rose.

I tapped the toe of my new boots, a smile inching up my face. They pinched a little, but I didn't care. These shoes were newer than the hand-me-downs I had been wearing for a few years now. A part of me wanted to spiral into self-loathing for allowing Filena to care for me financially. The other part of me, the more practical side of me, knew she was right.

My eyes hunted for the silky waves of her auburn hair. But I had yet to catch a glimpse of her lithe form or hear her boisterous laugh since the revel began. Disappointment gnawed incessantly at my gut with every candlemark she didn't show. Each year, I looked forward to stealing her away for a dance or two. This year, I wanted to dance with her until I was breathless and spent.

Candlelight flickered off my lute and my gaze slid to the instrument resting against a chair at my feet.

I didn't think there were any pieces of my heart left to break since Bryok "pulled" my name from the elder's hat. But when Cian walked away with my family's instrument, I couldn't stop the grief-stricken fury. Tears had burned trails down my cheeks. If I defied Bryok, Filena would be forced onto her knees before him. My fingers had wanted to claw into the tree trunk I leaned against, uproot it, and toss it over the mountains.

And then my mate marched the lute right back to me with the three prettiest words to have ever stolen my breath.

I choose you.

I repeated the words in my head over and over. An endless loop of her soft voice claiming me as hers.

I choose you.

I choose you.

I choose you.

I would do anything to protect you.

The stunned, furious look on Bryok's face when he strolled into the revel and found me among the musicians was the beginning of many revenges. I lowered my eyes in required submission—for Cian's sake, for Filena's too, but only until I secured their safety.

The music slowed and the lead dipped his head in a visual cue that the song would end in 4 . . . 3 . . . 2 . . . I lowered the drum and grinned as the crowd applauded and whistled. The four of us on stage bent in shallow bows. We had played a full fifteen song set in a row. Replacement musicians walked onto the stage for the next two hours. But we would return after them in a rotation until sunrise.

"Drink up, lads," the lead said. "Rhylen, you'll sing next set, aye?"

I grabbed my lute and slung it across my back. "Aye," I answered over my shoulder as I jogged off the stage toward the felly and slave area, to Cian and the boys.

"There's the broody arse," Cian said with a slight slur and lifted his pint. The other lads lifted theirs in salute. "To girls and—wait." Glennie walked by and Cian plucked a fresh mug of ale from her hands and put it into mine. My sister's mouth fell open but Cian ignored her. "There. Now where was I?"

"To girls!" Sean volunteered with a grin as Glenna playfully glowered.

"To girls!" Cian lifted his pint again and we clinked our mugs.

I took a sip, barely suppressing a laugh, then returned the ale to my sister, who rolled her eyes and pushed the mug back to me as she stepped up to Cian.

My best friend bit his bottom lip in an impish smile. "Breaking hearts, darlin'?"

"All of them," she tossed back.

"Where's Jerry?" He said the boy's name with an innocent blink.

"Jimmy," Glennie corrected. "And probably crying a river behind the food tent." She heaved a long, dramatic sigh. "Time to find me another mortal blond lad to spend the evening with now."

Cian slowly nodded his head and my sister narrowed her eyes. "I need your dress."

Sean whooped and Corbin slapped Cian on the back.

I quickly downed the ale, shaking my head. Cian was such an eejit, especially when sloshed.

"Corbin," Glenna said without taking her eyes off Cian. "Be a hero and ask your brother for another round, aye?" Corbin dipped his head with a large, humored grin and dashed through the crowd to the outdoor pub. "I need your suit."

"Want my boxers too?"

"Why not? You'll need my drawers and corset."

"Obviously. I'm no hussy."

Glenna leaned in until she was inches from his face. "Even if you're the village strumpet, you still won't break as many hearts as me."

Cian shrugged. "You're running out of blond lads, darlin'."

My sister reached up and brushed a lock of fair hair from Cian's gray eyes. "Am I, pet?"

"Nice try, Raven Folk witch—"

Glenna flicked his forehead.

"Ow!"

"Lady of Man," she cooed, "bets."

"Gent of Fem," he cooed back equally as syrupy, "bets." Cian grabbed Sean's top hat and plopped it onto Glennie's head low over her eyes and on an angle. "A proper, saucy gent now."

She tipped the hat at Sean with a touch of her fingers and he pretended to tip an invisible hat in reply.

Cian grabbed Owen's pint mid sip and shoved it into my hands, then draped an arm across my shoulders and pointed at the crowd. "They're all frothing desperate for a Traveler lad, you lucky bastard." Placing a hand beneath the mug, he lifted it to my lips. Owen gestured for me to finish off his drink with a drunken, lopsided smile. I quickly downed this mug too. "Look at them," Cian slurred in my ear. "Girls are circling close, as if any wing feather you shimmy into view will be the most orgasmic peep show experience of their life." Cian sighed. "I need feathers."

He wasn't wrong, though, and my skin crawled at the unwanted attention. All evening, single Raven Folk lasses and village girls had been wolfishly staring at me and other unmated males as if we were meaty buck carcasses still fresh from a kill. Their meddling mams and nans too.

"Where's Filena?" I asked him, but it was my sister who answered.

"Gran was feeling poorly."

I nodded. Since both she and Filena worked at night, they took turns caring for Gran when Gran wasn't well enough to also attend events. Glenna enjoyed revels far more than Filena so it made sense that Filena stayed behind. This past year, especially, it had been less common for Glenna and Filena to be together. They never complained—we would all do anything for Gran—but I could see how much they missed having more carefree time for each other. Probably one of many reasons why Glenna leaned more on Cian for friendship lately.

My sister took Sean's hat off her head and put it on Cian's. "Be a dear, Rhy, and bring her and Gran Ring Cakes?"

"And miss the Lady of Man and Gent of Fem Heartbreak Show?" A corner of my mouth tilted up.

Cian kissed my cheek and whispered, "No talons for you tonight," just as Glenna tugged him by the suspenders and dragged him toward the woods.

"She's going to sacrifice me to the gods, Rhy," Cian shouted over his shoulder. "I'm too pretty to die young!"

Owen and Sean whistled and hooted suggestively and I laughed. Since fledglings, those two had humorously competed with each other, their bets growing more and more ridiculous.

"Off to swap clothes, are they?" Corbin asked, trading the empty mugs in my hands with two fresh pints. "Musician's tip," he said with a wink. Thank the wishless stars, I was thirsty. "Bottoms up, lads."

Sean, Corbin, Owen, and I lifted our ales and, in a matter of seconds, drank until only the foam remained. I would savor the other pint, though. If I didn't pace myself, I wouldn't be able to walk back up onto the stage.

"Fellas," I said with a dramatic bow, "need to check on Gran." I took another pint from Corbin with a kissy face, this drink for Filena. Corbin patted my cheek before playfully shoving my face away, sloshing some of the ale over the mug's rim.

Grinning, I began angling through the crowds toward the

confections stand, a mug in each hand, my lute strapped to my back.

The meadow was thick with people—flirting, dancing, kissing. The lantern-lit night wrapped around me in a cool caress. I could almost feel the soft breeze flutter my wing feathers—I kept them shifted out of sight, though. The girls were terrifying enough without flashing more of my masculine beauty for their viewing pleasure. But stars, my wings itched between my shoulder blades for release. My head was starting to spin, too, from the three ales I threw back on an empty stomach. Thankfully, I remained light on my feet, still floating from the magic rushing in my veins. A breathless laugh filled me. I loved this feeling, this high. A musician's high.

I slowed at the confections wagon and greeted Glenna's co-workers. Ring Cakes were arranged on platters, individually wrapped in tissue. A younger lass, helping from a different tribe, balanced two in the crook of my arm. Then, with mugs balanced in my hands again, I sauntered off toward my family's wagons once more . . . and nearly lost my balance when an older man with shaggy auburn hair, a graying beard, and bloodshot gray eyes stumbled into me.

"Piss off, tramp," the mortal slurred.

Sweat and food stains covered his shirt. The long hair of his beard was matted in parts. His equally unkempt hair shone with several days, or weeks, of grease. I lived among the poor, our clothes were often dirty and in patches—not many spares we owned—but drunkards were an entirely different animal. They were pig slop, from head to toe.

"Step aside, sir," I warned with a biting smile.

The mortal leaned into my space, teeth bared, and I nearly

gagged at his stench. "Ye owe me an apology, drifter trash."

No, I didn't. Disgusting men like him didn't deserve my kindness.

Pulling my coercion magic to the front, I growled, "Leave," while baring my teeth in reply, "and do not return to the Night Market or I'll peck your mind to insanity."

He laughed, a loud, raucous sound. Then he spit at my feet and staggered into the revel.

A muscle worked along my jaw.

Rowan berries. The mortal had to be wearing a strand or two—one of the only forms of protection against fae magic.

Shite, if my hands weren't full, I'd illusion a leaf from my pocket into a raven to attack his head. And laugh I would, louder than that arsehole when he ran away screaming. I loosed a hot breath. Another Folk would deal with that slop bucket.

Stepping around the crowds, I ambled into the market proper toward the back wagon lots. My head was still light and airy from magic and from drinking with the lads. The Harvest Moon was almost full, but bright, and I was on my way to see my beautiful mate. I wouldn't let that man ruin a perfectly good evening after a shite of a day.

I dipped my head at the middle-rank hawkers as I passed by, my eyes lowered in submission. Tables sprawled around me, filled with potions, especially love potions, trinkets and jewelry, many "charmed" to catch the eye of a handsome lad, dried herbs for tea, for freshening garments, for spells—

A tug pulled on me, a violent urge to stop as I passed a table with hair combs, lace gloves, handkerchiefs, and . . . ribbons.

My gaze rested on a pretty lavender piece and the strangest sensation moved through me. It was almost as if a faint voice whispered "Filena" in my head in a maddening loop over and over again—my moment with that town drunk all but forgotten.

"Rhylen Lonan," a familiar voice greeted me, but I kept my eyes lowered. "Sweet on a girl already, are you?"

For ten years now . . .

"Or preparing for your required nuptials?" She bit out the last word. The whole tribe was displeased, but what could we do? We were on the brink of bankruptcy and the elders bound their decision in magic. "Pretty things, aye? And you can look at me, felly."

"I have no coin for gifts, lass," I answered, meeting Gwen's dark eyes, a female in her late twenties. But I found I couldn't leave. I *needed* this ribbon. "Will you bargain?"

If only there were cobblers among the Caravan fae to also bargain with. But making shoes required leather and tanning leather was a difficult trade when traveling to a new town every few days—an odorous affair too. Easier to send slaves to purchase our shoes when needed.

"What caught your eye, darlin'?" Gwen gestured to all her wares.

"The purple ribbon."

She lifted the lavender satin in her lace- and ring-adorned hand and I nodded. "I have two broken spokes. Repair them this week?"

My shoulders relaxed and I smiled. "Do you have new spokes already?"

"That I do. Is it a deal then?"

"First," I said with an arch of a brow, "prove the ribbon isn't a trick."

Gwen chuckled. Grabbing a hand mirror, she draped the satin inches from the front and held both objects next to the smoke from her lantern. Smoke and mirrors were the only way us fae could see through another Folk's illusions.

It was indeed a real ribbon.

"Aye, I'll come by this week if you promise to not say a word or judge when you see who wears this ribbon."

A delighted smile stretched across her lips. "Your scandal is your own, Rhylen Lonan."

"Agree, Gwen. No tricks or riddling words."

"Aye, I agree to not say a word or judge when I see who wears my ribbon." The smile didn't falter, though.

"Then deal." I set a mug of ale on the table, shook her hand, and pocketed the satin beside the rose quartz Filena had gifted me. Beside the button she gave me eight years ago too.

Tipping my head, I picked up the mug and continued onward. Past thinning crowds. Through the edge of the meadow where the grass was taller and wildflowers slept beneath the moon.

My head grew lighter the closer I approached our wagons. A quiet laugh left my chest. But it died quickly on my tongue when I took in Filena, curled up on a step, barefoot, in a cream chemise, corset, and dark blue shawl, her cheek resting on Sheila and her shoulders shaking. Barry leaned against her leg and licked a tear off her chin. Had the little hedgehog died?

Or . . .

My heart dropped to my stomach.

Chapter Thirteen

RHYLEN LONAN

Lena?" I asked softly.

She startled and reared back, blinking rapidly. "Oh," she said when recognizing me. Quickly, she wiped her cheeks with her sleeves. Sheila lifted her little nose in the air and sniffed—which made the twinge of nausea in my tightening stomach spasm stronger and my eyes shot to the door.

"Is Gran—"

"What?" she asked, cutting me off. "No," she quickly reassured, shaking her head. "No, she's asleep. Muscle aches and weakness this evening. Rubbed her legs and hands with liniments to ease the discomfort. I emptied the last of the jar . . ." She swallowed thickly and pet Barry on the head between his ears. "She's finally resting."

Pushing my brows together, I knelt before Filena and was about to ask what was wrong when I saw a brush stuck in a tangle of her hair. A corner of my mouth hooked up in a ghost of a smile. Gently, I set our ales and the wrapped Ring Cakes on a step, then removed my lute and rested it against the stairs.

"May I?" I pointed to the brush.

Her shoulders caved in, then her bottom lip trembled. "I tore her ribbon, Rhy . . . I . . . I didn't mean to—" the words were cut off with a heavy sob.

"Oh lass . . ." I knew this pain. Only hours earlier, I feared losing forever a piece of my family. Not caring who saw us, I pulled her to me, wrapping my arms around her upper back, careful not to squish wee Sheila.

Filena pressed her face into my neck and my eyes slid closed at the heady feel of her lips and shuddering breaths falling across my skin, the feel of her corseted softness against me. Feck, this girl. She would be the death of me. And like a tipsy fool, I leaned my cheek against her head and savored every forbidden touch of bare skin.

"It belonged to my nan first," she said between hiccuped sobs. "A gift from her mam . . ."

"And a gift from yours," I whispered into her hair.

"I own nothing," she whispered back. "Nothing is mine. Not one stocking. Not one day dress."

"The dress is yours, *a stór*." I tucked an untangled strand behind the rounded shell of her ear. "The costumes, headdresses from the tribe? They're all yours. I give them to you. Every inch of lace and yard of cotton."

"But the tribe—"

"I already worked off the debts." Her mouth fell open. "Filena Merrick, I would make a hundred bargains to give you just that one day dress, if it's what you wanted. I would make a hundred more to give you a trunk full of dresses."

"Rhylen, you can't—" she took in a shaky breath. "Your mate . . ."

A tiny smile curved my lips. "She won't mind."

Filena pushed back, a horrified scowl between her pretty brows. "Grand promises to a mortal slave your clan owns? Of course she'd mind!"

"If I promise you anything, I also promise her."

"That's nonsense. How much ale have you had?"

"Not enough," I drawled.

She chewed anxiously on her bottom lip. "And Glenna? You'd make bargains for her as you would for your wife?"

A humored smile tilted on my lips. "Aye, Cian too, if he wanted a trunk full of dresses."

Filena sputtered a quiet laugh at that. Cian would ask for stockings and heels too. And a box of cosmetics just to upstage his sister and mine. He was, undoubtedly, the prettiest male bird of us all—or would be if fae.

The wobbly smile on Filena's face faded. I wiped a tear from her cheek, then stood and walked around where she sat on a lower step and studied the tangled mess of her long strands. Gods, how did one get a whole brush knotted into their hair? I fingered what was left of her mam's ribbon. A muscle in my jaw tensed as I thought of the one in my pocket.

Was that the mate bond speaking to me earlier? Had her mam's ribbon snapped the moment magic pulled me to a stop in front of Gwen's table? Goosebumps raced down my arms.

"There's ale," I said softly, to distract my thoughts. "And Ring Cake."

"I hope I bite into a stick," she muttered. My lips twitched. "You'd have to tell everyone, naturally, so they can gossip about my unhappy, unlucky marriage." She unwrapped the small cake. "Poor *fáidhbhean*," she lamented on a sad sigh, "destined to divine the happy love lives of Carran, she is, but fated to live a tragic life scorned by romance. Not even her wild hair could entangle her a mate or save her heart from the agony of unrequited love."

"Unrequited?" I gently gathered her hair and began un-knotting what was left of her mam's ribbon. I almost mentioned that my fingers were currently entangled in her beautiful lantern-lit tresses. Her wild hair had done a fine job of trapping her mate.

"Aye, no feral swine husband for me, pet." Filena bit into the confection and moaned around a mouth full of cake, "I only want a love affair with this. Forever." She took another dainty bite. "You are my one true love—" Her entire body went rigid. Swearing, she yanked the cake from her mouth. An old tin ring was nestled into the crumbs and I burst into laughter. "And now you too have betrayed my heart."

"I can find you a stick," I said, unable to hide the ale from my voice. My head was buzzing lightly. "I'll even put it in the cake for you to bite down on."

"Gran's superstitious arse will wake her from sleep to haunt me, bet you my last button, she will. 'Walk up the stairs backward three times fer good luck, me wee Filly girl,'" she said, mimicking Gran and I grinned. "At least she's not requiring me to put apple peels beneath my pillow."

She winced as I unknotted the brush from her hair.

"Males have it easy," she adorably grumbled. "Do you lads gather by the well to braid each other's hair in-between markets?"

"And share beauty secrets."

"Terrible burden, it is, darlin'."

124

"We care for each other's feathers too."

"In a secret ritual bird bath?"

I laughed. "Only beneath a full Harvest Moon."

"The best feather care magic, aye."

I laid her mam's ribbon pieces on my thigh and then began working through the tangles in gentle strokes.

Her hair . . . I wanted to bury my face in the silky strands and trail kisses down her neck, breathe in her wildflower honeyed scent. Then slowly, reverently, lose my soul to the delicious taste of her lips on mine.

To kiss her, to intimately know the rhythm of her singing pulse as I touched her . . . Stars, help me. I could think of nothing else. And she was in only her underpinnings, which wasn't helping. I have never begged the gods for a shawl to suddenly blow away in a strong gust of wind until this very moment. Filena in a corset . . . a moan lodged in the back of my throat.

Unaware of my suffering, Filena broke a small crumb from the traditional apple pound cake for Sheila and gave the rest to Barry.

With a final stroke, I lowered her brush. She didn't move. Neither did I. A tense silence strung tight between us. Tense but thrumming by our tethered heartbeats. No . . . this was the high I craved, the swelling feeling of completeness I loved.

The tattered remains of the blue ribbons fluttered in a light breeze. I gathered the pieces in my fingers while pulling out the lavender satin from my pocket with the other hand.

"The lad who loves you," I said softly over her shoulder, "will love you madly, obsessively. He'd be willing to burn his world to ash for you."

Her breath was quick, shallow. Affected by me.

These were the words she told me in the woods a week ago. Words I hoped she recognized. I wanted to say more, to confess everything, but I wasn't sure if Bryok sent Ravens to spy on me, or on her. Instead, I hugged my arms around her body until I found her hands and placed both ribbons into her fingers.

"Nothing could ever replace your mam's ribbon. But I hope your daughters and granddaughters will wear a ribbon in their hair for you too and smile when remembering your love for them."

She opened her fingers and gasped. Filena turned to peer over her shoulder and our eyes locked. Tears glistened on her cheeks and I knew, without question, I would need to start a jar to collect hair ribbons for her beside the jar of buttons.

"Thank you, Filena Moira," I whispered. "For protecting me today."

Her gray eyes rounded. "Rhylen, don't you dare indebt yourself to me, you stubborn eejit."

My gaze caressed the sweep of her candlelit-painted cheeks, the tiny freckles dotting her skin like stars in the sky, the flushed part of her mouth, the vulnerability in her teary eyes. In a moment of weakness, I wove my fingers with hers, the ribbons pressed to our palms, and leaned in close.

"Lass," I whispered in her ear, "now you own me too."

Chapter Fourteen

FILENA MERRICK

A lively tune echoed around where we sat. The bodhrán's melodic drumbeat raced beside my pulse—the one aware of Rhylen's hot breath on my flushing skin, the feel of his strong arms wrapped around my body, the way his thumb slowly caressed my inner wrist in slow circles.

Now you own me too.

Since the fires, he had been uncharacteristically affectionate with me. But nothing compared to the intimacy in how he embraced me this very moment, breathed me in, held my hands . . . how much did he drink before wandering over to our wagons? I could smell the ale on his breath. His voice held an easier, looser rhythm too.

A frayed end of my mam's broken ribbon dangled from our joined palms and my lungs constricted. The satin ends of Rhylen's gift brushed our fingertips. The material was cool to the touch and gleamed in the moonlight.

All my life, I possessed only passed down articles of clothing,

Filena Merrick

shoes, and hair adornments. This ribbon was truly the first brand new item I owned, a wondrous thought.

But this . . . *this* was a courting gift, not a mere gift between friends. Not a missing button, not a piece of cake his sister had baked. He had bargained for this ribbon. And it was meant for *her*, his True Mate, not me.

Now you own me too.

I should refuse the ribbon. Go into the wagon for the night.

I was a silly girl, though. A silly girl who wanted to believe a silly story about a star-crossed faerie boy and mortal girl fated for one another.

My heart was falling, always falling, and would shatter on the gravestone of my longings by the end of this week. But I was a desperate fool. Sitting under the stars, with the revel's music floating around us, his arms circling me, I could do nothing else but completely indulge in every forbidden desire.

Twisting on the step, I angled more toward him and our noses brushed.

Fire raced beneath my skin. My chest heaved for breath.

A slow, teasing smile crept up his handsome face. The satisfied look a boy gave a girl when he caught her unraveling pulse sighing over him. And I was completely under his thrall; he didn't need to use coercion magic on me. Every burning nerve-ending was entirely at his command. Carefully, he unwound our fingers and pulled the lavender satin from my hands, his eyes searching mine. His ale-sweetened breath teased my lips.

Stars, why was I so selfish?

This was probably why the gods didn't provide me the magic to curse because this day would be plagued with curses.

128

I leaned away from him, ready to push off into a stand, when Rhylen gently gathered my hair in his hands once more. I stopped breathing—again. My heart was pounding so violently in my chest, I feared my ribs might break. A flirtatious glint darkened those beautiful eyes as they fell to my lips. He slipped the ribbon beneath my tresses and began knotting the satin at the nape of my neck.

Was he about to kiss me?

Had he kissed a girl before?

Would I be his first like he would be mine?

I wanted to kick myself.

Of course, he had kissed a girl. My brother probably made sure of it at some point.

Rhylen straightened the bow he tied, then he leaned in closer, closer—*goddess of love help me*, I wasn't this strong. I could feel my shawl slipping down my arm with the brush of his body. Our mouths were a mere breath apart, and . . . my spiraling anxiety came to a screeching halt.

Was he reaching into my lap?

What in the three kingdoms was he doing now?

Rhylen, apparently done with making me gasp for air like a desperate, dying fish, scooped Sheila from my lap before I could squeak one awkward word.

"She's cute," he said softly and brought her up to our faces. "A wee thing, isn't she?"

"Aye," I croaked out. Stars, I was a mess.

Sheila didn't once glance my way, only having eyes for him. *Me too, lass. Me too.*

"She needs a bow."

I blinked. "A . . . *bow*? Rhylen Lonan, how many mugs of ale have you had?"

"Three and a half," he answered with a side-smile. "You want a tiny one behind your ear, don't you?" he said in an adoring voice to Sheila. "Lavender to match Lena?"

Sheila's nose kissed his and I couldn't help the little laugh that left me. I swore hearts were shooting from her tiny black eyes.

"She's faerie touched like Barry." Rhylen rubbed his nose with hers, like one would a bairn.

What in the moon blasted stars had gotten into that lad? Rhylen was a happy drunk around his family, though. He had always been more playful when in his cups—adorably so.

Wait.

His words caught up to me.

Faerie touched?

I had *two familiars*?

Barry peered my way, his yellow eyes pinched into a prayer for perseverance. Poor Barry . . . of all the faerie foxes, he was tethered to a slow, mortal eejit like me, one who stupidly believed that he'd make a forest friend for reasons other than the gods' business.

"Muffin Moo," I cooed in a saccharine voice and scratched behind his ear. "My fluffy red rain cloud." If foxes could roll their eyes, that was exactly what Barry would be doing. Ignoring his narrowed, indignant gaze, I studied Sheila. "What's her magic?"

"Happiness and courage." Rhylen grinned. "A hearty hedgie full of happiness."

I snorted. Now who was the eejit. A smitten one at that.

No, a happy fool from holding a happy hedgehog.

"Barry." Rhylen turned his head toward the fox who looked

at him, his yellow eyes sliding to me next, then back to him. "Keep your wee friend warm for a spell." He leaned down and placed my newest familiar onto the ground. Sheila appeared to lick Rhylen's finger before waddling up against Barry.

My stomach knotted.

The gods had gifted me a pocketful of happiness and courage. A small creature I could carry on me and cuddle with at any given moment. I started to unpackage why, but I already knew why. I just didn't know why the gods cared so much about a poor girl's broken heart.

"Drink." A mug was suddenly thrust into my hands, yanking me from my spiraling thoughts, and my gaze snapped to Rhylen's crooked smile. I rolled my eyes and took a sip. "To the bottom, *fáidhbhean*," he commanded with a devilish wink.

Sighing, as dramatically as possible, ensuring he knew what a terrible burden it all was, I lifted the mug to my lips and quickly downed the drink. Rhylen pushed off the step, finished his ale in a few gulps, and jumped to the ground.

Barely had I lowered my mug when he grabbed my hand and tugged me toward him. The smile playing on his lips was rascally, the glimmer in his eyes mischievous, until they fell down my body to a revealing stretch of skin. My chemise reached mid-calf—bare, wanton calves. Well, there was no help for it now.

Sorry, petticoats of death. You can't protect me from every dangerously handsome lad.

To act casual, I quickly tied a knot in the shawl, then tucked my mam's ribbon down the front of my corset and lifted my chin.

His gaze slowly traveled back to mine and that cocky half-smile returned.

"Dance with me," he mock demanded, as if a gov.

Alone, beneath the trees and stars? In my underthings? Flutters took flight in my stomach. My entire body screamed, YES. But I shook my head to not encourage him. "There's too much drink in your fluthered head, darlin'."

"It's our song," he murmured with a tipsy lilt.

My brows pushed together. We had a song?

"You were eleven," he began, "your first Caravan Áine's Day revel."

Oh rotten stars above. *That?* My face scrunched up in a groan, making Rhylen bite back a laugh. "Don't you dare go there, *Rhylee Lo*, or I'll curse your blanket to make you itch all night, I will."

His grin widened. "I'll just steal Cian's."

"I'll make his itch too."

"Then I'll steal yours."

"If you force me to also curse Gran's blanket, I'll curse your knickers next."

Rhylen's black brow arched, a sensual curl to his lips as his gaze roamed down the length of me once more. "If you want to undress me—"

Gods, yes . . .

"I want you to never bring up that memory again, pet." I planted a hand on my hip to hide my blush. Was he flirting with me again?

A small canine caught on his bottom lip and his eyes flashed to mine in a single blink. "Curse my knickers, then. I dare you."

Well, shite. Of all the times to lack the magic necessary to curse underwear, it would be with him. Just the thought of him shirtless, tracing his tattoos with my lips and tongue, unbuttoning

152

his pants—

No.

He would *not* distract me.

Seven suns, that was such an embarrassing night nine years ago.

Irritated at my then fourteen-year-old brother for ditching me to make-out behind the haystacks with a mortal girl from a different tribe, and lonely without Glenna's company, who was in bed sick, I had shouted Rhylen's name over the crowd with demands that he dance with me—as if I were the tribe's princess. When I saw him with a pretty Caravan girl, a thirteen-year-old like him, I had stomped over, shoved her out of the way, hard enough that she fell into the dirt, then pointed in his face and said, "This is our song."

Gran hauled me off the floor before we could dance with an earful about how to behave in public, especially as a mortal.

I had only been with West Tribe and Gran for five months and didn't really understand how I was a slave. Brenna Meadows had never once treated me and Cian as property. We were her mortal grandchildren, as she called us. And living with her, with West Tribe, was the first happiness and sense of safety I had known. My da was violent and took out his cruelty on Mam and Cian often, and me on occasion.

For a couple of years after that night, Rhylen's and Cian's friends shouted Rhylen's name in high-pitched voices at revels, demanding he dance with them, then laughing when I would blush and stomp away.

My eyes narrowed and Rhylen's grin grew more playful—a flirtatious dare. But I didn't have a chance to scoff, let alone march out of sight for memory's sake. He wrapped an arm around my waist from the side and pulled me into the dance. I squealed and swatted at his chest, but he just laughed and spun us around.

And . . . more memories came tumbling back.

Each Áine's Day revel since that night, Rhylen had danced with me—to this *exact* song. I hadn't remembered the song, not even when reeling with him since, only my mortifying public demand that he dance with me, the possessive jealousy I had felt when I found him smiling at a felly faerie girl from a different tribe, and . . . how those furious wings of longing in my stomach soared as he grew older and older, how my pulse trilled at the touch of his hands joined with mine while dancing, how my entire body ached in the most tantalizing way when he smiled at me—like right now.

He was right. This *was* our song.

And he remembered, each year.

Why did it have to be the most Traveler of Traveler songs, though? I would choose *our song* to be the liveliest jig of the night, wouldn't I? But stars, one look at him and I no longer cared if I tripped over my own feet.

Moonlight caressed his obsidian hair, the masculine angles of his cheekbones, sensual lines of his jaw, and dusted his berry wine-hued eyes in silver. The charms and beads in his hair clinked with our movements.

Standing side-by-side, we formed a knot with our arms and hands and stepped to the lively melodic beat in a wide circle, lift-ing a kick and hop. A couple of measures later, Rhylen released one of my hands and lifted the other up above our heads. I moved around his body, holding up the thin cotton hem of my chemise for the jig's bouncing footwork. When facing him once more, he wrapped an arm around my waist and held me close, one hand still clasped in mine. The next beat, we side-stepped in a skip for four paces, ending in a spin, before side-step skipping back.

I was laughing so hard, I could barely hear the music. But I could feel the drum vibrate through me. And feel Rhylen's thundering heartbeat pressed to mine.

Leaves blew around our bodies in a cool autumn wind. The trees around us swayed to the melody. Strands of dark hair blew across Rhylen's face as he kick-stepped backward, holding my hands as I kick-stepped toward him. Then we reversed. The threadbare cotton of my underdress pressed to my legs with another light gust. Our eyes were lost in the building intensity of each other's stare, our grins wide and cheeks flushed.

The song ended a measure later and Rhylen tugged on my hand until I fell against him, both of us breathless with laughter.

Forgetting myself, forgetting everything, I pressed my face to his chest and inhaled deeply his sunrise skies and spiced wine scent. I didn't want ale; I wanted to drink him in and him alone—his beautiful, kind heart and vibrant soul, the smooth, hard lines of his sculpted body, the musical sound of his deep laugh, the heady, intoxicating taste of his lips.

Lips I wanted to worship every inch of my skin.

"Dance with me all night, Filena." He locked me in with his arms and rested his cheek atop my head. "Just you and me and Sheila and Barry."

"Can we change *our song* to something less robust?" I asked him.

"You just need more ale first." I could feel his smile in my hair.

Suns above, I loved his boyish smiles.

I closed my eyes and tried to calm my wild pulse. He was holding me. I was truly in his arms. I had dreamed of this for so long.

"And if the ale doesn't help?"

"Then, me wee Filly girl," he whispered in a thicker accent, "I will make a new *our song* fer us."

"Rhylen?"

"Hmm?"

"The ale didn't help."

He softly snorted. "You only had one mug."

"The gods showed me a vision, pet."

"Of a handsome lad writing you a song?"

"Who am I to question the will of the gods?"

He quietly chuckled. "For fate, then."

"Well, don't sound so forlorn about it," I teased.

"Fine," he added. "For fate and for Sheila."

"And Muffin Moo."

"*Our song* is dedicated to all the faerie forest animals."

I sputtered a laugh into his vest. "Except George."

"Feck George." Rhylen tightened his arms around me and pressed his lips to my head. "But first," he murmured, "*our song* belongs only to us." And then he began singing in a low, melodic hum.

My eyes snapped open.

Was he writing a song? This very moment?

I was merely jesting. Well, the silly part of me that continued to cling to girlish dreams wanted to believe our back and forth was genuine.

Oh my melting heart, *Rhylen* . . . his voice.

His gorgeous, otherworldly voice.

It smoldered with emotion. The sound always stripped me bare and left me panting, even when singing a simple ditty or bawdy pub favorite. This song, however, stirred the ever-present ache in my chest. Haunting, lilting notes, born from a thousand pining lovers, breathed between us. The melody trailed kisses down my skin; the rhythm caressed my pulse in sultry touches.

He could easily sing me into his bed on any day. This song, however? It was strangely familiar, spookily so, though it wasn't a Traveler Folk song. Where had I heard this song before? I couldn't place it, but I was also far too distracted.

His soul was reverently making love to mine with each sensual note.

Delicious, curling heat pooled low in my belly and I clenched my thighs at the feel of his roughened breath feathering my hair. A flush spread like fire across my tightening skin. I wanted him. Gods, how I wanted Rhylen Lonan to know every part of me.

Taking one of my hands, Rhylen pressed my fingers to his chest, above his heart, and then guided us in a slow dance beneath the trees. If this was what it felt like to die, I embraced my end. I was so in love, filled with such intense, exquisite agony, the speed of my falling heart accelerated. The ground I would shatter upon was rushing up to meet me.

Yet . . . I no longer cared.

Let me obliterate to nothing in his arms.

This was *our* song, *our* midnight dance among the autumn wind-tossed leaves—

A memory slammed into my mind. One that violently shivered in my pounding pulse. Rhylen's humming voice grew distant and warbled in my ears. The scenery around me faded in and out of focus.

I . . . I had *seen* this moment before. I *did* know this song.

Last week, while sitting in the tree with Rhylen, I had *seen* a vision of him slow-dancing with his faceless, nameless wife beneath the moonlight to this same hauntingly romantic melody he was currently humming into my hair.

This song was meant for *her*, not me. Just like the Alder card vision. He should have called *her* name, not mine.

Dark starless nights, I was going to be sick. Why would the gods be so cruel?

I drew in a painful breath, ready to push away from Rhylen when a voice echoed in my head. A soothing, motherly voice who spoke my birth name.

> *Fáiléanna MacCullough, you'll only see in part unless you change the view.*

Fáiléanna—a name that meant "bird-like fate" in the fae tongue.

My surroundings slipped away and I was suddenly walking backward up the wagon steps. Rhylen leaned against a tree in the far distance, shirtless, plucking at his lute.

> *"Do ye see yer future husband?"*
> *"I can't see my future, remember?"*
> *"That's because yer not using yer eyes, Filly girl."*

The night returned to me, the warmth of Rhylen's arms, the gorgeous, toe-curling, smoky sound of his otherworldly voice.

My breath caught. This . . . this was his call, the song he sang only for his mate.

Our song.

My jaw slackened.

Promise me, Filena Merrick. The very moment you know, you'll tell me.

Fáiléanna—bird-like fate—my mam's name for me. She saw my future. She knew I would one day live among the Raven Folk Travelers. That I would be . . .

My eyes went wide.

Holy Mother of Stars, *I was his mate!*

I was that feathered arse's mate! All this time, he knew. He knew and let me suffer too.

Tears crested my lashes and I buried a smile into his chest.

The buttons, the cake, visiting me before each opening night, playing with my hair . . . *a stór*. He was blissfully, heart-wrenchingly, beautifully mine and had been telling me for years. The gods, too. Every damn vision was *my* future told through *his* eyes.

Feck, I was so joyfully angry right now—at myself, at him, at the gods. I could scream and laugh simultaneously.

Rhylen Lonan was mine.

He was mine.

The satin ribbon tickled the back of my neck where Rhylen had tied back my thick, wavy tresses, and a thousand wings took flight in my stomach.

Now you own me too.

Chapter Fifteen

RHYLEN LONAN

My heart was on fire. Her honeyed scent was intoxicating my senses to the point of delirium. My equilibrium was already spinning fast enough from the ale. For years, I had starved to hold her. It was torture to keep a platonic distance. And now I wanted to forever drown in the feel of her body curving into mine.

Until this moment, my magic hadn't serenaded a girl romantically either. I knew the mate bond pull would be intense with any true ritual, but I didn't know it would be ecstasy. Seven suns, I was dangerously on the verge of writing my name across the pulse in her neck with my lips and tongue and teeth.

The only barrier holding me back from marking her as mine, besides Filena's consent, was Bryok. I didn't know how to riddle myself out of the lottery. But, if I wanted to marry Filena by Samhain, she needed time to decide if the consequences would be worth it to her too. Not just banishment but inviting a curse from the tribe for breaking a decision our chieftain and elders bound in magic.

I sighed, long and slow.

Despite my ranting thoughts, Bryok was the last person I wanted to discuss while floating in these intense, arousing pools of pleasure. She hadn't asked about our brawl since the night of the fire, though. Perhaps she believed it only had to do with Gran after I challenged Bram Fiachna. But Filena had a right to know about the prince's designs on her—should know for her own safety.

"Bryok," I began quietly and her body stiffened. Had he already approached her? Rage began simmering just beneath my skin and I clenched my teeth. "I need to warn you, lass."

She pushed away to lock eyes. "Is he going to sell Cian?"

A scowl appeared between my brows. "It's been threatened, aye." Her face drained of all color. "It won't happen. Bryok knows I'm coming for him and that I'll *not* be merciful. To him or his da. He—" I stopped to gather myself before my territorial rage painted my vision in blood. "He controls me through you."

"Me?" New fear widened her eyes.

"Bryok seeks to make you his mistress."

Her mouth parted. "He marked your clan and stripped you over . . . *me*?"

"Over *me*." With the tip of my finger, I trailed a possessive line down her cheek, along her jaw, then lifted her chin. "He's *not* allowed to touch you, Lena. He's *never* allowed to own you. I would pluck his feathers one by one for just looking at you if I could."

"Gran suffered because—"

"Because Bryok knew I would refuse him before he even asked."

She absently rubbed the raven bond mark on her wrist and the muscles in my jaw tightened. I was ready to rip the sky from this world to shatter each backwards, wing-beaten mating rule Travelers possessed. Fae had married mortals since the creation of their kind. Halfling lines possessed magic. Even mortals, like Filena, whose fae line was centuries back, *still* carried strong elements of their ancestor's magic.

Feck it.

Let them try and banish me. I will fight each person who dared.

I leaned in close to her face and roughly whispered, "You are mine, Filena Moira. You belong to me."

"You own me, aye."

There was a contented acceptance in her voice that seemed at odds with the flinted sparks in her sharp gaze, and my shoulders fell. She still believed I spoke of her indentured servitude. Skies, I never wanted to make her cry again, for any reason. We were playful and witty together, that was our way since children. This grief, this heartache wasn't us, not then and it wouldn't be now. Not anymore.

Tenderly, I played with a wayward lock of her auburn hair. "Do you still not know, lass?"

Her lips pressed together, and I couldn't tell if it were to suppress a laugh or in annoyance. "I haven't *seen* her in a vision, no."

"Then I'll show you, *a stór*."

Her eyes rounded in that melodramatic way of hers. "You've met her? And didn't tell me?"

My brows pushed together once more. Was she . . . *mocking* me? Why would she—and then it hit me. The sparking steel in her gray eyes hid a smile.

She knew.

She knew and was cleverly riddling her words to watch me ignorantly riddle mine back. A laugh settled in my chest. This fecking girl. She really was going to be the death of me.

I bit back a smile. "She is more beautiful than a dream."

"Is she now?"

"Aye, quite a looker, my lass." Fixated with her pretty, unkissed lips, I cupped her face and brushed the pad of my thumb across the corner of her mouth. "She sacrifices buttons for wisdom from the gods and to cheer up a poor lad with a broken wing."

Filena leaned into my touch. "Does she give him pretty rocks too?"

"She rescues lutes and climbs trees to talk to wood ravens she believes are me."

"And coos over their darling hackles, she does."

Lifting her mouth closer to mine, I continued. "She stays home from a revel to care for an ancient without complaint and dances to *our song* beneath the trees, barefoot, with a besotted felly boy."

Her expression comically flattened. "You drank *far too much*, pet."

My lips quirked to the side. "She yearns for the cake I bring her more than me. But I will *always* bring her comfort cake with berries despite my pitifully pining heart."

Filena rolled her eyes. "Have you tasted your sister's cake? It's witchcraft."

I leaned in until our noses brushed, her teasing smile nearly kissing mine. "Your heart," I whispered softly across her mouth, "belongs with mine."

"Your heart," she tossed back with a pointed arch of her brow, "belongs with your True Mate's."

I couldn't help my grin at her cleverly riddled reply and leaned back. "You're cuter than Sheila when stubbornly blind, *fáidhbhean*." She narrowed her eyes and I bit my bottom lip in a goading taunt. "Only took you seven years to finally *see*, pet." I winked.

"Pet?" She wrinkled her nose in mild disgust. "*Now* you call me 'pet,' *Rhylee Lo*?"

"Feral swine, then?" My grin widened. I kissed the palm of her hand. "Bill." Then kissed the palm of her other. "Phil."

She puffed a laugh at me. And then a strange, stricken look crossed her eyes, as if puzzle pieces clicked together in her head and she didn't know if she should feel horrified or laugh.

"*See* something?"

"My mam's last name," she began and stopped with a long, disbelieving sigh. Filena pulled a hand from mine to point a finger in my face. "You're not allowed to laugh."

"If you say 'so.'"

Seemingly satisfied, she opened her mouth to continue . . . and groaned. "Really? Back to riddling like a bairn?"

I shrugged. "You managed to insult your entire race in just two questions, *pet*."

Her eyes playfully narrowed. "So."

I tipped my hat to continue, already struggling to hold back my mirth. Per the age-old riddled words mortals *always* fell for, I hadn't agreed to anything. Fae must use exact language for a true bargain. I wasn't allowed to laugh *so long as* . . . but she never qualified the terms of her request.

She eyed me in warning for several long seconds. "Her last name," she began again, "is . . . MacCullough."

Her surname was—

I threw my head back with a loud laugh. I expected something embarrassing, but this was divine comedy.

"I agreed to your fake bargain!"

"Feral swine?" I laughed even harder. MacCullough meant "son of a wild boar" in the fae tongue and I was on the verge of wheezing. "You had . . . a brush . . . stuck . . . in your hair!" I could barely get the words out and doubled over when her face scrunched up and daggers shot from her eyes. "Descendant of . . . Torc Triath . . ."

"Do your fake bargains mean anything?!"

"Oh, Lena," I said with a delighted sigh. "My only disappointment is that—"

"Don't you dare offend my girls, darlin'."

I pulled her closer to me and murmured low across her mouth, "I'll make it up to them."

And then I kissed her.

Sweet gods, *I was kissing Filena Merrick.*

A gentle, chaste kiss at first, but one so charged, I swayed on my feet. Night skies, I was so madly, feverishly in love with her, I was on the verge of falling at her feet—over a simple kiss.

Simple, aye, but my first kiss *and* the sealing of a promise.

There was nothing that would separate me from her—ever. She belonged to me.

Mine . . . the word echoed in my heart, growing louder and louder with each throbbing beat as I lost myself to the feel of her soft lips, her softer curves, the press of her hand in mine.

And our kiss ignited.

My tongue branded hers in slow, sensual sweeps. The fingers once gripping my vest now explored the muscles of my chest, drifting lower and lower, to rest at my waist. At her territorial touch, a quiet moan left me and breathed into our kiss. My body was tipping upside down. I didn't know I could fall harder for my mate, but I was consumed by her, by us.

Why should we be punished for what the gods had Fated? It was a gift, not a curse. Caravan fae had traveled the same roads for so long, Folk believed the ruts made from our wagon wheels were to keep us from the dangers of traveling new paths. But we needed change. And I would paint new stars across the night sky to navigate a happier future, to give Filena wings to fly free beside me.

At the very thought of her forever by my side, warm, melodic magic drizzled down each limb, to the fingers I sank into her silken tresses, to the palms now cradling her face. My wings unfurled at my back to protectively circle our bodies and I deepened our kiss. This moment was ours. I refused to share her, not even with the moon.

She was mine. *Finally* mine.

And we were kissing.

My body was thrumming. Every inch of me was hard and aching for her. My fingers itched to unlace her corset and worship the slow reveal of her skin—

Oh gods.

I sucked in a sharp breath.

The tips of her fingers slid down my wing feathers and I moaned, a deep, gasping sound I couldn't contain as my body shuddered in wild pleasure.

"Lass," I panted, unable to think straight for a few seconds.

"I've dreamed of touching your wings."

"I'm already struggling to remain a gent, Lena."

She smiled. A wicked little grin.

Oh. Feck. Me.

"Filena . . ." I begged, struggling to form my words. "If I didn't agree to lead the lads in song next, I would tie you to your bed, like you teased." I lowered my lips dangerously close to hers once more and whispered, "And you would sing my name, *mate*."

A flushed breath left her and feck, that sound. I had never cursed my songbird line as I did just now. But if I didn't leave, I would carry her to my bed. And I really did have to return to the revel.

"Tomorrow," I murmured into the barest of kisses, "I dance for you." Slowly, I pulled away before I truly lost all control of my senses. "I won't see you before opening night." Which she already knew. Males performing in the Fire Dance were hidden away for the day.

My wings curled back to fall behind me once more and Filena blinked, as if in a drunken haze. She was so beautiful, I couldn't breathe. My gaze lingered on her red, just-kissed lips then drifted to the lavender ribbon in her hair before finding her storm-cloud eyes. The hand I cradled her face with trailed down her cheek to play with a strand of auburn hair draped over her shoulder. A soft smile tipped the corners of my mouth as I held her gaze.

Then I gently tugged on her hair and walked backward a few steps, turned, and jogged into the shadows, leaving my mate in her corset, bare feet, skin flushed, lips swollen, and her pulse trilling for mine.

Chapter Sixteen

FILENA MERRICK

That shiny black bead fell into my eye—like always—and I held back a dainty growl. I was already struggling to see beneath the black lace veil I wore. The one Cian insisted I wear every Autumn Night Market to add to my mysterious, fortune teller allure. But mostly to hide my exhaustion. The crowds were thicker and I remained continually busy with long lines through dawn, unlike weekly village markets.

My fingers itched to fidget with that errant bead. Alas, I was in the midst of a card reading.

"Your question, pet?" I tugged on the black lace fingerless gloves on my hands to distract my customer's eyes while I smothered a yawn with a grimace.

Only two hours since the market opened and I was ready to curl up with Barry and Sheila and take a nap. I didn't sleep much this day. I was too busy reliving each heart-thrilling moment with Rhylen. The dance, his voice, the ribbon, his gorgeous wings, the way he shuddered and moaned in my arms, the heady feel of his lips on mine . . . I could blissfully fall through the sky until my last breath just from kissing him alone.

Sweet silver moons, we actually, truly kissed.

We *kissed*.

It should have been awkward. But it felt like I had kissed him for a thousand eternities before last night. Maybe I had.

In one hour was the Fire Dance. Ripples of pleasure pulsed low in my stomach. Rhylen would dance for me and . . . and I wasn't prepared for the erotic experience. This mating ritual was entirely to display a male's virility and masculine beauty—any sense of propriety and modesty nonexistent. I might possibly die tonight.

But oh what a delicious way to perish.

Yet, despite the melting starlight in my veins, dread tugged on my gut. Last night was perfect. But I already knew the future and it confused me.

"Will my brother return home?"

I winced.

The card reading . . . I really couldn't concentrate right now.

The nervous woman across from me was far too thin. A tangled, dirty-blonde braid draped down her back, past her waist. The knuckles on her fingers whitened from clutching her skirts in anticipation of my answer.

I loathed questions like this one.

What if I said yes and gave her false hope? Did she depend on her brother for care and safety? Like me? Did he have children who needed him? Was he a good man?

Please gods, let me see true.

Swallowing thickly, I turned over the card.

Beith. The Birch tree ogham rune. A symbol of new beginnings, restoration, and cleansing.

> A man with short, dirty blond hair and two-colored
> eyes—one blue, the other brown—kneels on a cobbled
> street in a large eastern village, his arms open wide.
> A little girl about two or three runs into his embrace
> with a delighted giggle. Slowly he stands, lifting the
> little girl with him, and faces a woman with brown
> curly hair, then softly kisses her.

Another vision gripped me before I could answer the girl across from me.

> Rhylen is wearing a nice, clean linen shirt, the sleeves
> rolled up to his elbows and a black arm garter around
> his bicep. A sharp purple and black pinstriped vest fits
> snug against his tall, muscled frame with a pocket
> watch chain dangling across his front. His long ob-
> sidian hair falls over his shoulders beneath a newer
> top hat. Villagers amble past him into a sprawling
> market. A horn blasts nearby and Rhylen turns to-
> ward the source. My perspective follows his eyes and I
> see the train and ferry docks. Just above this market is
> the floating luxury island of Seren.

I blinked and the vivid floral and interlocking knot designs inside the temporary divination wagon came into focus. The wom-an leaned forward in her chair, eyes wide. My fingers rested on the Birch card with a slight tremble. The last vision, the one with Rhylen, came at a cost. And I knew it was entirely because of me.

The Blackthorn card viciously gnawed at the corner of my mind even though my heart still slowly danced beneath the moonlight with Rhylen. I would be put in danger. I would be harmed. And, to protect me, he would mark me as his. That decision would result in one ending: banishment.

But calling me mate, like he did last night, pursuing me instead of a Traveler girl with a dowry would also result in banishment.

Nausea churned in my middle.

Still, the vision showed a Night Market beneath Seren and Rhylen in newer, finer clothing. Rarely did I have a vision of just him alone. They almost always included his wife . . . and why I had to force myself to breathe. Did something happen to me? Was I not his mate, after all?

The way he pulled me into a kiss last night, after loudly laughing at something I said, was the second romantic vision come true between us. A future I saw while sitting up in the tree.

But what if I wasn't really meant to be his?

What if the visions were of both me and his True Mate? A warning from the gods?

The buttons, the cake, the card readings could have been gestures of friendship, a doting foster brother. And, in his shock and grief, he would rather face banishment with me than trick a girl with a dowry into marrying him, and then be banished by Bryok or Bram for other reasons—

"*Fáidhbhean?*" the woman meekly asked, snapping me from my spiraling thoughts. "Did ye *see* my brother?"

I swallowed back the rising bile. "Does your brother have two colored eyes? One blue and one brown?"

Her face brightened. "Aye, he does."

I pulled my trembling fingers away from the cards. "He appeared to me in a large village, one that is near the eastern cities. He held a little girl around the age of two or three and kissed a pretty, young woman."

A sad smile touched her lips. "He's not returning to me, then. But he's happy."

My chest squeezed for her. I normally didn't engage further but knowing that Cian could be sold to pay off our tribe's debts, I couldn't stop the question before it tumbled from my tongue. "Is he your protector?"

She shook her head. "I have another older brother, *fáidhbhean*."

"Is he kind?"

"Aye, he is. But he's not my twin, ye ken?"

My shoulders relaxed.

Rising from her chair, the woman dipped her head and turned to leave.

"Pet," I said, leaning over my table. "Go to the magical confections wagon. Ask for Glenna and tell her the *fáidhbhean* said the gods will for you to receive a slice of cake with an extra helping of berries."

Her mouth parted. "Thank ye." She dipped her head again. "Thank ye gods."

The woman smiled sweetly at me as she disappeared behind the wagon's sheer cloth door.

I deflated against my chair. My heart was twisting inside my constricting chest faster than the bodice button twisting in my fingers.

Should I go to the Fire Dance?

I knew how the evening would end. Gods, how I ached for his

confession of love. How I ached for him—

The button popped off my bodice with a threaded snap.

Lovely.

My eyes closed for two exhausted beats as I sank farther into the chair. Barry rested his head on my leg, but only for a second. He jumped to attention, his yellow eyes narrowing on the wagon's curtained opening.

Sighing long and slow, I sat back up and straightened my skirts. A part of my corset showed from the missing button. There was no help for it now. Nor time to fix that irritating black bead, either.

Quickly storing the button in my pocket, I cleared my throat and opened my mouth to greet my next customer. But a large body staggered into my wagon before I had the chance.

Oh gods . . .

Every drop of blood in my body iced solid.

"Barry," I whispered. I didn't need to say more. He was on his feet and trotting along the shadows unseen, then ducked from the wagon to fetch Cian.

"Fáiléanna," my da spat with a sneer. "Ye owe me, daughter."

A sob settled in my throat and I blinked back the building panic.

He was different than my memories, larger if that were possible, more gray now peppered his beard, the temples of his hair too. But the weathered cruelty scowling into sharp lines at the corners of his lips and eyes were the same. Gray eyes like mine, like Cian's. But colder and glassy. He stumbled closer to my table and I fought back a whimper.

Would he drag me back to that disgusting man?

Would I even interest him anymore at my ripe age of twenty

compared to the young girls he typically married? Though, legally, per the Kingdom of Carran's betrothal contracts, I *was* married to him because he *bought* me. He just hadn't collected the goods he owned yet, per the terms of my arrangement to him.

Fury spilled into my frozen veins. Fury and terror. I wouldn't go with my da anywhere. I would rather die than be yoked to that monster of a man or be my da's property again.

But Hamish MacCullough also hadn't seen me in ten years. Aye, he was married to a seer and knew his daughter would become one too. There was always a chance word of a young, red-headed fortune teller who traveled with the Caravan fae might one day reach him, despite the Night Markets not setting up anywhere near our old backwood's village on the skirts of the Greenwood. Still, I would play ignorant.

Plastering on a fake, mysterious smile beneath my veil, I somehow managed, "Coin first, pet."

"Ye and yer mam cost me everything, ye traitorous witch!"

I shuffled my cards to hide the shake of my hands. "Shout at me again, pet, and I'll curse your remaining days. Pay coin for a reading or leave."

Hamish darkly chuckled. I swallowed thickly, keeping my chin lifted high, my mouth set in a firm line. Thank the wishless stars he couldn't see the tears gathering on my lashes behind my veil.

"I owned ye," he said in a growling slur. "Not these drifter trash."

I gritted my teeth to hold back the fight-or-flight response quivering down my spine. "I'll curse you to dig the earth with your bare hands until you die in the grave of your own making—"

"—I owned every red hair on yer whoring head until ye were fifteen. Ye think I don't know the young *fáidhbhean* is me dau—"

"Sir, you need to leave."

My gaze whipped toward the wagon's cloth opening. My lungs heaved a short, sharp breath. Never had I been so grateful to see Bryok. But a new dread spasmed in my gut. Did Barry fetch the prince? I looked around for my fox and didn't find him.

"Not without me daughter, tramp."

Bryok's brow lifted and his dark eyes slid my way a beat before hardening his gaze onto my da. "Is this your father, *fáidhbhean*?"

"No, sire."

A corner of Bryok's mouth curled in disgust. "Do not threaten my property again if you value your sanity, sir."

His property?

Fresh rage clawed at my thundering pulse.

The prince whistled low, a bird's call, and his lads entered the wagon. "Show this mortal out. I'll escort him to the exit."

"She is married!" my da bellowed. "Legally purchased."

Bryok's head cocked to the side but he said nothing as my da was yanked from the wagon, red-faced and sputtering.

A cold sweat dewed my skin, my hands had grown clammy and visibly shook. The wagon spun in nauseating circles. I reached for my table, to steady my balance.

Bryok watched me closely, his eyes narrowed ever so slightly. Long, black hair, decorated in a half-dozen small, gold-threaded braids with ruby beads, draped down his shoulders and arms. A crisp black vest hugged his slender frame. Rings graced the fingers holding onto a shiny black top hat and gold hoops lined his pointed-ears. A dainty chain dangled from one hoop to a ruby post in his lobe. A thin line of gold curved the edge of his lids, eyes that were also rubbed in ash. The prince was beautiful in the way of most Raven Folk single males. Perhaps more beautiful than most. But where he was elegant, Rhylen was handsomely rugged.

I preferred the dirt beneath Rhylen's nails, the frayed edges of his shirt vest. His rascally, boyish smiles, his playful wit. His kind heart. His felly boy ways, too—hardworking, always willing to help his neighbor, often brawled to claim and reclaim what belonged to him. Fellys didn't own much, but they fiercely protected the treasures they did.

There was nothing kind about Bryok, except being kind on the eyes.

I knew why he was really here, too, and I wasn't sure if I could stop myself from retching if he asked me to be his mistress.

"Fáidhbhean . . ." The wagon's curtained door flapped open and Cian rushed in. "You sent for me? I can't believe the gods demand, *again*, that you read me *another* card—" Spotting Bryok, my brother slid to a stop and immediately lowered his eyes. "Sire."

The prince twisted toward Cian. "You just missed your father, slave."

Cian's Adam's apple noticeably bobbed. "Our da is dead, sire."

"Who is your sister's husband?"

"Our da," Cian repeated in a low, emphatic voice, "is *dead*. There is no husband, sire. That greedy, lying bastard you speak of isn't the first to claim the *fáidhbhean* as his daughter either." He paused, a muscle in his jaw moving. "Males, mortal and fae, want to own her gift and profits, aye?"

A sickened breath loosened from my chest. Thank the goddess

moon Cian didn't fall for Bryok's trick. But I knew he wouldn't. My brother smiled easily and flirted and shamelessly teased, but he was grounded beneath the Lord of Fools reveler exterior, clever like a trickster fae too.

The prince's eyes flicked back to me. "I will walk you to your wagon after the market closes, *fáidhbhean*. Alone."

I clutched my oracle cards. "Aye, sire."

Cian watched the prince exit beneath lowered lashes, lifting his eyes to mine a moment later. A muscle ticked along my brother's jaw, his eyes hot with anger. But it drained to fear within a blink.

Our da found us. And I didn't know if I wanted to run or scream.

Chapter Seventeen

FILENA MERRICK

N ow about that card reading, darlin'." Cian casually fell into the chair across from me. This was our strategy whenever a handsy gent had to be removed—Cian or Rhylen would pretend they were naturally interrupting and then follow through with a reading for those eavesdroppers in line outside. Yet despite my brother's attempt at putting on a brave face, his skin was sickly pale.

I nodded my head and replied equally as loud, "The gods favor you an additional fortune this night."

Bryok could be listening near the door, peeking in through the curtain too. Or others Bryok had posted to spy on me after our da was dragged away.

"It really was him," I said in a thin whisper. Moons and stars, I wanted to retch. My fingers were shaking so bad, I could barely slip a card from the deck.

Cian leaned forward. "You're safe, sister."

"I've never been safe."

I flipped the card face up before my brother.

Ceirt, the Apple Tree ogham rune. The symbol of the Other-world and choice, often choice in love and why apples were ritu-ally used to determine one's mate at Beltane, Áine's Day, and on Samhain.

> *Cian is sitting on a stone fence, wearing Glenna's fa-vorite dress, the one we weren't allowed to touch. And Glenna, who is in Cian's clothing, stands between his legs and dabs rouge onto his lips with the tip of a finger. Both are laughing so hard, it is difficult for Glenna to work. My brother's humor suddenly fades to sorrow a minute later, an almost pained pinch to the corners of his lips.*
>
> *Noticing, Glenna brushes a lock of blond hair from his eyes. "You're not a filthy Molly," she says quiet-ly. "Your da can rot for all eternity for beating those words into you."*
>
> *He searches her face, an ache in his eyes.*
>
> *Glenna cups his cheek and draws him in until their lips touch. "Break my heart, Cian Merrick. But I will never break yours."*

New tears lined my lashes. Oh my sweet brother.
Wait.
They kissed. Glenna all but confessed her love for him.
My brows shot up. Why I found this shocking, I wasn't sure.

She only kissed blond lads and preferred them with blue eyes. I wanted to grin despite the terror and disgust still ripping through me. Sometimes, I really was blind for a seer . . .

"Lena?" Cian placed his hand across my shaking fingers. "Rhylen won't let anything happen to—"

Forgetting our act, I shot from my chair and dashed around the table toward my brother, a sob loosening in my throat. Cian stood up in alarm and yelped when I threw my arms around his neck. My momentum unbalanced him for a split second. But then his arms crushed me to him.

"You're safe," he whispered into my hair. "I'll kill him before I let him touch you. Rhylen's territorial broody arse will probably kill him first, though."

"I'm so sorry," I hiccuped into his neck. "I'm sorry he beat you for—"

"No." Cian's arms around me tightened. "He doesn't deserve our memories or our pain. We only speak of our happy futures, aye?"

"Aye," I replied softly.

"He's *dead*. There is no him. Only us."

"Do you think Mam is still alive?"

He paused a moment. "Aye, I feel it. She's looking for us too."

My brows pinched together.

"Now," Cian said, guiding me toward the exit. "Let's get you to the bonfire so painted up, undressed lads can cheer you up." He winked at me and added, "Cheer me up too."

"But—"

"No," he said again. "Mam gave us a new life. Let's not waste it on a ghost. He's dead, Lena. *Dead*. That man can't claim you." Then he dramatically gestured in the direction of the field. "Painted up. *Undressed lads*. With wings." He bit his bottom lip and playfully let his head fall back onto his shoulders. "I love the Autumn Night Market," he whispered in a strained, croaking voice.

I smothered a laugh, though my stomach still bubbled with nausea—over seeing Hamish MacCullough and Bryok in my wagon. Over going to the Fire Dance knowing how this evening would end.

Another wave of fear washed over me. I needed to stay here and work. I couldn't go to the bonfire.

There would be no turning back if he danced for me. Our fate would be set—his banishment and . . . and would I survive to see him standing beneath Seren with his own Night Market?

Maybe I could buy myself more time before committing to a decision. The sideshows, like mine, closed for the Fire Dance. But that wasn't for another spell.

I tugged on Cian's suspenders and he paused. "Workers are on the clock for another two candlemarks. I can't leave."

Cian snorted. "You can do better than that, sister dear."

I lifted my chin. "Barry would be scandalized if I walked away from my duties. His poor wee, dessert-stealing heart might fail."

My fox huffed a disgruntled sigh and lowered his head.

"See?" I said, pointing at Barry. "He can't even bear to look at me this moment."

"Glennie Lo will have treats on her."

Barry perked up.

Traitor.

"May George never return your glove," I muttered.

Cian's mouth fell open. "How dare you bring George into

this. Look Barry in the eyes and tell him that treats make you sad."

"You're a monster, Cian Merrick."

"A dashing monster."

Grinning, Cian pulled me from the wagon and out into the night. I swore under my breath. He was incorrigible. Though, in a few ways—*fine*, most ways—so was I. Outside of the colorful wagon, a long line of faces peered at me with round, hopeful eyes.

Cian squeezed my hand.

"The *fáidhbhean* is commanded by our merciful, benevolent, all-knowing gods to restore her magic before a ritual bonfire." My brother leaned in close and said, "What did you say, great and powerful *fáidhbhean*? Your legs grow weak?"

I pretended to cling to Cian to stay upright. "My magic drains into the earth whenever the Harvest Moon grows full, pet."

Barry groaned and took a few steps away from us. I couldn't blame him.

"Naughty *fáidhbhean*, telling fortunes barefoot again, are we?" Cian tsked while pointing at the toes peeking out from my skirts. "You know your magic leaves through your dainty, adorable feet, darlin'."

I rolled my eyes, thankful for the veil. He was such an eejit.

Attendees parted for us, though, several wishing me well and praising the gods as I ambled past. Barry trotted along at my side, still on alert despite our playfulness a few minutes earlier. Did he search for Hamish? For Bryok?

"Thank you, Muffin Moo." Barry peered up at me with softened, yellow eyes. He was truly worried for me and my heart stilled a beat. Not wanting to be left out, Sheila poked her head from my pocket and I softly pet her.

It didn't take long to reach the field. The twenty foot or so bonfire washed the surroundings in flickering ambers and shadows. People huddled in groups, talking, laughing. Smoke hazed by my face, obscuring my already veiled view.

And my mind spun back to last night.

To the sensual, possessive way Rhylen's wings curled around our bodies. To the way his ale-sweetened breath tangled with mine.

For a thrilling moment, I could imagine the phantom feel of Rhylen's lips searing my heat-kissed skin and his body, flushed from dancing, pressing into mine.

Why was I always so selfish?

I knew the cost of openly claiming his love—for both of us.

I started to turn around and Cian held me firm with a humored shake of his head. The mischievous smile he tossed my way still sat on a complexion that was far too ashened. A paleness not even the firelight hid. He was shaken up too. Despite his insistence that I was safe and that Da was dead, Hamish MacCullough was Cian's tormentor as well.

We always knew he might find us one day.

What if he actually could claim me as his property still?

My gaze darted around the hundreds gathered, looking for the red hair and beard, for a pair of hateful, cold gray eyes. When I didn't spot him, I allowed my body to relax a smidgeon. Bryok's gang forced him from the market. Did they coerce him not to return, though?

Bryok.

A shudder wended down my spine. I almost forgot that he would walk me back to my wagon—alone—at dawn when the market closed. Well, he couldn't if I were already home. Time to devise a new escape plan.

"Oh dark, veiled one," Glenna greeted me with a mild grimace of disgust. "Why am I here?" She patted the log beside where she sat for me and Cian to join her. "Tell me you *saw* a future where I escape seeing my brother dance."

"Let's go play cards with Gran, instead," I suggested. *Please.*

Ignoring me, Glenna grabbed my hand, yanked me down onto the log, and then leaned her head onto my shoulder. I leaned my head on hers in return, soaking up her presence. Despite not wanting to be here, I really needed my friend, even if I couldn't tell her why.

"Why are the gods punishing me?" she asked with a dramatic sigh.

"Don't watch him," Cian said to Glenna with a flirty grin and a wink. "Plenty of lads dancing for a mate. Oh wait," he drawled in a low, mocking tone and pretended to pout. "You can't marry this year, Gent of Fem."

Glenna flicked his forehead and Cian stuck out his tongue. Sitting back up and twisting toward me, she took in my still veiled form and tilted her head. "Are you feeling poorly?"

Cian gave me a subtle shake of his head behind Glenna.

"A touch peaked from readings, I am." Barry rested his head on my knees and lifted pleading eyes my way. I bit back a snort. "Any treats on you tonight?"

Glenna scratched behind Barry's ears. "For this handsome lad? Always," she cooed. Sheila poked out from my pocket and Glenna giggled. "For you too, darlin'." Reaching into a small bag attached to her belt, Glenna pulled out chunks of oatmeal berry cookies and fed them to my familiars. "Now," she said when finished, gesturing at my black veil, "why are you still looking like the banshee goddess Clíodhna?"

"Naturally," I said with a little shrug, "I live with three songbirds who have been eating apples for the past twenty-four hours." And Clíodhna had exactly that, three colorful songbirds who lived on faerie apples picked from a tree in the Otherworld.

If only my keening wails could announce the death of a family member. My da didn't deserve to draw another breath.

Ceirt, the Apple Tree ogham card came back to my mind and I considered my best friend a moment before sliding my gaze over to my brother, who watched Glenna from the corner of his eye, a soft smile on his lips. A bittersweet feeling filled my chest. They, too, would be stuck in a situation of love or banishment. But I couldn't think of anyone better to love my brother and all his unique layers than her.

"Dark one," Glenna said with a mischievous grin, "let us transform you into Clíodhna's goddess form of love and beauty."

"I prefer to be feared by males. Far more entertaining."

"Oh aye, we'll start rumors that only regular offerings of cake will keep your death wails asleep and their fortunes happy." Squinting her eyes, Glenna carefully unpinned my headpiece first, followed by my veil and . . . grimaced—*again*. "Oh Lena, keen for your hair, lass," she said with a long, dramatic sigh. "It needs a proper wake, it does."

My expression fell flat, making her grin wider as she fussed over my manufactured curls and corded braids. Reaching into a hidden pocket, she grabbed a tin of rouge and dabbed a bit onto her pinky finger for my lips.

"There," she said, squishing my cheeks, "now you can face him."

"*Him*?" A blush crept up my neck. Did she know?

"Well, someone has to watch him for us."

"And I need rouge-painted lips for that?"

Cian shrugged. "I planned to wa—"

"Shhhhh . . ." Glenna released my face to place a finger to Cian's mouth. "You're watching other lads with me."

He pretended to bite her finger and Glenna rolled her eyes.

A low drumbeat started up. Goosebumps raced down my arms and I shifted on the log. Was it too late to escape?

"Gran probably would enjoy—"

Cian gently shoved my shoulder from around Glenna's back and both snickered at me. I clenched my skirts in my fists and forced myself to face the bonfire.

Raven Folk males, with their backs to the viewers, wings out, spread in a circle around the large, curling flames. Skirted wraps, similar to what the wild fae wore, fell down their thighs to just above their knees. Each male had feathers or antler crowns made from leaves, sticks, and berries woven into their silky tresses.

I couldn't find Rhylen. Was he in the shadows of the bonfire? On the other side of the circle?

The females around me giggled and whispered excitedly as the drumbeats grew deeper, more seductive. My fingernails dug into the moss covering the log. My heart lodged painfully in my throat.

I shouldn't be here.

But to feel him whisper *True Mate* on my fevering skin? This would seal his fate. Mine too. I would never forgive myself if his banishment destroyed Gran and Glenna.

Mo shíorghrá.

My eternal love.

If he danced for another, married another, I would shatter.

Your heart belongs with mine.

More drums added to the sultry beat and fresh panic seized me.

Was I breathing?

I wasn't sure if I knew how to involuntarily draw in breath anymore.

And then I saw him and . . . I forgot my own existence. I forgot *everything*.

In the distance, I swore I heard a banshee keen. An omen of my impending death.

Falling stars above, he was more beautiful than the moon, more breathtaking than the first pale lights of dawn.

A corner of his mouth tilted in a knowing, flirty smile.

And I officially died.

Chapter Eighteen

FILENA MERRICK

irelight reflected off delicate lines of gold paint that thinly traced along the tattoos inked across his chest and arms. His obsidian strands and beaded braids were pulled up into a messy knot, decorated with two raven feathers. A black, pleated wrap hung dangerously low on his waist. Stars, I was growing faint at the heady sight of him. Growing dizzier as the accentuated V of his hips drew what air I still miraculously possessed from my lungs.

The Fire Dance was a deeply scandalous courting tradition that dated back to a time before mortals built the eastern cities and renamed the Greenwood Wilds to Caledona Wood. It was mortals who introduced the idea of modesty and petticoats of death. But the fae didn't view bodies or sexuality as something shameful or to keep hidden—not then and not now. Yet it was mortals who, once a year, mostly flocked to the Autumn Night Market to watch unmated Raven shifter males give into their carnal, wild fae origins while they lost control to their courting magic.

The grip I had on my skirts tightened as I continued to take in the rest of the faerie boy I loved.

His feet were bare, one ankle decorated in a small wreath of dark leaves. My gaze slowly drifted up, and I bit back a sigh at the curved muscles of his calves. Stars above, maybe hiding calves behind petticoats or trousers wasn't a bad idea, after all.

Amber limned the soft feathers of his wings and glinted off the gold hoops lining his ears up to the gold paint that tipped both points. Dark leaves circled each wrist along with braided leather bracelets. And a black chain draped down his chest, with a pendant of a black feather falling between the defined lines of his pectorals.

The satisfied tilt of his lips deepened. His ash and gold lined eyes flashed to mine right as the drums paused in a long, dramatic beat.

Then he was moving.

They were all moving.

"Feck me," Cian groaned.

Glenna gagged. "I think I just threw up a little in my mouth."

"Why are you looking at *him*?" Cian asked on a laugh. "There are at least thirty undressed lads. Stars, look at *them*."

Cian's and Glenna's voices faded away, the people around me too. I saw nothing else but him.

Rhylen's body moved in slow tandem with the flames seductively licking the night sky. The flexing roll of his abdominal muscles pulled a soft moan from the back of my throat. He locked his wine-hued eyes onto mine, his small canine biting an edge of his lower lip, as he erotically pulsed his hips in seductive circles to the drumbeat.

Sweet goddess . . .

Molten pools of unadulterated want heated in my core.

In this moment, I knew, without a shadowing doubt, that I was the most selfish girl to have ever existed. I could never refuse dessert. Nor did I like to share. And Rhylen Lonan was incomparably, irresistibly delicious.

That richly muscled body owned every throbbing inch of mine.

Those soft, honeyed lips were made to kiss me and me only.

His fierce heart sang my name with every fiery beat.

No matter how our cards played out, I would burn for him until my soul's last breath. The Caravan fae and their ridiculous social rules could go pound rotten stardust. I wanted him. Midnight skies, how I *wanted* him.

Golden light and shadows caressed the hard, sculpted planes of his muscles as he trailed fingers down the corded lines of his chest, down the ridges of his abdomen, lower, lower. A slow, sultry grin curved his lips when my mouth parted in a flushed breath.

Dizziness continued to float drunkenly in my head and down my limbs. I knew he was strong, otherworldly beautiful, but seven suns . . . I had never wanted to be a drip of sweat so badly as the one rolling down his chest.

The banshee wails were growing louder in my head. I was dying at this very moment. The rising intensity in my core ached and I shifted on the log to find relief.

Blond hair caught the periphery of my vision and I pulled my eyes away from Rhylen to find my brother leaning around Glenna toward me. Both Cian and Glenna watched me with large, knowing grins and a hot blush warmed my cheeks. Then, to my horror, Cian pretended to wipe drool off my chin and I swatted his hand. Wrinkling my nose at him, I rolled my eyes with a huff and returned to the performance, dismissively brushing strands of my auburn hair off my shoulder for extra emphasis.

My brother laughed, normally a sound I loved. I ignored him, though, and gnawed the inside of my lip as I shyly focused on Rhylen once more. But another pair of eyes caught mine through the flames—dark, possessive eyes that flicked to Rhylen then back to me.

Bryok.

Chills pricked the back of my neck.

The prince tipped his head at me, a haughty curl to his biting smile.

Before I could properly react, movement snapped my gaze back to the dance and the white-knuckled grip on my skirts grew painful.

The males on display simultaneously stretched their wings in a soft fluttering beat. The bonfire sparked higher, a loud, roaring whoosh that rolled over the forest clearing. For a second, their winged forms became black silhouettes against the flames while the gold paint on their bodies shone in the brighter light. The crowd murmured excited gasps.

When the bonfire calmed, the dancers pivoted to give the audience a view of their profiles.

Cian groaned, "I love the Autumn Night Market," making Glenna giggle.

Rhylen's heated gaze held mine as he slowly leaned back in a suggestive display of his upper body. His long fingers sank into his knotted hair, accenting the defined muscles of his arms, and the sinful, arcing motion of his hips . . .

I was undone. All burning, anguishing sensation.

I no longer cared if Bryok, my brother, or Glenna saw the lust on my face.

The throbbing ache low in my belly quickened my breath.

But, if I had to watch another erotic flex of Rhylen's muscles, another provocative swing of his hips and he wasn't truly mine to love, to worship . . . a crack splintered behind my ribs at the very thought. I placed a hand to my heaving chest. I was so dizzy, the world around me began to blur. My corset was far too tight.

Air.

I needed air.

What was I thinking? His name was called in a decision the elders bound in magic. It wasn't just about banishment. He could be cursed by the tribe—by Bryok—for not fulfilling the magic's bargain.

"Oh gods." I wrapped an arm around my stomach.

What had I done? Last night should not have happened. I should not be here.

Stumbling to my feet, I pushed past Glenna and Cian, lifting a hand over my shoulder in a gesture to not follow.

Tears flooded my eyes.

If the gods had another chosen for Rhylen, I wasn't sure I'd survive the breaking pain. I wasn't sure I wanted to. Without his protection, I could be claimed by my da, despite Cian's reassurances that I was safe. I could be handed over to that vile man I was sold to as a child. Or perhaps sold to Bryok and forced to become his mistress.

Bile burned the back of my throat as fury curdled anew in my stomach.

How dare any male believe they *owned* me.

How dare they believe I existed *only* for their profit and pleasure.

Was it enough that I was also owned by the gods?

My body had never once been my own. Nor my future.

I leaned my forehead against a large, gnarled oak on the outskirts of the market. My lungs gasped in tear-stained breaths.

"Lena?"

My eyes cinched shut and I grimaced back a sob.

Rhylen.

It was too late. I didn't leave the Fire Dance for him to follow. In my panic and grief, I had forgotten that he would join me in the woods. I hadn't even realized where I was walking. I had just needed to get away from the crowds. And if Gran were still awake, she would question me too.

"Filena . . ."

His melodic voice shivered down my body. Skies, how I loved the soft, resounding timbre of his deep voice. Slowly, I turned toward the only person who was allowed to own me—who owned me body and soul.

Holy Mother of Stars . . .

The Heather card vision barely conveyed the absolute beauty of the male striding toward me—a creature of fae still drunk on his primal courting magic. The bonfire in the far background gilded his feathers and hair from behind while moonlight whispered silver across his bare torso, arms, and face. Desire darkened his eyes; his mouth flushed with arousal.

I swiped at the tears on my face. Then, in a moment of quick thinking, I plucked Sheila from my pocket and set her beside Barry.

Slowing before me, Rhylen cradled my face—a reverent, soft

touch. But his muscles were trembling, his chest rapidly rising and falling. He was holding himself back. Another tear slipped free and a scowl appeared between his black brows. His dark purple eyes furiously searched mine. "A *stór*?"

"If you're banished—"

"Let the Fiachnas try and banish me, lass." He gently leaned me against the giant oak at my back. "I will challenge them, if they do."

"You're bound in magic to marry a girl with a dowry."

Rhylen pressed a kiss to the fluttering pulse in my neck and I melted into sighs. "Aye," he whispered into another kiss. "I *will* marry a girl who brings in more profits to West Tribe annually than any middle-rank girl with a one-time dowry."

His tongue flicked out to taste my skin and my eyes fluttered closed.

Stars, I couldn't think as he moaned breathless kisses along my jaw. As his fingers trailed down my neck, around the curve of my breast, to grip my hip and pull me in closer. Lightheaded, I rested my hands on his bare chest and practically fainted. I was touching him. I had dreamed of exploring the warm, smooth contours of his body for so long.

"The magic is for a Traveler girl not . . . not a mortal slave."

"I don't care what you are," he growled into another kiss beneath my lobe. "You belong to me and I am yours. I have only ever been yours, Filena Moira."

"Rhylen—"

"I am *desperately* in love with you," he whispered, his breath hot in my ear. "True Mate."

Then his feather soft lips crashed into mine and I . . . never

174

wanted to breathe again.

Chapter Nineteen

RHYLEN LONAN

My blood rushed hot in a primal state between my animal and
my elven form.

The courting magic spellbinding me was pure ecstasy. I was falling through the wing-soaring skies of being drunk on love and flaming territorial desire, a sensorial high made all the more intense by the building Harvest Moon and the thinning veil as Samhain drew nearer.

I had glimmers of this possession in Autumn Night Markets past when in Filena's company, sometimes when gifting her small treasures throughout the year as well, or when playing with her hair. Raven Folk males were ruled by courting magic, unlike other fae. I had to suppress my urges for years around Filena. But finally dancing for my mate around a ritual bonfire? I was flying in an entirely different plane of existence right now.

The ancestral wild fae part of me craved a hunt too. I *needed* to chase, to corner, to devour. To crow in victory over my catch. But

I was in new territory with Filena. The other Fire Dancers would begin their hunt for a mate tonight, unlike me. I had also secretly courted Filena's heart and mind for years. But I didn't know her physically. And *that* was what the wild magic that danced for my mate tonight hunted—her pleasure.

Did she want me to whisper in her ear each fevered confession I carried?

Want me to bring her to the edge of release and not let go?

Kiss every erogenous place on her body until she prayed my name aloud?

I tightened my hold on her waist, deepening our kiss, as I rocked my hips in a slow, aching grind into hers. Stars burst behind my eyes. My lungs gasped for breath. Then I moaned, long and deep . . . and feck. I might actually pass out. Just that small amount of friction had me swaying on my feet. I was far too intoxicated by her wildflower honeyed scent, her trilling heartbeat, the mate bond . . . *her*.

"Holy gods . . ." she whispered.

A smile of pure male satisfaction tipped the corner of my mouth. "I still plan to tie you to your bed."

Filena blushed but she narrowed her eyes to playfully push back. "I was taunting your pride."

"You made a bargain, lass." I swung her into my arms, making her squeal, and my grin widened. No such bargain truly existed and she knew it. But I couldn't resist teasing her back. I stole a gentle kiss, then walked us farther into the forest, away from the bonfire, until I found a patch of moss where I lowered her beneath me. "This will have to do until then."

She arched a brow. "I share a bed with Glenna, pet."

"Then I'll tie you to mine. Cian can sleep with the horses."

Filena chuffed a laugh that was more like an eye roll.

The trees swayed around us in a cool breeze, shifting shadows across her face. I was so lost in her beauty, I couldn't speak for several seconds. But there were three questions I wasn't able to ask her before the market officially opened tonight and I was dying to ask them now.

Nuzzling my nose against hers, I murmured, "Does my mate love me back?"

"She loves you with every breath in her body." Her fingers caressed the edge of my ear to the point and I shuddered a soft moan. "She loves you more than every drop of water in the oceans, more than every leaf on every tree. She loves you endlessly, passionately."

I leaned into her touch and closed my eyes in a long, languid blink. "You just love the cake I bring you." I could feel her smile and I pressed my mouth to hers in a sweet, chaste touch. "Does she think me handsome?"

"He is the most beautiful male she has ever known and he knows it."

I smiled back against her lips. "Will we have children?"

"That's not your real question, Rhy." I stilled. Goosebumps raced down my arms. Sometimes, Filena's intuitive giftings were spooky in their accuracy. "What have you been really asking me all this time?"

I searched her gray eyes. "Will I marry my mate?"

A strange emotion shadowed her face, a guarded expression that seemed more like grief, and my brows pushed together. Were the gods showing her a vision right now? I waited patiently, caressing her cheek, softly kissing the underside of her jaw, grazing my nose along her neck.

"Aye," she finally said and drew my lips back to hers. "You will be with your mate and you will be happy together."

A week ago, in the tree, she had shared the same future and I grinned. I had already planned to make Filena my wife, no matter the consequences, but to hear it from the gods . . .

She was mine.

And I was hers.

Always, forever hers.

I would tear down this world and make her a new one, if that was what it took to be together.

"Mate," I whispered and my heart broke at the beauty of calling Filena the other half of my magic aloud.

Since the very moment she wandered into West Tribe, dirty, too skinny, eyes wild and hair wilder, I had loved her madly. A mortal girl I had yearned to call my own for seven years now—not as master and slave, but raven marked as bonded lovers. A mortal girl whose heart, I believed, would never truly belong with mine.

"My beautiful, clever mate," I whispered again, my voice rough with tears. I could grow addicted to the courting magic bolting through me each time that one thrilling word fell from my lips.

I kissed the corner of her lips, her cheek. Her nails possessively roamed over the flexing muscles of my back to where my wings sprang from my shoulder blades. The tips of her fingers then gently stroked down my feathers and an eruption of searing pleasure exploded down my limbs.

I moaned, "True Mate," into her ear, falling into the rush of magic rippling through me.

My wings flexed beneath her touch and I groaned again. Her chest heaved a hot, shaky breath. The seductive drumbeats, carrying on a cool breeze from the bonfire, heated my blood even more. My mouth savored the smooth skin of her neck. My tongue wrote confessions of love across her pulse.

I was deliriously obsessed.

"Your scent, your pounding heartbeat"—I nipped at her skin, unable to stop the animal side of myself, the wild fae on a hunt—"you consume me. Gods, I want every inch of your skin to taste of me." The urge to sink my canines into her was bordering on madness. But I would never mark Filena without her consent.

Already we played a dangerous game. One I would win, but first I needed to secure Cian's safety. I could mark Filena at any point. Once I did, though, every male would smell me on her. There would be no hiding what was forbidden. Not to mention, I would lose a sliver of magic when marking her too. I needed full magic and strength when challenging Bryok.

But I could make her mine in other ways until then. The fae were intimate with their willing mortal slaves all the time, even among Raven Folk. I should care about Bryok finding us, though. He had an agenda and would use anything against me. But I was driven by primal instinct to physically bond with Filena right now and could think of nothing else.

My fingers brushed over her breasts to the buttons of her bodice and I waited for her to stop me. When she didn't, my mouth collided with hers in a claiming I felt soul deep, to the very marrow of my bones. She was my sky, my endless horizon. My everything.

Crashing my hips into hers, I unfastened the first button.

She inhaled sharply at the feel of me through our layers of

clothing. My tongue branded her mouth in slow, sensual sweeps. The world around me tilted and I craved more. Needed more. Pure, molten starlight dripped into my wild pulse with each grinding arc of my body, a rolling rhythm set to the slow, sensual tempo of the drums.

The next button slipped free from my fingers.

Her nails dug into my chest and I continued to move, harder, faster, both of us practically panting. The moaning sounds loosening from the back of my throat vibrated from my body to hers. Midnight suns, I was unraveling, becoming more and more undone each time my hips collided with hers—and she was still fully dressed. But I was too pent up after years of physically keeping my distance to stop myself.

I played with the next button until it slipped open, then the next and the next and . . . my fingers fell into a large gap in her bodice, startling me from my aroused haze.

I leaned back, took in the mussed, breathless state of my mate, and laughed. "Lose another button, lass?"

She arched a dramatic brow and I laughed again. Feck, she was so cute. Gifting her buttons was one of the few things that genuinely made me happy.

"Aye," she drawled, attempting—and failing—to sound put off. "Popped off while thinking of you dancing tonight."

I grinned. "Only *one* button?"

Filena humorously rolled her eyes.

I slid a finger down her exposed corset and unfastened the final two buttons. "Did you enjoy my dancing?" My eyes flitted to hers in a single, flirtatious blink.

Warmth crept up her neck and cheeks. "I didn't know you

could move like . . . like . . ."

"Like how I want to worship you?" I gently tugged on her corset laces. The veins in my arms were throbbing. Everything about me was hard and throbbing and I was slowly losing my mind. "Tell me, *fáidhbhean*," I murmured, pulling on her laces again until the corset opened to her thin camisole. For a moment, I failed to form words as I took in the breathtaking shape of her curves. Swallowing thickly, I asked, "Have you *seen* me make love to my mate?"

"Yes." Her voice was feather soft and gasping.

"Did she fall apart in my arms as my body danced with hers?" My fingers traced the soft swell of her breast while my other hand slipped up her skirts, slowly, slowly trailing up her leg.

Her eyes slid closed. "Yes."

Gods, she was beautiful, utter perfection. From the constellation of freckles my lips wanted to map across her creamy skin to the beguiling feel of her body curving into mine to the silky locks of auburn hair spilling around her head.

I brushed my thumb across the breast I cupped in my hand. "I ache at the sight of you. But when you're beneath me? Flushed and breathless?" My other thumb drew light circles around the inside of her thigh. "I am—"

"Filena Merrick."

A Raven swooped down from a branch, startling us both. I quickly covered Filena with my body, teeth bared. Every protective animal instinct in me flared to life. Bryok shifted into his fae form before landing on the ground.

The prince cocked his head. "Stand up, felly."

I darkly laughed, refusing to lower my eyes. "Feck off before I tear your wings from your back."

Bryok stepped toward me and the muscles down my body flexed in warning, making him pause. Fear flashed in his eyes for half a raging heartbeat. Aye, I was still in a primal state, wildly territorial for my mate. I hoped the eejit came closer so I could make good on my promise.

A smirk curled his lips. "Did Filena tell you?"

This game again? A quip sharpened on my tongue but Filena's body went rigid beneath mine. My gaze slid to hers and the blush warming her cheeks only seconds ago had grown paler than moonlight.

My wings snapped wide, rage pumping in my veins. What had he done?

"Ah, she didn't." Bryok's smirk widened and I saw red.

In a single leap, I launched into the air and was on him. But, before we could tumble to the ground, the arsehole shifted into a raven and flew out of reach. I landed on my feet and spun toward where the coward materialized once more.

While Bryok was distracted, Filena sat up and began quickly refastening her bodice despite her unlaced corset. My mate's continued bloodless complexion flamed my fury.

"If you touched her—"

"You know I can't *touch* another's property without consent."

My gaze flicked to Filena's and widened. She would never consent to anything with that preening arsehole unless she was under duress and my stomach sickened. I reined in my anger, though. Or tried to. Bryok was tricking me into thinking there was a possibility to rile me up further. If he had coerced her in any way, she would have told me. Or at least told Cian, who would have then told me. Barry would have fetched one of us too.

Filena began to stand and Bryok commanded, "Stay on your knees, slave."

Oh, feck no.

I growled and launched myself at the prince. Once again, he shifted into his raven form and flew out of reach, laughing. He would be branded a cheat and coward for making that move if challenged. But there were no middle-rank or gov witnesses to declare me heir if I challenged him now.

Filena remained on her knees, as instructed, the ashened fear coloring her skin now burning humiliation, and I wanted to tear Bryok's head from his body and toss it into the bonfire. The prince's eyes flashed with fear for another wild second as he took in my bared teeth and flexing muscles. Then he settled on an arrogant smirk and I could roll my eyes at his attempt to illusion being the bigger male.

"What did I promise you when stripped, felly?"

I remained silent, refusing to play his games.

"Slave," he said to Filena and I charged again.

He would *not* speak to her. Look at her. Think of her.

But, just like before, he shifted and flew out of reach. When materializing back into his fae form, he sang a bird call whistle and more Ravens descended from nearby trees.

My shoulders sank. One by one, the prince's gang shifted around him. Six lads in all. They would interfere with any challenge I issued Bryok and join the brawl to take me down too.

"I'll ask you again, felly," Bryok sneered at me. "What did I promise you when stripped?"

I didn't answer him, but he could see on my face that I remembered. Filena would be forced onto her knees before him and a pain cracked behind my ribs. He had used my post-Fire Dance state to dominate me and humiliate Filena, and I fell for the trick.

I lowered my eyes in submission and blinked back the aggression before he tried to use me to hurt Filena again. The guilt bleating in my chest was stealing my breath.

Bryok's lads circled me and blood began to paint my vision. My fists clenched and unclenched. Sweat dripped down my forehead.

"You were instructed to marry a Traveler girl with a dowry," Bryok bit out. "Not rut your slave in the woods like a filthy felly animal."

Anger pounded in my head. The intensity was a splitting pain across my skull and I gritted my teeth.

"Fly to the bonfire and hunt for a mate," he instructed me.

"I will *not* leave my ma—Filena behind," I gritted out, then added, "sire," in a mocking tone.

Bryok's brow arched at my slip and he considered Filena from the corner of his eye. "You didn't tell him anything, did you? A slave who keeps information from her master but opens her legs for him . . ." His dark eyes glittered. "I wonder how many secrets, pet?"

My gaze shot to Filena's, but her eyes remained downcast. Fury, however, pulsed hot along her jaw.

"Felly," Bryok said to me, his voice thick with warning, "join the bonfire or your slave will spend the entire night on her knees before me—"

"—I will *not* leave—"

"Rhylen," Filena said in a pleading tone. "He can't touch me without my consent and he doesn't have it nor will he. Nor does he have yours."

My constricting chest heaved for breath. "Filena . . ."

"Go," she said softly, pleading . . . and something inside of me shattered. What did Bryok mean by secrets?

No.

I wouldn't allow that fecker to peck at my mind. I trusted Filena. I didn't give her much of a chance to tell me anything after the Fire Dance despite her distress. That trickster may force me to leave—and I would to protect Filena from paying for my defiance—but he wouldn't deflect my anger onto her.

"You feel safe?" I asked, my voice cracking.

"Aye," she replied back, though her voice cracked too. "The prince would be a fool to harm a *fáidhbhean* and anger the gods"—she paused—"any more than he already has." Bryok slightly flinched. "Or harm the tribe's much-needed profits." Her body relaxed and her gaze unfocused. "Faint voices whisper in my ear about a fire curse over West Tribe, sire. By another tribe or the gods, I am not yet sure. The fires are only the beginning. I see flames before me. Tall, building flames."

The smile playing on Bryok's lips slipped and I almost snorted. She was facing the bonfire. And govs were responsible for curses over a tribe. Bryok's lads peered at him with growing discomfort and the prince shifted on his feet.

Stars, I loved that girl.

"And . . . I heard the faint voice of our chieftain saying that Rhylen must do anything to secure a girl who brings in money to the tribe," she continued in the mysterious, soothing voice she reserved for fake card readings, still staring unseeing, as if in a trance, ". . . when you find her, Rhylen Lonan, tie her to your bed and feed her magical confections before wooing her in other delicious ways. That's how she'll agree to marry you." Filena gave her head a little shake, then arched a brow. "The gods' scandalous words, not mine, pet." Her hand fluttered in the air, a dismissive gesture.

I bit the inside of my cheek. There were so many replies begging for release. But we had an audience. Instead, I tipped my head. "Whatever the gods will, *fáidhbhean*."

Despite the territorial rage still pounding in my ears, I shifted into a raven and flew toward the bonfire to find Cian and Glenna before Bryok could order me again and I lost all control of myself. But I wasn't as worried about leaving her as before.

Filena Merrick was more a trickster fae than all the Fiachnas pooled together.

And fecking hell, I had never been more turned on.

Chapter Twenty

FILENA MERRICK

The early afternoon autumn sun chased away the morning dew. Still, the wagon step I sat on was damp and cool. But I didn't care. The cloth in my lap, a gift from Bryok last night, held all my attention. I unrolled the embroidered cotton for the hundredth time, still unnerved by the small, beaded braid. One with a silver feather pendant—the ornament I hadn't noticed missing from Rhylen's hair until I held it in my hands.

> "You have power for a slave," Bryok had spoken low, his voice tight and sinewy. "The power of the gods and power over males."

> The underlying threat in his words rose the hair on my arms.

> "Sometimes I wonder if you are truly a fáidhbhean or a cailleach in disguise."

188

The Night Market

Cailleach—*a fae witch.*

Alas, I only had the Sight and nothing more.

How I wished I were a cailleach, though. I would curse his feathered arse to drag across a field of jagged rocks until he begged me to shave his head in a plea for mercy.

"Your brother is a pretty mortal, strong and healthy too," Bryok had casually tossed out next. "The handsome price we would fetch for him at the Autumn Night Market would feed several families through winter, pet."

The ever-present panic rising in my chest spiked and I bit back angry tears. I had remained silent, however, my eyes cast to the forest floor.

"You have until Samhain to convince Rhylen to trade you to me or I will sell your brother for the good of the tribe." I flinched when I felt Bryok gently place the cloth into my hands. "A courting gift for you, Fáiléanna MacCullough."

My heart lurched. "Filena Merrick, sire."

"You and I both know that isn't true."

My eyes had dangerously met his in warning. "The

gods are already displeased with you, Bryok Fiachna.
Do not anger them more by calling their fáidhbhean
a liar."

The prince had paled a little at my words.

"Lower your eyes, slave." I did as he had bid, but not
before noticing a cruel smile tipping the corners of his
mouth. "Your da is desperate for coin—"

"My da is dead."

"—if unwed, you are still his property. If wed, you
are your husband's. Mortal laws not even the fae can
dispute. Either way," he continued, his voice growing
more confident, "you will be traded from Rhylen to
me or I will purchase you from whichever man owns
you." He tapped the cloth I clutched in my fingers.
"Do not forget my bargain, Fáiléanna."

"Do not forget the fire curse on West Tribe, sire."

He froze for a couple of beats. I wanted to smile as he
fought to hold back his fear. Despite his arrogance,
his blasé show of disregard, my pretend warning had
struck true.

In the end, I suspected he would still rather keep
Rhylen from challenging him than please the gods—
Bryok cared only for himself.

The prince stepped in closer and I worked hard to not move a muscle. But my fight-or-flight was a wild wind of tumbling leaves through my body.

"I'm a gentle lover," he breathed in my ear, careful not to touch me, and I had swallowed back a shudder. "I wouldn't take you in the forest like a wild animal." He pointed at the missing button on my bodice. "You would have the finest dresses too and belong to a master who could afford to repair your gowns."

Before I could reject him—spit in his face, cut braids from his hair, rip the buttons off his vest and wear them on my bodice as victory badges—he instructed one of his lads to escort me back to my divination wagon where I had remained the rest of the open market.

I didn't wait for Bryok to show up when the market's opening night had closed.

"Filly girl," Gran said from the doorway, yanking me from my thoughts.

I quickly rolled up the cloth and stuffed it into a spare pocket not occupied by Sheila, then twisted toward her as she sat beside me on the step. Glenna must still be asleep or she'd be out here too.

"Ye look a sight, lass."

"I didn't sleep much."

A teasing smile softened her face. "Oh aye? A Fire Dance lad keep ye company past dawn, did he?" Then she winked.

The old fae *winked* at me with a little knowing smirk.

Mortification burned my skin. Did she speak of Rhylen? Falling suns, I hoped she wasn't prodding me about bedding her grandson.

But dear, sweet gods in the big blue sky, how I wished I had last night.

"Morning, Gran," Cian mumbled, and our heads snapped up. Speaking of looking a sight . . . my brother's suspenders hung down his legs, his shirt wrinkled and partially unbuttoned, with smudges of dirt streaking his forehead and cheeks. As he lumbered toward our wagons, the toolbox in his hand hit his thigh in a rhythmic clank. "Morning, Lena."

"Brawl?" Gran asked.

Cian nodded. "Always."

My brother paused before us and ran a hand through his messy hair. He wasn't wrong. Each Autumn Night Market, there was an "incident" that led to a brawl, which *always* ultimately resulted in a partial tent collapse.

Cian sighed. "A drunk mortal tried to ride the unicorn out of the menagerie."

I burst into laughter. I couldn't help it. The "unicorn" was a grumpy, farsighted cow that was illusioned into the rare mythical faerie creature of The Wilds. The poor thing couldn't see the feed in front of her half of the time.

"Old Orla mooed her oath of vengeance first, decidedly not a mystical unicorn sound, spooking the visitors," Cian continued. "Then she ran straight into a tent post. Knocked herself out, she did, and half the tent too. Threw the lad on her back over the fence in her fall." Cian leaned against the side of the wagon and lit up a cigarette with a book of matches from his pocket. "Fecking Orla bit a billy goat before charging."

"What was a wee billy do'n in the unicorn pen?" Gran asked, wiping away tears.

"No one knows." Cian shrugged. "Probably belongs to another tribe and wandered in to steal food from that blind grumpy arse cow."

"Cowicorn," I corrected, our nickname for Orla since we were children.

Cian's mouth kicked up. "The goat leapt over the pen, right into the arms of a wealthy gent from the eastern cities, who screamed at the same time as the goat."

Gran and I howled with fresh laughter. I was cackling so loud, my chest hurt.

"The gent tossed the goat into the running crowd"—Cian dragged on his cigarette and slowly blew out the smoke—"knocking down a different drunk mortal." He pointed his cigarette at us. "But the lad did not stay down."

"He brawled with the stately gent?" I asked, picturing it all in my head.

"No," Cian replied while puffing on the cigarette. "The drunk lad who was hit by the goat swung at the drunk lad who tried to escape on Cowicorn. Apparently, the former had taken the latter's sister's maidenhood behind the men's loo. Classy, that one."

"Romantical location," I said on a wheeze. "Lucky lass."

Cian grinned. "Ballads will be sung in her honor."

"The Legendary Maiden of Loo Woo," I practically squealed in belly laughter.

"And the Angry Moo," Cian finished.

We both lifted our pretend mugs and shouted, "Cheers to her health!"

"Cian, darlin', yer too rich," Gran said, wiping at tears again as she stood. "My sunshine boy." She tussled Cian's mop of golden blond hair. "Ye make an ancient feel young again."

"You are young," Cian murmured and kissed her forehead. "Still a looker too."

She patted his cheek with a sweet smile. "Time to rest my young, hollowed bones." Gran slowly made her way up the two steps, bending to kiss the top of my head, then disappeared back into the wagon.

And still, Glenna didn't appear. Our laughter didn't wake her up. What time did she crawl into bed?

Cian dragged on his cigarette for several beats after the door shut. "Little ol' Rhylee Lo is going out of his ever love'n mind. He got into two brawls last night himself."

My mouth fell open. "Is he hurt?"

"Only his territorial rage." A slow, rascally smile lifted on my brother's face and I rolled my eyes. "Beat the shite out of a Traveler Folk from South Tribe for making a crass comment about Glenna. Called him Bryok accidentally at one point, he did." Cian eyed me curiously and cocked his head. "What's going on, sister dear?"

"Rhylen and I—"

"Are True Mates, aye."

I paused a beat, confused. "Did he tell you?"

A laugh rumbled from my brother. "No, darlin'. I've known for years."

"*Years?*" I asked, eyes wide. "How?"

He looked away with a little shrug and puffed on his cigarette.

"Sometimes I *see* things too."

"You have the Sight?" I felt the blood drain from my head. "How often?"

"Rarely. Perhaps two dozen times since I was ten or so."

I blinked. Two dozen times? I thought back over the years, to how Cian always knew the best way to care for my needs as a seer. All this time, I had thought our mam had instructed him on how to guide me as I grew into my giftings. A scowl pinched between my brows.

"I thought it only passed down through the women . . ." my words trailed off when my brother flinched, then looked up at the sky. "Oh, Cian." I stood from the step and walked to where he leaned against the wagon. I pressed my ear to his chest, to listen to his strong heartbeat, and wrapped my arms around his waist. "The gods don't make mistakes. You're not a filthy Molly. There's nothing filthy about you."

"Aye," he said softly. "I'm happy here. I would gladly be a slave my whole life to never live in a mortal village again."

I leaned back to peer up at Cian. For as long as I could remember, my brother had always enjoyed dressing as a girl and a boy, calling himself a lady at times too. The backwoods mortals of our village thought him possessed by a wild spirit, an excuse for our da's violence. I was young, but I remembered the sadness and fear my brother worked hard to hide.

I nuzzled back into my brother's chest. "You are exactly where you are meant to be, Cian Merrick."

We were quiet for a minute or two, content to just hold each other while Cian finished his cigarette.

"Tell me about Bryok," Cian said, breaking the silence.

"Rhylen could barely utter a word without swinging at someone nearby for just breathing funny. Do you know how many people breathe funny in the animal pens? Especially when watching a muscled lad in his prime fix a broken tent in only a bare scrap of fabric around his waist?" He dropped his voice to a stage whisper. "He wore gold eyeliner around his smoky purple eyes, Lena. The people couldn't breathe."

I peered around the woods by our wagons, biting back a laugh. Cian was such an eejit. No sign of any blackbirds. Most Traveler Folk were sleeping at this early afternoon hour, though. Normally I would be too after a long night of work.

Drawing in a deep breath, I shared Bryok's plan to own me, the "courting" gift he gave me last night, Rhylen's confession that Bryok was using me to control him, Bryok's insistence on using my birth name and speaking of Hamish as our confirmed da, as well as Bryok's threat to sell Cian if I didn't convince Rhylen to trade me to him.

When I finished, Cian cupped my face and his lowered until we were eye to eye. "I get first dibs on that fecker's feathers."

I let my mouth fall open in a mock gasp. "How dare you try to wear *my* victory better than me!"

He kissed my forehead then drawled, "They'd look prettier on me anyway," ending with a wink. "Now darlin', I need to sleep before enduring another night of saving innocent bystanders from breathing funny around Rhylen's territorial broody arse."

He sauntered toward his wagon, loudly "whispering" over his shoulder, "Gold eyeliner . . ." and I bit back a smile.

Those poor, dear souls who passed Rhylen working in the animal pens. I understood their suffering. He stole my breath even before I saw him undressed and prettied up for me. Fairly certain I would perish at the merest glimpse of him now.

Falling stars, he truly was the most beautiful male to have existed.

And he was mine.

Chapter Twenty-One

RHYLEN LONAN

The Autumn Night Market surrounded me. Overhead in the sprawling tree limbs, candlelit lanterns flickered various colors and patterns over the wide-eyed visitors—but not oil lamps, thank the wishless falling stars. Hawkers shouted their wares behind carted booths or from their wagons, from cures to love potions to magical items. By the outdoor pub, musicians sang a drinking ditty about a drunk lad who had mistakenly married a veiled Crone instead of his forbidden love.

Normally, I took in all the sights with a level of familiar appreciation. This was my tribe, my home. Traveling from village to village was the only life I knew. But, lately, I couldn't shake the notion of setting down roots instead of being constantly uprooted. I peered over my shoulder at Seren and blew out a quiet sigh.

No Bryok.

No slaves.

No banishment for marrying a mortal.

Children compensated fairly.

"I always loved this smell."

I turned my head back toward Gran, whose arm was looped through mine. We had been drifting slowly through the market for a single candlemark now.

"The faerie floss?" I asked her.

"Aye."

We walked by the spun sugar vendor and I slowed our steps. "You want one, Gran?"

"Nae, lad. Save yer coin for oats and feed."

"He owes me a favor. Fixed his wheel a few weeks back." I leaned in close and winked. "And, I have a pretty lass on my arm with a sweet tooth."

She smiled at me, then dipped her head.

Filena and Glenna had put dainty wildflowers in Gran's black and gray hair, which she wore down to her waist, the sides pulled back into a knot. The girls had ironed her prettiest dress, too, and applied a soft touch of rouge to her lips and cheeks before they left for work. Promenading Brenna Meadows around the Autumn Night Market was a date I looked forward to every year.

With my eyes downcast, I approached the vendor who happily handed me a paper cone of blackberry flavored faerie floss—but as a gift to Gran. She was the oldest member of our tribe, a true ancient. While some regarded her felly class, most held to the tradition that the gods favored the ancients among us. Brenna Meadows, however, would be embarrassed to receive preferential treatment, from anyone, for any reason. And, so, I let her believe the candy was still a bargained trade.

Gran pinched a tuft of spun sugar and plopped it in her mouth with a delighted sigh. "Ye spoil me, Rhylee Lo."

199

"Not nearly enough." I kissed her cheek. "You need a new hair ribbon too."

"I'm not a maid to be wear'n new ribbons in me hair."

"Well, if I have to find a mate, it's only fair you do too."

Gran barked a laugh and I couldn't help my grin, winking at her again. She had such a lovely laugh, melodic and rich. It reminded me of Glenna's in many ways.

With a happy sigh, she reached for another bite and startled when a little Raven Folk girl around two or three tugged on her skirts. The wee hen pointed to the faerie floss, making Gran laugh all over again.

"Baby birds," she said softly, "always hungry."

I knelt before the little girl. "Where's your mam, hennie?"

She eyed me warily and leaned into Gran's skirts. Gran's wrinkles deepened with her smile. She placed a protective hand on the wee one and offered her a cotton ball size of faerie floss.

"Caelie!" a frantic female voice called out, a felly around my age from a different tribe. "My niece likes to wander, she does . . ." Her words trailed off as I rose. The little hen's auntie blushed as she took me in, her rounded, worried eyes fading into a well-practiced bashful look. Gran's lips pulled in humor and I had to hold back the urge to roll my eyes. "I hope she was no bother," she said to me.

"None at all." I tipped my hat before offering my arm to Gran again. I wanted to get away before I had to endure any flirtatious attempts to keep my attention.

The girl placed a hand on Gran's shoulder. "Ancient wisdom to pass on?"

It was common for younger Folk to ask ancients for advice as a form of respect. But I wasn't sure if she was sincere or wanting to please me by honoring my gran.

Gran still eyed the little hen with amusement, who was now clutching her auntie's skirts. "Love doesn't wear a face, lass," she said softly. "It cares not if yer fae or mortal. It doesn't know yer sex or gender." Gran lowered her voice and met the felly girl's eyes. "Fear only a future without the one yer heart beats for." Her eyes then slid to mine. "Not the rules keeping ye apart."

The hair on my arms stood on end.

She knew.

Gran held my eyes a beat longer before smiling at the little girl again. Then, with a dip of her head at the felly still blushing up at me, she guided us forward to keep walking the market as before.

"Oh, lad," Gran said on yet another laugh a few seconds later, "she had it bad fer ye, she did."

I grunted in reply, too annoyed to say anything.

Also, too distracted by Gran's ancient words of wisdom.

They were easy words to speak. Much harder words to live by. It wasn't safe to always choose the one we loved. But . . . I also understood the deeper truth being spoken *to me*. I would suffer more for choosing a fear of banishment over Filena.

She *wanted* me to choose Filena over her, over Glenna, and my heart twisted in my chest. I had already planned on marrying Filena, knowing there would be consequences. It was unthinkable to marry another. The very idea made me physically ill. But I also couldn't shake the guilt in possibly abandoning my family by doing so.

What kind of grandson did that make me? What kind of brother?

Male faerie Folk were driven to protect their mates over any other in their care, Ravens especially. Still, the fear of being separated from the only family I had left consumed me, even though I would make a new one with Filena—if we weren't forced to live on Seren, that was. I loved my gran and sister with every beat of my heart. I loved Cian too.

And I was pissed to be put in this situation.

It shouldn't be a choice.

I shouldn't be punished for what the gods chose, nor should my family be punished alongside me.

"Yer thoughts are loud," Gran said around another bite of floss. "What troubles ye—"

"Rhylen Lonan," a deep voice interrupted and I bit back a groan. From lowered eyes, I watched as Connel, one of the elders, approached us with a Caravan lass at his side. "Brenna." The elder greeted Gran with a shallow bow. Returning attention back onto me, he said, "I've been looking for you since early evening."

"I was working. What can I do for you, elder?" I shifted on my feet, pulling Gran closer to my side.

"A family from North Tribe has asked for your hand in marriage to their eldest daughter and our chieftain has agreed to the match."

My heart stopped beating.

They had matched me *without my consent?*

"Bram Fiachna doesn't bother himself with the meddling tasks of mams and nans. Neither do the other elders." My eyes narrowed. "Why did the family approach the elders and not me directly?"

Connel cleared his throat. "Your marriage is set for Samhain Eve."

For a few stabbing seconds, the betrayal iced in my veins. The market around me blurred in and out of focus. Panic was a living, breathing beast stomping on my chest.

Then my anger exploded.

"Ridiculous. What middle-rank clan would willingly choose to marry their daughter to a felly boy?" I gestured to the market. "There are dozens of middle-rank lads hunting for a mate! Why me?"

I knew why, though. And rage raced beneath my burning skin.

"Allow me to introduce you to your betrothed, Braelin Cormac." He took the girl's hand and guided her closer.

Cormac?

"You may look at me, Rhylen."

Shame burned through me hot and bright. The girl I was arranged to marry had to give me permission to even look into her eyes—a middle-rank girl Bryok selected for me. I knew it was him. The elder refused to answer my question. But I didn't understand why any family would let their daughter from good standings marry a felly.

A Cormac, no less. A fecking *Cormac*.

My panicking pulse spurred into a full gallop.

Gran gently patted my arm and my furious gaze snapped to my betrothed's.

Braelin was pretty, with more delicate elven features, long black hair decorated in soft curls, fair skin, and dark, kind eyes. The lantern light and soft moonlight only accentuated her beauty. Any lad would be lucky to have her on his arm . . . which was what pricked the hairs on the back of my neck. Something didn't feel right. What had Bryok offered her family? How much would his decision cost the tribe?

Did she even want this? Was she forced into this arrangement too?

Not that it mattered. I wouldn't be marrying her beside all the other newly mated Raven Folk that evening.

"I'm sorry, Braelin," I said, trying to keep my breathing calm, "but I will not wed a girl I didn't choose for myself."

The elder's lips dipped into a frown. "The dowry is—"

"Not my problem now, is it?" I snapped. "I agreed to nothing. You can't marry me against my will, or hers."

"Aye, we can." The elder's gravelly voice grated on my waning self-control. "Your name was pulled in the lottery, a decision we bound in magic for the good of our tribe. To refuse is to invite a curse, not just on you but on her too."

My mouth fell open. "You would curse an innocent girl who has *nothing* to do with our tribe?"

"She's now your betrothed, Lonan."

Gran took the girl's hand and gently squeezed her fingers. "Do not fret, lass. Me grandson won't let anything befall ye. That's not his way."

My gaze flitted back to my "betrothed," a muscle in my jaw flexing. "You are not to blame for West Tribe's fire or the elders foolishly binding a harmful decision in magic. I'll not let anyone touch you or your family. But we are not marrying." Perhaps I imagined it but, despite the twinge of fear in the girl's dark eyes, her shoulders relaxed. The pinch between her brows smoothed too. "Now, if you'll excuse me." I tipped my hat first to her, then met the elder's narrowed gaze in challenge for one, hard second, before angling past both to continue my night with Gran.

It was uncouth of me to dismiss Braelin as I did just now, let alone as middle-rank Folk with a gov at her side. But I was on the verge of splintering apart. My pulse was a thunderclap, every breath a lightning strike. The storm raging in my head was seconds away from hunting down Bryok and pounding him into the dirt.

Maybe now was the time to challenge him—this very night. Make him a felly before he married the Chieftain of South Tribe's daughter tomorrow evening. Better yet, as the challenge winner, I would sell him to Seren. To never see his preening arse again would warm the cockles of my heart all the remaining days of my life.

But, without elder magic, I wasn't sure how to win a challenge against Bram. That reminder cooled my blood some. That and how he would find a way to remove me as heir to avenge his son. As the challenge winner, Bram would decide my fate. The fate of my family too.

"Rhylee—"

"I know, a kinder gent wouldn't have left the girl like I did."

"Nae, lad." Gran pulled me to a stop and took my face in her free hand. "Yer fire heart burns only fer one lass."

I drew in a hiccuped breath. "I love her, Gran. I have loved her for so long."

"Careful not to burn the world around ye to ash in yer pining."

"It's more than pining." I blinked back the angry tears. "She's a part of my magic," I whispered hoarsely.

Gran nodded her head slowly, her dark purple eyes boring into mine. "She is magic, lad, aye."

A scowl furrowed my brow. By the way she was looking at me, I gathered she wasn't talking about Filena's seer ability. Earlier she instructed me, hidden in her ancient wisdom, to choose

Filena over her and Glenna. But I didn't understand *this* disguised message.

"My hollowed bones are tired," she said and pointed to an empty bench near the outdoor pub.

Wrapping an arm around her shoulders, I supported her steps as she slowly walked to the seat. We lowered ourselves onto the bench and I twisted to face her. Warm lantern light bathed Gran's skin in gold and amber as she quietly ate her faerie floss while watching the visitors pass by. I didn't know what to say, too worked up for casual conversation. And so I distracted myself by watching the visitors too, yet I saw nothing but my own dread and fury.

"Rhylen," she began when finished with her treat and I swallowed thickly. I could count on both hands the number of times she called me by my full name. "I have a tale fer ye, lad." She wove her fingers with mine and the muscles in my stomach tensed. I leaned in closer to hear her over the music with an encouraging nod to continue. "A week before the Merricks arrived, I had a visit from the Mother while tending to our horses."

My forehead wrinkled. "The Merrick's mother?"

"Nae, a Sisters Three in the Mother's form."

My eyes widened. A Sisters Three was a triple goddess who walked Caledona Wood while shifted into her Maiden, Mother, or Crone form. To see one was rare. To speak with one was unheard of anymore—

Oh gods.

My mouth parted on a quiet gasp.

I could see it now.

Filena's unruly auburn hair and her seer's ability—like the

Maiden.

Her forest familiars and caregiver nature—like the Mother.

Her cackling laugh and clever wit—like the Crone.

"She's the Mother's daughter?" I asked, barely breathing.

"Great-granddaughter." Gran squeezed my fingers. "Cian is her great-grandson."

"Does Filena know this yet?"

"She will know when the time is right."

"But—"

"Nae, lad. Promise me ye'll say nothing until then."

She didn't have to finish the rest of that bargain. Only a fool would cross a Sisters Three. "I'll not tell the Merricks of their fae ancestry and speak of it only with Cian and Filena after Filena knows."

Gran squeezed my hand again.

My Filena Moira was a fáidhbhean and a cailleach . . . did Bryok know this? Was this why he obsessed over making Filena his property? And why hadn't we seen her magic as a fae witch yet? Maybe she didn't have any despite her lineage.

"The Mother told me to buy the Merricks when they arrived and keep them safe," Gran continued, her voice nearly drowned out by the nearby music. "She handed me a heavy coin pouch and . . . and placed a hand on me barren belly, saying that Filena and Cian would bear my descendants." A tear slipped down her cheek. The muscles in my gut tightened more as I kissed the back of her hand. The loss of my mam nearly destroyed Gran. "I was to tell no one, lad. But a fortnight ago," she whispered, her voice shaking, "the Mother visited me again, before the tent fire." Gran leaned in even closer. "I know who ye are to her, Rhylee Lo. I've known since before the Merricks arrived."

It all made sense now. She had always treated Filena and Cian as if they were her own grandchildren instead of slaves. My heart was so full, a swirling sea of emotions, I didn't know where to settle my thoughts. But I did know this . . .

"I'm going to marry her, Gran. They'll try to banish me—"

"The Mother has a message for ye," she said so quietly, I almost didn't hear her.

I paused a beat. "A message for *me*?"

"She says ye are to marry her great-granddaughter the night following the Fire Dance."

"Tonight?!"

"Before midnight, lad."

"Why tonight?"

"She didn't say."

My pulse was rushing in my ears. It was less than an hour before midnight. I couldn't believe Gran was just now telling me this. Or was that also part of her instructions? "Did the Mother say anything else?"

A pretty smile fluttered across Gran's lips. "I'll live long enough to hold me *chlann clainne*." Warmth spread across my chest at the image of Gran holding my child. "Make me lots of grand-babies before I walk me last." Gran winked at me and I started laughing.

"Well, if the Mother commands me . . ." I said with a crooked smile.

Gran cupped my cheeks with both hands. "They'll be such beautiful bairns. Build a new world fer them, me Rhylee boy, not burn it to ash."

I leaned into her touch and closed my eyes. "You're so bossy."

She quietly laughed. "Now go to yer lass."

My eyes opened and I sat back. "Do you need me to take you home first or would you like to sit with Glenna?"

In answer, she kissed my cheek, then shifted into her raven form and flew back toward the wagons. I watched her disappear into the night, chuckling to myself. My Gran was the best meddling, matchmaking nan walking Carran.

I pushed up from the bench and turned toward Filena's divination wagon.

We had crossed several lines already.

Now to cross the one that may cost us everything.

I was to marry a demi-goddess this night, my True Mate, and my heart couldn't soar any higher if it tried.

Chapter Twenty-Two

FILENA MERRICK

An elderly gent and his wife left my divination wagon in slow, trundled steps. I rubbed my eyes beneath my black veil. I could go weeks without a true vision from the gods. I was often dry during the Autumn Night Market. But tonight? I had *seen* over a dozen—minimum. I stopped counting, honestly.

When a new customer entered my space, I flinched too. Would I see my da again? Bryok? The disgusting man I was sold to as a child?

I pressed a hand to an aching spot on my chest where it increasingly hurt to breathe. Guilt was gnawing at my conscience. Rhylen deserved to know my true origins. But if he knew we weren't orphans when Gran purchased us from the tribe, he could no longer claim us as property per Carran's laws. Cian would be fine. Me, however? I would lose all protection.

I would lose *everything*.

Rhylen would have no legal rights to claim me back either. Only the fae recognized True Mates. Mortal laws cared not a whit about mating rituals save one detail: the newly married had fifteen days of no work to strengthen their bonds and relationship. This was a safety precaution. Many fae males were unbearably territorial for their mates at first. Well, *always*, but especially at first.

Rhylen needed to know I was still possibly married, though, before we took another dangerous step forward together. The constricting pang in my chest tightened. If the Fire Dance night were any indication, Rhylen will explode into action—he would want to hunt to kill—and I would need to carefully dance around his territorial rage to protect what I couldn't yet share. Not until I figured out how to maneuver around Bryok's threat.

Moonless stars, it was all so exhausting.

Barry rested his head on my leg and snuggled into my stomach. Sheila climbed from my pocket and nuzzled into Barry so my hand could trail from his head to across her back. Efficient little buggers.

The muslin curtaining the door rippled open a sliver and the candles around me sputtered. I held my breath, afraid of who might enter next, and without my invitation to do so. A few seconds later, when no one entered, I blew out a slow breath, fluttering my veil, then reached for my cards—and paused.

Was that a . . . *squirrel*?

Why was a squirrel in my wagon?

The fluffy little rodent began speaking in rapid-fire chatter. As he spoke, his adorable bushy tail twitched and I bit back a smile. Was he speaking to me? And how did I know it was a *he*?

Barry groaned followed by a long-suffering sigh.

Oh.

Ohhhhh.

Our little visitor was faerie touched.

I was so delighted by the scowl my fox was currently sporting, I was on the verge of manically giggling. Outside of raccoons, his least favorite forest creature was squirrels.

"Muffin Moo," I cooed, "you have a new forest friend, darlin'. Be a good lad now and introduce yourself. Remember to use your nice voice."

I swore the fox peered up at the wagon ceiling in a plea to the gods.

The squirrel scampered up onto my table and offered me a hazelnut, still chattering away. Amused, I accepted the hazelnut—a wild kind that was absolutely delicious, just like Barry's suffering—but, before I could pull away, the squirrel's little paws grabbed the nut and it broke in half. I was too startled to question how the wee fella and I managed to break a nut with so little pressure. Too startled *and* too distracted by the tiny wisp of folded paper that floated to the table.

I unfolded the paper and gaped. Words were writing themselves onto the strip.

"Say 'yes,'" I murmured aloud. I peered at the squirrel. "Yes to what? You can't expect me to agree to something without more information."

The strip erased and new words began to appear.

To your mate.

"My—" I cut myself off. My attention drifted back to the hazelnut and I almost rolled my eyes. Cheeky gods. Of course they would use a hazelnut to reveal the lad I should marry. I almost cracked an appreciative smile at their irreverent humor. Almost.

I considered the little furry messenger again.

"Do you have a name?"

The squirrel began squeaking at me, like earlier, and a name appeared on the paper.

Lloyd.

"Well, Lloyd, it's lovely to meet you. Who do you serve?"

The Mother.

Lloyd

"The Sisters Three?" My heart stuttered a beat. "That Mother?"

Your hair is pretty. Can I stay with you forever?

Barry let out a low warning growl and the squirrel lifted his paws.

I glanced at my fox, who had narrowed his eyes onto Lloyd, the latter who was now gazing at Sheila, his little paws clutched to his chest as if she were the most beautiful forest creature he had ever laid his little squirrel eyes upon.

A loud cackling laugh erupted from me.

I wasn't sure if Lloyd was meant to become my permanent messenger squirrel or if he were only here to deliver his one message from the Mother—a wild thought. But Muffin Moo was *clearly* in favor of becoming best friends forever . . . and I cackled harder.

A knock on the wagon's doorsill rattled me from my humor and I cleared my throat. "One moment, pet."

Break time was over, apparently.

I shooed Lloyd off the table, but the rascally lad scampered around my hands.

"*Fáidhbhean?*"

My hands froze mid-air. That voice . . . deep, soft, musical. Since last night, since the feel of his breath forming words across my body in-between feverish kisses, the slightest whisper of his melodic voice sent warm shivers across my skin.

But why was he here while the market was open?

Did something happen to Gran?

"Come in," I answered.

Rhylen angled into the wagon and halted at the sight of Lloyd, his black brow pointing into a humored arch. But only for half a beat of my rapid pulse. A soft smile touched his lips, one that warmed the candlelit elderberry wine hue of his eyes as he took in my veiled form. It was a look of tender affection, but of something else too. Almost as if he were looking at me for the first time—a curious tilt to his head, a feathered blink as his gaze roamed over my hair then the faerie-touched forest familiars at my side.

Well, he didn't look distressed. Why was he here?

I rose to my feet and placed Sheila on the table beside Lloyd. "Do you seek your fortune, Traveler?"

"Aye." He approached where I stood, removing his tattered top hat. "But I have no coin, *fáidhbhean*."

He was dirt poor and perfect. A prince of paupers. I was so in love with this felly faerie boy, I thought my pounding pulse might tear through my chest just for the chance to beat beside his.

A corner of his mouth hooked up in a flirtatious smile.

Those lips . . . those delicious, kissable lips.

"Will you accept this, instead?" Rhylen opened his palm and—

Oh my stars . . .

My mam's button.

Ten years ago, the day before Cian and I had run away, she had removed the pretty mother of pearl button from her dress and sewed it onto mine. Not even two years later, I had given Rhylen this treasure when he broke his wing.

"You still have it," I whispered in disbelief.

Taking my hand, he placed the pretty piece into my palm and cleared his throat. "Do you remember when you built a house of sticks for the wee injured field mice?"

I nodded my head. The tribe's foremen had instructed the

setup crew to scythe the meadow before tents were built. I was eleven at the time and still new to Caravan life. My heart grew sick when I spotted a hurt mouse, then angry that their home was being destroyed.

"I collected twigs and tied them together with bramble vines."

Rhylen's playful smile softened. "You asked me to help you find any mouse that needed shelter."

I studied the mother of pearl button. "I left acorn cap bowls of water beside each bed of moss."

"Aye, a wee fussy mam, you were."

"I wove wildflowers into tiny blankets too." I huffed a humored laugh. "The only time my lack of feminine skills actually created something half functional."

Rhylen snorted. "Then Cian showed up."

My then fourteen-year-old brother was such an eejit. The mice, he had said while tapping the tip of my nose with his finger, couldn't share the same mossy roof unless they were married. Such a mortal thought, too. The fae didn't give two shakes of a stick about any of that nonsense.

"I was so scandalized." I placed a fluttering, dramatic hand on my chest. "To think I had caused injured mice to live in shame."

"You were inconsolable, lass." Rhylen was laughing now. "And we didn't know what to do. Cian thought he was being funny but you wouldn't stop weeping about the poor, unmarried, now homeless mice."

Glenna showed up shortly thereafter and quickly helped me organize a quick wedding . . .

My thoughts slowed and my eyes lifted from the button to Rhylen's warm gaze.

Say yes.

"You wore a light green dress that reached your knees," he said softly. "It was so old and thin, dirty from constant use. But it had these pretty wee mis-matched buttons. This one," he said, brushing a finger across the one in my palm, "was my favorite."

"You remembered my dress?"

"When Glenna began reciting the marriage vows, I . . ." he drew in a quiet breath. "I watched you the entire time. I saw the moment your horror became happiness. Your smile was so beautiful. *You* are so beautiful, Filena Moira, *a stór mo chroí.*"—*treasure of my heart.* He paused. "I didn't understand at thirteen that I was already in love with you. All I knew is that I had never wanted to be an injured mouse living in shame so badly." I spurted a laugh and he grinned that rascally, boyish smile I loved. "Because, if I were, it meant those vows were for me. And I wanted to tell you, desperately, how I would always be yours."

My head was so dizzy I feared I might float away in bliss. "Tell me now."

He stepped around the table toward me, drawing the air from my lungs the closer he came. Stars above, he took up so much space in my narrow divination wagon, his tall frame well-built from years of hard labor. If his wings were out . . . A lightning bolt of pleasure ached low in my belly at the thought of his wings and I gripped the table.

"Filena," he whispered and I blinked, "*mo shiorghrá.*"

True Mate.

"I would level mountains and reshape the seas for you." He slowly lifted my veil. "I would capture every star in the sky to light your night." Our eyes locked and I could faint at the intensity of longing burning in his gaze. "I will *always* be your family, your shelter, and your protector." Rhylen lowered his face closer to mine and whispered, "I am so foolishly in love with you, Filena Moira."

"Yes," I breathed in reply.

"Yes?" Rhylen quietly laughed and leaned back. "I haven't even asked you yet, my wee feral swine wife-to-be." He kissed my palm. "Phil. Or is this one Bill?"

"Will. This one"—I wiggled my fingers—"is Swill." Rhylen's lips trailed up my wrist and I almost forgot how to form words. But, from the corner of my eye, I could see Lloyd's bushy tail and I remembered . . . "Ask me if you like, pet, but the answer is still yes."

My stomach clenched, but I shoved away thoughts of that horrible man. I would tell Rhylen before we truly exchanged any vows. But, right now, I just wanted to marinate in the headiness of his courtship.

Rhylen's smile faltered and a crease appeared between his brows. "I didn't bring my da's ring."

"I don't need a ring." I kissed my mam's button. "Not when I have a boy who gives me buttons and ribbons."

Exchanging rings was a mortal tradition, anyway. It was sweet of him to think of my humanness. The fae, regardless of Folk kind, only exchanged vows when wanting to mate bond to another—and often in private. No witnesses needed. Or rings. To their magic, it was the same as agreeing to a bargain. One bound by ravens, as they called it, a primal magic connected to the old fae, to a time when they couldn't lie. Also to a time when ravens were sacred creatures to faeries . . . before Lugh, our sun god, made them into Folk to honor his two magical pets.

But still, to this day, when bonding, a raven mark appeared on the wrist, just like the bond struck between a master and their indentured slave. For it, too, was an agreed upon form of ownership. He would be mine and I would be his, sealed in magic. Most faeries built their lives together without marrying, though. The fae were fickle creatures by nature.

But not Raven Folk.

They came from the oldest magic in Carran and mate bonded for life.

"Whatever you want," Rhylen whispered hoarsely, caressing my ring finger, "I would—"

"Bargain away your happiness for mine," I cut in with a shake of my head. "But I only want you, Rhylen Lonan. *Only* you."

He rolled his bottom lip into his mouth and blinked back a sudden flash of fear. "Today, the elders and chieftain," he began, his voice tight, "betrothed me to a girl from North Tribe."

The blood rushed from my head.

"You're betrothed?" The words were thick and sharp in my mouth. Tiny knives that pierced me over and over again.

"I refused her, Lena. I rejected the match," Rhylen quickly explained.

Unlike my situation, however, where I could ignore a contract made between two men so long as neither man could find me, Rhylen had no such escape despite his refusal. The elders had sealed their decision in magic.

Bile coated my throat and I pressed a hand to my middle.

For a few breaking beats of my heart, I couldn't think, only feel—plunging fear, coiling fury, jagged grief, white hot betrayal. Then a crashing wave of awareness rushed through my spinning mind all at once.

The murmuring voices of waiting customers echoed loudly in my ears.

The wagon's interior vivid colors and interlocking knot designs, washed in candlelit amber, swirled in my darting vision. I needed to focus on breathing, but it hurt too much.

Say yes.

Could we still marry? Clearly the gods thought so, otherwise they wouldn't have sent Lloyd. And it was that knowledge that began easing my spiraling grief.

I rested my zipping fear onto a candle's dancing flame. Wax dripped across the next fifteen-minute line cut into the relatively new taper. By the candlemark and by when I heard the village bells last, I estimated it was near midnight.

Midnight . . .

My dying heart jumpstarted in my chest.

The first five days after being bound by ravens, the bargain could be dissolved. On the sixth day, it was set. Rhylen wasn't required to take vows with the North Tribe girl for another six days, when the courting pairs stood beneath the Truth Telling Tree, a romantic Autumn Night Market attraction for visitors.

If we exchanged vows now, before the midnight bells tolled, our bond would be set by Samhain Eve, but we would be cursed and banished before the ceremony could take place—

A pull tugged on my mind, a familiar sensation belonging to only one creature.

My focus slid to Barry's waiting, insistent gaze. Yellow eyes that flashed with a reminder: no one could use their coercion magic against me, not with Barry assigned to my protection. I couldn't be cursed either.

My jaw slacked.

I couldn't be cursed.

As my bonded True Mate, would this protection extend to Rhylen since any curse he received could also harm me?

The nausea in my gut eased and intuition gripped me instead.

No, he couldn't be cursed if we were bonded.

I took Rhylen's hand in mine and squeezed his fingers.

We might be slashed from the field, like those poor mice, but we wouldn't be injured. Nor was there shame in a Raven Folk lad choosing a mortal slave to be his wife.

But he needed to know that I may be married first.

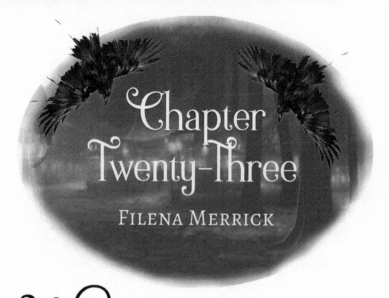

Chapter Twenty-Three

FILENA MERRICK

"We have twenty minutes, Rhy," I said in a low whisper, "or we'll miss the full five days—"

Rhylen's mouth parted. "That's why tonight."

"This wasn't your plan?"

He shook his head. "I just . . . knew . . . I needed to marry you before midnight."

My lips pressed together in a tight line. *Knew?*

I would ask him later. It didn't matter at this moment.

The nausea in my stomach came roaring back and I had to will myself not to vomit. For ten years, I had dreaded this confession—just the thought of saying I was married aloud made me shudder. The man I was sold to, however, may not still be alive. Gods, I hoped he was rotting six feet beneath the earth.

I wobbled over if I should also mention that my da was alive and here too. But if anyone overheard me confirm that Hamish Mac-Cullough was indeed my da, Rhylen would be required to pay reparations for owning property not legally his for ten years.

I blew out a slow, uneven breath.

"Rhylen," I began, and blew out another steadying breath.

His black brows pinched together but he waited for me to continue.

"When I was a girl of ten, my da . . . my da—" Stars, I was so dizzy. A clammy sweat flushed across my skin.

Rhylen gently cupped my elbow and guided me to sit, then knelt at my feet. "What did your da do to you?" His whisper was laced with unspoken, razor-sharp threats and my pulse spurred into a gallop. The rage building in his gaze while his hand tenderly held mine was my undoing. A tear slipped down my cheek.

"My da sold me in marriage to a man in his grandfather years."

Rhylen's fire was instant. A sudden whoosh of flames. The doting, affectionate male now a full predatory creature of fae, his eyes ablaze and canines bared. "Did he touch you?"

"No—"

"He will not survive me if he tries to claim you, Lena. Ten fecking years old!" Rhylen's wings appeared and snapped open. A couple of candles snuffed in the sudden breeze, plunging us into dusky shadows. "I will kill him."

"I—I know."

"Mate . . ." Rhylen held my face and leaned his forehead onto mine. The pad of his thumb brushed the tear from my cheek in a soft caress. "You sicken before each opening night because of him, aye? You fear he'll find you?"

"Aye," I whispered back.

"And why you and Cian ran away?"

"He couldn't collect me until I was fifteen, but I—I was terrified. I had no protection except Cian."

The muscles down his body flexed and trembled, but the fingers cradling me were gentle. "You are *mine*, Filena Merrick." His quickened, hot breath brushed over my lips. "Not that fecker's, not Bryok's. Not anyone's but mine."

"You're not upset at me for not telling you sooner?"

"Why would I be mad at you?" his voice strained, as if he were in pain. "He's to blame for your terror, him and your da. You've done nothing wrong, lass. Of course you ran away and hid. Of course you wanted to remain another's property." Rhylen's chest rose and fell in a furious rhythm. "And I would destroy the Otherworld to protect you, Filena," he whispered. "I would destroy Carran too."

Despite the disgust still souring my stomach, his possessive words drizzled starlight down my limbs, to my curling toes. I was a few heaving breaths shy of swooning. Seven suns, to kiss him while he was territorially aggressive for me—it would be molten and passionate in ways that would sinfully destroy me. I wouldn't want it to end.

But also, at the mention of Bryok's name, fury crackled to life in my veins. Sharp, bolting arrow points of vengeance. Bryok Fiachna was involved with Rhylen's betrothal. I could feel it in my gut and the anger inside of me was building and building. How dare he force his Caravan to mate bond for life against their will! He was a monster and deserved nothing, least of all me.

I pushed to my feet. The button in my hand cut into my palm, my fists were clenched so tightly. "I will curse the prince to fly until his wings molt to ash."

The dark broody line between Rhylen's brows was making my heart violently flutter. The flexing muscles in his exposed, tattooed forearms too. Why did he have to roll up his sleeves? I couldn't concentrate, even in my protective fury.

Rhylen rose to his feet with the predatory grace of a wild fae hunter stalking prey. And every handsome feature on his face sharpened into deadly stillness. "Cian," he practically growled, low, "told me about Bryok's gift and threats."

My gaze flicked to Rhylen's long, obsidian hair, to where he had hidden the missing braid.

Another wave of fury rolled through me.

"I will also curse the prince to go bald on his wedding day, in front of everyone." My hands fluttered in the air. "Imagine every strand of hair on his body falling to the ground just as his bride finished her vows."

"Every hair?"

I nodded. "On his body. He'll be barer than a bairn and cry like one too."

Rhylen threw his head back and laughed. "Bryok with no eyebrows or eyelashes."

"And ash for wings."

"Oh lass, the things you come up with."

I sighed, deflating into myself. "I desperately want to curse something. I feel it rising inside of me."

The strange look he wore earlier returned as he peered at me—head cocked, eyes gently squinting, his lips softly tipped downward—as if seeing me for the first time and not sure of what to think.

"Perhaps one day you will," he said simply. "And I hope I'm there to witness his hair-raising destruction." He winked at me and I bit back a soft snort.

Lloyd scampered over and nudged our hands with his head, then pointed at the paper.

Ask her already.

Rhylen's lips pressed into a humored line while reading the slip beside me.

"A messenger squirrel?"

"A chatty one. Muffin Moo and Lloyd are best friends already."

Rhylen chuckled and eyed my irritated fox. Then his attention slid to Sheila and he genuinely grinned. "Look at you, lass." He scooped her up and brought her close to his face, completely smitten. And, like last time, Sheila's nose kissed his. "Pretty bow, pet," he murmured. I had taken a tiny strip from my mam's ribbon and tied it behind Sheila's ear. "I'll find you more hair ribbons too."

Goddess help me, if we ever had a daughter, he would be ridiculous from moonrise to sunset each day . . . and I would completely melt into a sighing puddle at the sight of Rhylen Lonan as a doting, playful, hard-working, protective da.

Rhylen lowered the little hedgehog back to the table and I fell into the intensity of his captivating, large presence. Candlelight limned his face in sultry shadows. Heat pooled hot in my core as I took in the fine sweep of his brows, the handsome planes of his cheeks, the sensual tilt of his lips. Stars, he was beautiful. I could gaze at him for an eternity and still not be satisfied, but we had ten minutes at most to say our vows.

"I ache for you, Lena." Rhylen's dark eyes rested on my lips. "I don't care if I'm betrothed to another or if you're already married. I'm meant for you."

"No one should be sold into marriage. We belong only to ourselves."

Sheila

"And to each other." He pulled me to him and tilted my head back. "Become my bonded wife, *a stór mo chroí*." His voice cracked. "Vow to be mine forever."

Say yes.

"Forever isn't long enough." I laced my fingers with his, my mam's mother of pearl button pressed between our palms, and began the words I'd heard a thousand times from others beneath the Truth Telling Tree. "I, Filena Moira Merrick, mate bind myself to you, Rhylen Lonan, my True Mate, for as long as my soul exists. I belong to you, husband, for now and for all eternity."

Rhylen caressed his thumb over the raven mark on my wrist. "I, Rhylen Lonan, release Filena Merrick from indentured servitude. She is free to own her life beside mine. Her debts are paid in full."

What?!

What was he doing?

No, no, *no* . . .

I watched in horror as the raven mark on my wrist disappeared.

Oh gods . . .

My rounding eyes jumped to his. Did he understand that I would be owned by—

My mind caught up to the fight-and-flight panic flooding my pulse and I could pass out in relief. Still, I wasn't sure if my heart rate would ever recover.

Per mortal laws, I could still be owned by my da or mortal husband for the next five days when our binds could dissolve. This risk was true even if I remained marked as Rhylen's slave.

Per fae laws, however, ones still honored by Carran, Rhylen would own me as his bonded mortal mate. Only more permanently on the sixth day.

The thought of not being his indentured, though? My alternate name plus being owned by his clan was all the protection I had known and for half of my life.

But . . . if Rhylen didn't release me from my indentured servitude, I would have two raven bond marks on my wrist instead of one. By releasing me, it would appear as if nothing had changed.

Confirming my thoughts, Rhylen's fingers moved over the

raven mark he now carried only for Cian and illusioned the mark away—a master had one mark regardless of the number of slaves he possessed.

"I never wanted to own you in this way." Gently, he took my hand and brushed his lips along my bare wrist. "Only in this way." He kissed my pale skin again, his eyes locked onto mine as he whispered to my beating pulse, "I, Rhylen Lonan, mate bind myself to you, Filena Moira Merrick, my True Mate, for as long as my soul exists. I put you above all others and will protect you with my life. I belong to you, wife, for now and for all eternity."

Warm tingles wrapped around my wrist as a new raven mark appeared—on his wrist and mine.

We were bound by ravens.

Holy Mother of Stars!

We were bonded lovers. As True Mates. This had really just happened. And by hurried, whispered declarations in my divination wagon. Perhaps other girls would feel disappointed by a less romantic situation. But I didn't care about any of that, not really.

Tears streamed down my face and I couldn't stop my soft laughter. How I would finish the remaining night of work, I didn't know. Especially as we still had more to discuss.

I was his. For forever.

Gods, this faerie boy . . . he consumed me.

Still, despite my joy, I couldn't shake the nibbling fear still gnawing on my gut. But nothing else needed my attention at this moment but him. Not any apprehension over what the next few days might bring. Not even those outside my door hoping for equally as happy fortunes.

I traced Rhylen's jaw with a single finger. "I love you, Rhylen

Lonan."

The midnight bells tolled from the nearby village and we smiled.

"I love you, Filena *Lonan*," he murmured, his voice rough, possessive. "I have loved you from the first moment I saw you."

Then his mouth lowered to mine in a kiss so sweet, so pure, my pulse became the soft beating of a thousand wings in flight.

And I would paint NEW STARS across the night sky to navigate a HAPPIER future, to give Filena wings to FLY FREE beside me.

Chapter Twenty-Four

RHYLEN LONAN

The sun was quickly setting behind the Autumn Night Market's Truth Telling Tree and my heart hitched a beat.

I belong to you, husband . . .

A hot, heady wave of desire pulsed through me and my awareness of Filena intensified. Her scent infused every breath I drew in. The waning sun glinted off the copper of her hair and caressed her face in delicate brushstrokes of gold. Stars, I ached to trace my lips down her neck and taste the fading sunshine on her skin. I could almost feel the salt on my tongue in my mind-spinning want.

But we were at a large celebration revel for Bryok's wedding. We fellys were tucked along the fringe of the gathering, near the slaves. Filena sat close to me on a fallen log, her arm pressed into mine, our fingers nearly touching, with Gran holding my hand in her lap on my other side. Across from us, Owen and Sean were joshing back and forth while Corbin snickered into his mug of ale.

"Aye me, she's a looker," Owen said, suddenly straightening. A felly girl from a different tribe ambled by with her friends. Her dark eyes caught onto Owen's and he grinned. "Evening—"

Sean shoved Owen from his stump before our friend could finish. Owen's legs flew into the air and his ale sloshed over his face. Corbin roared a laugh, laughing harder when Sean winked at the girls who giggled at their antics before moving on. Owen lifted a rude gesture at Sean, but he was grinning. Upstaging each other's attempts at flirting was old times.

Normally I would laugh too, but I was fading in and out of wanting to throw Filena over my shoulder and haul her back to my wagon like a complete brute or wanting to start a fight with another male simply to get the fire and angst out of my blood—particularly one male. I was only a hairbreadth away from not caring that it was his wedding day too.

From the corner of my eye, Gran held a barely contained smirk at my suffering.

There was a reason the mass wedding and The Wild Hunt were on Samhain Eve, the final day of the Autumn Night Market. Many Fae males were known to turn into animals for a fortnight after bonding—even when bonding without physical intimacy. And my kind? Raven Folk courting magic not only made us over-the-top territorial but temporarily mad too. I certainly felt like I was losing my godsdamn mind.

I would be embarrassed by Gran's taunting smile, but I was struggling to remain a gent in public. Moons above, I wanted a fight.

Swallowing thickly, I peered around for Cian's blond hair. Families gathered around communal cookfires or in small groups, like ours, deep in conversation, playing games, and laughing. In a sea of black hair, Cian's golden locks were a beacon. But no sight of the lad or my sister. Soon after Bryok's and Doireann's vows had finished, he had trotted off to walk Glenna back from the confectionery wagon—she and others had worked overtime to bake desserts for the govs and middle-rank. I had a feeling they were doing more than walking back, though.

And I was suddenly envious of their disappearing act.

If not for Gran, I would steal Filena away as well.

If not for the gathering and social class rules, I would bring my wife to the Truth Telling Tree and repeat my vows to her too.

The tree's Otherworldliness truly was beautiful.

Ceremonial sashes adorned the large, mossy trunk in an intricate knotted pattern, with handfasting bindings tucked into numerous places for mass weddings. Dangling from the sprawling oak branches above, lanterns dotted in-between an endless sea of fluttering Beltane and Samhain ribbons the elders from all four Caravan tribes had enchanted in lover's magic—a spell for happiness in marriage, a spell for passion in the bed, and a spell for luck in love.

This tradition was completely unnecessary for the fae. But the courting magic of Ravens craved the romance of claiming a mate in a ritual ceremony veiled in beauty and tree magic.

And so all four tribes stood before the giant oak to honor the royal wedding.

As top govs, Bryok's and the South Tribe's princess's marriage was its own spectacle outside of the Samhain Eve event, despite any territorial madness he might display afterward. That, too, was considered part of the show for the attendees. Only mortals would pay coin to be entertained by a fae male becoming primal for his mate.

Actual Truth Telling Trees, not the ones we recreated at each Night Market, were from old magic. It was said that *only* the Maiden, one of the Sisters Three, could grow a Truth Telling Tree and *only* from the coercion magic a faerie willingly gave up. Beneath the tree's bows, a mortal couldn't lie. Not in bargains struck in trade, in marriage, or in politics.

But now the fae could lie too.

Folk magic was weakening as humans expanded their cities into The Wilds, the heartbeat of our elemental origins on the mortal plane. Magic that was growing weaker still each time Carran's military slaughtered another clan of wild fae. So much so, faeries had been able to lie like mortals since just before Gran was born.

A cool autumn breeze brisked through the gathering and the hundreds of tree ribbons stirred into an aerial dance. With the sinking sun breathing golds and pinks across the dusking sky, the image was dreamlike.

I slanted my head toward Filena.

My wife.

My bonded True Mate.

We'd had little time to spend with each other since our hurried, whispered vows. Two days had passed and only a handful of stolen kisses. The Autumn Night Market was simply too demanding on our work schedules and . . . we needed to be careful.

The same night we were bound by ravens, I was called in to fix broken boards on one of the stages, a few mirrors had knocked loose in the fun halls, and a fence in the animal pens was missing. Where it went? Nobody knew. A bet among drunk mortals, most likely.

By the time I returned, I was dead on my feet and stank of

sweat and barn animals. Filena had fallen asleep waiting for me on her wagon's steps and, for a few wondrous seconds, I stood before her beauty completely humbled that she belonged to me.

My wife was a mortal demi-goddess. Her fae ancestry came from a powerful creature of legend.

I was nothing.

Just a felly boy with buttons and rocks in his pockets.

Why had the gods chosen *me* as her husband? My magic was little compared to trickster Ravens. I possessed no real material wealth either.

Tilting my head, I studied Filena's profile.

I felt the barest bump of her hand against mine from inside the folds of her skirts in reply. She continued to stare straight ahead while pretending to give a shite about Sean's, Owen's, and Corbin's antics. Just as I started to swing my head back toward the lads, her pinkie finger curled around mine.

Just that simple contact sent me spinning. With the autumn leaves tumbling by the lanterns and ribbons and the sleepy stars twinkling just above the horizon . . . the gathering faded until it was just me and Filena beneath the Truth Telling Tree, our hands bound together. She deserved to stand before our tribes in a beautiful gown, flowers arranged in her hair, as I declared before all that she was mine.

I glanced around our circle again. Everyone was pre-occupied, so I lowered my mouth to Filena's ear, unable to resist an opportunity to flirt. "What are you thinking about, *a stór*?"

"Glenna's new recipe."

My lips twitched.

"And ropes," she added, pausing a beat, "to hang the laundry."

I bit back a laugh and, instead, whispered, "I'm fantasizing about undressing you, *slowly*." My tongue flicked out to tease her lobe and I could moan. But I reined in my longings before I kissed her senseless in front of everyone. Filena's breath softly caught. She kept her gaze fixed straight ahead but curled her pinkie around mine tighter in warning. Wanting to laugh again, I continued, "Only so you can do the laundry, lass."

She angled her head toward me and I knew she was rolling her eyes. Satisfied, I pulled away and flashed her a flirty smile.

But she wasn't looking at me anymore.

Her sunset rose gold complexion grew moon pale, her eyes rounded, her mouth parted in a stricken look. I slowly turned to see what had gripped her. Gran's brows pushed together as I peered over her head.

A large man with red greasy, tangled hair and a long scraggly beard bellowed at another mortal incoherently. Food and ale stains mottled his threadbare shirt and his boots were barely stitched together. My eyes narrowed. He looked strangely familiar. Where had I seen this mortal before?

I swung back to Filena and stilled. An animal stillness that raised my hackles at the terror on her face. This was more than being shocked by a drunkard's hostility.

"Who is he?" I asked, almost not recognizing my voice. It was guttural and sharp.

She snapped out of her trance at that moment and shook her head. I released Gran's hand and cupped Filena's face before she could look away, no longer aware of anyone or anything else but her. My tilting madness was in full flight now.

"What did that mortal do to you?"

She blinked back the building tears. "He . . . he c-came into my divination wagon b-belligerent before the Fire Dance."

Was this why she had been crying? Besides the fear of losing me to another?

In my periphery, I could see that my boys had quieted and were watching us.

"Did he touch you?"

"No," she answered quickly. "Bryok stepped in—"

"Bryok visited your wagon?" My skin pebbled in white-hot fury.

"Aye, I t-think," she said and stopped, darting her eyes around the gathering. "I think," she continued, her voice now a whisper, "he planned to give me his gift then. But Cian showed up."

My gaze slid to Barry's and I murmured, "Good lad." The fox dipped his head. Searching my wife's still pooling eyes, I asked, "What did that man want? Do you know him?"

Her entire body stiffened and my nostrils flared. I would kill him. I had no idea who he was and what he'd done but—

A memory surfaced. That fecker's slurring threats continued to echo in the background, making Filena wince. But I remembered where I had seen that mortal before. It was the slop bucket who stumbled into me at the Áine's Day revel. A hot-tempered, drunk man with red hair and gray eyes . . . my thoughts slowed as I stared deeply into my wife's gray eyes.

Similar . . . gray eyes.

This was the secret Bryok spoke of and my heart thundered— Filena and Cian weren't orphans. I tried to calm my rage before Filena believed I was angry with her. Quite the opposite. I had only compassion for her and Cian. If my sister were in Filena's situation, I would want her to do whatever was necessary to protect herself and survive too.

Plus they were children. How would they know Carran's laws about faeries who owned mortal slaves? They were innocent. But not the Mother who asked Gran to risk her own family to save the Mother's kin . . .

Now I knew exactly the power Bryok had over us both. My family couldn't make any reparations to Filena's da if he demanded them. Based on his pub gutter appearance and behavior, he certainly would. The tribe would sell me and my sister to Seren to pay for the debts, if Filena's and that man's relation was proven in court.

I was surprised Bryok hadn't used coercion magic for that retaliation alone—the Merrick's da could be compelled to speak only the truth. But, if I remembered correctly, the mortal resisted mine. He must have rowan berries on him or a charm to ward away fae magic.

Filena was trembling, her breaths coming quick and short. I needed to ease her without saying words that would confirm anything. If anyone heard her admit the truth and reported the confession to Bryok, we would be doomed.

"Remember the opossum Cian found when you were fifteen?"

Her throat visibly swallowed. "A-aye, he had l-laid still for hours. We thought he had run under a wagon's wheel."

I nodded slowly. "Your brother tried to protect your sensitive nature." I smiled sweetly at her. "You're like a fussy mam around wild animals, a protective one too."

"Cian told me the opossum was dead and t-to move on." She blew out a tight breath.

"You had wanted to give it a proper burial, you did."

"But he wasn't dead."

"Aye," I said, struggling to hold in my anger. "He wasn't dead."

My parents, good Folk, died senselessly when a horse spooked and bolted. The horses and wagon had trampled my mam and then my da when he tried to protect her. But then feckers like Filena's da still stole breath from this world's air.

My mate watched her da with owlish eyes and it took everything in me to not charge after that disgusting man, fists raised. Gods, I wanted a fight. But I wouldn't publicly take him on, not with Bryok suspecting the truth. Filena's and Cian's secrets were their own and no one was entitled to them, not even me. I trusted them both explicitly. Knowing the truth changed nothing, anyway.

Filena Lonan was *mine*.

She had *always* been mine.

"He wasn't dead," she repeated softly under her breath.

Those beautiful gray eyes of hers snapped back to mine in understanding and new fear took root in her widened gaze. She seemed to struggle for words. My wife was rarely afraid and never this frightened. She was fire and sass and brilliance and laughter.

I lifted a tender smile, despite the animalistic rage battering my self-control, and caressed her cheek with my thumb. Leaning in close, I whispered under my breath, "I love you, Filly Lo."

She tried to blink back the tears but one fell anyway. "Rhy, I'm sorry—"

"No," I quietly stopped her. "You did nothing wrong and everything right. I hope you curse that pig slop's arse too."

A tear-choked grunted laugh left her. "I already threatened to curse him to use his bare hands to dig the grave of his own making."

A corner of my mouth hooked up higher. "You're truly terrifying, lass, you know that?"

"Getting cold feet about the laundry ropes, pet?" A single auburn brow kicked up and my relief was immediate. She was baiting me for an emotional distraction.

"A bargain is a bargain." I leaned back with a wink. "I'll push through."

"You broke a different bargain with me this week. Why should I believe you?"

I threw my head back and laughed. "But you had a brush stuck in your hair! That wasn't fair and you know why. Next time prepare a lad."

I almost said something aloud about boars and Torc Triath but decided to keep that just between us. She was my wee feral swine wife and I would never stop being delighted at how one of her ridiculous, dramatic "futures" circled back to her—and us—so perfectly.

The boys were watching us closely. After the Fire Dance, they now knew I had feelings for Filena, if they hadn't suspected earlier . . . which I was sure they did. Regardless, we were protective of each other's families.

Corbin lifted his mug. "Want me to fetch you an ale, Lena?"

Before she could answer, Gran jumped in. "Aye, I'll take one, Corbie lad."

"Anything for you, Gran." Corbin jumped up from his stump and dashed through the gathering toward the brewery wagon.

"I think he's sweet on you, Gran," Sean said with a teasing smile. "Haven't seen that fella run so fast to fetch an ale."

"Oh hush, ye rascally goat," Gran replied with a laugh.

"Aye," Owen piped in. "Ancient struck, he is. We have to beg for a drink. Terrible times." Owen shrugged dramatically. "But if *you* asked him to bring the wagon here, I bet he would."

I cracked a smile and turned back to Filena while Sean and Owen continued to tease Gran. The pensive line between my wife's brows deepened. Her skin was still far too pale. She was watching her da again, who was thankfully stumbling off in the opposite direction toward the exit, a few Raven Folk males on his tail.

Flames rolled through my already boiling blood. Tonight's wedding was private and why it was held a few hours before the market opened. Had Bryok invited him to antagonize the Merricks?

I leaned forward to block the view. My wife's eyes lifted to mine and I could swim in her stormy sky gaze forever.

Another light gust of wind ruffled through us and the hundreds of ribbons danced around the Truth Telling Tree. I was suddenly grateful the real trees were now rare. It may be the only way Bryok could get a true confession from Filena's da and from the Merricks.

Chapter Twenty-Five

RHYLEN LONAN

G lennie Lo," Cian drawled, "that wasn't happiness you in-fused into the cake you *made* me eat."

The two ambled into our circle—*finally*—setting down a large slice of cake for us to pass around and share. Corbin walked beside my sister, holding a tray. He quickly passed out fresh mugs of ale before slumping onto a log.

Whatever special occasion food was left over after the mid-dle-rank and govs feasted would be divided up among each felly family clan. If none remained, my small clan would make our usual fare of vegetable soup for dinner. We had enough barley saved up to throw into the pot too.

"No?" my sister replied to Cian, her voice ringing with false innocence. "Happiness is my specialty, it is."

Cian snorted. "Darlin', you're about as cheerful as a wild pack of sparkly rabid mountain goats—" Glenna flicked his forehead. "Ow!"

"Sparkly, aye. More than you."

"What did you put in the cake?" he demanded more seriously this time.

"I didn't put anything in the cake."

Cian groaned. "Bloody Ravens."

"What are you feeling, lad?" Owen eyed the slice of cake as if the cinnamon that dusted the whipped cream frosting might be poison.

"Angst!" Cian practically shouted. "Like I'm a fecking, awkward teenager wanting to kiss a crush for the first time. I'm twenty-three, godsdammit. And never been nervous to kiss anyone! This . . . this . . . weird crawling, bubbly feeling in my chest is going to be the death of me." He fished around for a cigarette in his pocket. "Glenna, I dedicate this angry smoke session to you."

My sister was practically doubled over in laugher. Filena too. The two girls shared a delighted look and then Glenna said in a singsong voice, "Maybe if you kissed someone, you'll feel better."

"Oh aye?" Cian snapped back. He struck a match and lit his cigarette, taking a long drag. "Why would *I* need cake magic to kiss someone?"

"But the *magic* of a *first* kiss . . ." Glenna trailed off and Cian's eye twitched.

I didn't know eyes could twitch so noticeably, but he looked about two seconds away from becoming completely unhinged. I had to tip my hat to Glenna, though. It was a very clever trick to do as part of their kiss and break hearts competition.

"Come here, Owen." Cian beckoned with his finger.

"Stars no." Owen shook his head, laughing loudly. "Kiss Sean."

Glenna's wings suddenly appeared and I knew what she was

about to do before she even fluttered a single feather. So did Gran, who began quietly chuckling. Cian narrowed his eyes at my sister, daring her to make a move.

And then she did.

In a light whoosh, she brought her right wing forward and nudged Cian forward. The lad lost his balance and fell onto Owen's lap, whose ale went flying from his hands. But not before spilling over his shirt.

"For feck's sake," Owen cried out with a disbelieving laugh.

"I just sat down," Corbin muttered. "Take Cian's ale."

Owen swatted Cian's arse to get up and my best friend rolled his eyes. "Owen, darlin', you spank like a lad who is more vanilla than—" Cian abruptly stopped. His mouth dropped open. "George?"

Our heads whipped in the direction of Cian's gaping stare. Sneaking up behind an unsuspecting female, about fifteen feet away, was the largest, fluffiest raccoon I had ever seen. The fella's little paw reached out and snatched a woolen fingerless glove atop the female's belongings.

"My son!" Cian called out, his arms stretched wide. "You returned to me!"

Cian bolted from Owen's lap and charged toward George. The raccoon chittered, startling the middle-aged female he stole from into a high-pitched scream. She shifted into a raven in the next blink and flew across her family, reappearing on a log opposite her cloak and gloves. Well, *glove*. The still chittering raccoon then sprinted on all fours toward the woods.

"George!" Cian yelled between clenched teeth, skidding to a stop. "You ungrateful, wee thieving bastard!"

And we lost it. All of us.

Filena was cackling so loud, Sheila waddled from her pocket into my wife's lap and nestled into her skirts to soak up the happy magic. Moons, I loved Lena's raucous laugh. The humor brought much-needed color to her fair skin after a half hour of skittish, paling fear.

The Mother's messenger squirrel, who was antagonizing Barry with an attempt at conversation, scampered up my leg, my arm, to rest on my shoulder.

"Lloyd!" Filena threw her hands into the air. "You need to ask consent first. You can't climb people like trees. Not even Rhylen!"

The squirrel turned to face her from my shoulder and began chattering. His bushy tail dusted my lips and I spat gray fur out of my mouth. I gently slid him over farther on my shoulder, and a fresh round of laughter left me.

The Merricks . . . one sibling was chasing a glove-stealing raccoon while the other was scolding a squirrel and holding a hedgehog that lived in her pocket.

Lloyd quieted while watching Filena pet Sheila and I swore the wee fella sighed. I understood. I fell in love with a girl wearing the same blue ribbon in her hair once.

"You can stare at your lass from my shoulder, lad." Lloyd's tail twitched and I leaned my head out of reach. "Next time ask before climbing up me or another, though, aye?"

Barry huffed.

The fox was probably right. Lloyd had the attention span of a drunken butterfly and the maturity of a nap-deprived toddling bairn who had eaten a dozen sugar cookies and drank an entire kettle of coffee.

Speaking of a drunken butterfly . . .

Cian strode back into our circle, glaring at Glenna, who winked at him in reply. A ghost of a smile flirted across my friend's lips. He plopped down next to my sister and puffed on his cigarette with a long, heavy sigh.

It didn't take long for the boys to turn back to each other. Cian leaned forward, his elbows digging into his knees and his chin resting in his palm as he eyed Sean, Owen, and Corbin from beneath a fallen lock of blond hair. The muscles in his shoulders were bunched, a leg was slightly bouncing, jostling the smoke dangling from his fingers. Was it the magic in the cake? I knew my best friend and something seemed . . . off.

It was then I noticed the knuckles on his right hand. Two were cracked and three were swollen. His complexion was a touch more bloodless than usual too. Cian didn't have the kind of injuries from a more involved fight than a punch or two. But also . . . a slave didn't hit Raven Folk. The curve of his lips tightened as his focus traveled to his sister. The fear that flashed in his partially hidden eyes told me everything I needed to know.

He had seen their da.

I couldn't fault my best mate. I was constantly fighting a rising rage to beat that man until he was nothing but food for the wolves. But if Bryok found out it was Cian, if Cian had indeed struck his da, then we were in a heaping pile of steaming shite.

Glenna gently elbowed him in the ribs. Cian angled his head enough to slide her a sly smile, his hair still fallen over his face. Was the whole cake story a fabrication to distract from Cian's paler skin and worked up emotions? Or was Cian just being Cian? He never could stay angry for long and he enjoyed practical jokes.

Lloyd scampered down my arm and my body flinched from the unexpected feeling of little feet. He then jumped to the ground from my thigh. In a few scurried steps, he disappeared beneath Filena's skirts. A second later, Sheila left the warmth of Filena's hands and burrowed back into her pocket. It was only when Barry lifted his head to look over Filena's shoulder that the hair on my arms rose on end.

Sean whistled low, a warbling sound of pleasure that quickly silenced my lads. A look of enrapture stole his features and I peered over my shoulder to see what had ensnared his—and Barry's—attention.

Braelin Cormac, my "betrothed," daintily walked toward us, accompanied by Elder Connel, a male I surmised was her da, as well as Bryok and his new wife, Doireann Brannagh-Fiachna.

Feck.

Me.

Sean openly stared a moment longer before respectfully lowering his eyes. Aye, Braelin was beautiful, there was no question.

"*Fáidhbhean.*"

The smooth, arrogant lilt to Bryok's voice made the wild fae inside of me sink its talons into the beating heart of my waning restraint. Just one word from him and I was already on the razor's edge of tearing whatever remnants of self-control I possessed from my body.

Gran slipped her hand inside of mine and gently squeezed. "Ye're an arrow tipped in fire, Rhylee Lo," she whispered to me. "Careful, lad."

My muscles shuddered; my teeth clenched.

He was speaking to *my* mate. Looking at *my* mate. Desiring *my* mate.

Filena rose to her feet with a quick warning glance my way to stay seated.

"Felicitations on your bond, sire." Filena bowed her head with an extra dip at his bride. "My lady."

"You will attend me and my bride, *fáidhbhean*."

The nails of my free hand dug into the log. Across from me, a muscle worked along Cian's jaw as he, too, fought to remain still.

Bryok stepped closer. "We wish for a card reading, pet."

"I do not carry—"

"You will also do a card reading for Braelin Cormac of North Tribe and her betrothed, Rhylen Lonan."

Glenna let out a quiet gasp and I blinked back the anger. I was married. Filena and I were bonded mates. The betrayal, however, was still a simmering fire low in my belly.

Sean's gaze shot to mine and widened. Then he mouthed, "Betrothed?"

The hands at Filena's sides curled into fists as her body froze. I couldn't tell if it was a real response or for show. Bryok would expect her to react.

"Oh forgive me," Bryok carried on, "allow me to introduce Braelin and her father, Brenden." Bryok paused a beat then, in a clipped tone, said, "Lonan, rise and greet your betrothed."

It was on the tip of my tongue to reiterate that she wasn't my anything. Bryok *wanted* me to react in front of all the tribes, though. And Filena would be the one to pay for my territorial temper. I wouldn't challenge Bryok on his wedding day, though. The tribes might reject me as heir if I did. Mate bonding ceremonies were sacred to Raven Folk. But, most of all, submission was how I protected my mate . . . for now.

I slowly rose from the log and turned; my eyes lowered. "Braelin," I grounded out. "Sir," I said to her da.

"You work on the set-up crew, Lonan?" her da asked.

"Aye, I'm one of two leads."

"How do you plan to support future children?"

I closed my eyes in a long blink, pulling in a slow breath. "West Tribe will have your daughter's dowry, sir."

It wasn't a lie, but I refused to answer questions of my low standing and instead deflected to West Tribe's cruelty. My pay, my clothing, my food portions . . . they were allotted by the tribe and Brenden Cormac knew this. The intentional dig at my rank was a thousand bees stinging me over and over again. I didn't have much, never would, but I worked hard and *loved* my family and would support my wife and future children the same way felly males had for centuries: through bargains.

"Rhylen," Braelin said, "you may look at me."

Mortification burned my skin. Willingly or not, she had shamed me before my clan and gang. The dirt of my station had never clung so deep until this moment. Point out the obvious that I am poor, fine. But remind me that I'm not to look others in the eyes? I could almost hear Bryok's satisfied smirk. The only shame greater than my supposed betrothed granting me permission to meet her eyes in front of my clan was having my head shorn.

My chest was heaving. Dizziness flooded my quickly unleashing mind.

Slowly, I lifted the sharpened steel of my gaze.

Braelin's voice was soft and sweet, her features dainty and almost too perfect. Was it an illusion? I couldn't reason why someone as beautiful as her would desire to bond to someone like me. The Cormacs were well-known trickster Folk. Her cousins came from a longstanding gov family who had helped build and settle Seren.

She smiled kindly at me, but quickly looked away—and abruptly stilled on Sean. Braelin's mouth parted in a breathless gasp, but she quickly recovered.

I peered over at my friend. Half of his dark hair was pulled up into a messy knot with a couple braids falling down his back beside his wavy strands. Ash was rubbed around his eyes, like most single males. But unlike anyone in our circle or in Bryok's circle, his wings were out . . . the black feathers fluttering in the breeze. My brow furrowed. He was putting himself on display for the girl introduced as my betrothed.

Did he realize this?

Or was he—

My jaw slackened.

Holy Mother of Stars . . .

I considered Braelin again. The sudden flush of her cheeks, the soft smile she tried to bite back.

An idea struck me like lightning.

If Bryok wanted a tricked wedding, I would give him one.

Chapter Twenty-Six

FILENA LONAN

A part of me was a touch miffed that Braelin Cormac didn't seem attracted to Rhylen. Now I couldn't have pretend fights with her in my head. Besides terrifying males by threatening a curse and cackling as they ran away, my petty arse adored imaginary arguments. I always had the best witty replies.

From lowered eyes, I caught Braelin smiling kindly at me. I found myself admiring the perfect symmetry of her lovely face. She was mesmerizing. Though, most high fae were preternaturally beautiful. Standing beside her, I probably looked like a boiled potato with yarn hair.

The gods clearly had a favorite.

Even the princess of South Tribe was otherworldly beautiful. I bit back a sigh.

Braelin probably was an excellent cook and didn't burn porridge too. Always kind to animals and gifted them desserts without a dragon hoard craving to keep the confections for only herself. Undoubtedly, she laughed just as daintily as she looked as well. My laugh scared children and old superstitious Folk.

I did have nice breasts, though.

Sorry, Braelin, darlin'. My girls are one of my crowning achievements.

Not that I had any control over their curviness. Still . . . I would allow myself this one daydream win.

I bit back another sigh. A happy one.

Rhylen could have looked at the face of a goddess all his remaining days. But he sought me immediately after rejecting her, desiring to exchange vows with me instead.

He was mine.

Only ever mine.

And territorially flexing beside me. The angry heat coming off his body was doing strange things to my pulse. Knowing he was borderline primal for me, defending what he had claimed as solely his, drizzled molten starlight into my veins. Suns above, just thinking about him was an instant intoxication.

I needed to close off my panting thoughts before it was obvious.

Bryok was studying me too closely. It was unnerving the way his dark gaze took in every blink of my eyes, fidget of my fingers, how my dress and hair fluttered in the cool evening breeze. I felt nothing but pity for his bride who, if her sudden stiff bearing were any indication, noticed the intensity of her groom's attention on me. It was hard to tell with my eyes lowered, though. But where was the territorial attention and protectiveness? Most Ravens mate bonded without being in love first.

A shiver crawled down my spine.

"If you wish for a card reading," I forced out as pleasantly as possible, "you'll need to follow me back to my divination wagon."

"No need," Bryok said, far too quickly, a congenial smile on his despicable face as he looked around the gathering. "My lads fetched your cards. You and Lonan are invited to our table for a reading."

My mam's cards. They *touched* my mam's cards.

The fury was instant. My eyes shot to his and narrowed. "My cards and runes are sacred and may only be handled by me."

Bryok's arrogance clawed into me. "Lower your eyes, slave."

I was an agent of the gods and no longer a slave. It was *he* who should be lowering his eyes before *me*. Taking a step toward him, Bryok winced. It was almost imperceptible, but I reveled in the way his Adam's apple bobbed at my approach while working hard to maintain a smug curl to his lips.

"I will need to perform a cleansing first, *sire*."

I was on the verge of snarling. I never snarled. But neither had I felt so violated either. What else had his gang rifled through? And did they also go through my personal belongings in my wagon? Perhaps looking for proof that Hamish MacCullough was my da?

A tug in my gut confirmed my latter fear true.

He was indeed searching for proof.

And tricking West Tribe's fellys into believing he was generous for inviting both me and Rhylen to his table—as a cover for rummaging through my personal things and to make Rhylen look bad for challenging him—pissed me off even more.

"Unless . . ." I dragged the word out, "you desire a reading from contaminated magic?"

Please say yes.

Bryok laughed, but there was no humor in it. "Why would a *fáidhbhean* need cards or runes for her magic to work? You are a supposed wise woman, touched by the gods."

Supposed?

His bride's eyes rounded and she gaped at the prince in horror. At least someone had a lick of reasoning and a healthy dose of self-preservation.

I returned the self-assured smile. "Illusion me a rose from nothing, sire."

A few smothered snickers sounded behind me and my taunting smile widened.

He couldn't. All Folk required an object to glamour, save the elders who had the ability to glamour the minds of the fae to see or not see things—a blinding curse, it was called. An effective trick in battle when they were wild fae. But Bryok, who was heir but not a top gov yet with elder magic, couldn't illusion a trick unless he used a leaf or rock or any other inanimate object. While I could have visions without my divination instruments, Bryok could think we were the same.

"What do you know of the gods' magic?" I challenged him further. "How many futures have you seen, *pet*? Where are your appointed familiars of protection?" When he didn't answer me, I slowed right before him and bared my teeth. "Do not *ever* touch my belongings again, and that includes my family, or the gods will allow more than a fire curse over West Tribe, sire."

"Filena Merrick," Elder Connel said in a falsely calm voice, "know your place, mortal. Step away from the prince and lower your eyes. It's an honor to be invited to his table. Show humility."

I turned the explosion of my fury onto him. That was his entire concern? Not my fake prophecy of a fire curse? At this point, I was convinced the govs of West Tribe were corrupt to the point of blindness. But before I could spit a fire curse at him next—or any threatened curse—Bryok spoke.

"Cian Merrick, attend me."

A boulder of fear hit my gut. I tried not to look shaken as I twisted toward my brother. Cian rose from his place beside Glenna, head lowered. The tendons in his neck flexed, his lips pressed together in a severe line. My gaze drifted to his clenching hand and paused. Why were his knuckles cracked? Who had he hit?

"Bryok," Princess Doireann said in a low warning tone as she swept a worried glance around the gathering. "We can wait for the *fáidhbhean* to cleanse her cards' magic."

The prince ignored his bride.

My pulse was pounding in my ears. If I lost Cian, if he were sold to a cruel family to punish me for standing up to a monster—

Rhylen's wings snapped open, sending a gust of wind around our circle. He moved to stand in front of Cian, rage tightening every beautiful feature of his face. "I will release him from his slave bonds if you even attempt to sell him off." His voice was gravelly and sharp. "West Tribe can't afford to lose an able-bodied worker to another tribe or Seren, either, especially before winter sets in. Why should they profit off our loss? New wagons will need to be built, aye? New tent pieces too. Don't put the burden of his absence on those already taxed from our loss just for revenge and a few coins." The fellys and middle-ranks pressed in close to watch, whispering to one another. "Your choice, sire."

Bryok blinked. A dismissive gesture that elicited a low growl from Rhylen. The prince looked a fool before the tribes. As a mortal man, Cian would no longer be able to live with the Caravan fae if his slave bonds were dissolved. But he couldn't be bought or sold by Raven Folk either unless he indentured himself again.

Bryok's gaze roamed down Rhylen, as if sizing him up. A condescending grin curved his lips, his canines now on full display, but he spoke to me. "My lads will escort you to my table for a card reading, Fáiléanna MacCullough."

People murmured my birth name in confusion. The prince was an eejit. No one had context for that name unless he revealed, with proof, that Hamish was my da. Matching hair and eyes wouldn't hold in court either. Perhaps using my birth name was merely to rattle me after seeing my da earlier, a reminder of his threat.

But I was so damn tired of feeling afraid—of him, of my da, of the man he sold me to, of entitled males everywhere who believed they owned me.

I didn't move a muscle save a carefully arched brow. "I will spare everyone but you a cursed vision. That is my bargain, Bryok Fiachna. A contaminated card reading only between you and me before witnesses, if you feel the gods will favor your disrespect."

A muscle worked along his jaw. "Lower. Your. Eyes. *Slave.*"

At the cruel edge in Bryok's voice, Rhylen charged, but Elder Connel stepped in and pushed Rhylen back with a low burst of elemental magic. My husband's entire body was heaving with unbridled rage. In the blink of an eye, Rhylen had become a dark creature of fae with sharp canines and glittering shadows in his brightening purple eyes.

Braelin openly gaped at Rhylen, as did the princess of South Tribe. Even Braelin's da stared wide-eyed.

Power was rippling off my mate. A strong magic I had only felt once—the day of the lottery when he strode toward the chieftain and prince after his name was called. People had bowed their heads when he marched by, both middle-rank and fellys. Even now, a few fellys lowered their eyes instead of watching Rhylen as before.

The vision of Rhylen at a Night Market beneath Seren floated back to the forefront of my mind.

He was destined to become a chieftain and Bryok was terrified . . . because he knew.

"Prince," Elder Connel said carefully. "Accept or refuse the *fáidhbhean's* bargain." He looked to both glaring males. "It is bad luck to invite challenges on a wedding day."

I almost rolled my eyes.

"In two days," Bryok drawled, as if Rhylen hadn't just undeniably displayed the greater virility and dominance, "you will read cards for me and my bride as well as all other mated pairs from West Tribe's lottery."

I stuck my hand in my pocket and pulled out the cloth with Rhylen's braid and thrust it into Bryok's hand. "A wedding gift for you, sire."

He recognized the cloth and his nostrils flared.

"To remember your future," I said sweetly, "before the gods confirm it in two days."

I was dangerously courting my own destruction. But the lifetime I had spent yoked to fear was snapping loose. I refused to bow before a male who denied an ancient warmth and care, who burned a felly's shirt and boots for defending his tribe and clan, who betrothed another against their will, who threatened to sell my brother if Rhylen didn't trade me to him, who used my da to torment me.

"Remember, Fáiléanna"—Bryok pocketed the cloth and smiled at the gathering for show—"I know *all* your secrets."

"Not *all* of them," I said a little too smugly. "And you clearly don't remember my name, *pet*."

At that, he grinned. A taunting, vicious grin that rose the hair on the back of my neck. He was within every right to dominate us publicly, however he pleased, for our irreverence—strip Rhylen again. Banish us from caravanning with any tribe. But he was clearly campaigning for West Tribe's approval. It was all he had left to remain in power: the illusion of being merciful.

Rhylen would win any challenge.

But the tribe could still refuse to follow him. Especially if he looked like the bully instead of Bryok.

I dipped my head at Doireann, then Braelin, but not her da and not Elder Connel, then I pivoted on my heel and stormed toward the wedding table to fetch my mam's cards. Not only would I have the last word, but I also refused to be dismissed by that preening arsehole or told where I was allowed to exist.

Stars, I wished I were a *cailleach*. If ever there was a time to curse someone and strike fear in the elders . . .

Still, I was the only known *fáidhbhean* in Carran outside of my mam and nan, if either were still alive. I had little choice but to indenture myself as a child for survival. But I was more powerful than Bryok and I would no longer let any male make me feel small and worthless again.

I lowered my eyes for no one.

Chapter Twenty-Seven

FILENA LONAN

I swiped a low-hanging tree branch from my face, then ducked beneath another. Brittle leaves crunched under my stomping boots as I marched to my wagon, my oracle cards gripped in my fist. Glenna offered to come back with me but I waved her off. If fellys received leftover banquet food, I didn't want her to miss out.

I needed to calm down before I worked tonight.

I needed to get into costume too.

The firestorm inside me, however, only desired destruction. A strange tingly sensation warmed my hands. I could feel magic-charged words on the tip of my tongue, but they didn't fall. If they did, something terrible would happen. I could feel it in my bones.

Which didn't make sense.

Perhaps it was all in my head. I certainly thirsted for vengeance right now.

"Lena," Rhylen called out from behind me.

I spun on my heel to face him, not aware that angry tears were streaming down my cheeks until I felt one drip over my lips. Bryok would punish us; my family might suffer for my defiance, but I was not his puppet on a string to manipulate. If the prince thought he could take me to his bed, I would only agree so I could murder him in his sleep.

"A *stór* . . ." the tenderness in Rhylen's voice was in stark contrast to the territorial rage still brightening his wine-hued eyes. He slowed before me and pulled me into his arms, pressing my face to his chest. "You were . . . feck, Lena. Your fury is so beautiful and fierce, lass."

"You will win," I murmured into his chest. Stars, he smelled so good. But I pushed back enough to see his eyes. "I have *seen* a vision of you and a Night Market beneath Seren."

The brooding anger on his face relaxed into slack-jawed surprise. "Seren?"

"Aye, and you were wearing newer, fancier clothing."

"I . . ." he swallowed thickly. "I have entertained the idea of a stationary market beneath Seren for a few weeks now. West Tribe could save money and resources—"

"This was *your* tribe, Rhylen."

"My tribe," he repeated softly.

We didn't have to say more. Either all or part of West Tribe would support him after beating Bryok in a challenge, followed by crowing victory over our chieftain.

Pride surged through me.

This strong, beautiful, protective male was *mine*. He loved his family and friends and showed it in so many little ways. He always supported his community. Never once regarded me as if I were anything else but his equal despite being my master and I his family's slave. Moons and stars, he didn't even reprimand me for going toe-to-toe with the prince. Or treat me as if I were untrustworthy for keeping my da and my contracted marriage a secret.

How I *loved* Rhylen Lonan and loved the way he *loved* me.

Rising on my tiptoes, I crushed my lips to his.

A moan left him.

We were on the edge of the revel. It was dark, but there was a chance others could see us. Bryok could have assigned Ravens to follow me too. But I didn't care. Apparently, neither did Rhylen.

He pressed me to a tree a few steps away. His lips trailed down my neck, his breath hot on my skin. My fingers explored the sculpted lines of his chest, slowing their descent to feel every ridge of his abdominal muscles through his shirt and vest.

"I want you," he kissed into the hollow of my throat. "Sweet gods, I want you."

"Then have me," I whispered back.

He straightened and studied my eyes, as if he were weighing if he should. There was a chance he could go mad with insatiable want if we completed a physical bond. A terrible idea right now. But I was selfish. So, so selfish. Goddess save me, I was already stumbling drunk on the idea of him craving me to madness.

Cradling his cheek, I dragged my thumb across his lower lip—a claiming. A tease. A declaration. He closed his eyes in a long blink as he leaned into my touch and kissed the raven mark on my wrist.

A sudden rush of air whipped his hair around my face and he tightened his grip on my waist. Moonlit blues and purples shimmered along the feathers of his large, unfurling wings, and I could sigh. He knew it too, stretching out his wings entirely for my viewing pleasure. A satisfied curl to his lips was my only warning before he lifted us into the air. I started to squeal, making him grin.

The night blurred past me as he flew us over the ruffled treetops to our wagons. The view was incredible. Behind us, lanterns and cookfires lit the field where the revel continued. In the far distance, snow seemed to glow off the mountains beneath the Harvest Moon.

And the stars . . . I lifted my hand and grinned when my fingers touched the sky.

A minute later, Rhylen lowered us to the ground beside his wagon . . . and Barry, who was stoically waiting for us. The horses nickered, startling me, and Lloyd scampered from where they lay beneath the trees. Ignoring the squirrel's antics, I scooped Sheila from my pocket and placed her next to Barry for warmth.

Besides the animals, the world around us was blissfully quiet. Everyone was at the wedding revel.

Rhylen took my hand, shifting his wings away, and led me up the short steps inside. I set my mam's oracle cards on a counter while he tied a small strip of tent canvas on the outside handle.

Rhylen noticed my arched brow and quietly chuckled as he shut the door. "Cian's way of telling me to take a longer walk."

"Have you—"

"You were my first kiss," he answered softly. "My first everything."

That confession flushed across my skin and dizzied in my head. I had never truly swooned before, but I was pretty sure I was too weak to walk this moment.

Rhylen gently held my face. "I have loved you for so long, Filena Lonan."

His lips savored mine, a soft, lingering kiss dripping with a thousand heady confessions. For several beats of our wildly fluttering pulse, we simply breathed each other in. Unlike the Fire Dance, where every touch was a lightning strike of explosive electricity, set to the rhythm of tribal drumbeats, this moment felt reverent, languid—vulnerable. As if nothing else existed but our bare hearts after years of hiding the truth.

The tips of his fingers twirled a strand of my hair. A slow, boyish smile crept up his flushed lips. Then he playfully tugged on the strand, like he always did, right as his mouth claimed mine.

Moonlight spilled into my body. A billowing, silken heat that possessed me completely.

We stumbled backward until he pressed me to the edge of his rumpled bed. I had been in this wagon hundreds of times, had even sat on this very bed. With the sultry way his hands skimmed down my lower back, the fevered sparks of his lips on mine, each familiar object suddenly seemed foreign and forbidden.

He began unbuttoning his vest, his shirt, only breaking our kiss to toss his clothing to the floor. Traces of light from the small window limned the defined lines of his muscles. I brushed my fingers across the warm, smooth expanse of his skin.

Suns above, he was achingly beautiful.

And so tall. I sometimes forgot how big fae males were compared to their human counterparts.

His darkening gaze roamed over my body. A territorial sweep of his eyes as he sank his fingers into my hair and gently tugged my head back. The point of his canine softly dragged down my neck. I clutched his arms. That dangerous reminder that he was, beneath the mortal clothes and assimilated life, a primal creature pumped the blood in my veins harder. Stealing my breath completely when he pressed a feathered kiss to the throbbing pulse in my throat.

I had heard that being fae marked by one's mate was orgasmic. And while his aroused courting magic teased me, teased the idea, I would be surprised if he permanently parted with *any* magic before challenging Bryok. The tremble of his body's need to claim me, though, the quickened breaths on my skin was a different kind of otherworldly pleasure.

The fingers of his other hand drifted up my side to caress my corseted breast. At this next possessive touch, I practically went limp, growing dizzier when he released my hair to unfasten my bodice, and I whispered his name in a plea—for more, for a lover's death, for relief from this building agony—and we had only just begun.

"Pray my name again," he begged in my ear, nipping at my lobe. "Rhylen . . ."

"That sound." He shuddered in my arms. "Gods, do it again."

I sighed, "Rhylen," on a breathy moan right as his mouth devoured mine.

My bodice piece slipped to the floor beside his clothing. His lips fell to where my neck and shoulder met, brushing fiery kisses across my collarbone. Corded muscles along his upper arms flexed beneath my fingers. The warmth of his body surrounded me in the cool darkness of his wagon. A mead-drenched heat that enveloped me still when he untied my skirts and petticoats next before helping me to step out of them.

Biting down on a corner of my bottom lip, I stood before my childhood love in only my corset, drawers, stockings, and boots. The faerie boy who owned me heart and soul softly blinked as he took me in, swaying slightly—like he had when he first kissed me after *our song*, then again at the Fire Dance.

Was he about to pass out? Because of *me*?

Gripping my hips, he fell to his knees and pressed a kiss to my stomach. "You make me weak, *a stór mo chroí*." Fire touched my skin at his words and pooled hot in my core. His dark eyes held mine, his chest heaving. "I would crawl on hands and knees across all three kingdoms just to worship you."

Chapter Twenty-Seven

FILENA LONAN

I couldn't speak. The hunger in his gaze silenced me. How the pale light reverently caressed the contours of his body stole every rational thought too.

Affectionately, he lifted my boot to rest on his thigh and began untying the laces, eventually removing both shoes. He kissed my calf while rolling down my stocking on one leg.

Calves really were a dangerous temptation. *Stars . . .*

I rested back on my elbows atop his bed, my head falling to my shoulder blades, my eyes fluttering closed. I wanted to bury my face in the covers and drink in his scent—the warm, ambrosial decadence of spiced faerie wine and the fresh, dewed air of a golden autumn sunrise.

An embered trail of kisses glided higher and higher up my thigh as he unrolled the stocking on my other leg. Kissing even higher, his hot breath dangerously pulsing close to my sex, his tongue—

Holy gods . . .

I sucked in a sharp gasp and slowly exhaled a moan. The feel of his warm mouth on me was . . . dark moons, I couldn't breathe, it was so unspeakably divine. I had heard of this act; Glenna had shared many juicy, scandalous stories of her trysts. But the ecstasy was beyond description. With each electrifying, curling lick of his tongue, I died a little. Sounds were leaving me I didn't know I was capable of making.

Fisting his dark hair, I held him closer to me, making him quietly laugh. Aye, I was greedy. But we already knew my behavior around treats and this was a sweeter pleasure than any dessert I had yet eaten.

Liquid sunlight began pooling in my quickly constricting core, growing and growing until I thought I might erupt. The intensity rippled outward. I released his hair to grip the bed linens. The indigo sky rushed into my veins. A dark, silken whisper to crest above the heavens.

I shattered into a million gasping pieces.

A starburst of hot, molten sensations.

Rhylen pushed up and captured my lips with his, holding me while I gloriously unraveled beneath the hard planes of his body. Tasting myself on him was an unexpected carnal thrill and my thrumming body lusted for more of these brazen delights, more of him.

Tossing me a flirty, earth-tilting smirk, Rhylen slipped out of his pants then dipped onto the bed over me. My gaze drifted downward. Swallowing thickly, I arched a brow at his playful arrogance, trying desperately not to blush, having never seen a fully undressed male before, which only made him grin wider. Then his mouth was on mine again. And the fevered way he kissed me was criminal, as if each profane stroke of his tongue and dangerous sweep of his mouth could be redeemed only by mine.

I didn't want to break the spell his sinful lips had over me but, at his gentle tug, I sat up to remove my undergarment and he lifted the camisole over my head. My auburn hair fell over my arms in springy waves and cascaded across my front.

"Wife," he breathed. The callous tips of his fingers traced around my breasts. "You are perfection."

Until this moment, I hadn't felt shy, not truly. He had distracted me too much earlier when removing my stockings and drawers to feel anything other than the soaring sensation of flying high above the moon and stars. But I had only ever been bare before Glenna and Gran. Despite living among the fae, mortal modesty still won out.

But that one word.

Wife . . .

How it gripped me.

Only a year and a half separated our ages. Though he was my brother's best friend, he had also always belonged to me. A few days ago, though, I believed Rhylen would never be mine. Every kiss in each vision, seeing him make love to his True Mate, broke my heart one painful, shallow fracture at a time. I didn't think I would survive watching him build a life with another.

Now nothing separated us.

In three more days, nothing could ever separate us.

"Mate," he whispered into a soft kiss.

"I'm yours," I whispered back. "Only ever yours."

"Forever mine," he branded along my jaw, my neck, as he gently laid me back onto his bed and kissed down my chest. "Feck, your body drives me wild."

He took my breast into his mouth and I gasped. I was already a puddle of pleasure-laden sighs from earlier. This new, honeyed torture would absolutely be my untimely end.

If the cards had shown me the way his wicked tongue would tease and play with his wife's soft flesh, how his warm mouth would set her every nerve-ending ablaze, I might have been more prepared for this early death.

Knowing full well I was on the verge of madness, he took his time exploring the curves of one breast while cupping the other, groaning at the feel of me.

And I *needed* him.

I didn't know a body could crave a feeling one had yet to experience.

But I was in agony and he was my salvation.

"Please . . ." The moment the whimper left me, I nearly begged again.

Rhylen pushed himself up, his nose brushing along mine. "Are you sure?"

"Yes," I breathed. "Yes."

"*Mo ghrá*," he murmured against my lips, "*mo cuishle*."

My love, my pulse.

Our eyes locked and . . . for several windswept seconds, our unfolding love story consumed me. We were eleven and thirteen all over again, catching frogs at a creek to scare Gran. Thirteen and fifteen, sneaking up on Cian to throw frozen creek water on his head while he kissed a village girl behind the tents. Sixteen and eighteen, dancing beneath the Strawberry Moon at a Midsummer revel, breathless and flushed. Eighteen and twenty, laughing over ridiculous gossip and cake drowned in sugared berries as I pretended to read cards to him. Twenty and twenty-two, exchanging hurried bonding vows in secret.

Making love in secret too.

Rhylen cradled my face, kissing the corner of my lips, my jaw, the soft spot just below my ear. Hooking my leg around his waist, he gradually pushed inside of me and stilled. Dizzying, pulse-throbbing pleasure filled my body, and his eyes drifted closed. My nails dragged down his abdomen, utterly mesmerized by the breathtaking strength of the male above me. I could stare at him forever, especially when he was bare, his lips swollen, and skin blushed. Opening his eyes, he caressed my cheek while pushing in farther and I obliterated into a night sky of glittering stars.

His head fell to my shoulder on a strangled moan.

His breathing was ragged.

His fingers curled into the covers.

"Gods, you feel good."

Kissing my shoulder, he then leaned up on one arm, rolled his hips and I . . . ceased to exist. There was nothing left of me but flickering stardust.

"Gods," he moaned again, his voice tight and breathlessly deep. "So fecking good."

The erotic stroke of his body inside mine once more was my utter ruination.

I was destroyed.

My fingers twisted into his long, obsidian hair and his mouth crushed mine.

This kiss . . . this soul-curling kiss rewrote the rhythm of my heart. The same pounding heart fusing to Rhylen's as his pining breath became mine, as my dancing pulse became his.

I didn't know anything could feel this incredible.

I didn't know I was capable of falling more in love with Rhylen Lonan.

The sculpted curves of his muscles stirred across his chest and broad shoulders with each languorous, elegant arc of his hips; the veins on his arms throbbed. Moonlight kissed the defined lines of his abdomen and the V of his hips. Long, decorated, silky black hair pooled around my face. The penetrating intensity of his unnatural purple eyes searched mine and I became lost in his adoring gaze.

"I love you," he whispered, his voice cracking with pleasure. "I'm so in love with you."

My hand left his hair to explore the muscular lines of his jaw. "I'm madly in love with you," I whispered back.

Trailing higher, the tip of my finger caressed the outline of his ear to the point. His eyes fluttered shut in a long, shuddering blink. That look of sweet suffering at my touch awakened something wild inside of me.

I had power over him.

I had the power to make him splinter apart in rapture . . . because of *me*.

Pushing on his chest, I rolled Rhylen over and slowly—so, so very slowly—sank back down on him.

The husky groan that left his chest, the drunken look on his face was my undoing. Any shred of mortal modesty and rules of ladylike decorum I still clung to vanished. I wanted him trembling beneath me. I wanted him to pray my name too.

Rhylen gripped my hips and furiously grinded me against him, up and down, up and down, his head arched back, his mouth part-ed, his breaths sharp and languid.

He was mine.

His joy, his tears, his laughter, his pleasure.

Rhylen Lonan belonged to me.

My mate.

My husband.

My best friend.

I rocked against him harder, faster. But I craved more. I had a feeling I would never get enough of him.

Grabbing his hands from my hips, I pressed them into the pil-lows. Our lacing fingers rested on either side of his face while my tongue traced his tattoos and drank in the heady taste of his skin. I explored every dip and rise of his chest with my lips, then the mesmerizing lines of his taut neck and jaw.

A Beltane fire was building and building inside of me the more I lost myself to the rhythmic feel of his body curving into mine.

A tempo that was growing more desperate.

A spinning carousel of friction and pleasure.

Molten heat seared where our bodies touched. Every breath heaving from his chest was laced with a moan so raw, so seduc-tive, I tipped over the edge and free-fell into his dark otherworldly beauty. My nails dug into his pectorals as I gasped. The riptide of pulsing intensity that hit me was decadently, devastatingly lush, a binding completeness in my soul I couldn't fathom how to compre-hend yet felt with absolute clarity.

I released Rhylen's hands and his fingers flew to my waist, gripping me as he increased his rhythm. Thrusting harder. Whis-pering my name over and over and over. His lower abdominals a salivating erotic dance of definition.

I nearly forgot how to breathe when pleasure seized him. The sight of each alluring, rippling muscle stiffening beneath me arrested my intoxicated pulse.

"Feck . . ." he cried out, his voice panting and rough.

A look of exquisite agony flushed across his features. And Holy Mother of Stars, I had never seen anything so beautiful and delicious.

I did that to him.

I made him feel pleasure unlike any other.

I couldn't help the flirty smile that teased my lips as his breathing calmed.

Our eyes met and he quietly laughed at my smugness.

"Come here," he whispered. He tugged me until I fell against him, then he rolled us over. Smiling, he buried his face in my neck and peppered me with playful kisses. "I wish you didn't have to work."

"Mmm," I quietly agreed. "Is that your fae way of thanking me?"

"You already own me, Filly Lo."

I brought his lips to mine. "Maybe I want another favor owed," I teased.

"Anything," he whispered. "Ask me for anything and it's yours."

"So you can have another bargain to break?"

He leaned up. "What bargain did I break, lass?"

"Where are the laundry ropes, pet?"

Rhylen threw his head back and laughed, a deep, rolling, melodic sound.

"You're lucky I'm not declaring seven years bad luck on you."

"Aye," he said, kissing me sweetly. "I am indeed a lucky lad."

With another sultry kiss on my lips, he rolled off me to lay at my side. But we couldn't stay away. My legs entangled with his and he drew me close until our noses touched. For a couple of minutes, we lay content, floating in bliss, unable to look away from the other. The intensity still burning between us was a wildfire in a windstorm.

Stars, I was addicted to him.

Rhylen nuzzled in closer and tucked a curl of auburn hair behind my ear. "I love you, *mo shiorghrá*."

His eternal love.

His True Mate.

These were the very words he spoke to me in a vision I had while up in the tree. A vision where he was shirtless in bed, where he tucked a strand of hair behind my ear too.

I closed my eyes and pressed my face to his strong chest. "I love you too, *mo shiorghrá*," I whispered back. But my happiness sobered.

There was one vision that continually haunted my pounding pulse.

The Blackthorn card.

Something terrible was about to befall me.

And I had this gnawing dread in my gut that publicly standing up to Bryok and rejecting his courting gift was the catalyst. But if I told Rhylen? I feared he would lose all control in his primal state. And, if he ended up in trouble, especially with the law, would he still be there to rescue me? Or would him losing control change the future?

My intuition was strangely quiet. Perhaps that was my an-swer—say nothing.

At least I knew he would rescue me.

That is, unless, the future hadn't already changed.

Chapter Twenty-Nine

RHYLEN LONAN

My hand skimmed the smooth length of Filena's bare arm and back up. The soft swells of her perfect breasts pressed into my chest. Her fingers explored the lines of my jaw, the muscles of my neck and shoulders, the beaded, decorated strands of my hair. Leaning in, I stole yet another tender kiss.

It felt like everything was happening so fast and, yet, like we had always been lovers. Stars, I was inside of her. I had yearned to drink from her lips for *years*. And now I knew the rhythm of her body, intimately, and she knew mine.

Pleasure was such a tame word for what I had felt, still felt . . .

I trailed the journey of my fingertip sliding across her skin and my blood billowed into flame all over again. I didn't want to stop touching her. She belonged in my arms—all day, all night, until the sun tired of chasing the moon.

But we didn't have much time before she would need to dress for work. Already I could feel panic rise at any thought of separation. Perhaps I might camp outside of her divination wagon unless

I was called away for repairs.

No, that would be too obvious.

"You haven't asked me," she said into the charged space between us and I repositioned my head to better see her in the darkness.

"What should I be asking you, lass?"

"The name Br—"

"Do *not* say *his* name in our bed." The words came out as a growl, a deep, guttural sound that even startled me. "*My* name is the *only* male—"

She pet my head.

She actually *pet my head*.

"Rhylee Lo," she cooed, the same saccharine reprimanding voice she used when talking to *Muffin Moo*. And, despite the involuntary territorial rage that demanded I sever that preening arse's head from his despicable shoulders, my lips twitched.

"First you patronize a male's heckles," I quipped.

"Fluffy throat feathers are adorable."

"Now you mock our mate bond?"

"You growled, darlin'." She wrinkled her nose. "That, too, was adorable."

Grabbing her wrists, I rolled her onto her back, making her squeal a laugh. "I haven't asked," I murmured playfully against her lips, "because I already know you're a 'feral swine with a bird-like destiny,' my wee Torc Triath."

She arched a single warning brow at me.

I wanted to say Fáiléanna MacCullough aloud while we were in the privacy of my bed, to feel her birth name on my tongue. The need to protect her, however, overruled all urges. I couldn't yet be familiar with this name.

"But I prefer you to be a 'little blackbird fire seer,'" I translated her chosen name with my clan name. "Especially the 'little blackbird' part."

"Filena Lonan," she whispered as a kiss against my mouth.

The sound of my name, *our* name, shuddered pleasurably through me.

My hands continued to pin her wrists above her head. Our breaths tangled. The feel of her softness pressed to the hard planes of me was quickly becoming a form of madness. I wanted every divine inch of her silky skin to taste of me, to smell of me, for every male in every kingdom in existence to know that she was mine. I buried my face in her neck and inhaled deeply, groaning at her wildflower scent.

"Your beauty"—I kissed along the underside of her jaw—"intoxicates me."

"I don't know," she said with a teasing but breathless lilt. "Braelin is *very* beautiful, she is."

I couldn't help my smile. "Aye," I agreed, finding her eyes. "But she doesn't have freckles in the faint shape of a rabbit on her left cheek."

Her jaw slackened in mock outrage. "It's clearly a cat. You agreed years ago."

I grinned now. "She keeps too many matching buttons on her bodice."

"I only have four different buttons, pet."

"She's never entangled a mate with her wild hair."

At this, she angled her head to glare at me. "If you mention the brush again—"

I nibbled on her bottom lip before sucking it into my mouth, silencing her. She let out a little moan that instantly pooled heat in my groin. An animalistic fever that surged through me. I wanted to nip at her skin and leave little marks. Feck, I would ask if I could fae mark her now, too, but I needed my full magic before facing off with Bryok. As a trickster, his magic didn't drain as fast as mine.

I released a wrist, lazily skimming my hand down the length of her arm, to cup her breast—*dark skies*, I loved her gorgeous breasts—dipping down to kiss her when her eyes flew wide. Fear cooled the fire in my blood and I removed my hand from her body. "Did I overstep?"

"No." She shook her head. "I just realized that I don't have herbs to prevent . . ." her voice trailed off and she swallowed thickly. "I'll find someone to bargain with tonight."

"Don't on my account," I whispered back.

"You want children . . . *now*?"

"Aye, lass." I winked. "I want wagons full of wild faerie bairns with you."

"*Wagons* full?" She snorted a laugh.

"Mhmm . . ." I glided my nose along hers. "To climb all over Cian just to make him curse 'Bloody Ravens' and for Glenna to spoil endlessly with cake. And," I added, brushing a fingertip along the shell of her ear, "so Gran always has a wee one to rock to sleep."

Though it was dark, I could see a constellation of tears gathering on her lashes. "Stars, you'll be ridiculous as a da."

I laughed under my breath. She wasn't wrong. Doting on Filena was my obsession and had been for years. But children? I would be a hopeless, smitten fool. There was *nothing* I wouldn't do for my family, even if it meant I bargained away my life to provide for and protect them. To see my own babe with my True Mate . . .

My hand slid down her body to her stomach. "But only when you're ready, *mo ghrá*."

"My life isn't as long as yours, Rhylen—"

"No," I interjected quickly. "You're a *fáidhbhean*. Fae blood is in your veins."

She was quiet for several long seconds. "I'm mortal."

"Where do you think your magic comes from, Lena?" If Filena led a mere mortal lifespan, I would be shocked. The Sisters Three were immortal goddesses. My wife might even outlive me. When she didn't answer, I sweetly kissed her lips and asked, "Did you know your maternal nan?"

Her brows bent together. "I met her once, in secret. Da didn't allow Mam's family to visit." The mention of that pig slop stoked the cooling territorial fire to life in my now thundering pulse. "When I was nine," she continued, "Mam brought me and Cian to The Wilds to pick berries. Our nan, and a woman whose belly was round with child, met us in a small meadow." The furrow between Filena's brows deepened. "No, an elf. She was fae. The . . . the lady's eyes were the cerulean shade of a faerie pool and her long golden braid was corded with ribbons and threaded with fruit tree blossoms and tiny crab apples. She . . ." Filena scrunched up her face and peered out the window, as if that would help her remember in more detail. "She had a pet fawn, aye, a darling baby bunny in her apron pocket, and a stellar jay sat on her shoulder."

The Mother.

Golden hair like Cian with an affinity to wild animals like Filena.

"While we picked berries, a fox brought her kit of three to the strange faerie. One of the kits romped over to me." A smile alighted across Filena's lips. "I snuck him berries and giggled each time he licked my chin." She sucked in a quiet breath. "Barry . . ."

A corner of my mouth tugged up. "Aye, Barry."

Her gaze flicked back to mine and narrowed curiously.

Shite, I forgot about her intuitive abilities. An irritated breath stirred in my lungs. I didn't want to keep anything from my wife, but I also trusted Gran—and agreed to a bargain. It was a strange shift in power, too. Though I knew Filena saw more into my life, my future than she chose to share with me, I also knew not being able to see her own future led to mindlessly twisting buttons off her bodice. She always fared better emotionally when stumbling upon the truth on her own terms rather than being surprised by a future she couldn't see coming.

Settling beside her on the bed again, I pulled her in close and asked, "What did your mam and nan look like? You've never told me."

"I can't entirely recall." Pressing a light kiss to my lips, she wove her fingers into my black strands and fingered one of my small, beaded braids. "But I believe Nan had auburn hair, like me. Mam has eyes in the loveliest shade of forest green and golden blonde locks, similar to Cian's hair."

Has? Her mam was still alive? Did her nan also still live?

"Did your nan appear young?"

She opened her mouth and promptly shut it. "Aye," she said softly, almost as if spooked. Goosebumps raced down her arms. "Fae blood . . ." she said under her breath and frowned.

"You do have an inhuman craving for sweets." I attempted to

keep a straight face but sputtered a laugh when she shot me a droll look. "Must be part pixie."

Her face fell farther right as she shoved her arms at my chest, but I caught her hands and rolled to my back, taking her with me. Filena squealed again and I couldn't help my rascally grin.

Now atop me, I had a full view of her playfully pinched expression. Her soft waves of auburn hair spilled onto the pillow around my face. My heart stilled in my chest. Her beauty ripped the breath from my lungs. Gods, I wanted an eternity of eternities with her. I was so obsessively in love.

At the feel of her bare body adjust above mine, my wings beat desperately for release—*again*. The whole time we made love, they ached to cover us, caress her skin, stretch to feel her fingers glide along the silky feathers. But the space was far too small.

The next time, I would fly Filena deep into the woods so my wings could curl with pleasure too.

"What are you thinking about?" she asked.

My hands caressed down the arrow of her spine and she shivered at my light touch. "I need to talk to Sean."

If I told her the truth, how I wanted to bury myself deep inside of her and climax from wing play, she wouldn't show up for work . . . and then I'd need to pay the tribe for a night's loss in profits. She wasn't my slave anymore, but they didn't know that—or that I had made a mortal my wife. I did need to share my plan with Filena though, and this was a perfect segue.

A corner of my mouth hitched up. "I have a real and fake wedding to plan."

"Involving Sean?"

"And my betrothed." I blinked innocently at her.

Filena rolled her eyes. "Can I pretend to be a territorial male?"

"You want to growl at me, *pet*?" I asked with a delighted grin.

She leaned her head on her elbow, her lips now next to mine. "Darlin'," she practically purred, "you would enjoy that far too much."

"Not as much as watching you talk to a wood raven while thinking he was me."

"I fed that wee bastard precious comfort sweets!"

"And fed me none, though my heart was breaking." I rubbed my nose against hers playfully. "I now question your love."

Before she could react, I wrapped my arms around her waist and captured her mouth with mine. For a hot second, I thought she would resist. But she melted into me without a single protest and I quietly moaned.

Gods.

How I craved her.

Every part of me filled with drunken moonlight. I could get forever tipsy on the seduction of her smooth, warm skin caressing mine, the slow, feverish way her tongue branded my mouth, her lips, feck her lips. But . . .

"Lass," I forced out, breathless. Between my aching wings, knowing she would spend the rest of the night with strangers instead of me, and gently setting her beside me on the bed so I could think, I was in agony. "We really do need to talk."

"I have something to share with you too."

I arched a brow and dipped my head for her to continue.

Filena gnawed on a corner of her bottom lip. "While you're bonded to me," she said in a low whisper, "you can't be cursed."

My face relaxed in surprise. "Because of Barry?"

286

She nodded. "Whatever curse you endure would also harm me."

"That lad deserves an entire cake and a mug of ale."

Filena groaned. "Don't go spoiling Muffin Moo, Rhylee Lo, or we won't be able to live with him."

I grinned, a look she knew meant no bargain, and she heaved a sigh. Not being able to be cursed stripped several layers of trepidation off me. Especially as the only way to survive a trickster Raven was to out trick him, even if he was a gov. And I had promised to protect Braelin from my tribe's cruelty.

"So," Filena said on another sigh, "tell me about your wedding plans, *mate*, and I'll try not to growl."

I brushed my thumb across her lower lip and leaned in for the barest of kisses, then murmured, "I'm going to stand beneath the Truth Telling Tree with Braelin on Samhain Eve."

Her eyebrows shot up.

The rest poured from me in threadbare whispers and her brows inched higher. And then a conspiratorial smile broke across her face.

At Filena's look, I should have felt relief. Instead, a spike of dread bolted through me. She hadn't *seen* what I had proposed? I didn't know if I should take that as a bad omen. Perhaps Fate intentionally left Filena blindfolded to this possible future. The gods would tell her if we were in danger, right?

I pushed up on my elbow and kissed my wife, deeply, infusing every melodic beat of my singing heart into the dancing sweep of my lips. Then forced my throbbing body from the bed. She needed to get ready for work.

And I needed to talk to Sean.

Chapter Thirty

RHYLEN LONAN

I leaned against a tree near the hawkers, not too far from Filena's divination wagon, and plucked my great-granda's lute. Cian and

the lads would find me eventually. Twenty minutes ago, Filena began reading cards and I felt myself descending toward the ruffled edges of madness at the separation. Keeping my fingers busy helped.

Visitors drifted by me, their lantern-lit eyes full of wonder as they took in cart after cart and endless tables of faerie made wares and enchantments. Several females—mortal and fae—slowed to study my wings . . . and *me*. Stars, it felt good to have my wings out. I ignored all the heated, blushed stares my way, though, despite my expectations to flirt as a "single" male, as part of the Autumn Night Market's courting magic charms.

After completing a physical bond with Filena this evening, my heart was too full of song to care about anything else. Magic was spilling into my veins. A melody of sky and moon and stars reeled across the black feathers of my wings to the rhythm of the dancing breeze.

In the far background, the ghostly wisps of Samhain ribbons rippled over several crowds of mortals who had formed lines around the Truth Telling Tree to take vows the same night a Raven prince and princess had.

Thinking about that fecker soured my stomach.

I focused back onto the market proper and locked eyes with a little mortal girl around seven or so. Her blonde curls were tied up with pink ribbons to match the flouncy, rosy-hued dress that reached her knees. And, for a heart fluttering second, my mind slipped back to the conversation with Filena about starting a family.

Would we have a daughter with golden locks, too? Like Cian, like the Mother?

Would our bairns have pointed or rounded ears?

Would they have Raven wings and fly away from their mortal mam when in trouble? A quiet laugh settled in my chest at that last thought.

My gaze once more rested on the strips of pink satin and my chest rose and fell in a settled sigh. I would work endless hours for my little lass to wear ribbons in her hair too. Or weave her flower crowns if she preferred those instead.

Stars, I really would be ridiculous.

"Your wings are pretty," the little girl said and took a step toward me. "Are you an elf or a faerie?"

"Marilee!" Her mam grabbed the girl's hand to yank her back.

"I am both, hennie," I answered the wee lass with a soft smile, still fingerpicking my lute. "Elves are a type of faerie who look the most like humans."

Her mam eyed me curiously then.

"What are you playing?" the girl asked next.

I crouched to be more eye level and extended my great-granda's lute toward her. "An ancient instrument of the Fair Folk." I plucked a simple melody and encouraged her to do the same. Touching the strings, her rounding blue eyes flew to mine at the haunting notes. "You just played a song on a nine-hundred-year-old lute, pet."

Her mam's mouth parted. "How does the wood not rot?"

"My great-granda carved it from an Ever Tree in The Wilds—"
Movement caught my eye.

Behind the girl's mam, Morenn—one of many wild fae orphans in West Tribe—sly-footed his way closer and reached toward the woman's belt purse. The lad puffed a strand of unruly blue hair from his eyes.

The boy tilted his head at me, a silent request to create a distraction.

I slid my soot-rimmed eyes to the lady from beneath my lowered lashes and gently fluttered my wings, not above using my masculine wiles in this situation. She blinked back a blush as I reached into my pocket to pull out a leaf, which I kept hidden in my cupped hands. Then, with a wink at the wee lass, I leaned on the body of my lute while still crouched and blew on my fingers. The little girl's curious eyes tracked my movements. Magic trickled down my arms in a rush and a brief lightheaded spin raced around my head.

Morenn softly gripped the purse, his sea blue eyes flicking to mine. I didn't look directly at him, not wanting to give him away.

Instead, a side of my mouth hitched up and I opened my hands the moment he yanked. A faintly glowing pink and purple butterfly fluttered its wings on my palms.

The girl gasped.

The woman looked behind her at the slight tug but Morenn had already melted into the crowd. Furrowing her brow, she returned her attention back onto my illusion and placed a hand to her chest, her eyes widening like her daughter's.

"A pair of pretty wings for you, hennie." I placed the illusioned leaf into the little girl's hands and she grinned. "She'll fly to the stars when the sun rises."

"Tha—"

"No," I cut her off quickly. "Never thank a fae, lass. You'll owe them a favor if you do."

She nodded and smiled at the butterfly.

The girl's mam, still unaware that she was robbed by a child the same age as her own, gently pulled the little girl toward her as I slowly rose to my feet. The woman's gaze burned across my body and then down my wings, her cheeks stained pink. Mortals who spent little time around the fae were easily elf struck. I was used to it—knew how to heighten the attraction. Still, I felt a tightening territorial response flame inside me.

"Rhylen!" Corbin waved his hand a short distance over the woman's shoulders.

I lifted my chin in quick acknowledgement, shifted away my wings, then swung my lute to my back.

"Enjoy the Night Market, pet," I said to the little girl, then tipped my top hat at the woman and angled around them.

My gang drew close with Cian in the lead, Glenna at his side and Gran on her arm.

Sean met my eyes for a fleeting second before looking away. His normally relaxed, smiling features were carved into stone. Brows pinched, he placed his hands into his pockets and raised his shoulders, pretending that the woods beyond the market were interesting.

"Rhylee Lo," Cian drawled, "we come bearing gifts."

Owen lifted a tied linen bundle of food, a wide grin stretching across his face.

"Sausage," Cian stage whispered. "Large, dripping sausage."

"Cian didn't want to deliver yours," my sister drolled. "I quote, 'Rhy-Rhy doesn't like juicy meat like I do.'"

The lads roared with laughter, except Sean, who managed a tiny appreciative smile before watching the toe of his boot draw circles in the dirt.

Cian suggestively winked at me. "I've never asked you to share your sausage with me before."

"Darlin'," I said, mimicking him, "it was you who asked for *my* girthy mallet earlier behind the tents."

"I do like to nail wood with a girthy mallet."

I smirked. "Especially mine and you never gently tuck it away when finished."

Cian squished my cheeks, the ale on his breath tickling my nose. "So, you'll share your juicy meat with me?"

"Don't, lad!" Corbin hollered. "He already flirted his way to Owen's sausage!"

A corner of my mouth hooked up. "What will you give me?"

"I don't bargain with broody Ravens," he said.

I lowered my voice so only Cian could hear me. "What about

with your *brother*?"

Cian's body stiffened. The reveling fool act sobered as he looked between me and his sister's divination wagon. Was that fear or disapproval? He knew I danced for Filena. He knew I was alone with her in the woods afterward . . . and why. Sean, Owen, and Corbin too. The prince and his gang as well. The risk of banishment, the threat to make Filena pay for my insubordination then was the same as now. So why did a muscle tick along his jaw and his eyes narrow at me?

A hot flash of irritation raced beneath my skin and my wings flexed to reappear.

She was *mine*.

My best friend didn't get to silently judge me as if suddenly a protective older brother. Not without also answering to me about his own behavior as of late.

I raised a mocking brow, peering pointedly at my sister then back to him . . . and a slow smile crept up Cian's face.

"Love birds," Owen sang out to us, "done with your lingering stare yet? You're blocking my view of a far prettier lass than the two of you."

Cian's smile tilted higher. "Rhylee Lo is peering into the depths of my lovelorn soul, he is." Trailing his fingers down the strap of my lute, he blinked up at me. "Play me a song, lad. 'His Talons Grip My Heart.'" He clawed his hand at me.

I rolled in my bottom lip for a long second, to keep my face straight. But a tight laugh spurted past my compressed lips. Stars, Cian was an eejit. I was grateful for the humor, though. If the tension inside of me didn't give, I would snap. This evening was far too intense and it was only going to get worse the more time I spent separated from Filena.

"The Cattle Maid's Drawers!" Corbin hollered his song request and the boys cheered, including Sean—surprisingly. "*I'll sing you a pretty tale so tragic you'll weep,*" Corbin began.

"*Of a farmer's daughter roam'n fields of cattle and sheep,*" Owen jumped in and sang next.

"*Who didn't wear drawers or stockings!*" they all shouted in laughter, even Glennie and Gran.

Cian, however, continued to watch me closely. To others, he looked bent on mischief. To me, I saw the reminder in the tight crinkling at the corner of his eyes, the way his gaze remained dead still on mine.

I understood the message: guard my territorial rage.

If I forgot my place, Bryok would punish me by making Filena kneel at his feet. Or attempt to sell Cian before I could release his bonds.

Just that reminder ignited a new wildfire in my veins.

We hadn't talked yet since I protected Cian at the wedding revel. But we didn't need to, not really. I already knew my brother would do almost anything to remain a tribe's slave, regardless of tribe, than be forced to live in a village without family. But Bryok would sell him to Seren. He would ensure we never saw Cian again while making the most profit off him.

"Rhy," Cian warned under his breath, "you had a strong primal display earlier . . . with *magic*. Bryok almost pissed his pants at your domination. But he wants scary Rhylen to manifest in front of the tribe. And feck did you look unhinged. Gird your monster's loins, darlin', or I'll kick you in the balls until you can control your territorial urges."

I nodded and blew out a slow breath.

"You can't play house forever, either," Cian added after a beat. "He'll figure it out. Your arranged mate too."

"Aye," I agreed. "I have a plan. Putting it into motion tonight. Trust me?"

Cian rolled his eyes. "If I say yes, do I get your sausage?"

"Are you going to tell me who you hit at the revel?"

Cian's body stiffened again, his smile strained as he gestured with his head toward our fellas, who were leaning in to hear us. "That will cost you more than letting me put your juicy meat in my mouth, Rhy-Rhy."

"You're the fecking worst," I tossed out with a breathy laugh, more for show. Cian and I would talk details when alone.

"Love you too . . . *brother*," Cian whispered, his eyes softening.

I cupped the back of his neck and drew him in until our foreheads touched. "You're also mine, Cian Merrick."

"Are they bonding over wedding sausage?" Corbin asked.

Cian pulled away and leisurely spun toward Corbin. "First time Rhylee Lo has shared his sausage with another male." Cian bit his bottom lip at me. "After care is everything, lads." In a couple of steps, he swiped the tied bundle of food from Owen.

The gobshite stole my dinner.

Chapter Thirty-One

FILENA LONAN

The crowds around us thickened. It would be a rowdy night, between Travelers still in their cups from the wedding revel and visitors celebrating their own Truth Telling Tree bonding ceremonies—both mortals and fae.

Not all Raven Folk would wait until the Samhain Eve mass wedding event either.

"Sean," I casually addressed my friend, "a repair needs attention." I beckoned with a hand to follow and Sean tensed.

Cian's steel gaze flitted to our friend. Wrinkles across my brother's forehead smoothed, the lines around his eyes too. I figured he would quickly put together part of my plan. Cian rarely missed a beat. He acted the fool, but Cian Merrick was sharper than a blade.

Now I understood his dual nature—both mortal and fae. Son of a drunk with the trickster wit of the Crone, mischievous playfulness of the Maiden, and the sexual nature of the Mother. As if he and he alone were responsible for the land's fertility.

Stars, once he knew his origins, that he was a demi-god . . .

The arse noticed my staring and took a large bite from the pilfered sausage just to crow his victory over tricking me. I lifted a rude gesture in reply. He grinned, then draped his arms across Owen's and Corbin's shoulders, the meal dangling from his fingers, and led them away.

"*Hey ho, my love, a bonny lad called out to she,*" Corbin sang.

Owen answered, "*Let me kiss you, my love, beneath the hawthorn tree.*"

"*And she didn't wear drawers or stockings!*" Cian shouted while lightly kicking Glenna in the arse as he passed by.

My sister whipped around and hissed mock threats at him, loud enough for the gawking visitors to hear. Cian's eyes gleamed with glee. With a roguish wink, he wrapped his arm around the front of Owen's face, making the lad squirm for release, and took another large bite of the sausage. Glenna tried not to react at first but burst into laughter a second later.

"You little shite hawk," Owen muttered. "You have to crow over my loss too?"

When they disappeared into the crowd, Gran murmured, "My sunshine boy."

"Troublemaking bargaining eejit," Glenna corrected. "Sometimes I think he's more fae than a flock of Raven Folk."

Gran's dark purple eyes drifted to mine. The love and pride in their depths warmed my chest. "Better get to yer repairs, aye?" To Glenna she said, "Take his lute, lass."

I strapped our family instrument around Glenna, who playfully stuck her tongue out at me. I stuck mine out in reply, poking her in the side until she huffed a laugh, then leaned down and kissed first her cheek followed by Gran's, whispering, "I'll check on you in a couple of hours."

"Guard yer fire heart, me boy," she whispered back. "Don't go look'n fer trouble."

"The tribe is worth defending, Gran." I paused a beat. "So is my family."

She patted my cheek, a spark of fear in her gaze, then tugged on Glenna's sleeve to head back to the wagons. I watched until they disappeared into the crowd before facing Sean, who peered at the visitors angling past us. But when I gestured with my head for him to follow me, I caught his attention. Our eyes locked for one loaded second and then I began walking.

"To the pub," I murmured.

"Fly to fetch our tools first?"

"I just want to talk, friend," I answered with a side-long glance. "Privately."

At the pub wagons, the music would cover our voices better than a clandestine talk in the woods where Ravens spying for Bryok might overhear us. Most people would be too inebriated to follow our conversation.

We wove through the meandering crowd in silence, our eyes downcast as we passed by middle-rank hawkers. They sang out to the visitors, promising anything from combs enchanted to add luster to one's hair to a cure for heart burn, both indigestion and grief. People ribboned around us in laughter and excited chatter. Mortal girls giggled behind gloved hands while young men shoved each other around in games for their attention. Mams with prams and tired eyes pushed wee bairns beneath the moon's lullaby. And fae from different kingdoms curiously eyed mainlanders from Carran's eastern cities who strolled the market to be seen in their outlandish, garish clothing styles.

Some truly did look ridiculous.

Sean and I slowed on the edge of the outdoor ale house. Tables dotted most of the space, where mortals and fae sang with mugs lifted, talked and laughed in loud boisterous voices, while a few danced to the fiddle, banjo, and bodhrán drum.

My breath formed clouds in the chilly autumn night. But my blood fevered, a hot branding knife that twisted mercilessly in my heart with each step I took farther away from Filena. It felt like I was dying—with want, with fear, with a need to guard what was mine. I could still taste the sweet salt of her skin on my lips. Gods, the softness of each curve, the intoxicating ecstasy of being inside of her, the heady feel of our bodies moving to the rhythm of our pounding heartbeats.

I was on the verge of pivoting on my heel and marching back to wait near her wagon when Sean stopped behind the makeshift stage. Candles in red-tinted lanterns painted the space around us in sanguine shades. A color that didn't help my present state.

Sean shifted on his feet. "Talk."

A single word but infused with a raging tide of emotion. The underlying territorial response ruffled the feathers of mine.

Drawing in a slow, calming breath, I stepped close, ignoring the urge to dominate, and whispered, "I'm already married."

Rage darkened his gaze and his wings flashed into view.

"Not to Braelin," I added and he stilled, a preternatural stillness that spoke to the primal wild fae nature controlling me right now too.

"Filena?" he asked, fear gutting his eyes. I nodded and his chest rose and fell deeply in a relieved but terrified, heaving exhale. "I'm sorry, friend. I shouldn't have—"

I grabbed him and pulled him into an embrace. "I would feel crushed and territorial too, Sean Byrnes."

"You *have* since the lottery," he corrected me. "And I'm barely managing a couple of hours."

"I've had years to accept what I thought would be my fate."

"Fecking hell, Rhylen," he snapped, leaning back, "you'll be banished. Bryok will purchase Lena after selling Cian off to Seren." Sean clenched his teeth. "I knew you were in love with Cian's sister but what were you thinking? Is it too late? Can you still break the bond?"

"That is *not* an option." Mates who broke their bonds before the sixth day could never be bound by ravens together again. That was the magic's rule. I crossed my arms over my chest. "If the elders dare banish me or my family, I'll destroy them all."

They would have to kill me to keep me from Filena or my family. I was done with Caravan rules on love and marriage.

"How do you plan to get out of the lottery, Rhylen Lonan?" A muscle along Sean's jaw ticked. "What if the elders bind you in a curse before you can challenge the govs? Bryok already has your beating heart in his fist."

"Not my heart," I said with a smirk. "He gets off on stroking my large fire until I threaten to come for his family."

"And then he forces you to marry," Sean said, pointing his finger in my face, "strips you before your crew, vows to make Filena kneel before him if you forget your place, denies Gran warmth, makes Cian attend him . . ."

"If you could mate bond with Braelin Cormac this night,

300

would you?"

"Aye," Sean rushed out in a soft breath, not even hesitating to answer. "I know that's madness. We don't know each other—"

"She's your True Mate," I said just as softly. "I understand."

A scowl darkened his brows. "Filena is your—"

"Aye," I whispered.

"Shite," Sean hissed violently. "What games are the gods playing at?"

Confessing that I had married a demi-goddess balanced on the tip of my tongue. Filena was both a mortal *fáidhbhean* and a fae *cailleach*—two powerful feminine magics. Regardless, Raven Folk didn't marry mortals let alone other fae. But to marry a mortal slave? I knew my gang didn't feel this way, the Merricks were one of us, but I might as well have committed murder in the tribes' eyes.

"You're arranged by the elders," Sean gritted out, pulling me back from my thoughts. "Already married or not, bonded to a fae or not, they'll curse you, Rhylen. Then they'll banish you and your mate will be left unprotected."

For a mere second, I weighed how much to tell Sean. I decided what Barry could or couldn't do for our family was Filena's secret to share, not mine.

"The magic binding the lottery is only through Samhain Eve," I countered. "I was told to find a wife who would bring money to West Tribe. The elders never said she had to be a Traveler lass."

Sean straightened and his mouth parted at the truth of my words. It was assumed we'd only marry our kind. But my marriage to Filena fell within the lottery's bargain—she brought in regular coin too, not a one-time dowry.

"I promised Braelin that I would protect her in my rejection."

"So you want me to marry her." It was a statement, not a question.

"If she'll have you, aye." I placed a hand on his upper arm. "Then she and I will pretend to exchange vows beneath the Truth Telling Tree. The elders will be none the wiser. Nor will the bonding magic bind us together since we'll already be bonded to our True Mates."

Sean slowly nodded, taking in my plan. "And after, when the Fiachnas realize you've tricked them?"

"They won't have long to ponder," I said with a wicked smile. "On Samhain, I'll challenge Bryok for the gov position, our chieftain too."

I still didn't know how I would fight Bram Fiachna, but Filena's vision of me with my own tribe gave me courage.

"Pluck the prince's feathers, one by one," Sean replied with a wicked grin of his own. "Give them to Cian. The poor lad has wing envy."

I quietly laughed. "Cian is already a prettier bird than the lot of us, he is."

"The mortal eejit." Sean chuckled under his breath.

The smile slipped from my lips and I cleared my throat. "No middle-rank clan, especially a Cormac, would willingly give their daughter to a felly boy, aye?" Sean nodded slowly, his lips pressing together. "They're clearly being blackmailed by the Fiachnas. But—"

"You speak true," a soft familiar voice said from the shadows. "But not entirely either."

My wings snapped out in reflex and spread in warning as I stepped in front of Sean. Braelin's hood covered most of her face, but her eyes were bright beneath the lantern light.

Baring my canines, I pinned her with a challenging glare. "How much did you hear?"

Sean's fury at how I spoke to his mate was palpable and I flexed my wings wider to protect him. They may be True Mates, but she could be in a bargain with Bryok. Thankfully, Sean was behind Bryok's small party when the mate bond awakened in him.

And, thankfully, he remained still despite the territorial rage heating off his body.

"I do not spy." She demurely lowered her head. "I snuck away from my mam and sisters to speak to you in private."

"And listened in on my *private* conversation first. For how long?"

She stepped closer without answering my question and my fingers shifted into talons. I didn't care who she was or what I had promised. No one would harm Filena, Cian, or my boys.

"Rhylen Lonan," she spoke calmly, "I swear on my life that I mean you no harm."

"Your life?" A dark laugh left me. "How do I know it is truly you and not a glamour?"

"Ask the Raven brother under your wing."

"Raven brother?" I asked over my shoulder, not wanting to give her an edge on my friend by introducing his name. A male's blood ignited when hearing their mate speak their name, especially the first time after an awakening.

"Aye," Sean replied, his voice tight. "It's her, Lonan."

"Bargain with more than your life, lass." I took another step toward her. "Swear your allegiance to me—"

"Rhylen," Sean growled low.

"She could sacrifice herself after sacrificing me or another in my care," I snapped over my shoulder and the blood visibly rushed from Sean's face. "Bryok arranged our marriage, lad. Do *not* forget."

Muscles were trembling down Sean's body, but he dipped his head in a single, curt nod. I faced my *betrothed* again, suddenly feeling like a fecking sod for suggesting Sean marry her in my place without first unearthing the truth of her family's debt to the Fiachnas.

She had *followed* me, had *listened* to me confess dangerous secrets to Sean. And she wanted me to know she had too.

Braelin lifted her chin. "I give you my life and my allegiance, Rhylen Lonan. I put you above all others, including my family, my mate, and the govs of both our tribes, upon penalty of death."

The moment she finished, Sean charged me from behind. But I was ready for him and quickly shifted into a raven. I flew into the shadows, then reappeared at his back. My friend spun on his heel, his chest heaving, his talons now out.

"She is *mine*," he growled. "Her allegiance is to *me*."

"She is yours," I agreed, lifting my hands. "But her allegiance is to me until *we* can protect our families."

Braelin gently placed a hand on Sean's arm and he practically moaned at her simple touch. "I do not fear Rhylen Lonan or his bargain."

Sean lowered his wings. "Who do you fear, mate?"

Their eyes locked and an intensity shimmered through the air as the word "mate" hung between them. The beginnings of a blush crept up what I could see of her neck and face. The look of longing in her eyes shuttered just as quickly as it appeared, though.

With one last lingering glance at Sean, Braelin exhaled a soft, quivering breath and dropped her hand. Then she turned toward me and slowly lowered her hood.

My stomach jumped to my throat.

A scar marred the porcelain expanse of her left cheek. The puckered skin slightly drooped down the corner of her dark eye.

Gods . . .

She was scorn marked. A barbaric tradition rarely practiced today, but one that allowed a male the right to scar a female in retaliation for permanently breaking a mate bond before the sixth day. Not only scar but, if a gov, curse too. Often a love curse.

Braelin Cormac began to open her mouth and I knew what she was going to say before the horrific words fell from her tongue. The pain in her bold gaze lit a raging fire in my breaking heart . . . and I just knew.

"Bryok Fiachna doesn't blackmail my family," she said, tears glistening on her lashes. "He blackmails me."

Chapter Thirty-Two

FILENA LONAN

Rory, one of a half-dozen collectors, pushed a stack of coins to join the others on my table and began counting another set from the fortune telling fees I brought in overnight. Lloyd scampered over from where he had been snuggling with Sheila to the new stack and sniffed the coins. Last night was largely profitable, even for me.

"Move your squirrel," Rory mumbled under his breath.

Lloyd lifted his messenger paper to me.

His breath reeks.

A tiny smile played across my lips, but I otherwise ignored Lloyd. He was capable of moving away if he didn't like the collector's breath.

Leaning back in my chair, I arched a tired brow behind my black veil and tried not to bat at the damn bead that fell over my eye. Why this bead? Always *this* bead. Gran had fixed my headpiece this week—twice. If I were alone, I would tear the costume from my hair with a clenched scream of frustration. Alas, I had company and must retain some semblance of ladylike deportment. But that stars-blasted bead . . .

Fáiléanna, a soothing motherly voice whispered around me, *you will only see in part unless you change the view.*

The hair lifted on the nape of my neck.

My gaze shot to each shadowed corner of my workspace. It was quiet outside of my wagon too. The market closed an hour ago and most had already collapsed into their beds. The crowds were thick last night and most Travelers, in celebration of the royal wedding, had drank like a parched horse at a trough. But I had to wait for one of the collectors to come around to fetch my coins and pay my wages before I, too, could turn in for the day.

I must have imagined the voice.

The night had been long and exhausting. Far too many intense emotions. If the male would hurry up, I could free my girls from this confounding corset, then curl up next to Glenna and pass out until near sunset. Though I wished it were Rhylen I could share a bed with this morning. To be cradled against the heat of his strong body . . . stars, I'd never sleep. Not after last night.

Rory finished—finally—and slid a single coin my way. My eyes jumped to his. For the amount I collected last night, I should have three coins, per the agreed percentage payout by the govs.

"Two more coins," I said to him.

"Only one, pet," he drawled out. "West Tribe needs the funds."

West Tribe could rot. I wouldn't starve for our govs to strut around in comfort.

Feeling bold, I helped myself to two coins off a stack.

Rory grabbed my hand and slammed it onto the table. "Slave," he hissed, "you steal from the tribe?"

A warm tingling sensation trickled down my arms and pooled in my stinging palm and fingertips beneath the collector's. It was a similar foreign feeling to last night's when I had furiously marched into the woods after facing off with Bryok. But I was too angry to truly take notice right now.

No male owned me nor would again.

No male would deny me what was rightfully mine.

I was a *fáidhbhean, not some mere indentured mortal.*

I lowered my eyes for no one.

"Two additional coins," I warned low, a fire dancing on my tongue, "or I'll curse your feathered arse."

"One coin, *slave*. Orders from the elders."

I cackled darkly. "Trick others out of their earnings, but you can't trick me, *pet*." Leaning over the table toward him, I lifted my veil with my free hand and grinned. A wicked, delighted smile that normally made arrogant, self-serving males run. "Last chance to honor my wages due or I'll curse the air to grow teeth and bite your ear for refusing to listen."

"One. Coin." He punctuated each word in a near growl.

A storm whipped in my veins. My blood buzzed; my fingers burned. "So be it." Three words, but they echoed with supernatural power in this tight space. Fear, for the first time, widened Rory's eyes. "I curse the air around you." The words spilled from my tongue before I could stop them. "You will know the bite of the wind for each coin stolen from my wages. Two bites, one for each ear."

The air around him fogged into visibility. Rory shoved back in his chair. Before he could stand, spectral ropes appeared and tightened around his body. His wings shifted in and out to beat against the restraints for release, but it was no use.

A laugh bubbled up from my gut, but I nearly heaved instead.

What was happening?

My body swayed. I felt wrong all over. Confused, I focused on the coins I was owed and quickly tucked them into my corset. Why was I so lightheaded?

A plea snapped me out of my stupor.

"No, no!" Rory whimpered. "Take the coins!"

In front of the collector's face, a mouth had formed. Its sharp teeth dripped blood-shaped vapors that melted into the unseen air. Terror skated across my chilled skin. All words lodged in the back of my throat. I gripped the table, to do something, anything. But the mouth attacked the male in a flash before I could and bit the pointed tip of his ear right off.

He screamed. The high-pitched sound clawed viciously down my spine. As I watched him, I felt both delighted by his pain and horrified that I had cursed someone.

I had *cursed* him.

For years I had wanted to curse a selfish mortal or fae.

But I didn't think I actually *could*.

Bile coated my throat.

Mortals didn't have this kind of spellcraft. Green witches, the women who healed through herbal magics, were the only mortal witches not feared by villages in Caledona Wood. But a mortal witch who could command the air into acts of violence?

I would be hanged for dark magic!

Oh gods, oh gods, oh gods . . .

Where was Barry? My gaze darted around. I needed my

brother or Rhylen.

Black edged my vision. I stumbled back a step from my table, woozy and sickened. "Stop," the words rasped from my gasping lungs. The mouth froze in the air. "H-h-heal him, p-please."

My teeth were clacking so hard, my body trembling so bad, I could barely speak.

The wind fogged into a hand and lifted the male's pointed tip. Another dizzy rush stole my balance and I squeezed my eyes shut. I was on the verge of blacking out from a sudden energy loss the likes I had never experienced before. Visions drained me, but in little trickles. Nothing like this.

Rory thrashed in his chair, screaming and screaming. I covered my ears and heaved a sob.

The wagon's curtain burst open. Cian ran inside, his face bloodless, Barry right behind him. My brother took one look at Rory, then me. Pulling his fist back, Cian punched Rory across the upper jaw, knocking him out in one swing. Silence replaced the cries—immediate and swift—but the void was deafening.

My brother rushed over to me and cupped my face. "Lena . . ." He kissed my forehead. "Are you hurt?"

"I-I don't k-know what's h-happening to m-me."

"Did he hurt you?"

The sob in my chest loosened and I leaned my head on his shoulder. My entire body was shaking. "I c-cursed him."

Cian's head angled toward Rory and I opened my eyes long enough to see the fogged hand putting the collector's ear back into place.

"Did he hurt you, Lena?" he asked again, this time more softly.

"He refused m-me my full w-wages."

"And so you cursed him."

I nodded my head, feeling the cool dampness on his shirt from my tears.

My brother remained silent, holding me tight against him.

"They'll hang m-me for d-dark magic," I hiccuped between sobs.

"No," Cian whispered, kissing my hair. "No one will touch you."

"H-he'll speak!"

Rhylen pushed into the wagon, murder in his eyes before they rounded at the sight of the fogged hand healing Rory's ear.

"Get blue mushroom," Cian commanded in a clenched whisper. My husband growled and stepped toward me and Cian quietly growled back, "Now!"

My husband's fingers transitioned into talons, his canines bared, his wings now blocking the wedges of early morning light filtering in from the curtain. Territorial rage flamed in his gaze as he held mine, and my tears fell harder.

"Don't make me kick you in the balls," Cian said slowly, emphatically. "If you want to protect your mate, fly into Caledona Wood. Place blue mushroom on the collector. Quickly."

Rhylen studied Cian for a wild second. Then he shifted into a raven and flew past the door's curtain into the dawn.

"Listen carefully, Lena," my brother whispered into my ear. "He was hallucinating. Ate too many mushrooms. You twisted your ankle when moving out of his grasp. You're crying because it pains you. Understand?"

"Aye," I whispered back.

"Forgive me, sister." Before I could make sense of his apology, he kicked my ankle and I quietly cried out. My legs buckled and Cian scooped me up. He kissed the side of my head. "Forgive me," he whispered again and settled onto my chair. I curled into his lap and buried my face in his neck. My ankle was throbbing and surely bruising now. Cian stroked my hair. "You're safe. No one was outside. You had to be one of the last on the collector's rounds."

"H-how did I c-curse him?"

"I don't know."

"Why are y-you still awake?"

Cian sighed. "I didn't trust Bryok after the large lady balls you grew last night and hung out nearby with Owen. I had sent Rhylen to the wagons a couple candlemarks earlier so he didn't mark his territory in the open after hours of separation."

"He's my husband," I whispered into his neck.

"Aye." I could feel Cian smile into my hair. "The broody arse is now insufferable to live with."

The tears burned the back of my eyes again. "I-I'm so scared."

"He ate too many mushrooms," Cian repeated. "He hallucinated. You twisted your ankle when defending yourself." Leaning toward my table, he fisted a small handful of coins and thrust them in my hand. "For your troubles."

I put the money down my corset, not arguing. My eyes were heavy and blurry, but I gently took Cian's hand and studied the cracked and bloodied knuckles. The same injured hand as last night. "D-did you hit Hamish last n-night?"

Cian sighed again. "He threatened to sell me to a Molly house on Seren if I didn't turn you over to him."

I pushed up. "He doesn't own—" I stiffened and a sudden gust of fury cut through my fear and magic loss fatigue. "West Tribe would sell you and pay him off?"

"You really think Bryok will hand *you* over to Hamish Mac-Cullough?" Cian laughed bitterly. "He would sell me to a Molly house and use those funds to buy you."

"He can't sell you into prostitution," I gritted out. "That's illegal."

"Darlin', the carrion crime syndicate doesn't care about the laws of mortal men."

A growing horror bloomed in my chest as I understood what he was really saying. Cian would let them sell him into prostitution to save me from Da. "Don't you dare," I gritted out. "Rhylen would free you first."

The sad smile that dipped the corners of his lips broke my heart. "If he knows first. But," he added, tapping the tip of my nose, "Da is dead."

"Cian—"

"Da is dead."

Rhylen flew into the wagon with blue mushrooms in his talons, dropping them onto Rory's chest, and gracefully shifted into his fae form before touching the wooden floor. Immediately, he knelt before the collector and put a torn piece of mushroom into the male's mouth, pinching his nose until he swallowed. Then he tucked the remaining mushroom into Rory's pocket.

It was a brilliant plan. The lower class fae really did like blue mushrooms. Cheaper than alcohol. And they bloomed around Samhain.

Fáiléanna . . .

Another dizzy spell spun through my head and the room tilted. My head lolled onto Cian's chest. Black crept across the edges of my vision again.

"Stay with us, Filena," Cian demanded. "We need any potential witnesses to see you limp home."

"Limp?" Rhylen asked, his voice dark.

"How many crime alibis have you staged, pet?" I slurred, poking Cian in the stomach.

My brother laughed. "Out tricking those feathered bastards gives me life, it does. Ready, darlin'?" Cian scooted me onto my feet. "Slow and gentle now."

Fáiléanna . . .

I hissed a breath when I put weight on my ankle.

Rhylen caught me before I fell over. I was too dizzy to move. "Magic loss?" he asked me. I nodded my head, grateful he didn't ask for more details right now. But, then, he was always attuned to my needs. "I'll brace you under your arms." To Cian he said, "Alert the cashier that a collector passed out."

"This is the story," Cian hurried out, "if anyone stops you."

My mind slipped in and out as my brother shared all the details with Rhylen. Then we were moving. My eyes squinted at the pale morning light. Pain shot through my ankle and I grimaced. But Rhylen moved slowly. The muscles of his arms, of the large body holding mine up, flexed with barely contained wildness.

I blinked and had to force my eyes to open.

Tired.

So, so tired.

Fáiléanna, the soothing voice spoke my birth name again, *you will only see in part unless you change the view.*

I wasn't going to make it to the wagons. My body was growing more boneless with each step. I meant to say Rhylen's name,

314

instead, "*Cailleach,*" whispered from my lips.

"*A stór?*" Rhylen asked, bending down closer. "Cian will be back shortly."

"*Cailleach. . .*"

His steps halted. One beat. Two beats. Then we were moving again.

"I know," he said softly into my hair, but I could hear ripples of fear in his deep, melodic voice. "I know, wife."

I didn't have a chance to react to that revelation.

The world around me turned black.

Chapter Thirty-Three

FILENA LONAN

A dull ache throbbed across my skull. I squinted open my eyes and grimaced at the streams of dusky evening light spilling in from a curtain-drawn window across from me. Intricately painted green and blue walls blurred in and out of focus. My body was a lead weight in a raging river of sensation. Dizziness, bruising pain in my ankle, tired, so, so tired.

Feeling pulled under toward sleep once more, I shifted to burrow into the comforting warmth cocooning me. An arm wrapped around my waist, another circling my upper back, pressed me closer to the heartbeat pounding in my ear. I could blissfully drown in the spicy scent filling my nose and I buried farther into the protective warmth.

"Lass," a sleep-husked voice whispered into my hair. "How do you feel?

My eyes widened at the unexpected sound . . . and landed on Cian, who was sprawled across a tiny pull-out bed opposite me in sleep, shirtless, a halo of blond hair spilling over his pillow. I wrinkled my nose at the sight and tilted my head toward the deep, melodic voice attached to the body holding mine. But I was laying atop Rhylen, my front to his, cradled just beneath his chin, and couldn't see his face.

"Mate?" he whispered again and my heart skipped a beat at the breathy sound of that word. Speeding up when memories quickly surfaced of this morning.

Cailleach.

Fae blood is in your veins . . .

I had cursed someone. I had commanded the elements to do my bidding. I'd always had an incessant itch to curse someone, an itch that had plagued me for years. But it was terrifying to behold, to know my words carried actual supernatural violence.

Rhylen kissed my head. "Do not fear yourself, *a stór*. Or the future."

The future . . . the one I *saw* of Rhylen beneath Seren without his wife. Was it because I was hanged? Who did he rescue in the Blackthorn card vision? No, it was me. I *knew* it was me. Perhaps I'd be hanged afterward for commanding dark magic.

Tears flooded my eyes and I drew in a sharp, hiccuped breath.

"Filly Lo . . ." He sighed my name as if his heart were breaking with each syllable. "Magic is a strange, wild thing, and at the whim of the gods just as much as us. But Filena Moira Lonan, *you* are still the same strong, clever woman you've always been. A beautiful, powerful storm of a lass. *My* lass."

Was I truly the same person as before? Because I knew in my gut that *nothing* would ever be the same now.

My mind snagged on a trail of his words. Magic was at the whim of the gods . . . had the gods possessed me in that moment?

Perhaps I wasn't a *cailleach*.

Sometimes I wonder if you are truly a fáidhbhean *or a* cailleach *in disguise.*

Bryok's threatening musings the night of the Fire Dance echoed loudly in my mind.

Why would he entertain such an idea after *years* of indentured servitude in his tribe? He had known I was a seer since I was four-teen, when Barry showed up on my wagon step. What possible clues had he picked up on that would suddenly suggest I was a *cailleach in disguise*?

Another thought hit me and bile coated my throat.

As his mistress, if he denied me herbal prevention, I would bear him children.

Was that why he recently obsessed over me? He wanted heirs with a powerful mortal?

Cailleach.

Where do you think your magic comes from?

Fae blood is in your veins . . .

Cailleach.

I know, wife.

Wait.

How did Rhylen know?

Anger curdled the racing blood in my veins. He knew and didn't tell me. There was no doubt a valid reason. Not a single bone in his body would willingly cause me pain or betray my trust. Still . . . fresh, hot tears streaked down my cheeks and spilled onto his linen shirt. My husband, my *mate*, kept this huge part of myself from me.

"I wasn't allowed to tell you," he said, tightening his hold around my waist. "A bargain."

Chills flushed across my anger-fevered skin. Rhylen Lonan was always so in tune with me, and another gust of fury tumbled through my shaking body. Which was entirely selfish of me, but we already knew I was a selfish creature. He would sacrifice all so I might live, be happy, have everything I desired. Not to mention, he had been a solid mountain of compassion and protection when I confessed two of my darkest secrets to him—ones that threatened his family's well-being.

Right now, though, I felt too raw and exposed.

This whole week had flayed my heart wide open.

And I was terrified.

The soul part of me connected to the soul part of him, however, understood he was aware that I wasn't truly angry with him, not really. Ribbons of grief and betrayal were quickly knotting up my ability to think straight. The thick fog in my head, the exhaustion bleeding out with every pained breath, wasn't helping.

"A bargain with who?" I demanded on a choked whisper, lifting my head.

He tenderly brushed a wisp of hair from my face. "Gran."

"How long have you known?"

"Since the night we married."

I stilled, my mouth ajar. Was that why he had looked at me curiously, as if for the first time? Why he *knew* he needed to marry me that night?

"How long has Gran known?"

He held my warbling gaze steady, but a muscle jumped along his jaw. "That is a confession you deserve to hear from her lips and not mine."

"You're still under a bargain?"

"Aye."

I rolled my eyes. "So you keep your bargains with Gran but not with your *True Mate*?"

The corner of his mouth kicked up. "You want to break a bargain with an ancient?"

Fair point. We didn't need the gods' ill favor right now. Or ever. But also, I wouldn't be able to refuse Gran anything either. And I knew she'd never harm a hair on my head too. That knowledge did nothing to lessen my building fear, though. Nor had teasing Rhylen.

Resigned, I sighed and lowered my head back to his chest and fidgeted with a button on his shirt.

Nausea rolled in my gut; the wagon around me tilted. The ache in my head tightened. Did Rhylen feel this way with major magic loss too? Had he ever spellcrafted this intensely before? I had seen him spin illusions many times, use his coercion magic too. If he felt drained, he would immediately shift into a raven and fly beneath the moon, singing to the stars until he felt replenished.

Fae blood is in your veins . . .

I thought back to my and Rhylen's conversation last night, of my mam, nan, and the strange faerie with the animal companions and a babe in her belly.

Was I related to this beautiful forest elf?

Were Rhylen's questions meant to riddle me toward a truth he couldn't share?

My gaze cut back to my brother and I studied his pillow-smooshed face. He had *seen* visions too. Could he also curse someone?

What were we?

Rhylen's long fingers brushed the thick waves of my hair and played with a few wayward auburn locks spilling over our arms. The movement was soothing and affectionate and lulled me deeper into his warmth. The tips of my fingers, however, held my entire body weight in anxiety and furiously twisted one of his buttons—and he let me.

"I have a piece of gossip for you."

Despite the fear, the heaviness, I couldn't help the tiny smile that stole my lips. He knew the way to my heart—and how to distract me from endlessly spiraling.

"Wickedly scandalous," he added.

"Does it involve romantical forbidden cheese?"

"What?" Rhylen's laughter rumbled down my body. "Please tell me you've *seen* a scandal involving romantical forbidden cheese."

I buried a smile into his neck, thinking of Glenna's gossip about Kaela Branwen and Cian the other day. "I only *see* visions of your obsession with—"

"You."

"—Pigeons, pet."

"Pigeons?" Another round of laughter quaked his body.

"Aye, you swoon over their white breast feathers, you do."

"Mmm," he playfully moaned into my hair. "I do like white breast feathers, *pigeon*."

I sputtered a breathy laugh, making Rhylen grin into my hair. Stars, those boyish smiles of his ruined me each time, even when I couldn't see them.

"Your gossip, then?"

"I perched in a tree this morning," he whispered conspiratorially, "to watch Barry when he scampered into the woods and . . . meet up with George."

My head popped up, making the room spin. But I was too surprised. "Are they in romantical forbidden love?"

Rhylen's dark purple eyes swept across my face, a doting look I felt in the marrow of my bones. "Our cake love'n fox seems to have an additional fetish."

My eyes widened, then slid to where Barry had curled up beneath a small nook table, both Sheila and Lloyd cozied up beside him. His yellow eyes were narrowed to slits. Oooh, Muffin Moo was *not* happy and I felt a cackle building. The cloud bank in my head, however, fogged my galloping thoughts and I couldn't possibly conceive what Barry would be—

"Gloves."

"Nooooo . . ." I gasped. "Where is the lad hiding them?"

"Check the underside of your wagon."

My gaze shot to Cian. His chest rose and fell in a slumbering rhythm and I bit back a snort. My brother could sleep through a war.

I twisted Rhylen's button again. "George is stealing gloves for Barry?"

"Aye, lass."

"So Barry," I said, side-eyeing my fox, "set up his wee thieving forest friend to steal Cian's glove?"

Rhylen grinned in reply, equally as delighted as me.

"What does George get out of it?" I asked next.

Barry growled low in warning.

Rhylen's lips pressed into a humored line. "Snuggling."

I burst into loud laughter. And immediately regretted my

cackling joy. Pain swooped in and thundered across my head. I adjusted my body with a groan, lowering my head. My injured ankle nudged against Rhylen's leg in the movement and I hissed.

Rhylen kissed my head and pulled me closer to him. "It kills me that you're in any kind of pain, *mo ghrá*."

Flashes of this morning reeled across my mind's eye.

For a few moments, I nearly forgot about the terror of this day.

I had watched air bite the tip of an ear clean off.

Air.

"I have another secret to share with you." His deep voice ended in a shaky breath. "About Braelin."

My body stilled. The saddened but angry way he said her name lifted the hair on the back of my neck. "Is she in trouble?"

"A year ago, at the Autumn Night Market," he began, lowering his voice to a near-whisper, "Bryok courted Braelin in secret."

"Preying on her," I corrected. My stomach clenched, already dreading every word of this story. "She's truly beautiful."

"And Ren Cormac's second cousin. Her older brother was Ren's righthand at Stellar Winds Casino."

Disgusted, I squeezed my eyes shut. Four weeks ago, Ren Cormac ran the floating island of Seren. Or the City of Stars, as mainlanders often referred to it as. Now Ravenna Blackwing, from the ancient Raven Folk royal line, ran the carrion crime syndicate.

"Two nights before Samhain Eve," Rhylen continued, "Bryok got Braelin drunk. She woke up the next morning in his bed, undressed, and mate bonded to him."

"Oh the poor lass. . ." I gripped the button on Rhylen's shirt, feeling furious tears sting my eyes—then my heart stopped beating.

Oh gods.

Braelin was now betrothed to Rhylen.

"Aye," Rhylen said quietly, confirming my growing horror.

Ravens mated for life. They didn't break bonds. Not without consequences. As a prince, Bryok could marry more than one Traveler, if he so chose. No male gov did, though. Not in hundreds of years. They either remained true to their wife or indulged in mistresses instead.

I was going to be sick.

"She's scorn marked, Lena," he gritted out, a raging fire in his voice. "Bryok disfigured her face when she broke her bond. He had tricked her into marriage and . . . more." Rhylen shuddered with fury. "In her drunken state, he also charmed her to vow on her younger sister's life that he would have governing power on Seren. And . . . he holds her sister's life over her still."

My jaw clenched. If I weren't so drained of magic, too horrified by my own violence, I would curse Bryok to slowly suffer in ways that would for sure get me hanged. I was so tired of females being collateral damage in the games of greedy, insecure males.

How many other girls had Bryok harmed? Threatened? Tricked?

"Do her parents know she's scorned marked by Bryok?" I croaked out. Surely, she couldn't illusion the scar away every second. "About her sister too?"

"They do," he answered soberly. "And why they consented to our betrothal. North Tribe doesn't know which male she rejected, though."

My heart was shattering for her all over again. "Her parents scorn her too?"

"Bryok love cursed her. To know love, she would need to embrace poverty. But not even the felloes of North Tribe will touch her, especially after Ren Cormac's fall." Rhylen laughed bitterly. "If she married a partner of her class or higher, they would despise her the moment the last vow was spoken."

"You would have been so kind to her," I said quietly.

Rhylen pressed his cheek to my hair. "No, lass. I would have scorn marked her in a different way."

Goosebumps fleshed down my arms. And his words from over a week ago, when up in the tree, came tumbling back with fresh sharpness.

This pain I will carry for the rest of my life. Bryok gave me a fate worse than death, worse than banishment.

Bryok knew that Rhylen and I were True Mates.

I squeezed my eyes shut as another wave of fear washed over me.

He desired for Rhylen to *always* yearn for me, even if he was bonded to another. Even if he fell in love with his Caravan fae wife, his courting magic would *always* crave me more. It would literally torment him.

And torment her too.

And if I were Bryok's mistress? Bearing him children that should be Rhylen's?

Save my da, I had never hated anyone. But I now loathed Bryok Fiachna with a fierceness that marched to war drums in my pulse. He knew what I was, knew the eternal anguish he would cause my husband and, yet . . .

The disgusting pig didn't fear my wrath quite as much as he should.

Still, I couldn't help but wonder a little also. Bryok punished Braelin—cruelly. The gods, however, redeemed her with the truest love she could know despite her curse.

Braelin's True Mate was a felly boy.

"Did Sean marry her?"

A kind smile softened Rhylen's lips. "Braelin Byrnes is now one of us."

Chapter Thirty-Four

FILENA LONAN

We grew silent after discussing Braelin. Rhylen continued to hold me tight, nuzzling his face into my hair and caressing the length of my back in soothing strokes. Raven males were exceedingly affectionate with their mates. My eyes fluttered closed and my mind began to drift.

Just when I thought I might slip back into sleep, a knock pounded on the wagon door and I squeaked a startled sound.

"Shite," Rhylen hissed under his breath.

Gently he placed me onto the bed beside him as he slipped from the covers, before scooping me up in his arms and depositing me beside Cian.

He wanted me to share a tiny bed with my *shirtless* brother?

The disgust must have played across my face because Rhylen tried to hide a humored smile despite the fear flashing in his eyes.

The knocking grew more aggressive. "Lonan, the chieftain demands you attend him!"

Cian lifted his pillow-creased head, his gaze bleary and

half-lidded. "Feck off," he mumble-shouted at the door. Noticing me beside him and the way Rhylen hovered over us both, Cian's eyes comically flew wide. "I do not consent to this kink."

"I'm being summoned, eejit," Rhylen rushed out.

"Thank the wishless falling stars." Cian started putting his pillow over his head, then froze. A half-second later, he whipped back to face Rhylen, suddenly registering what he had said. "Shite."

Another round of loud banging on the wooden door. "Lonan, open up!"

"Well, sister dear," Cian said, throwing an arm over his face, "it's showtime."

I wrinkled my nose. Did he have to choose the arm closest to me? I started to sit up and a dizzy spell hit me hard. Stars . . . I felt sick.

And scared. What would happen to Rhylen? To me?

"Better in his bed than mine if they enter the wagon, aye?" Rhylen murmured. I arched a disgruntled brow to hide the icy claws squeezing my throat, but he was right. Leaning down, Rhylen kissed my forehead, whispering, "Remember the story." Then he was striding toward the wagon front, new boots in hand, and pulled the door open a crack. "Elder Connel," he greeted, a thread of warning in his tone.

"The chieftain demands your and Filena Merrick's presence."

There was a pause. "I'll attend him, elder, but Filena needs to rest longer before work tonight. Her ankle is bruised and swollen."

"Lonan," Elder Connel began to correct but Rhylen interrupted him.

"Does he want the *fáidhbhean* to work?" Rhylen snapped. "Or for West Tribe to lose money on her final exhibitor night? It will be on his head and not mine. The tribe will not claim lost profits from me."

Another pause. "Fine, lad. Come along, then."

Rhylen peered over his shoulder at me and mouthed, "I love you"—both a confession and an apology—then left, closing the door behind him.

Silence.

But Cian's thoughts were riotously loud. My brother didn't move a muscle, as if anticipating someone might slam through the door in Rhylen's absence. I wouldn't put it past Bryok either.

A minute or so later, I started to relax. "Help me to Rhylen's bed."

"Not yet."

"Why not—"

Cian quickly sat up and moved to climb over my legs when Glenna peeked her head inside. My brother froze, his eyes locked on Glennie's, every muscle in his body coiled tight, before settling back on his heels, exhaling loudly. "I thought you were one of that pecker's arsehole fellas."

Glenna's face flamed with color. "Gran is in the . . . the woods . . . Gran . . ."

My brother finished crawling over my legs to stand on the floor—in low-hanging knickers. *Goddess save me*. I really was going to retch now. Had I not suffered enough today?

Oblivious to my scrunched-up face and Glenna's lip-biting, roving gaze, Cian grabbed a pair of trousers strewn on the floor and began pulling them up. "Gran not able to shift and fly home?" Cian asked while buttoning up and Glenna's pale complexion blushed even hotter.

"She's foraging for . . . wild onions," Glenna answered in a weirdly breathless voice.

I thought for sure my best friend and brother were already physically involved with each other. But, from the way Glenna seemed stricken by his undressed state, apparently not.

"Your visit is about . . . *onions?*"

Glenna awkwardly nodded.

Cian raked long fingers through his bed-mussed hair with a yawn. "Glenna, darlin'," he drawled in a flat voice and my best friend seemed to snap out of her trance at the mocking tone, "I was dreaming about riding that farsighted arsehole cow that has escaped thrice"—he thrust three fingers into her face—"into battle against a host of angry—"

Glenna flicked his forehead.

"Will you stop doing that?!" he practically bellowed.

"Not until you start using that big mortal brain of yours, *darlin'*." She grabbed his arm and yanked him toward the door. "Now shoo!"

"I need a shirt."

"No."

"No?"

"Go cuddle with your magical cowicorn to stay warm." Glenna swung open the door and shoved Cian outside and dropped her voice to a stage whisper. "Hear that distant battle moo? Orla's calling for you . . ."

Her words trailed off in a disapproving cluck as she took in his barely awake, rumpled state. Cocking her head to the side, she reached up to fix a messy lock of blond hair falling over Cian's eye—preening him like courting Ravens did, clearly forgetting herself—and he grabbed her wrist.

A slow, flirty smile hooked the corner of his mouth. "Glennie Lo," he said, leaning in close to her face, "you either get to play with my hair or stare at my bare chest. But not both at the same time."

Glenna rolled her eyes, yanked her hand free, and slammed the door in Cian's face.

Then bolted the lock.

"Bloody Ravens!" A muffled thunk echoed in the wagon, as if he had plopped his forehead against the door.

Glenna spun toward me, hands on her hips. "You didn't tell me."

My brows rose. "Wild onions?"

My best friend's cheeks blushed again. "Don't deflect, darlin', or I might send stale bread home with Rhylen instead of dessert. The bitter, extra seedy kind."

I sighed long and slow, exhausted, and closed my eyes for a couple of heartbeats. "I *see* futures, cake witch, not read minds."

"It's colder than a corpse's pulse outside!" Cian shouted through the door.

"Mooooo!" Glenna shouted back at Cian. Arching a perfectly sculpted black brow, she lowered onto the bed beside where I lay. That accusatory brow inched higher as she gently took my hand in hers and tapped the raven mark. "We are sworn blood *sisters* since age eleven. You tell me everything. But your hidden *Buttons* affair?"

Buttons affair? I had to bite the inside of my cheek to keep from laughing. At least she was discreet. And now Rhylen would be henceforth referred to as Buttons.

"I didn't know how to tell you about my eternal love of *Buttons*."

Her lips inched into a conspiratorial smile. The fae didn't get as emotionally twisted about things humans did. A mortal might feel grieved that I hadn't shared something as important as marrying their brother, but faeries saw the world through tricks and bargains. They married in secret all the time.

Glenna scooted off the cot and opened a drawer beneath her brother's bed and pulled out a jar. One filled with . . . My mouth fell open. He had a collection? Just for *me*? Oh my heart, I think I just fell in love with Rhylen Lonan even more.

All Ravens had favorite objects they collected. But he found buttons because I not only needed them, but because they made *me* happy. Because I first gave him one in comfort, in affection.

A stór.

My treasure.

Stars, he really had been courting me in secret for years.

And knew the pining rhythm of my beating heart.

"How did you learn about my Buttons affair?"

Glenna swept a hand toward the window right as my brother growled. "Gent of Fem—"

"Check the underside of Gran's wagon!" I shouted at Cian to hide my laughter and grimaced against the pounding ache in my head. "Barry left a gift for you!"

Muffin Moo lifted his chin but lowered his lids in a single, dismissive look. I grinned at him, the sly wee rascal. Now I wondered what other secret lives he led.

How many forest friends worked for him to thieve . . . other things?

What did he do with the gloves?

And how had we never noticed them in the undercarriage?

"Well, sister," Glenna said, curling up next to me on the cot, "Gran foraged wild spinach and dandelion greens to feed you bitter soup."

My friend tried to subtly inhale Cian's pillow and my amusement grew.

"Kissed any blond-haired, blue-eyed mortal lads lately?" My voice was falsely innocent, my expression even more so. I was in love with my best friend's brother and my best friend was in love with mine.

Glenna's face slackened into playful unamusement. "You have been cut off from my romantic life for the next day, forbidden Buttons lover." I snickered and she gave me a gentle shove. "You do look ghastly, Lena," she added, eyes narrowing. "It's not your monthlies, though. Ill, are you?"

My stomach clenched. Everything in me wanted to tell Glenna. How I needed my friend right now.

But Gran hadn't told her.

Yet, Brenna Meadows knew what had transpired today if she was making bitter soup to enrich my blood and restore my magic faster, common for female faeries during their moon cycles or . . . during critical magic drain.

As a *fáidhbhean*, it was assumed I needed blood healing during my monthlies too. I didn't. But, per usual, I let Raven Folk believe what they would to protect both me and my brother.

Where do you think your magic comes from?

Fae blood is in your veins . . .

I cleared my throat. "Rory had one too many blue mushrooms

before ending his rounds at my wagon."

Glenna propped herself up on an elbow, her eyes now sharp. "Are you injured?"

"Aye, sprained ankle. Woozy from the pain."

Her head twisted toward my swollen, bruised foot. "He attacked you?"

I winced. *No, I attacked him.*

My stomach lurched to my throat with the reminder.

"An accident when moving away from the table."

"Can you walk?"

"Barely."

"Bitter soup to speed up healing, then," she said more to herself, as if it all suddenly made sense. "Well, we need to ready you for work, aye?"

I nodded my head, too consumed with growing fear to reply.

Would I even work tonight?

Would the chieftain turn me over to the nearest village magistrate?

"Berry Barry Muffin Moo Lonan-Merrick!" Cian's muffled shout came from outside. "What kind of dirty paw operation is this?"

Barry groaned and I giggled.

I couldn't see him from where I lay. But, before I could crane my neck and tease my adorably grumpy familiar, he appeared at my side, carrying Sheila by the scruff, and gently plopped her onto the tiny pullout cot. The little hedgehog waddled over to me and licked my finger until I scooped up the wee pocket of happiness and courage and drew her close to snuggle, cheek to cheek. Peace trickled down my limbs and my pulse bolstered. Not wanting to be left out, Lloyd scampered onto the bed and cozied up at my side. And fell asleep within a twitch of his tail. That squirrel had two modes of operation: hyperactivity or comatose.

Just like my brother.

Trying—and failing—not to laugh at Barry's attempt to sweeten me up, I threw him a taunting side-eye.

"You are the fluffiest, smooshiest red rain cloud," I cooed at my fox and he turned his head away with a disgruntled chuff. "But why did you steal from Cian?"

I swore a tiny smile played at his lips.

Glenna reached over me and scratched behind Barry's ear. "Lad, what did you do to that exasperating dolt? And how much cake do you want in payment?"

The knob jangled and our heads whipped toward the door. Cian must have grabbed the spare key in Gran's wagon. A heartbeat later, he burst inside, wearing Glenna's favorite dress and carrying an armful of gloves.

Despite the pain in my head, and the dread stabbing my gut, I burst into a full cackling laugh. Glenna was howling at my side too. The thunder in my brother's eyes, first at Glenna, then at Barry, was so intense I laughed louder.

Then Glenna realized what dress he was wearing and her humor came to an abrupt stop. A bow and rosette adorned plum-hued satin gown she convinced an elf struck village lad to buy her from a used dress shop.

The dress not even I or Gran were allowed to brush or iron.

He swaggered over to us with a knowing smirk and dumped the gloves over Glenna's face. She squealed in outrage, grabbing a fistful and throwing them back at him.

"Take my dress off!" she scolded.

"You left me in the cold, barefoot and shirtless, over *onions*."

"Take. It. Off."

Cian's grin turned impish. "Darlin', take it off me."

Glenna launched herself from the bed with a growl. Cian swore under his breath and charged from the wagon.

Those two were going to kill each other in their ridiculous, endless competitions—

An image sharpened in my foggy mind.

Cian sitting on a stone wall and Glenna between his legs as she tried to apply rouge to his lips while they were laughing.

In my vision from a couple of days ago, Cian was wearing *that* dress.

Did that mean, tonight, Glenna would confess her feelings for him? And kiss him?

Yes. The word hummed inside of me. She would have sudden boldness encouraged by my and Rhylen's forbidden mate bond.

Happiness swelled in my chest.

As if summoned by my thoughts, a shadow passed by the door and then Rhylen stepped into the wagon. His eyes rounded when spotting me covered in a mound of stolen gloves and my animal familiars cuddled up to me with Barry standing guard, a glint in his yellow eyes daring Rhylen to say one word about the pilfered stash. The side of Rhylen's mouth quirked up. But my lips dipped into a frown. A wrinkle formed between my brows and I had to force myself to breathe. He didn't look distressed. Still . . .

"The chieftain sends his apologies and well wishes," he said quietly. Scooting a couple of gloves to the side, he lowered himself beside me. "He agreed you were owed three coins too. Apparently, it wasn't the first time Rory had tried to trick other wage-earning female mortal slaves. Or"—Rhylen paused to dangle that one word a heavy beat—"consumed blue mushrooms while on the job."

My mouth parted. "Cian knew."

Rhylen slowly nodded his head. Then, my husband leaned down and gently kissed my lips, murmuring, "The chieftain gave me permission to sit with you tonight, too."

Relief flooded me and a knotted breath in my chest loosened. I wasn't sure his company, in his post-bond territorial state, was the best decision, however. Especially given the amount of strangers who would interact with me. Unless . . . "I need a bargain from you, mate."

"Lena, you only have to ask me for—"

"For the duration of my last shift tonight, you will not interfere with my work so long as I am not in actual danger." Wary surprise sparked in his gaze. But fae couldn't resist bargains. It was woven into the very fabric of their being, so I continued. "You will not react to non-physical threats or comfort me should I *see* a difficult vision. You will only step in if a customer becomes physically violent."

A scowl deepened between his brows. "If I agree to your bargain?"

"I won't interfere when you challenge Bryok, no matter how much my . . . magic will want to." My voice caught, the reminder that I could curse another still raw. Rhylen's gaze sharpened on me, noting every nuance of conflicting emotion flitting across my face. To lighten the mood, I tossed him a half-smile and added, "And I won't publicly call you Buttons."

"Buttons?" Reluctant humor twisted his beautiful lips.

I tapped his nose. "I reserve the right to do so in private, though."

His smile faltered and he drew in a tight breath.

"Please, Rhy," I asked softly. "Make this bargain with me."

He kissed me, his lips possessively lingering on mine for several long, anguishing seconds before he murmured, "You slay me with your request. But I can deny you nothing, *mo shíorghrá*. Aye, I agree to your bargain."

My body relaxed. "Tell me our chieftain was eager to appease you."

He leaned away just enough to see my face. "Oh aye, very eager, he was."

"Poor gov," I cooed, "afraid of a felly boy's fury."

The smug tilt to Rhylen's smile flamed in my racing pulse.

Sweet moons, he was so pretty it ached.

If I were not hanging on by a fraying thread or ready to kick Cian's ankle in gratitude, I would sink my fingers in Rhylen's silky black strands and lose myself as he slowly unraveled beneath my touch. Just the reminder of his breathy moans, the way his tongue danced with mine to the thrusting rhythm of his body, the feel of hard muscle beneath my fingertips—

I forced my mind to a screeching halt.

Stars, I could barely sit up without help let alone do anything else.

To distract myself, I lifted a glove and faced Barry. "We'll discuss this later." Then to Rhylen, "Help me to the cook pot."

I had one night of work left before we set up camp for the winter months ahead. And Gran had lovingly prepared me bitter soup.

But even as Rhylen carried me outside, and as Gran kissed my head and caressed my cheek, and as the chieftain's apology settled warmly in my frightened bones, the dread didn't go away.

I was injured.

And the Blackthorn vision had yet to come to pass.

Chapter Thirty-Five

RHYLEN LONAN

Filena swayed slightly and my muscles stiffened, ready to spring from my chair to catch her if she blacked out. Several hours had passed since the market's final night opened. Tomorrow was the mass wedding and The Wild Hunt.

Until participating in the mating rituals this week, I didn't fully understand how the primal need to hunt for a mate would consume me. The intensity of courting magic was a drug I craved and fought in turn. The Wild Hunt was a wedding game West Tribe sponsored to honor this very ancestral magic—and for Ravens to secretly mock males who weren't pretty enough to attract a bride. The whole event, though, was packaged around the story of hunting Torc Triath to appease mortal laws.

The Hunt disgusted me. Perhaps if I wasn't raised beside mortals as my equals or a True Mate with one, my fae nature wouldn't care and would probably find it all entertaining. But fae males hunting unwanted indentured women in the woods to mark as a slave or bride was vile to me.

Filena shook her rune staves and gently tossed them to the table, bringing my mind back to the present.

Lloyd, who had curled up on my shoulder a candlemark earlier, squeaked a yawn and I forced myself to relax. The rose quartz Lena had gifted me rolled between my fingers, back and forth, back and forth. Normally I didn't fidget with objects, not like my wife, but I was too wound tight from watching her endure these past few hours in pain, in exhaustion, using up what little magic stores she possessed after Gran's bitter soup.

It seemed like every little thing was setting me off lately. The only time I felt right, felt any kind of inner-balance, was when I was holding Filena while we slept. She belonged in my arms, with her heart pressed to mine.

Filena's fingers brushed over the ogham rune staves scattered across the table and rested on two with runes facing up. "Does your love have a small scar above his left brow, pet?"

"Aye, his brother hit him with a rock on accident when younger." A woman, with earthen brown hair and olive skin, absently rubbed at the place above her heart and choked out on a whisper, "Will he survive the war?"

"He's alive," Filena answered, but I could hear the slight tremble in her voice. "Carran is sending his unit to an uncharted area of The Wilds in the spring."

The woman's expression of hope fell. "Will . . . will he . . ."

"Write him a letter and include a lock of your hair." Lena reached over the table and gave the woman's hand a gentle squeeze. "It will give him courage until he sees you again, pet."

"Thank you, *fáidhbhean*." The woman stood up and dipped her head with a wobbly smile.

347

Filena crumpled the moment the woman disappeared behind the curtained door. Her shoulders shook and she furiously swiped at tears beneath the black veil covering her face. I wanted to scoop her up, but she made my territorial arse promise not to interfere except if she were in actual danger, not the threat. Or coddle her from the pain of any vision the gods willed her to *see*.

And it was killing me.

Barry, who was not under any such bargain, however, eyed me with smug glee as he laid his head on Filena's lap. Her hand stroked behind his ears and he purred, not for her, though. The lad had been attempting, quite humorously, to make me suffer for outing his secret.

But I also knew the rest of his secret.

I knew exactly what the gloves were for and why I pretended to be outraged by his little acts of joyous retribution.

Barry's yellow eyes flicked to mine, to see if I were still watching. I narrowed mine in reply, then clenched my jaw for added mock-angry fun. A how-dare-you-touch-my-woman look the furry lad ate up. Believing me pissed, he happily chuffed and buried his head into her waist to encourage her to pet down his back.

"He will be slain." Filena's voice was so quiet, I almost missed it over the crackle of the wood stove. "A blue-haired male the wild fae call *Bogha Báistí Cáelen* either kills him or tries to save him. I couldn't tell. But . . . but I *saw* him die. He was clutching a letter with tomorrow's date and kissed a lock of brown hair before his last breath."

Bogha Báistí Cáelen.

Slender Bow of Rain.

A water spirit name.

My heart sank. How often did she *see* the death of another's loved one? Or *saw* other sorrows? She rarely spoke of her visions. Not that she should. Those futures were private moments owned by others.

He's alive.

Write him a letter.

It will give him courage.

Filena had always been a clever creature. But, as I recalled the words she gave the woman, the depth of her riddling skills had never seemed as sharp to me.

. . . until he sees you again . . . in the Otherworld.

Did she comfort people like this often?

I didn't feel the slightest twinge of pity over a mortal who slaughtered the fae or stole our lands and doused our magic. But I could sense, to Filena, it wasn't about if the young man was deserving of death for his crimes against innocents, but how his dying would shatter the heart of a mortal who couldn't imagine a future without him.

The beauty of my wife's kindness struck me hard—often. Not that I wasn't capable of kindness or compassion, regardless of race. But, right now, her humanity confused me. I didn't understand this mortal act of mercy just shown. As fae, I wasn't sure I could ever fully understand.

She was allowing a man who had stolen the happiness of so many to have one moment of happiness before he breathed his last and all to comfort one woman. I could hear Lena's humanity now argue that the lass was not responsible for her lover's crimes. But, to the fae, the man made his choice. To knowingly, intentionally kill an innocent was to invite a curse. For his love to forever feel the unbearable, tearing pain he had forced others to suffer was only fair in the eyes of the Folk.

I desired to understand Filena's duality. The human nature that showed compassion to those deserving of a curse her fae side would just as easily make. My mate was the richest riddle. But, right now, that overly gracious compassionate nature of hers mercilessly dug into the fury writhing just beneath my skin. She wasted much-needed magic to show kindness to the very mortals who would see her hanged for being a *cailleach*. For possessing the blood of gods. The same gods they worshipped.

I curled my fist around the rose quartz and exhaled slowly. Whoever Bogha Báistí Cáelen was to the wild fae, I hoped he ended that soldier's life.

Filena straightened her shoulders—wincing when adjusting her foot's position—then lifted her chin and cleared her throat.

"Enter!"

An older gent stepped into the wagon. In the low candlelight, shadows danced across his neatly combed white hair and weathered skin grooved by age and years of labor. He lifted a corner of his mouth, a friendly look, until he spotted me and the smile slipped. I tilted my head in silent greeting and . . . warning.

Touch my mate and I'll crush your brittling bones.

No mercy. No kindness.

"Sit, pet," Filena said and gestured to the chair across from her. When the old man lowered himself into the seat, she asked, "Cards or runes?"

Barry slipped into the shadows beside me.

I placed a hand onto his back and whispered low, "Good, lad."

The fox side-eyed me suspiciously.

"One card," the man answered.

"Two coins, pet."

I leaned in closer to Barry. "I saw you deliver a pair of gloves to a wee orphan slave in a tattered dress. The new foster, aye?"

Barry turned big yellow eyes my way.

"What answer do you seek?" Filena asked the older man.

"You have a good heart, lad," I continued. "But Gran knitted Cian's gloves. Tease Cian all you like, feck, I'll join you, but don't cause an ancient grief, aye?"

Barry lowered his head in apology.

"Looking fer a girl," the older man answered and the hairs down my arms rose. "About yer age or so, lass. She ran away from home a couple of years ago. Her poor mam's keening soul, she's worried herself sick, she has."

Both Barry and I snapped to attention.

"What is your question, pet?"

Filena's voice was stronger than I had heard it all night, the only clue that she, too, was fighting animal fight-or-flight instincts.

The man lifted a corner of his mouth in a grandfatherly look that was both sad and sweet. The type of fake smile meant to invite pity. From the subtle way he shifted in the chair, he could feel the heat of my stabbing gaze. But he kept his eyes pinned only on Filena's shadowed, veiled form.

My wife.

He was studying *my* wife.

"Does the girl still live?" he asked.

Filena placed a black lace fingerless gloved-hand on her mam's tree oracle cards and tapped once. Twice. A move I learned was to hide her trembling. Slowly, she pulled a card off the top and turned it over.

Fearn, the ogham rune for Alder.

The celestial Tree of Ravens, strength, and shields.

The pop of wood in the stove echoed in the small space. The air tightened, a taught string that would snap if plucked.

"Does she have a chipped front tooth? The right one?"

The man's eyes rounded slightly. "She does."

"Aye, she lives, pet."

"Where is she?" he asked, his voice catching.

"That was not your question." Filena opened her hand. "A coin per question."

He leaned back in his chair and pulled out a coin. "Then I ask ye this, lass." He pressed the money into her palm. "Is she safe?"

Filena removed her hand and tucked the coin into the pouch fastened to her chair. "Tell her mam she is safe and . . . happy too. Tending chickens."

"She loves chickens." His body deflated and he scrubbed a hand down his face in relief. "Thank ye, lass." Scooting the chair back, he rose and left the wagon.

The silence that followed roared in my thundering ears.

Was that all a ruse?

Did Filena trick him in return?

"The lass's brother has a wicked temper," she whispered to me over her shoulder. "The girl is an indentured with East Tribe now, using a different name."

And tending to their chickens.

My shoulders unclenched, my jaw too. The Tree of Ravens card made sense now.

"I thought—"

"I know, Rhy." Her voice was tired. "His face is viciously etched into my memory."

Words that were meant to reassure me, but it only made me more furious. "He was *staring* at you, Lena."

"That's what eyes do, *Rhylee Lo*," she said with a half-snort.

"No, he was staring at you like a male wanting to dominate a female."

"Or a man who is losing his sight in his older years and trying to focus on the mystical *fáidhbhean* before him." She sighed. "I'm a curiosity to some and intimidating to others."

I gritted my teeth. "Then why did you feel fear? Why did your fingers start to tremble?"

She was quiet a long heartbeat. "Because I *fear* what the gods will show me and *fear* they won't. Girls run away for two reasons. For safety or for love." My heart grew heavy once more. Lena was one of those girls. "And if I do not see an answer?" she continued. "The burden I bear all night long is . . . exhausting."

Her body swayed slightly and she gripped the table.

And the building fury inside of me snapped.

"Fecking stars, I want to close down this wagon right now and—"

"Darlin'," she cooed over her shoulder, "break our bargain and I'll clean the horses' teeth with your toothbrush."

My brows shot up.

"Then tie you to your bed and tickle you with your own feathers."

I threw my head back with a loud laugh, startling Lloyd, who leapt from my shoulder to my lap. "And after you torture me with my own feathers?"

She partially lifted her veil. A wicked little smile curled her lips and an entirely different fire heated my rushing blood.

"Tempting." I winked.

Gods, she was going to be the death of me tonight.

But only one night left—of work, of our five-day bargain period.

At sunset tomorrow, marking Samhain Eve, while I stood beneath the Truth Telling Tree with Braelin, my and Filena's raven mate bond would become unmovable.

And the next day? I would destroy Bryok and begin the new year with a future that would set me and Filena free. Set others free too.

Filena reached for her oracle cards, her black veil now in place. Drawing in a deep breath, she exhaled slowly. Lifted her chin. And then said to the next person waiting in line, "Enter!"

The curtain parted and my wife went deathly still.

My eyes whipped to the large, bearded silhouette in the doorway.

Oh. Feck. No.

He was *not* allowed to speak to her.

Baring my canines, my wings snapped open as I shot to my feet. Candles sputtered out around Filena's table.

"Fáiléanna," her da greeted her but with cold, bleary eyes locked onto mine. And, when they drifted to hers, violent shadows gathered in my raging pulse. He lifted two copper coins in the air. "Read me a card, daughter."

Chapter Thirty-Six

FILENA LONAN

A woman with blonde hair is running through the nightfall woods. I can't see her face, only the back of her head. She lifts a hand to grip a branch while stepping over a large stone. A strange iron bracelet catches the moonlight. No, not a bracelet. A cuff. There's a keyhole. I can feel her panic as she searches the underbrush. Fog is freezing in the air and she doesn't wear a coat or cloak. Bruises mottle her arms. She slides to a stop beside a hollowed-out log, clapping a hand over her mouth.

And then I see her face.

A sharp breath wheezed in my lungs.
Reality flashed back into sight.
My fingers were clawing into the table.
I didn't recall falling into a vision. Stars, my heart, it

was trying to beat through my rib cage. A dizzy spell floated through my head. I was on the verge of retching.

"*Fáidhbhean*," Rhylen growled.

I twisted to meet his eyes over my shoulder. All traces of the playful, affectionate, brooding faerie boy I fell in love with were gone. In his place was a dark, primal creature of fae with talons for fingers, sharp canines, and dark purple eyes bright and reflective in the dim light cast by a single remaining lit candle. His glorious black wings took up most of the wagon's back, the black feathers shimmering midnight blue as he shifted impatiently on his feet.

"Release me from my bargain." The deep timbre of his growling voice rumbled through me.

At first, I didn't understand what he was asking me. What bargain? My eyes moved toward the doorway and bile crept up my throat.

I opened my mouth to reply but a sob squeezed my throat shut.

Mam.

I *saw* Mam. She was alive.

Why was she wearing a cuff? It didn't look like a manacle used to cart away criminals either.

As I gaped at my da, Rhylen's plea faded back into my mind. I wasn't in any actual danger *yet*, only threatened. But, mostly, I feared what Rhylen would do if I released him from the bargain. I didn't have the energy to fight either. And, so, I made a split decision I would probably later regret.

"Sit, pet."

Rhylen hissed a breath behind me.

I spoke those two words hundreds, thousands of times

each year. But, this time, I spoke them to protect my husband. I would do anything to protect him, as I promised. Even protect Rhylen from himself.

But, dying suns, how my body was shaking right now. How my stomach wanted to heave up every horror I had endured as a child because of this man.

Hamish stumbled toward my table, a smug curl to his lips and his lower jaw sporting a bruise. From Cian? The man was completely and utterly unafraid of Rhylen too. Magic was rippling off my husband, a commanding, dominating power that I now knew was the awakening of elder magic the top govs carried. He hadn't won a formal issued challenge yet and already the gods favored him. But combined with his newly bonded primal state? He was combustive.

Wisps of smoke twisted into the air around me from the snuffed-out candles. I needed an occupation to gather my wits before facing my da. Plucking a taper from a holder, I angled the wick into the one still lit until it caught flame. A small burst of light spilled into the space. I continued to light other candles, my hands shaking.

A quiet violence simmered beneath Da's calm.

I lowered the final taper, then tapped the table in a gesture to leave the coins. Normally I had fortune seekers place them into my palm. But this man wouldn't touch me.

Da forcefully plunked the money where I indicated.

"What answer do you seek, pet?" I asked, surprised by the steadiness of my voice.

His ill-humored chuckle pricked tears behind my eyes.

That sound.

I remembered that soft, mocking laugh right before he

would strike. And suddenly I was ten-years-old, hiding beneath the table all over again, hoping, praying, that he wouldn't see me in his temper. That my brother had escaped through the back door, still too weak from the last beating. That my mam . . . gods, my mam . . .

I bit back a whimper and forced myself to remain ram-rod straight.

"Will me daughter save her waste of a pansy brother?"

He threatened to sell me to a Molly house on Seren if I didn't turn you over to him.

Closing my eyes in a long blink, I swallowed thickly and pushed back the rising tide of terror building inside my icing pulse. But not even the empty well of magic could drain my body of the gathering fury. Cian was a beautiful, strong, intelligent man who brought mischief and happiness to everyone around him. These past ten years, he was my rock and shield and laughter. I owed him my life.

No, the *only* pathetic coward in our family was Hamish MacCullough.

Warm tingles flowed to my fingers, a sensation I recognized from when facing off with Bryok, when standing up to Rory. Words drenched in spellcraft danced for release on the tip of my tongue. The ache of magic loss swirled in my head, though. Dizziness swam vengeful circles down my body. Black blurred the edges of my vision. Still, I shuffled the deck, then fanned the cards over the table.

"Choose one. But do not touch the card."

My voice carried a supernatural quality that filled every nook and cranny of this drafty old wagon. Hamish's bloodshot, bleary eyes lifted to study my veiled face.

"Those are Moira's cards, minnow," Da said, using Mam's term of affection for me, and I shivered.

"Choose."

"Ye can't coerce me, witch." He pushed up his shirt sleeve and my mouth parted. An intricate tattoo of berries and leaves wrapped around his wrist. "Rowan." His grin widened. "Made from rowan berry ink, it is. Got it shortly after marrying Moira."

I didn't recall these markings as a child. But I also tried not to look at him.

"Know how I found ye, daughter?"

I clenched my jaw. "If you do not choose a card, *pet*, then you will leave."

"Daughter—"

"—I am *not* your daughter."

He leaned back in his chair with another harsh laugh.

I preferred him sloshing drunk, when all he did was yell and slurred belligerent cruelties at us. But when more sober than not? Like now? That was when he truly became violent.

The coiling snake of hatred in his cold steel gaze leveled on me. "Ye cost me everything, ye whoring witch." Spittle flew from his mouth and I winced. "When ye didn't return, yer husband seized the cabin in payment and put a bounty on me head, he did." He leaned in and lowered his voice. "Five years, *daughter*. I have searched fer ye fer *five years*."

Horror welled up inside of me.

That disgusting old man was still alive? Or did he speak only of the past?

Behind me, Rhylen's breath was ragged. I could feel the heat pouring from his blistering fury. But he held to our bargain. This was my fight, anyway. My monster to slay—

My thoughts skidded to a hard stop.

Flickering candlelight glinted off one of the coins he deposited onto the table. Where did he find the money for a card reading? For drink this week too?

My gaze narrowed on the doorway.

Remember, Fáiléanna, I know all your secrets.

Was Bryok out there listening?

I couldn't reason how else Da had coin enough for a card reading.

Bryok knew Rhylen was sitting with me tonight too. Killing a mortal market guest was *not* how to earn West Tribe's support after defeating Bryok . . . if he could challenge the prince before being tried for murder by the local village first.

A knowing tug pulled on my gut.

That was exactly what Bryok wanted: for Rhylen to lose complete control of his faculties, but on Hamish before he could on Bryok.

Another trickle of magic pulsed down my arms and pain bleated in my head. The wood floor beneath Rhylen's boots creaked. I threw out a hand in a silent plea to stay back.

"Would ye deny yer da or sell Cillian to Seren, minnow?" my da taunted. "Let's see what yer mam's card predict, aye?"

He pointed to a card.

Another ripple of defensive magic stirred in me and I had to force myself to remain upright. Rhylen growled, a low plea at me, a warning to Hamish. The guttural sound was like a cannon shot to my head. My body was fighting to remain conscious. The *cailleach* side of me warring with my mortal limitations. But I pulled the card Hamish indicated, my grip steady despite my rapidly declining state, and flipped it over.

Straif.

The Blackthorn.

The tree of death and suffering.

The wagon tilted and spun. Then I was slipping from my chair as the last of my strength faded to darkness.

Chapter Thirty-Seven

RHYLEN LONAN

I barged past that pig slop, Filena limp in my arms. Red—that's all I could see.

The blood I wanted to spill stained my vision.

I ducked past the curtain into the still dark early morning, barely able to squeeze through with my wings still out and my mate nestled against me. The man I regretfully left alive in the wagon was shouting at my back, his words unintelligible in my rage.

To no surprise, Bryok loitered at the bottom of the stairs, his dark eyes fixed onto Lena. "Magic loss?" His tone conveyed concern, but his gaze glittered with satisfaction.

"Feck off," I hissed under my breath.

"Felly—"

"Grab the night's coins before your pet does."

I didn't slow to see if he followed my directive.

Gasps at the sight of Filena, followed by shocked whispers, murmured down the long line of attendees who awaited their fortunes. Then regular market attendees who openly gaped as I stormed past. I ignored them. I ignored everyone, including that traitorous pecker who now trailed behind me.

I made a promise to Filena. One I planned to honor though it killed me.

Filena was no longer working. The stipulation of her bargain, however, bound me to the duration of her last shift. And she was, technically, still on the clock.

But something feral writhed just beneath my skin.

A magic of shadows and light, of earth and wind and water and fire. I felt more akin to a wild fae from the Greenwood than a mere Raven Folk Traveler.

My boots ate up the ground as I marched toward our wagon. I could fly, but it was against Caravan rules during an open market. The wind our large wings created was hazardous. Objects gusted off tables; lanterns snapped from branches.

In my periphery, a train of black lace from the back of Filena's headpiece fluttered in the breeze of my movement. The rustling skirt layers of knitted black lace and satin too. I peered down at my wife and the protective beast coiling around my hammering heart constricted. The front of her veil covered her face down past the neckline hem of her bodice, held in place by a band of two black peonies that covered each ear. Long, wavy auburn hair spilled over my arms and bounced with my furious strides.

I started to look away when Sheila poked her wee nose from a skirt pocket. I nearly startled, forgetting about Lena's familiars. A tiny smile touched my lips at the scrap of blue ribbon tied behind the hedgehog's ear. Her mam's ribbon. I quickly peered around for Barry and Lloyd. But they could easily find their way back to our wagons.

"Felly," Bryok's voice slithered behind me. "A word with you."

The threadbare strip of relief Sheila gave me dissipated.

My jaw clamped until my teeth ached. But I didn't break stride.

"Stop and face me, felly," he demanded.

A growl lodged in my throat. But it was no use. He would dog my steps until I acknowledged him. Not to mention, if I acted like a territorial male in his mate bond period, he would grow suspicious—and exploit my primal state until the courting magic blinded me in a possessive rage. More so than I was already feeling, that is.

The success of this evening depended on my ability to control myself. Barry protected me from curses, but Braelin was vulnerable. Sean too.

I pivoted on my heel and charged Bryok, teeth bared, wings out. He peddled back a few steps until I was within inches of his face, my thundering gaze pinned to his. Dark strands of my hair blew across my face in a chilly breeze. The beads and charms clinked in the electrified silence sitting heavy between us. This close, I could smell the rosemary scent of Bryok's soap, the ale on his breath, and revulsion shuddered through me.

I adjusted Filena in my arms and pressed her tight to my body. "Sire?" I scraped out, aware of the curious, whispering passersby as well as the middle-rank hawkers within earshot.

"You are invited into the groom's tent this early afternoon. No charge." Shifting on his feet, Bryok cocked his head and lifted a smug corner of his mouth. "Bring your lads to attend you."

An ill-humored snort left me. "Oh aye and owe West Tribe

a favor for this generous offer?" I clenched my teeth and gritted, "I've sacrificed enough, you'll not trick me into another."

"No tricks or bargains." The words were delivered amicably but the smile was baiting. "A favor owed you from the elders for performing your duty for the good of the tribe."

"Why would the elders ask *you* to act as messenger to *me*?"

Bryok leaned in and lowered his voice. "You are a disgusting, uncivilized animal, Lonan. I could strip you again for not lowering your eyes. I could banish you for allowing your slave to disrespect me before all the tribes. Sharing a tent with a rutting felly is not what us gents want. And yet, here I am, delivering you an invitation." His black eyes rested on where he had cut my braid. Then, in a soft blink, his gaze lazily drifted down the length of Filena's veiled form. My muscles flexed. "Don't insult the elders, Lonan," he whispered, "or my fellas will personally deliver this invitation to you too."

Bryok spun on his heel, took two steps—and paused. Over his shoulder, he added, "The card reading planned for the lottery couples is canceled. I wouldn't want the *fáidhbhean* to . . . *bite my ear off* for disregarding her delicate state." Our eyes locked for a fleeting second, then he strode in the opposite direction. Back toward Filena's divination wagon and that mortal pig.

I loosed a ragged breath. I nearly lost it when his gaze slowly roamed over my wife.

After tomorrow, he would never look at her again.

After tomorrow, I would never look at him again either.

"Rhylen?" Owen said, pushing through the crowd, Corbin and Sean at his side. "What happened?"

I drew in a slow breath and blinked back the anger. "She's

been woozy and exhausted over the sprained ankle." The lads nodded their heads, as if that made perfect sense. I started walking and they fell in line around me. "The elders invited me to the groom's tent this afternoon."

"A felly?" Corbin asked. "When have they ever allowed us fellys in *there*? Not that we could afford it."

Sean's brows drew together. "More like when have the elders ever given a hawk's arse about us fellys? Slaves get more attention than us lowly Folk."

"A favor owed for my sacrifice to the tribe," I answered, but Sean was right. The gift both made no sense and seemed too gracious. "I was told to bring my lads to attend me. No charge."

Owen grinned. "Do we get to eat the food too?"

Corbin, however, grimaced in mild disgust. "You want us to bathe you? And clean your wings?"

I rolled my eyes. "Kiss my arse too."

"Well, if I get to kiss your pretty feathered arse," Corbin said with a mocking wink.

"What favor do the middle-rank lottery lads receive from the elders?" Sean asked.

My brows knitted together. It was another fair question.

"I suppose we'll find out, aye?" Owen said.

"Aye," Corbin agreed. "Suppose so."

Our steps slowed at the edge of the woods, just beyond the outskirts of the market. The felly and slave wagons weren't too far on foot. But I preferred to fly at this point. "See you this afternoon, lads."

My boys replied with a single nod, then casually stepped back as I leapt into the air.

When I landed, Cian was leaning against our wagon and staring up at the stars, still in Glenna's dress and smoking a cigarette. A smudge of fading rouge smeared the corner of his lips, his hair messier than usual. I would crack a smile if I weren't still fighting with my self-control.

"I didn't think she'd last this long," he murmured, blowing out a stream of smoke. "Poor wee lamb."

I sighed. "The elders invited me into the groom's tent."

Cian's brow furrowed. "What's the catch?"

"Aye," I said with a dark chuckle. "Bryok assured me there were no tricks or bargains. A favor owed by the elders for my sacrifice."

"You believe the elders care?"

"I believe they want to keep me happy for now."

Cian slowly nodded his head, lifting the cigarette to his mouth and puffed a long drag. "Darlin'," he said, the smoke curling from his mouth bright in the moonlight, "they're afraid of *her*."

My pulse stuttered.

Did the elders believe Rory's claim despite their apologies to me?

I wouldn't want the fáidhbhean *to . . . bite my ear off . . .*

The hair on the back of my neck stood on end. Or was Bryok just pecking at my mind? He didn't act possessive of her during our conversation either. Not like in days past. Though, perhaps, his mate bond with Doireann redirected his obsessive behavior. Unless that, too, was a trick.

Muscles down my body flexed. "A certain drunkard visited the wagon for a reading." Cian's cigarette paused mid-lift. "When you're done, let's talk inside," I said and took a step toward Gran's wagon.

The door swung open before I reached the last step and Glenna first looked at Lena with growing horror, then me. "You stood outside talking with Cian while holding her in this state?"

I rolled my eyes. "I plan to hold her inside while talking to Cian too. How is that any different than now?"

My sister humorously eyed me and drolled, "Not looking like an insensitive brute. You think Lena wants to dangle in your arms while you make social calls?"

I shifted my wings away to angle past Glenna, sliding her a wry smile as I moved into the small living space. Gran was curled up asleep on the pull-out cot, insistent that Glenna and Lena share the big bed in the back. Gently, I lowered Lena atop the thin covers and began unfastening her bodice. Glenna sidled beside me and untied her skirts. Between the two of us, we stripped my wife down to her camisole and petticoats for better comfort.

"You can sleep in my wagon tonight," I whispered.

"Why not sleep—"

"Because it's easier on Gran and I need her assistance with Lena."

Glenna nodded her head. "Aye, true."

Cian crept in and tip-toed his way around Gran as I crawled onto the bed and gathered Lena into my arms once more. When he reached the bed, I quickly explained everything to Glenna in low whispers. Filena would need her tomorrow and I didn't want my mate to feel like she had to hide anything from our sister.

Glenna's dark eyes rounded as she gaped at Lena. "She actually cursed Rory?"

Cian lifted a finger to his lips as a reminder to lower her voice.

"Extra slices of comfort cake, it is," she tossed out with a nervous, disbelieving laugh.

I was grateful she wasn't offended for just now learning. Though, I knew she wouldn't be. We fae didn't usually get upset over withheld information like this. Especially dangerous secrets. Glenna took Filena's hand in hers and then nodded for me to carry on.

I continued, describing the events with Hamish MacCullough. Cian's face darkened; a muscle worked back and forth along his jaw and the tendons along his neck tightened.

"In a moment of idiocy," I whispered, "he confessed that her contracted husband put a bounty on his head. Cian—"

"On it," he gritted out.

"On what?" Glenna asked, looking between us.

Cian whispered close to Glenna's ear, "Alert the authorities in the local village later today."

"While I'm in the groom's tent, go," I continued. "Slaves weren't invited. People will be too busy to notice your absence then. Plus leaving will keep you safe," I added, "should Bryok try anything while I'm distracted in the tent."

"Aye."

"But not completely safe." I removed the illusion over the second raven mark on my wrist, the one I had kept hidden since I married Filena. Then I grabbed Cian's hand and whispered under my breath, "I release Cian Merrick from indentured servitude to me,

363

my family, and to West Tribe. His debts are paid in full."

The master mark finally faded from my skin. The slave mark on his too.

"Rhylen—" The sheer panic in Cian's eyes startled me. "You'd cast me away?"

"No, brother." I released his wrist to cup his face. "You're my family, not my slave."

"How can you afford to purchase me back?"

"There'll be no need after tomorrow." I pulled him close until we were both leaning over Filena, our foreheads pressed together. "When I'm chieftain, mortals can work for my Night Market without indenturing themselves. Plus," I said and paused a beat, then reemphasized, "you're my *family*."

Would ye deny yer da or sell Cillian to Seren, minnow?

My thoughts slowed before spinning into a memory.

I was twelve when Cillian MacCullough arrived in West Tribe at thirteen. Bruises had mottled part of his face and arms. But he stood in front of his sister, to protect her when speaking to the elders. When speaking the name Cian Merrick, his steel gray eyes sharp and unafraid. He had wrapped a comforting, protective arm around Lena's tiny shoulders as they walked to our wagon—now our purchased slaves—whispering reassurances in her ear. "We're finally free, *Filena* . . ."

A single tear slid down Cian's cheek. "Don't abandon me," he whispered.

"Never," I whispered back. "I couldn't imagine a life without you in it, Cian Merrick."

Glenna circled her arms around Cian's waist and kissed his cheek. "You're *ours*, Lady of Man."

He sniffed back his tears and straightened, pulling away from me. A corner of his mouth tilted up in a familiar impish smile. "Well, Gent of Fem, as my first act as a free man, I'll select the perfect pair of George-thieved gloves to wear, the wee bastard."

"You'll need help, lad," Glenna replied, yanking him toward to the door. "No one should save their reputation alone."

"Aye," he said with a serious nod of his head. "Respectable ladies don't flash their bare wrist around town. I'm no hussy."

"Maybe a little bit of one."

Cian's mouth fell open. "That was hurtful."

"You're right." Glenna shoved him out of the door. "You're all hussy."

"Thank you."

Cian shut the door behind them and I blew out a slow breath.

The immediate silence wrapped around me. My thoughts, however, were loud. I leaned my head back against the wall and studied the knotted patterns on the ceiling.

Tomorrow would test every shred of patience I possessed.

A banshee wail of wind howled outside. A low keening cry that ripped through the trees and tumbled with the decaying leaves. The veil between the mortal plane and the Otherworld was thinning, the Harvest Moon above now full. And, from the sounds of it, an autumn storm brewed as the sun began to rise.

I stretched out beside my wife and tucked her in close to me.

At sunset, the spirits of our ancestors would walk among us.

At sunset, Filena Lonan would become eternally bound to me.

Chapter Thirty-Eight

RHYLEN LONAN

Scented hot water lapped against my flushing skin. Around me, other West Tribe grooms sat in copper tubs surrounded by their attendants. Boughs of woven fall leaves and berries dipped and swooped across the ceiling above, dotted by lanterns. The purple, dark-red, and gold striped canvas walls of the tent, decorated with artfully placed branches, flickered in golds and ambers beneath the candlelight.

This was, by far, one of the oddest experiences of my life.

The baths, the grooming tools given to each party, the tables laden with meats, cheeses, fruit, ale, and mead . . . overwhelmed me.

One moment, I wanted to raze this tent to the ground for the opulence while fellys and slaves lived on so little. The next breath, I fell into the exotic wonder of it all. I hardly paid attention to the privileges of middle-rank and gov males. What was the point? Our lives were so enormously different, the list of comparisons too grand.

But most of all, I couldn't fathom the upfront costs. Even with fees to enter, how did West Tribe afford this extravagance year after year? *This* year?

Owen dipped his fingers into the tub, pulling me from my thoughts, then flicked water at me. I splashed water back at him and he jumped back with a laugh.

"Want to join me?" I asked with a flirty smile.

"I will," Corbin volunteered with a teasing grin of his own.

"What's it like?" Owen asked.

I leaned my head back on the edge of the tub. "Like the time we snuck away to the mineral hot springs."

"A dream then," Owen said with a sigh.

"I thought foreman would pluck our feathers," Corbin muttered with a quiet laugh.

Sean looked up from where he was brushing dirt from the skirted wrap, the one I had worn at the Fire Dance, and grimaced. "Our fate was far worse, lads."

We were on call that open market night five years ago. A tent partially collapsed. The main day crew was asleep. And we, the on-call night crew, were swimming in hidden hot springs we had discovered earlier that afternoon when gathering firewood. Cian had lifted jugs of wine from mortals at the pub wagons and we were well into our cups before we were discovered.

Stars, Gran was livid.

But foreman was spitting feathers. The lot of us, aged sixteen to eighteen, were required to empty the visitor latrines for a whole month—in addition to our regular setup and break down work. I thought we'd always smell like shite.

I sighed. I wished my boys could experience a bath too.

Fellys didn't have copper tubs. We heated water in a cook pot and bathed in rivers. Or lathered up in heavy rainstorms with scraps of soap. This was the first time in my twenty-two years I had sat in a proper bath and it was strangely embarrassing and relaxing.

But suns above, I would give my left wing to gift Filena a copper tub. To watch my wife bathe . . . I could moan.

My eyes drifted closed and I tried to steady my breathing. But the familiar unease fisted in my chest. It didn't help that I was grooming for a bride who wasn't my wife.

Separating from Filena, for any reason, set me on edge. My heart was so wildly in love, just the slightest glimpse of her smile, her riot of hair, the freckles sprinkling her skin, sent me spinning. I couldn't stop touching her, never wanted to stop holding her. Gods, I craved her to distraction. Even now, I could feel the ghost of her lips on mine, on my skin.

I had to force myself from the bed before she woke, if she woke this night. Who knew how much rest the magic loss demanded. I then left her in Gran's and Glenna's care to see Cian off and to meet up with the boys.

I wasn't sure if Filena would be strong enough to see me stand beneath the Truth Telling Tree this night. But, as I prepared myself, I thought only of her.

Would she find me arousing? Would she feel honored by the care and attention given to pretty up for her pleasure?

"Sir," a voice said at my side and my eyes fluttered open. A mortal slave knelt with a tray, his gaze downcast, as if I weren't a felly. "Your adornments."

An array of feathers, twigs, berries, leaves, ribbons, and beads spread across the platter. Raven Folk males were considered the most beautiful of all the fae, from the way we decorated our hair, the cosmetics we wore to accent our eyes, the elaborate tattoos we inked into our skin, to the jewelry that graced our ears and fingers. I had very little jewelry, only what had been passed down from my granda and da. Since my da was middle-rank, he had a decent collection, though, including a fine pair of cuff links. Ones I almost traded away for a used shirt and boots.

"I'll take those," Sean said and accepted the tray.

"Can I attend you in any other way?" the slave asked.

Owen leaned forward. "A tray of food. Couple pints of ale too."

"Aye," the man said with a bow before walking away to do Owen's bidding.

He *bowed at me.*

Sean, Owen, and Corbin sputtered tight-lipped laughs and I slid them an equally reserved but humored expression. "The mortal can't tell my fine feathered arse's class from all the other bare arseholes in this room."

"We get to eat their food," Owen said, practically falling out of his seat in excitement. "Gods, I don't think I will eat so fine again. They have cheese. I might swoon, fellas."

Does it involve romantic forbidden cheese?

I bit the inside of my cheek to keep from smiling at that memory. Before leaving, I would pocket forbidden cheese for Filena. A couple slices for Gran and Glennie too.

A round of laughter caught my attention and I turned toward the sound. Bryok and his boys were joshing back and forth not too far away. The prince's eyes slid to mine, a pleased curl to his lips. At my side, Sean stiffened.

"Hold steady," I whispered.

"Are they laughing at us?" Corbin asked.

Bryok dipped his head at me, a friendly gesture, before turning away. But I knew it was all for appearances. Light laughter circled from his gang once more as they sauntered toward the tent opening, slipping outside one by one. Bryok peered at me casually over his shoulder one last time, a delighted glint in his gaze, then disappeared into the afternoon light.

"Food, sir," the slave announced as he slowed.

"Holy Mother of Stars," Owen whispered.

Another mortal slave set a small table next to our group to hold plates and a platter that was mounded in prepared food. A third mortal appeared with ale and offered a mug to Owen, Corbin, then Sean.

"From the prince," the same mortal said and handed me a wine glass. "Honey mead for the groom."

"How else can we attend you?" the first slave asked and I swallowed.

There was more they could do for us? I took note of the adornments and cosmetics, the grooming brushes for my clothing, the food and drink, the bath.

A shiver ran down my spine. Past the slaves, three elders watched me closely. Were they waiting for my answer?

"We are"—I cleared my throat—"We are well."

The slaves bowed and left.

My gaze flitted around the tent beneath lowered eyes. Several males, ones I had known my whole life, watched us with disgust. We were the only fellys in this space. The middle-rank lads pulled in the lottery didn't appear to receive any preferential treatment, not like us. At least, none that I could see. And the slaves . . . they bowed to me as if I were not practically one myself. As if we didn't wear patched up, old, fraying clothing just like the indentured mortals who served us.

A flush crept up my neck and face, but I shoved away the shame.

I had nothing to be embarrassed about. If my father were still alive, I would be middle-rank like them. I wasn't born a felly. But I was one, through and through. And proud to be surrounded by my best friends. I would rather be the dirt of the tribe than one of these preening arses any day.

Water sloshed the sides of the tub as I pulled my knees up to my chest.

My boys were gaping at the food. And, I realized with a pang, they were waiting for permission from me to eat.

"Dig in," I said quietly.

They jumped from their seats and grabbed plates. It was then I noticed that tables and platters were not brought to other groups. The groom's attendants fetched food from the banquet spread. Did the middle-ranks and govs believe we'd sully their food? Or was Bryok mocking us, treating us like govs to make a spectacle of the *uncivilized animals*, as he called me?

This was why they had laughed.

Sean shoved slices of meat into his mouth and moaned.

"This might be better than sex," Corbin murmured as he bit into melon slices wrapped in thin slices of smoked ham.

"I'm going to eat until I retch," Owen bit into a slice of cheese. "Sweet gods . . ."

Angry tears bit the back of my eyes.

People were watching them eat like starved dogs and quietly laughing. But my boys, who lived on watered down vegetable soup, porridge, and days old stale bread, were too enraptured to notice.

The amber hue of the mead in my hand glistened the color of gold coins and my stomach clenched. Feck Bryok. Feck the elders and the unkindness of Ravens in this room. Gritting my teeth, I set the drink on the ground beside the tub.

Sean glanced my way and I forced a smile. "Not hungry?"

"Too nervous to eat." A believable sentiment for any eavesdroppers. I stood and stepped out of the bath, wrapping a thick linen round my waist. "But save a few slices of cheese for Lena, Glenna, and Gran, aye?"

Corbin grabbed a cloth napkin, filled it with food, then placed it beside my belongings. Perhaps this was considered rude and uncultured to these better fed swine, but my family would enjoy the favor owed too.

A slave appeared before I could sit. "Finished with your bath, sir?"

I dipped my head, unable to meet his eyes.

He and another lifted the tub and carried it from the tent.

"What adornments do you want?" Sean asked me.

"Hair up or down?" Owen asked while chewing.

"Up." I lifted my chin. "Make me into the night. I want the stars to sing of my beauty and the moon to sigh. I want," I said with a pause, looking at each of my boys in turn, "to be revered a king in rags."

They grinned.

Lowering my voice to a whisper, I added, "Make Bryok tremble in fear and jealousy at my masculine display. I *will* dominate him in *every* way."

A couple of hours later, as the sun began to slip behind the trees, I joined the procession of grooms.

Like several other males, I chose to go bare chested, my tattoos traced in gold to match my granda's golden arm band circling my bicep. One worn by wild fae Raven Folk males before mortals "domesticated" us to assimilate to their life. My da's rings graced my fingers and gold hoops lined my ears. A crown, made from leaves, twigs of various lengths, feathers, and berries, rested on my head. My hair was pulled into a complicated knot of beaded, threaded loops and braids. Ash heavily lined my eyes and streaked toward my temple—war paint.

I would destroy.

I would walk among my ancestors proud of my heritage.

Attendees who paid to watch the mass wedding ceremony clustered around the torch-lined path. Women feverishly whispered behind gloved hands as we grooms strode past, our wings out.

In a few minutes, the bonding ceremonies and The Wild Hunt would begin, each held at opposite places of the Autumn Night Market. While Raven Folk exchanged vows, drunk on their courting magic, other fae would hunt the woods to mark a mortal female as their mate or slave.

I shuddered with anger. No woman would be sold into an ancient wedding game in my tribe. *Those* fae were the true uncivilized animals among the Folk. Blowing out a slow breath, I focused on marching toward my own forced arrangement.

Braelin Byrnes waited for me beneath the Truth Telling Tree

in a beautiful midnight blue gown, flowers woven into her curled hair. Around us, Samhain ribbons danced from the lantern-lit tree branches. I took Braelin's hands in mine, but all I saw was my true bride before me. I would speak these vows to her. Only speak her name for the autumn wind to carry to the gods.

Tribal drumbeats echoed throughout the field just as several bonfires whooshed into flame, officially heralding it Samhain Eve.

The veil between the mortal plane and the Otherworld was at its thinnest. The Harvest Moon above shone with Danu's favor. But all I could feel was the warmth trickling down my arm to my wrist where I bore a raven mark—and I smiled.

My mate bond with Filena was now eternal.

Chapter Thirty-Nine

FILENA LONAN

"My true love followed me to River Brook Fair,
There I bought her fine ribbons to tie in her hair,
I promised to marry and stay by her side,
But she says come morning, she sails with the tide."

A soft lilting voice sang above me. The comforting stroke of a hand caressed down my hair to my back. I sank into the motherly touch while floating somewhere in the twilight of sleep and wakefulness.

"Oh if I were a blackbird, I could whistle and sing,
I'd follow the vessel my true love sails in,
In the top riggin', I would there build my nest,
And I'd flutter my wings o'er her lily-white breast."

Gran continued to sing a familiar Traveler Folk ballad. I could almost hear Rhylen playing his lute as she sang, with both Rhylen and Glenna harmonizing. It was the song she would sing when I was little and afraid. When the monstrous shadows of memories haunted my dreams. Many nights she held me as I cried, terrified after nightmares of Da.

My eyes popped open.

A rush of panic gripped me.

Would ye deny yer da or sell Cillian to Seren, minnow?

The Blackthorn card—the card he chose.

But I had passed out before I saw a vision.

A sob knotted in my throat. He was in my wagon and Rhylen—oh gods, where was Rhylen?

I slowly rolled to my back and grimaced back the bleating pain in my head.

"Rhylen?" I croaked out. "Is he safe?"

"Me wee Filly girl," Gran said sweetly, cradling my cheek with her long, slender fingers. "Yer True Mate is grooming for ye."

Grooming for me?

"He . . . he didn't kill Hamish MacCullough?"

"Nae, lass." Gran leaned down and kissed my forehead. "Ye pale wee thing," she softly tutted. "Let's get a warm meal in ye."

Turning away, Gran moved to the woodstove, softly humming the familiar ballad under her breath. Atop the cast iron was a small cook pot and kettle. Had she made me bitter soup again? The thoughtfulness bloomed warmly in my chest. It was harder for her to move around let alone forage and wildcraft in Caledona Wood. Most days, just striking a match to light a fire was too hard for her arthritic fingers.

Gran's gray-streaked black hair fell down her back in a loose braid. An apron older than me was tied snug around her waist.

The points of her ears were slightly wrinkled, the knobby fingers tending to dinner too. Sensing my inspection, she flashed me a kind smile while humming louder and I smiled back.

Not once had she ever treated me like a mortal slave, but as one of her own. I missed Mam fiercely after Cian and I ran away. Gran would hold me, ask me to tell her about Mam, sing me songs, save spoonfuls of coveted honey just to drizzle over my porridge. She would gently brush my hair and pin it up in a faerie tale fashion using whittled sticks, decorating the strands in wildflowers and leaves, then send me and Glenna out to play long lost fae princesses.

And when I would escape to the woods to process my grief alone, she tasked Rhylen to find me. Not my brother, not Glenna . . . but Rhylen. I may not be an orphan, but it had felt like my mam had died. For years, the certainty that I would never see her again ached until it hurt to breathe.

Rhylen would sit beside me, sometimes quiet as we watched the trees bend to the wind. Other times, he helped me care for the wounded animals I found or had found me. Never telling me I was ridiculous, not even when I insisted the adorably fluffy rabbits were cold and I should knit them winter coats from grass and stems. Or how butterflies required different colored pollen to paint their wings. Or that field mice needed a home and flower blankets to sleep beneath. Other times, he shared how he also missed his mam and I would cry for his loss too. Sometimes he would sneak me treats or bring me rocks and then buttons. And many times he would tease me until I couldn't stop laughing. Then we would fall into mischief, playing jokes on Cian or telling Glenna wild stories.

Stars above, how I loved laughing with Rhylen.

He always seemed to know what I needed, when I needed it. And Gran always seemed to know I needed him too.

Do ye see yer future husband?

Yer True Mate . . .

"Gran," I said from the bed, "how long have you known about me and Rhy?"

She looked up from the soup she stirred with a soft smile. "The moment I heard of ye. The moment I knew ye'd be forever mine."

Fresh tears blurred my vision. Until Brenna Meadows, I hadn't truly felt safe or wanted or seen. I knew Mam loved me, but our relationship was tethered in fear. There wasn't time for cos-tuming hair for pretend play or finding joy in spoonfuls of honey. With Brenna Meadows, I was a faerie child that danced beneath the moon, spun tales and riddles, believed ladybugs brought good luck and wishes were made on dandelion fluff. That true magic was the earth, the sky, that the gods whispered in the wind and wept when it rained.

You have fae blood in your veins . . .

"How—how long have you known what I am?"

"And what are ye, lass?"

I hiccuped back a sob. "*Cailleach. Fáidhbhean.* And . . . and the daughter of a mortal monster."

The kettle began to whistle. Grabbing a linen, she lifted the handle and poured hot water into a mug. "I'll ask ye again," Gran murmured. "What are ye, lass?"

I blew out a tight breath and peered out the window. Gran was trying to pass on ancient wisdom and I was tired. So, so tired. My ankle throbbed, my head pounded, my stomach could retch for days. But I also knew these moments with Gran were fleeting. I didn't know when she would walk her last and I didn't want to waste a single shared moment, regardless of how poorly I felt.

What was I?

I thought back over the day, of how I had stared down my trauma while my body and magic were failing me. A few days before last night, I stood up to another tormentor before all the tribes. My blood had rushed hot, my hands shaking from rage, but I refused to let Bryok dominate me or anyone in my family.

"I lower my eyes for no one," I whispered to myself.

And Rory . . . the violence in my magic surprised me but, also, there was a rightness I couldn't quite reconcile within myself. As if I were the whole of autumn, the season of dying, the end of harvest, the beginning of the long dark. The threat of curses had fallen off my tongue since I was a wee child. Each curse growing wilder and wilder in strangeness.

It was in such contrast to my playful, mischievous, nurturing side that I sometimes felt like two different people. *A wee fussy mam*, as Rhylen often teased. *A wicked mortal*, Cian quipped in approving delight. *Or a clever trickster fae*, I would quip back. For one who couldn't *see* her own future, that line now twisted inside of me in disbelieving, ironic humor.

I spent my nights *seeing* into the lives of hundreds each year and every waking hour endlessly craving desserts as if I were an expectant mother. I carried a hedgehog in my pocket and a fox trotted at my side. And the Mother's messenger squirrel—

Wait.

Why had the Mother *really* sent me her squirrel? Besides ensuring I married Rhylen? Lloyd hadn't returned to her yet.

I squinted my eyes at Barry who had his tail curled around

Sheila and Lloyd while they slept against him. The fox opened a single eye and spared me a quick glance before returning to sleep himself. Barry, whom I had met in The Wilds when picking berries when he was just a little pup. Had the Mother also sent me my other familiars?

The elf in the Greenwood with the long, golden braided hair, animals surrounding her, and a belly round with child . . . was I related to her? Both Mam and Cian had the same sunny summer locks.

Was this beautiful forest faerie connected to the Mother?

What are ye, lass?

My mind raced back over the past two weeks—Bryok's threats, marrying my forbidden true love, seeing my da, my magic blossoming into something as wondrous as it was horrific—and I sensed what Gran was really asking me.

"Strong," I finally answered. "I am strong."

She set a mug of tea on a counter beside the bed and then cupped my face. "Aye, Filly girl. Ye are so *strong*."

"And brave." A tear slid down my cheek. "Clever," I continued. "Kind and unkind."

"What else?"

"Witty." I drew in a shaking breath. Another tear crested my lashes. "Protective. Nurturing and playful."

"Fierce," Gran added.

"And magical."

"Aye, magical," Gran said so softly, my heart cracked at the gentle sound. "Ye are magic, lass. So is Cian."

"I'm . . . I'm a halfling. Am I a wild fae? An elemental spirit?"

Gran brushed a tear from my cheek, then dropped her hands

from my face.

"The gods are ancient and weave fates we cannot begin to fathom, Filena Moira Lonan."

Chills prickled the back of my neck. She rarely spoke my full name. But I also didn't miss the lilting dance on my middle name, Moira—my mam's first name and the word for "fate" in the common fae tongue.

Was I related to a Fate?

"It seems like chaos and suffering at times, aye," Gran continued. "It seems unfair and cruel. We're not always ready fer the information we seek and the knowing before our appointed time opens paths not meant fer us." She kissed my forehead. "Ye will eventually know the fullness of yerself, lass. It won't always be bits and pieces cast to the wind."

Though I was still laying down, I took her hands in mine and kissed her fingers before pressing them to my cheek. "I love you, Gran," I whispered.

"Ye're now a true granddaughter of mine, me Filly girl," she said, her eyes twinkling. "Love ye as long as the endless sky, I do."

I softly laughed.

There were times I still couldn't believe that I was Rhylen's wife.

And Brenna Meadows was now officially my nan.

"Drink up, lass." She tapped the mug. "We have another hour before the bonding ceremonies begin."

My eyes rounded. I had completely forgotten. This wass why Rhylen was grooming. My cheeks warmed at the very thought of him prettying up just for me, even if it was in secret. Silver moons, I wanted him to always wear ash around his eyes, decorate his hair, and wear jewelry even though he was now a mated male.

"He's in the groom's tent." A frown appeared between Gran's brows. "Invited by the elders as a favor owed fer marrying a girl with a dowry."

The fae didn't use the word "thanks," but rather "favor owed." But a felly in the groom's tent? That seemed far too generous. The paying grooms would consent to sharing space, food, and amenities with a felloe rank?

The persistent twinge in my gut wouldn't lessen, but the door opened and Glenna strode in before my fatigued, magic-drained senses could intuit why. The long, plum-hued gown we were not allowed to touch, the one Cian wore last night, draped neatly over her arm. Gran slid her a knowing smile and Glenna narrowed her eyes.

"Don't you dare say a word," she said and fisted a hand onto her hip.

"Hope ye found some sleep, Glennie Lo," Gran said innocently—too innocently—her smile saying everything she wasn't. "We have a long night ahead."

Glenna's face flushed bright red and I, also far too innocently, said, "Wild Onions."

My sister's mouth dropped in mock-outrage. "Forbidden Buttons lover," she tossed back, pointing her finger at me and I started laughing. Gods, it hurt. But gods, it was so worth it.

"Help Lena sit up," Gran instructed Glenna. "Bitter soup is ready—"

A loud knock echoed in the small space and our rounding eyes whipped to the door in unison.

Glenna, closest to the wagon's entrance, turned the knob and slowly opened the door.

My painfully thudding pulse dropped into my churning gut.

The prince stood on the top step, his dark eyes snapping to mine before possessively drifting down my bare arms to my petticoats.

"Fáiléanna MacCullough, the chieftain summons you."

Chapter Forty

FILENA LONAN

Everything happened so fast.

Bryok gave a whistle and, within a furious blink, his lads had flooded the wagon.

Gran and Glenna were restrained, my animal familiars boxed beneath a wooden crate before they could escape, all while I was yanked from the bed and hauled outside.

But not before I was cuffed.

A strange iron manacle was clamped around my uninjured ankle, my hands first bound by ropes. The moment the metal touched my skin my body arched. Only seconds passed, but the agony seemed a lifetime.

And then nothing.

I felt nothing but the evening chill biting my bare arms and rocks from the forest floor digging into my feet.

The ever-present tug in my gut, the one I could listen to or ignore at will, was eerily silent.

No energy danced just beneath my skin or buzzed in my head. I was utterly, terrifyingly silent.

I tried to scream, to thrash in Bryok's hold as he dragged me away. But I was too weak. Too dizzy. The cruel pace he kept sent pain flaring up my leg from my still-swollen ankle. Suddenly realizing this in his frenzy, he scooped me into his arms and I swung my bound hands at his face. But he ducked before I could hit him.

"Cian!" I shouted in a raspy scream. "Cian!"

"You don't call out for your True Mate?" Bryok taunted. My True Mate, who was currently in the groom's tent. The one whom Bryok had arranged to marry the girl he had scorn marked and love cursed.

So, he did know about me and Rhylen all this time.

Fury whipped through me at his delight. I would melt his feathers one-by-one when my magic returned. I would make him suffer until he begged for the soil to bury him alive. I didn't care if I was hanged as a witch afterward. So long as he left this world first, it was a sacrifice well made.

The pounding of hammers echoed behind us, shoving me from my raging thoughts. I tried to peer around Bryok's arm, but I couldn't twist my body enough.

"What are they doing?" I demanded.

The bastard didn't answer me and my panic began spiking again. I kicked and twisted in his arms until he adjusted his hold enough in the fight that I could see.

The blood drained from my head.

They were boarding up the wagon door and windows.

They were trapping Gran, Glenna, and my familiars inside.

"Merciful stars . . ." the half-sob, half-whimper curdled from my gut. "You are caging in an ancient? And an innocent girl?" I cried out. "The gods curse you, Bryok Fiachna. May you only know bad luck all the remaining days, no *minutes* of your *short* life."

His hold on me tightened and squeezed until I audibly gasped in pain.

"The gods, who chose Hamish MacCullough as your mortal sire? The same gods who chose a Raven Folk felloe as your True Mate?" He darkly laughed. "The very gods who allowed one of their own to be enslaved by mere fae and mortals?"

One of their own?

Was he suggesting . . . I was related to *a god*?

No, that demented bird brain of his had lost all threads of sanity in his obsession to own me. No one in their right mind would harm an ancient—or threaten to. And now he had twice.

"Fáiléanna, you've been cursed by *these gods* since before you were born." Bryok's eyes slid to mine. "But I'll redeem you, pet."

That dark, cruel gaze lingered on my lips for a half a second before focusing on the path once more.

Violent shivers skittered across my skin.

Every instinct in me screamed to run, to swing my arms at his face again and again. But I had no energy. My lolling head was bleating. My limp body ached.

Trying to calm my breathing, I peered around and my heart jumped to my throat once more. We were walking away from the market proper and onto the marked path through the woods leading to The Wild Hunt. Was he going to sell me?

He couldn't. I was legally owned by Rhylen, per the Kingdom of Carran's interracial marriage laws between the fae and mortals. Though, did that still count if I was a halfling?

Then I remembered his words at the door: the chieftain had summoned me. He oversaw The Wild Hunt while a few of the elders governed the mass wedding beneath the Truth Telling Tree.

I forced another gulp of air into my burning lungs.

A few minutes later, we walked from the trees and into a field thick with attendees. The majority made up of mortal men and fae males in fine suits and top hats, many with cigars and tumblers of whiskey in hand. This was a gent's sport, to watch women be hunted and claimed by creatures.

Bryok walked along the edge of the makeshift camp toward an ornate tent. Spectators studied me as we passed, taking in my bare arms and legs, the thin, tattered undergarments I wore. They leaned into one another, smiling and chatting, as if approving of the next victim. Perhaps readying bets on which fae male in the running would list me as his claim.

Bile coated my throat and I swallowed back the urge to vomit.

I needed my wits about me . . . and all my remaining strength.

West Tribe put on The Wild Hunt each year and it was lucrative. Those selling their indentures were compensated upfront. They would also get a share if their bet won. The exorbitant fee to attend, though, the wagers pocketed . . . it was why our tribe was the wealthiest of the four.

Until the fire, that is.

Until we had less exhibits, less supplies, and more overhead.

The candlelit dimness in the tent relieved some of the pounding in my head. Bryok deposited me onto a chair, then quickly circled the back and placed a hand around my throat so I wouldn't attempt to flee.

Not that I could. They had wings. I could never outrun them.

"Where is Cillian?" the chieftain asked. I recognized his voice.

"We couldn't find him," Bryok answered.

"Guard the tent," Bram said and a shuffle of feet dashed by me. "Send a group of men to find him. You know the rest."

I blinked rapidly and tried to focus. The chieftain and two elders sat directly across from me. Were the other five at the Truth Telling Tree? Next to the elders was Hamish and . . .

No.

No, no, no, no!

My heart was beating so fast, my lungs panting for air in my terror, that black began to edge my vision.

The old man who had purchased me as his child bride regarded me with cool detachment, a barely-there slant to his lips. In my child's mind, he was much older. But looking at him now, he appeared somewhere around his mid-fifties. Maybe early sixties. His dark gray hair was slicked back beneath a brown bowler hat, his wrinkled face clean shaven and ruddy in the candlelight. The drab brown wool three-piece suit he wore appeared new, nary a speck of dirt or frayed thread. My eyes squinted against the polished gleam on his black shoes in the flickering candlelight.

How was he here?

My village was from the backwood, along The Wilds up north. A Raven or two must have flown to Kelkerry, then escorted Brady Sullivan to the station. It's an easy two-day travel from Kelkerry to the train stop located in the village near the Autumn Night Market.

Still, how was *he* here?

My da confessed the man took our home to compensate for

a broken contract Hamish couldn't pay back. Then had a bounty placed on Da's head.

As if reading my thoughts, Hamish's gaze twitched. His jaw moved back and forth as he shifted on his feet. He was nervous.

Bryok's fingers adjusted on my throat and a new wave of rage burned through me.

It had to be the prince who found my contracted husband.

But how did he learn his name? Hamish wouldn't have told anyone where to find me. He was too desperate for reparations himself.

"Fáiléanna MacCullough," Bram Fiachna said, his black eyes boring into me. "It has come to our attention that you are already the property of Mr. Brady Sullivan of Kelkerry village."

"My name," I seethed through clenched teeth, "is Filena Merrick."

"The prince was witness to a conversation between Brenna Meadows and a Sisters Three over a fortnight prior."

A Sisters Three?

Why would Gran be talking to a Sisters Three? That was absurd.

"From what he overheard, Bryok shared concerns that you were both a *fáidhbhean* and *cailleach*, but we needed proof. You are a liability to us now, Fáiléanna."

I tried to twist in my chair, but Bryok was unyielding. Drawing in a barbed breath, I shouted, "You denied Brenna Meadows warmth, stripped Rhylen, and other atrocities just to provoke me—"

Bram cocked his head. "For the safety of the tribe."

"The gods didn't show you, *fáidhbhean*?" Bryok whispered in my ear. "Our children will be powerful, mistress." The fingers around my throat gently slid down my neck in a sensual, possessive caress.

I refused to take the bait and stared straight ahead.

But my muscles were shaking with the effort to not shudder.

My intuition was right. He wanted to bind himself to my magic by siring children with me, even though the only acceptable Raven was a purebred one. Apparently, there were exceptions for mortals carrying the blood of the gods.

A corner of Bram's mouth lifted at his son before addressing me once more. "Your father, Hamish MacCullough—"

"He's not my da!" I spat and Bryok re-tightened his hold of my throat. "My da is dead," I choked out.

"—*Your* father," the chieftain spoke over me, "then appeared with claims that you're his daughter and . . . that you're married. Per law, we couldn't ignore that claim and summoned Mr. Sullivan."

No intuition magic was needed to know my da sold me out once again. This time to keep his repulsive arse from jail. Or had West Tribe paid for the information?

I narrowed my eyes, hoping the fury oozed from every line on my face.

"You deny your name is Fáiléanna MacCullough and that this man is your father. Do you also deny Mr. Sullivan is your husband?"

"I'm *not* his wife."

I was Rhylen's. And as soon as the sun set, I would be his eternal bonded mate.

"Mr. Sullivan," Bram said, turning toward him. "Do you consent to questioning under coercion to speak only truths? Four questions I would ask under magic. Four questions, no more, no less."

My heart stopped beating.

It must have registered on my face because Brady Sullivan's gaze flicked to mine with a victorious smile. "Aye, I consent."

A sob knotted in my chest.

The chieftain and elders must have tried to coerce Hamish and discovered his rowan berry ink tattoo.

An elder stepped forward. "Brady Sullivan," he began, the words tipped in magic, and the man's body relaxed. "You will answer four questions and speak only the truth."

The elder stepped back and dipped his head at the chieftain to continue.

"Mr. Sullivan," Bram began, "is Hamish MacCullough of Kelkerry village this mortal girl's father?" he asked, pointing at me.

"Aye, that he is."

"And what is her name?"

"Fáiléanna Moira MacCullough."

"Was she sold to you in marriage at the age of ten?"

"Aye, to be collected at age fifteen." Bram opened his mouth to speak again, but Brady cut him off. "I have our marriage contract."

The chieftain's brows raised at that, his gaze darting to the elders before settling on Brady once more—the only visual cue that this inquisition wasn't staged. And my heart sank farther into my churning gut. Brady dug out a rolled-up document from his coat pocket and handed it over to the chieftain.

"One last question under coercion," Bram said, opening the contract. "Is Fáiléanna MacCullough a mortal *fáidhbhean* and a fae *cailleach*?"

Brady's expression sobered. "Her family's magic wasn't dis-closed when Hamish approached me. Desperate fer money, he was." Brady shot my da a smug smile. "Gambling debts and drink."

My mouth slackened.

"To ye!" Hamish bellowed. "Ye ran the dice at the alehouse, ye fecking—"

"Per the contract, Mr. Sullivan," Bram said, interrupting Hamish, "Mr. MacCullough's properties were forfeit if he didn't deliver his daughter on her fifteenth birthday?"

"He took all I had, he did!" Hamish sputtered.

"So you've been compensated, Mr. Sullivan?"

"Keep reading, Traveler," Brady answered, that smug grin of his growing.

Silence roared in the tent. I fixed my gaze on the chieftain, un-able to peer at my da or that vile older man. The official wax seal from the Kingdom of Carran glared back at me.

"Did he pay you the additional penalty fees?" Bram asked Brady as he lowered the contract.

"Nae, there's a bounty on his head," Brady answered. "But ye'll compensate me for making profits on me property too, per the law."

"Of course," the chieftain said, his gaze darting to the elders once more. "Allow me to pay you what's due, aye?"

Bryok laughed quietly under his breath and chills clawed down my spine at the sound.

Bram stood from his chair and tucked a long strand of black hair behind the point of his ear, one decorated in a line of gold hoops. The elegant black suit he wore, with a red and purple striped vest, to match the colors of West Tribe, fit snug against his large frame—

large when compared to Hamish's and Brady's mortal sizes. A top hat tipped low on his head, shadowing part of his face. A fine hat made of silk that shone in the low candlelight.

"Brady Sullivan," the chieftain intoned once standing before the man and a wave of magic washed over the tent. "You believe you are fairly compensated and do not seek additional payment for Fáiléanna MacCullough. But you are willing to sell her back to West Tribe. Until you annul your marriage, you relinquish all rights to her as her husband and will sign off as so on your contract."

The chieftain took a step back and Brady blinked his eyes.

"Do we have a bargain?" Bram asked him, hand outstretched.

Brady's brows narrowed as he studied the hand. Then his gaze slid to Hamish. My da's cold eyes were wild, a bloodthirsty gaze directed entirely at me.

"Aye, I'll sell her. First," Brady said, sticking his hands in his pockets, "I'd like a word with me wife. Privately. We'll just step outside—"

"Speak to her here," Bryok commanded.

Brady chuckled, the sound an adult made when indulging a small child, and Bryok stiffened. "Legally, lad, ye're touching *my* property." The man turned back to the chieftain and, with a roll of his hand, said, "Remove her slave mark."

I couldn't breathe.

Gods help me, I couldn't breathe.

Every male in this room believed they owned me. What would they do to me when they learned the truth?

"Brady Sullivan," Bram spoke, the air thick with magic once more, "you will—"

"Kelkerry is one of the last mortal outposts before the Greenwood." Brady plucked the marriage contract from the chieftain's fingers. "Men near The Wilds get rowan berry ink tattoos to ward against yer trickster kind. Ye can't coerce me, lad. Now," he said, tucking the document into his suit coat, "ye'll remove *my* wife's slave mark."

Bram didn't even blink an eye. "You lied about answering questions truthfully under coercion. How can we believe your claims now?"

I paused at that. Bram didn't believe the marriage contract was real?

"I never lied to ye. Aye, waste yer coercion magic on me all ye like, doesn't mean me mind can be glamoured." Brady chuckled again, but there was no humor in it. "Ye must think me a fool."

"On the contrary," Bram said, a little too amicably. "You seem a shrewd businessman."

"Aye," Brady said and leveled a dark gaze onto the chieftain. "Authorities from Den Merrow should arrive any moment now. Do we understand each other?"

Bram stilled.

But Hamish bolted.

"Feck," Bryok hissed. "Grab him!"

I couldn't move to see the commotion behind me. But Hamish's belligerence scraped down my skin in familiar torment—the sharp sound of his voice, the slightly slurred words. I winced. Another shout and I winced again, as if he were swinging at me instead of the guards who were tackling him to the ground.

Brady grinned at Bryok as he slipped on a pair of brass knuckles. "Overplayed yer hand, boyo."

"Name your price."

That disgusting old man openly studied me, his gaze drifting to the dips and curves of my body while Hamish was dragged past me to the center of the room. I lifted my chin and glared at Brady down my nose.

"Your. Price," Bryok clipped.

Brady snorted, a condescending sound directed entirely at Bryok, right before he pivoted on his heel and swung at Hamish. The brass knuckles on his stubby fingers collided with Da's jaw in a sickening crunch. I shot back in my chair and screamed. Bloody spittle flew in the air. Brady threw another punch and I squeezed my eyes shut. I couldn't look. I didn't care if my da was deserving of the same violence he had shown his own family. Hot tears rolled down my cheeks.

Would Brady do this to me too?

Would Bryok treat me any differently?

"Rhylen," I quietly sobbed under my breath. "Rhylen . . ."

"Remove her slave mark," Brady demanded, his voice straining for breath. "And I'll not report ye to the authorities for harboring a runaway and profiting off another's property."

"Why didn't the authorities come with you?" Bryok snapped.

I squinted open my eyes and bit back a whimper.

Bram nudged Hamish with his boot until my da rolled over, his face bruised and bloodied. Was he dead? Or just unconscious?

When Brady didn't answer, the scowl between Bryok's eyes deepened. "How do we know you're not tricking us?"

"Ye don't." Brady threw him a patronizing grin. "Tricky business is always a gamble."

The chieftain studied Brady for a couple of seconds. "Once you sell her back to West Tribe, you'll not seek additional monetary reparations from us?"

"Her mark," Brady gritted out. "Before the authorities arrive and I change me mind."

Bram slowly turned toward me and I drew in a pained breath. Tears continued to stream down my cheeks. Not a flicker of sympathy rested in his dark gaze. "Filena Merrick," he commanded, using the name my mam had told me to use—

"Don't give her to him!" Bryok interrupted. But his da ignored him.

"—your debts to West Tribe and to Clan Lonan are dissolved. We release you from indentured servitude and into the hands of your rightful owner, Brady Sullivan."

I couldn't cover my wrist with my hands bound.

I could do nothing but fight to remain conscious in my fatigue and terror.

"Father," Bryok growled, his voice tight with white-hot rage. "She's not a slave."

Bram's eyes flicked back to mine and darkened. "Change of plans. Banish him now," he snapped at the elders, though he looked directly at me. "Still do a blinding curse."

The elders at his side shifted into ravens. A tendril of twilight curled around my bare arms and legs in an icy shiver as they flew from the tent.

Yet, despite the chills wracking my body, and though I wore a cuff that blocked magic, a soft rush of warmth trickled down my arm and pooled around the raven inked onto my wrist. And I almost laughed through my tears. My childhood best friend and forbidden love was now eternally mine.

Horns heralding the rise of Samhain Eve blared through the

woods.

Then drumbeats, in a seductive rhythm, beckoned our ancestors to dance around bonfires and walk amongst us.

"How many days?" Bram asked me.

A satisfied smile begged to curl my lips but I had no form of protection against their dominating anger. So I simply answered, "Six."

"Banish who?" Brady strode toward me, a feverish wildness in his eyes at my trembling.

"Rhylen Lonan," the chieftain growled, baring his teeth. "Her bonded mate."

Chapter Forty-One

RHYLEN LONAN

I adjusted my hold on Braelin's hands to better see the raven mark on my wrist.

Dread nipped at my mind.

My thoughts were always full of Filena. Her boisterous laugh, her sass and fire, her mischievous wit. The burning feel of her fingers sliding down the bare skin of my back. The hungry press of her lips on mine.

Dark skies, how I craved my wife.

But this maddening separation anxiety felt different. It was as if I could hear her voice sobbing my name.

Had Bryok pecked at my head too much today?

I couldn't tell if I was just being paranoid from Bryok's games, more primal since my and Filena's bond became eternal, or if Filena was truly in danger and calling to me. And the not knowing was sending me into a spiraling panic.

My gaze drifted back to Braelin.

If I walked away now, breaking the bargain I was under with

West Tribe, she could be cursed. And I promised no one would touch her or her family.

But what if Filena was actually crying out for me?

Sean may never forgive me for failing Braelin. But I would *always* choose Filena, no matter how much my heart shattered for my Raven brothers and their mates.

I angled my head to scan the crowd for Gran, Glenna, and Lena—though I knew the likelihood of spotting them was slim. There were hundreds upon hundreds who lined the field to watch the seventy or so couples circling around the Truth Telling Tree. As a felly, I was near the back outskirts with Braelin, closer to the forest than the attendees.

Heady courting magic twined through the males waiting to exchange ancient vows. Each new pulsing wave captured my senses more intensely than the last. My blood rushed hotter. My mind sharper. Unrelenting desire for my wife, to inhale her scent and let it drug me, was quickly obliterating my self-control.

Images of Filena's curves molded perfectly to the contours of mine filled me. Feck, how I ached to make love to her until our lips were raw and our bodies spent.

Braelin watched me with rounding eyes and a flush crept up my neck. My chest was heaving with ragged breaths. My gaze felt ravenous, searching, searching, endlessly hunting for my wife.

"Sorry," I whispered. Shifting on my feet, I attempted to shove back the courting magic possessing me. "I don't know how Sean can watch you with another. I would tear him limb from limb right now if the roles were reversed."

"I told him not to come."

I nodded. "Good."

Rhylen . . . Rhylen . . .

My head snapped back up. Her sobbing voice echoed in my fraying mind once again. I lifted my ear to the wind on instinct. Every muscle in my body went preternaturally still, a hunter's stillness.

Was Bryok tricking me into leaving my "betrothed" in a primal rage? I would look like a frothing mad fool before all the tribes. And then who would follow me if I challenged him and our chieftain and won?

Elder Connel walked by with a quill and scribbled a note on a sheet of paper when seeing both me and Braelin. A tight smile pulled on his lips when our eyes connected—the look of one concentrating on his task. But his eyes quickly darted away, as if he were nervous.

Or was I reading into his look in my growing paranoia?

"Ladies and gents," an elder from North Tribe shouted over the crowd and I blew out a shaky breath. "Welcome to the Autumn Night Market's Samhain Eve Wedding Event."

The crowd's clapping rumbled over the field.

"Most traditions long held by the fae have been traded for the customs of mortals who now live among us. But the ceremonies held by Raven Folk are ancient."

The attendees spoke to one another in excitement.

"Unlike our fae cousins, we are ruled by courting magic. Our legendary romance is why you are here, aye?"

The field erupted into cheers and a muscle jumped along my jaw.

"You traveled across mountains and rivers to participate in the hunt, to watch males display their masculine beauty and virility to win a mate."

More cheers roared around us.

"To know the courtship of a Raven male is to know the magic of True Love's kiss. Other fae love like the frolicking wind. But a Raven's love is eternal. He is possessed by his mate from their first encounter and long after he brands her pulse with his vows." The elder turned from the crowd to face us. "For to be bound by ravens is a form of ownership before the fae, one that is eternal. Ladies, he is yours until the end of time."

The crowd fell into an enthralled silence.

"Turn his palms to the night sky."

Braelin gently moved my hands so they faced the Harvest Moon.

"Wrap your fingers around his wrist as he embraces yours."

Her fingers were trembling, but she did as instructed.

"Confess to him the sacred words spoken by our ancestors, who bear witness as they walk among us this Samhain Eve."

Braelin blinked. The fear we both shared was tight between us. I gave a reassuring dip of my head. She replied with a nervous smile, then began the old words.

"I, Braelin Cormac, mate bind myself to you"—she dropped her voice to a breathy whisper—"Sean Byrnes, for as long as my soul exists." She cleared her throat and spoke more loudly, "I belong to you, husband, for now and for all eternity."

We both grinned. This was almost over, our trick almost complete.

"Lads," the elder called out, "bring her wrist to your lips. Speak your vows. Her pulse will carry your words to the heart you now own."

I lifted Braelin's wrist to my mouth, but at a respectable distance. For a moment, as I nervously stared at my friend's wife, I saw only mine. My mind faded to the low-lit divination wagon, to the mother of pearl button pressed between my and Filena's palms, to the black lace veil draped down her auburn curls, to her gray eyes that shone with happy tears as she peered up into mine—

—Her tears.

Rhylen . . . Rhylen . . .

The hairs on the back of my neck lifted.

A sickening wave of blinding terror hit me.

Something was very, very wrong.

For a second, I couldn't breathe. My heart was hammering violently in my chest.

I lowered Braelin's wrist just as two Ravens swooped over the crowd and shifted before the elders who were overseeing the bonding ceremony. Grooms, who were in the middle of reciting their vows, fell silent. But the roar of whispers rippled over the crowd.

"Braelin," I said under my breath. "You knew nothing, understand? You're innocent."

Her eyes startled wide.

Gloved hands grabbed me from behind. My wings snapped out, knocking one of the chieftain's lackeys to the ground. I launched into the air. The other Raven anticipated this move and jumped, wings out. Before I could shift, a gloved hand cuffed enchanted cold iron onto my wrist and . . . let go.

The sudden loss of shifter magic hit me like a flame-tipped bolt. Every nerve-ending caught fire and I cried out. My wings disappeared mid-air. And then I was falling—fast. Pain splintered through my head with the impact. I didn't have time to brace my fall.

I didn't have time to care about any injuries either.

Rolling over, I pushed to my feet.

Filena.

All I could think about was Filena.

"Rhylen Lonan," Elder Connel shouted from the wooden platform. "The elders summon you."

The chieftain's lads gripped my arms and hauled me through the circle of couples. I peered over my shoulder at Braelin and mouthed, "run!" Then faced forward once more. I shoved at the lackeys until they lost their balance and it was I who pulled us toward the stage. Folk parted as we cut through the couples. I kept my head high, back straight the entire time.

The earth seemed to tremor beneath my bare feet. I knew it wasn't really, not in a way most around me could sense or Folk would be reacting. It was as if the magic of nature echoed my anger. Connel tried to mask his fear at my furious approach, but not fast enough. Could he feel the wisps of elemental power thundering from me with each footstep despite the cuff on my wrist?

The sensation was so natural to me I didn't consider how or why I connected to the magic of earth so viscerally.

Unless . . .

I drew in a quiet breath.

Elder magic.

I was wielding elder magic.

This was the magic that seized me at the lottery and when Filena stood up to Bryok. Folk had lowered their eyes to me then, some had even bowed. Now, while dressed and decorated like our wild fae past, with a power only the gods could take away, I became the dark of night.

The stars were singing of my beauty.

The moon's sighs feathered my hair as I slowed before the elders.

There was no question I was one of them now—appointed by the gods to govern and protect the tribes. By the stiff, guarded looks on the chieftains and elders present, they knew it too.

Yet, no one intervened.

They could temporarily revoke the use of elder magic for a trial if five or more elders agreed, regardless of tribe. Were they too shocked to see a felly with god-appointed magic to react?

Good.

Baring my canines, I faced Connel and asked, "Where is she?"

"Did you marry a mortal slave, Lonan?" Connel asked.

Gasps moved through the Raven Folk in attendance. Aye, I had committed one of the greatest crimes of my kind, though the gods clearly disagreed. And I would rip through anyone who dared try to keep us apart.

I stepped closer to Connel, my muscles flexing. "Where is she?" I growled.

"West Tribe dissolves the debts of both Cian and Filena Merrick," Connel shouted for all to hear. "They are no longer indentured servants to West Tribe or Clan Lonan."

He grabbed my wrist and lifted it for all to see—and I let him. I wasn't ashamed of Filena. A glimmer of satisfaction flashed in Connel's eyes, brightening when Caravan Folk erupted into horrified cries and began chanting for banishment.

I yanked my arm back and shouted, "Where is my mate?!"

404

When Connel didn't answer, I charged. But a net, made from thin threads of enchanted cold iron, was thrown over me before I could attack. Searing pain scorched down my body. My fists curled. My jaw clenched. My muscles stiffened.

Where in the feck did the net come from?

Had Bram pre-planned to publicly shame me before the tribes?

Of course, he had.

Outside of Filena, I was his and Bryok's greatest threat. But with us together?

We would destroy.

Even knowing this, I didn't know why I was surprised that Bram and three elders acting against me aided Bryok's schemes. The clues were there all along. The rigged lottery—no one would put fellys in the running to secure doweries. The elders binding their decision in magic, thus forcing my hand. Bram's threat to do whatever was necessary for a girl with money to marry me or be banished, a move that could have resulted in legal repercussions. Bram's and the elder's involvement in arranging me to Braelin, to give me Bryok's castoff while Bryok stole my heart and soul. Hamish tormenting Filena and threatening to sell Cian to incite and redirect my violence. The invitation to the groom's tent—a trick to distract me.

Did they also plan for the fire? It was conveniently near Filena's tent.

The lottery wouldn't have happened without the fire . . . and that thought alone writhed inside of me until I thought my rage would explode in a soul-shattering war cry.

They had to know Filena was a demi-goddess.

And those greedy feckers wanted the Fiachna line tied to the gods.

West Tribe would boast the most exotic sideshow of all: a woman who was the mortal manifestation of the Mother, Maiden, and Crone.

The cold iron's enchantment eased as my earth magic took over. My lungs heaved for breath. My fingers relaxed. Any remnants of shifter magic in me were now completely doused. But the lush, storm-charged elder powers continued to build inside of me. A magic given to the oldest line of Folk still walking Carran to preserve and protect tribes, not one to abuse fellow Caravan fae.

Connel towered over my kneeling form. "You stood beneath the Truth Telling Tree with Braelin Cormac as an already mated male—"

"What choice did you give me?" I snapped. "West Tribe threatened to curse her and her family if I didn't marry her *after* I refused the arrangement. *Your* words, elder."

The crowd around me silenced at my confession.

But Connel ignored me. "Rhylen Lonan, son of Garen Lonan, grandson of ancient Brenna Meadows, per the orders of Bram Fiachna, Chieftain of West Tribe—"

"The elders bound in magic a decision that forced me to marry against my will or face banishment!" I continued. "Filena Merrick is my True Mate!"

"—you are hereby banished from West Tribe for marrying a mortal slave and for refusing to and failing to marry a Raven Folk girl as directed by your chieftain."

I pushed to my feet, my canines on full display, my muscles rippling in barely restrained rage. Connel stumbled back a step. The elders, who held onto the corners of the net, tugged hard to force me back to my knees. But an entire mountain range of fury was rising in the marrow of my bones.

I gritted my teeth. "I didn't break my bargain with West Tribe. Bram Fiachna instructed me to do *anything* necessary to secure a girl with money. I married my True Mate, who brings in more profit for West Tribe than a girl with a dowry ever could." I drew the wind into my lungs and shouted, "I refuse to trick a girl into mate bonding with me and I refuse to let West Tribe curse any girl I decline to marry."

"No tribe will take you in," Connel continued, his words growing hurried. "No Folk will face you."

At his words, Caravan fae began turning their back to me. But not all. I was surprised that more than half of the Folk in attendance hadn't moved. Emboldened, I took another step forward, pulling the elders and the chieftain's lackeys with me.

"You dare punish me for marrying the girl the gods chose for my mate?"

"West Tribe curses you, Rhylen Lonan."

I grabbed the net and tugged until the gloved elders and lackeys collapsed at my feet. With another yank, I pulled the net from my body and threw it atop two of the fallen elders. Their bodies arched in pain beneath the enchanted cold iron's grip on their shifter magic. I expected the other govs present to wield their own elder magic to subdue me—or revoke it all together. But none present, from the remaining elders in my tribe nor the elders from the three other tribes, stepped in to interfere. They were allowing me this challenge?

Connel gaped at his fellow govs, then me when I used a thread of earth magic to open the cuff.

My wings snapped out and flexed with the release.

Not even a second later, an inferno of power flamed through my veins. And seven suns above, my skin was flushing hotter than Samhain fire.

"Where is my wife?" I growled, a deep guttural sound.

"A blinding curse," Connel rushed out, his eyes locked onto my fingers as they shifted into talons. "From this point forward until your last breath, Caravan fae will be struck from your sight. You will not see nor hear the Traveler Folk before you." I took another step forward and his mouth fell open. Aye, I couldn't be cursed. "From this point forward until their last breath," he barked out while peddling backward, "Rhylen Lonan will be struck from the Caravan fae's—"

I grabbed his throat and leaned into his face, flashing my canines.

"Bram's tent," Connel choked out. "The Wild Hunt."

I shoved the male to the ground and faced the four tribes. "Bear witness all," I shouted. "I officially challenge Bram and Bryok Fiachna for West Tribe."

The crowds gasped and some cheered. Those with their backs to me began to turn.

"Do *not* touch Braelin Cormac or her family," I commanded the elders.

My large wings alighted my body into the sky and then, when I was sure everyone could see me, I shifted into a raven with a thunderous caw.

I'm coming, Filena . . .

Chapter Forty-Two

FILENA LONAN

I screamed for Rhylen.

Then for Cian.

Barry was locked up on the other side of the market. I didn't know if proximity played a part in my familiar's protection magic. He was always at my side. But what if Rhylen could now be cursed? What if he could never see another Caravan fae again? His sister? His Gran? If they could never see him? I had witnessed one blinding curse before and the banished Folk's keening wails haunted me still.

Drawing in an aching breath, I tensed to scream again when a rag was stuffed in my mouth from behind. My limbs were heavy, the fog circling my thoughts thick. Still I thrashed. Arms held me and I screamed again when the fabric was tied behind my head.

Brady lowered until we were eye level. "I've no need for a girl who'll kill me with her magic. But I'll not let slavers own what's legally mine either," he said in a mocking lilt. "Yer mate will never touch ye again."

I went deathly still.

The disgusting bastard's gaze devoured the shape of me in my thin camisole. I kicked out my uninjured foot to shove him away. He laughed at my weakness, easily angling out of reach, then righted his posture.

"Ye there," he said to one of the chieftain's attendants, "fetch the registrar." To Bram he said, "Ye'll pretend she's yer slave and sell her fer me."

I whipped my head toward Brady. Fresh panic clawed at my pulse. He was selling me to The Wild Hunt?

Bryok stepped from behind the chair. "I'll pay more than the Hunt."

"I don't give a shite about what ye want, whelp."

Bryok leaned into the man's face and quietly seethed, "You want a fecking animal to own a *cailleach*?"

Brady's barbed grin was instant. "Not a fecking Traveler one."

Bryok's wings flashed into view. A low growl rumbled from his chest. His fist shot out and he grabbed Brady by the coat and yanked him close. "Mortal—"

"I'm a gambling man," Brady spoke over the prince, a cruel curl to his lip. "Lived me whole life making wagers. Ye learn when to cut yer losses." Brady sniffed Bryok's neck in a taunt. "And ye reek like shite luck, boyo."

Bryok shoved Brady away and grabbed me from the chair, a feral, unhinged gleam in his darkening gaze. I tried wriggling from his grasp, using my uninjured heel to kick at his legs. But his hold on me was too firm. A slight spark of magic warmed the tips of my fingers. Words built on my gagged tongue. The sensation surprised me so much, I moved my ankle to see if the cuff was still there— it was. The very next breath, it sputtered out. I didn't have time to contemplate what had just happened. Fisting my hair, Bryok yanked my head back. I screamed, knowing what was coming.

He would *not* mark me.

Barry could protect me from external magical attacks and co-ercions, but being marked was internally imparted, directly into the bloodstream, and not always malicious. It was about intention. If Rhylen marked me, it would be to let other males know I was his—no magic to control me would be involved. If Bryok's attempt worked, though, he would use the magical signature of his I'd carry to enthrall me. And if I had no will, I couldn't refuse him *anything*.

Drawing on what little strength I had, I threw my elbow back into his gut at the same moment a sudden, violent burst of wind knocked us both to the ground.

Bryok immediately jumped to his feet with a flap of his wings. "She's not a slave. I'm not hunting her—"

"Lonan will come for his True Mate and he'll be feral," Bram spoke slowly, as if speaking to an eejit. I would laugh if I weren't in so much pain. The great Fiachna trickster clan needed to spell out the obvious to their heir. "She's not Caravan. He'll see her and she'll see him."

The prince's eyes slid to mine and narrowed. A muscle jumped along his jaw.

Oh aye, just figured out I wasn't Raven Folk?

"Mr. Sullivan's plan is sound." Bram's dark gaze widened in warning and Bryok's jaw clenched tighter. "She's not fae marked and the raven on her wrist will pass inspection. The Hunt is the best way to ensure Lonan doesn't challenge us in his primal rage. Or *worse*." A muscle ticked along Bram's jaw. "He'll do *anything* to keep her safe. His family too."

So this was why Brady wanted to quickly sell me to the Hunt. It wasn't necessarily about my magic killing him. He feared my bonded mate would kill him first. A fear Bram shared as well.

"It's the only leverage we'll get right now," Bram stressed.

"What leverage? Lonan is banished," Bryok all but shouted. "And if he figures out he has—"

"—Then we distract him—"

"And if she's marked during the Hunt?"

"Bryok Fiachna, you *will* pretend she's your slave and sell her like Mr. Sullivan requested," Bram said, the warning clear in his tone, "and then give Mr. Sullivan the money. If the blinding curse fails, and it might because of his bond with a *cailleach, this* is our protection." Bram hauled me to my feet then pushed me into Brady's arms. The chieftain snapped his fingers at an attendant. "Tell the registrar to not close the entries until Fáiléanna MacCullough is loaded onto the cart. Be quick." Bram then turned back to Brady. "Will our debts be settled then?"

"We'll talk after she's sold to the Hunt and no sooner." Brady sized up Bryok, a smug slant to his lips. "Try anything, lad, and I'll press charges against yer family." Brady gestured to the tent opening. "Go ahead."

"You do not give me orders, mortal."

"Walk in front of me." Brady's voice lowered. "Both of ye." He gestured between the prince and chieftain. "Or we wait here for this Lonan fella and the authorities."

Bram glanced at one of his attendants, a muscle in his jaw ticking. "Watch Hamish MacCullough. He's not allowed to leave this tent, understood?"

"Aye, sire."

With that, Bram forced Bryok toward the exit.

My da was still alive?

"Come, lass," Brady said and yanked me forward by my bound hands.

I hissed with the sudden weight on my ankle. Pain flared, bright and hot. My legs started to give out, but I refused to let any male in this room touch me beyond the ropes on my wrists. A cold sweat dewed on my forehead. My hands were chilled and clammy. I took a limping step forward. The tent tilted.

I would *not* fall.

I would *not* be weak.

Ye are so strong, Gran's melodic voice soothed from my memories. *Ye are fierce.*

The rag in my mouth made it difficult to breathe. Dizziness raced around my head. But I took another step, then another. Eventually I found a rhythm I could manage, thankful Brady didn't drag me outside or force me to crawl on hands and knees.

The final, faint light of the sunset warmed the horizon when we exited the tent. Just a tiny stroke against a sea of star-flecked blue. Lanterns shone above our heads. The embered orange glow of cigars dotted the field around me.

The mortal registrar from the Kingdom of Carran's constabulary wasn't too far away from the chieftain's tent. Panicking, I peered around for Cian. No one here would help me if I screamed. They hoped I did. They wanted to watch me be dominated by another male while in a state of primal terror.

We slowed at the ornate gate. The wooden arch was decorated in the way of Caravan fae with bright colors in knotted patterns, dotted with moons, stars, flowers, silhouettes of ravens, enchanted stones, and scrolling wrought iron filigree.

Similar gates were placed around the hunting grounds, marking north, south, east, west—a gate for each tribe—to ward the square game space connecting each gate from attendees and Raven Folk. The only Travelers allowed in this sectioned forest were those who were tagged to enter or those with elder magic.

Ravens, especially, were forbidden from entering the game or the hunting grounds. This sport was in celebration of their wedding event and meant for everyone else. Plus, they rarely fae marked a mortal. It ruined slave trading. The fae didn't like owning a human who carried another's scent and signature. Ravens also only married their own kind and they especially didn't marry mortal slaves.

Unlike my True Mate.

My soul was tearing in half.

The ache, the obliterating pain stabbed me mercilessly.

Rhylen wouldn't find me. I would probably never see him again.

With me locked behind The Wild Hunt's wards and with Gran and Glenna boarded up, Rhylen would yield and cave to their demands—

You will only see in part unless you change the view, a motherly voice whispered in my mind.

The familiar words jolted me from my spiraling grief.

What view?

The next throbbing beat of my rending heart, a vision of Rhylen beneath Seren floated back to memory. Images of middle-rank and fellys lowering their eyes and heads as Rhylen walked past the day of the lottery carouseled by afterward. Then I recalled the dark, commanding primal creature of fae he became to protect Cian when I stood up to Bryok.

Elder magic . . .

My pulse stuttered to a stop. I had nearly forgotten that he had begun manifesting elder magic. He was fated to become chieftain of a Night Market beneath the City of Stars.

This was what Bryok was starting to say before Bram cut him off.

They knew Rhylen Lonan was an elder and why they feared him so much. The gods had appointed my husband to protect the tribes.

The Blackthorn card reading whipped through my memories next. Rhylen found me, then marked me. Which he could only do if another had not marked me yet.

A sob knotted in my heaving chest.

Gods, please don't change your mind.

I didn't think they would. So far, every vision they had shown me since the Alder card had come true.

A few minutes later, Brady pocketed a hefty bag of coins and blended into the crowd. The trick had worked. My raven mark passed the detection magic and the registrar recorded me as Bryok's slave while Bram shook hands and spoke with the hunters, leaning in to whisper something in each ear before moving onto the next.

Then I was tagged with an illusioned sigil of a boar on my forearm and escorted through the warded gate. A non-player picked me up and shoved me into a cart, my hands still bound, the cuff still on my ankle. Girls around me were sobbing and pleading for release.

"Ladies and Gents," Bram announced from atop a small, brightly lit stage, a showman's smile lifting the corners of his mouth. "Welcome to The Wild Hunt."

Bram opened his hand and blew across his palm. Glittering light, probably illusioned sand, caught in a tumbling breeze he made with a flourish of his fingers. A second later, a burst of twinkling stars appeared above the gala in a rainbow of colors.

Those in attendance clapped and lifted tumblers of whiskey. A few reached out to catch the stars falling around their feet before they flickered out.

Bryok's gaze locked onto mine. Grabbing the rag with my bound hands, I pulled it down to smile sweetly at him. I knew how this night would end.

His lip curled and wings twitched.

"Long ago, on Samhain Eve," Bram began, "when the veil was thin, the fae would cross into the mortal planes . . . and we would hunt."

The crowd ate up his opening with robust cheers.

"Now the faerie and mortal worlds are one. The Kingdom of Carran made hunting mortals punishable by death except for one hour on Samhain Eve. The rules . . ." he said with a dramatic pause. "Unlike our wild fae past, when we hunted for ownership, the women must already be indentured slaves legally owned by the fae. Their slave mark must remain until claimed by a hunter for this reason, which is inspected and confirmed by a registrar for the Kingdom of Carran. The hunter will fae mark the mortal woman, as either his bride or his slave, per our ancient tradition, and then the trade from one fae owner to another is complete per the bargain made at the gate."

The crowd clapped and murmured in excitement to one another.

"The last rule," Bram spoke with a humored grin, "we cannot legally call it a hunt for mortals. And, therefore, we hunt boars." He gestured to the cart and the attendees whooped and hollered. Some squealed like pigs.

"The boars will be released into Caledona Wood," Bram continued. "The fae who paid to hunt must claim a boar within the allotted legal hour or"—Bram's dark eyes slid to mine—"she will be returned to her original owners."

And I was registered as Bryok's.

A shudder wended down my spine.

How can we believe your claims now?

Bram had a trick up his sleeve, one he wanted me to know was in motion. But I refused to be cowed by his threats and lifted my chin. The cards predicted a far different evening for us both.

Bram gestured to the driver with a dramatic sweep of his hand. Appointed guards moved around the cart, each bearing a raven shield on the back of their hands, allowing them access to the game field. Once all were in place, the driver clicked his tongue and the horses jolted forward.

The cheer at our departure was deafening.

Lanterns, hanging off hooked poles, swayed with the jostling cart. Fog misted low on the ground and writhed around trees. Weeping girls bumped into me with the juddering motion of the large wheels rolling over the uneven ground.

Bryok was shaking with rage. His burning black eyes held mine as I began to fade into the woods, as I smiled at him the entire time. His da had apparently not yet shared his plan to ensure I was returned to Bryok unmarked.

"Filena!"

My gaze shot past Bryok. Cian charged the wards screaming my name.

I gripped the edge of the cart. A whimpered cry left me.

"Filena!"

Folk grabbed my brother and yanked him away.

Before I could scream his name back or see what Bryok and his gang would do to my brother, the dark of the forest swallowed our cart and the gate disappeared from view.

Chapter Forty-Four

RHYLEN LONAN

My wings cut through the night sky.

Beneath me, sparse trees, smudges of colored lantern light, lines of wagons, and milling people blurred by me. The Wild Hunt was on the clear opposite side of the market, down a marked trail through the woods. I couldn't figure out how to increase wind speed for more drag to fly faster. Commanding the elements was still too new. Or maybe it didn't work when in my raven form.

Filena, Filena, Filena . . .

Her name played on an endless panicking loop in my mind, my heart, screaming from my soul. What were they doing to her? Her terror hit me in waves. The guilt that followed shredded me into a million dying stars.

I was her mate. And I had failed to protect her.

A caw sounded to my right, followed by one on my left and another just behind me. I turned my head slightly. Moonlight caressed silver along Sean's black wings and reflected in his eyes. Owen and Corbin were with me too. Just knowing my gang had my back pumped the blood harder in my veins.

We angled our wings to descend closer to the ground. The Wild Hunt's west gate came into view. But I focused on Bram's tent, my heart pounding as the opening drew closer and closer. In a woosh, I flew past the canvas into the interior and shifted to a stop.

Two attendants jumped back, wide-eyed. No, not slaves. They weren't dressed like Caravan mortals. Indentures didn't startle when Ravens shifted either. These must be lawmen from the village and . . . they had tied up Hamish MacCullough to a chair.

Heat rolled down my muscles. A growl lodged in my throat. I wanted to rip into him. But someone else already had. Blood dribbled from his nose. His jaw and cheek were black and blue and swollen. Had Bram ordered this? It was no less than what that pig slop deserved. If the lawmen weren't here, I'd finish him.

A flicker of recognition registered in Hamish's bleary, pinched gaze as he took me in.

"Brady," he rasped, "Sullivan. Kill him."

Who the feck was Brady Sullivan? That wasn't a Traveler name.

"Moira . . . was right," he quietly spat. "Brady—"

"Filena?" I snapped.

"Don't . . . know."

Now I growled and my fingers curled into fists.

"Authorities . . ." Hamish slurred out in a grimaced whisper, "not from . . . Brady."

Not from Brady?

Kill him.

I narrowed my eyes.

The mortals exchanged a wary look. One appeared like he was

about to ask us to leave. Pulling my gaze from Hamish, I turned to my boys and gathered them close.

"Corbin," I whispered low, "go to Gran's wagon. If she's not there, find her and Glenna, aye?"

"Aye." Corbin faded into a raven and flew from the tent.

"Owen"—I cupped his shoulder—"find Cian and stay with him."

If the authorities were here, Cian was successful. Dipping his head first, Owen then flew away a second later, leaving only me and Sean.

"The Wild Hunt has already begun," Sean whispered, his eyes darting around the empty tent. "Or they'd be in here."

I tilted my head. Had Sean been at the wedding event? There's no way he would have caught up to me in the sky otherwise. "Only interfere if he's cheating and I'm not able to fight back, aye?" I hurried out. Sean nodded. "I have elder magic, though."

Sean's smile was instant. "I saw."

A smile trembled on my lips in reply but my gut was tearing apart. "If they've hurt her—" my words choked to a stop. No, I couldn't give into my worst fears yet. I needed to focus. "You," I addressed both villagers, "seen a mortal lass with long auburn hair? By the name Filena Merrick or Fáiléanna MacCullough? She was in this tent earlier."

The men shook their heads.

"She's my bonded wife," I clipped out. "If you see *my* property in the custody of another, you're duty bound by the Kingdom of Carran to arrest them, understand?"

"Aye," a lawman said, his eyes large as he took in my taloned fingers and my wild fae dressed and decorated state. "Who . . ." He cleared his throat. "Your name?"

"Rhylen Lonan," I answered, my canines on display. "The next chieftain of West Tribe."

I shifted into a raven and cawed for Sean to follow.

Outside of the tent, the night glided off my wings. My heart gathered shadows while my eyes hunted for the prince in a dark sea of silk top hats—and found him. Blood painted my vision. War drums beat behind my ribs. I swooped around a group of men and gracefully shifted into a full run, Sean behind me. Dead leaves crunched like bones beneath my bare feet. Spectators startled out of our way. A few lifted cries of alarm.

The Fiachnas were off to the side of a small stage, talking to a group of men. Lantern light glinted off the gold paint lining my tattoos. At the metallic gleam, Bram's eyes blew wide. Bryok pivoted to peer over his shoulder.

He didn't have a chance to react.

Hot pain ricocheted down my muscles at the impact. I immediately dug my taloned fingers into the earth and snapped my wings wide to break my speed.

The force threw Bryok back several yards. He hit the ground rolling with a hard grunt. But he didn't stay down long enough for me to launch another unguarded attack. With a roar, he flew to his feet, flexing his wings in an act of dominance over me. I started laughing. Of all the illusions, that was one every Traveler could see through.

The black eyes locked onto mine glittered with rage. He flashed me a flinty grin as the top hats around us began making bets on who would win.

Asking him about Filena formed on the tip of my tongue.

He fought by pecking at the mind instead of with fists, though. I wouldn't give him weapons to use against my already waning sanity.

Instead, I shouted, "I officially challenge Bram and Bryok Fiachna for West Tribe!"

"You're banished!" Bryok shouted back. "No tribe will claim you."

"Am I struck from your sight, Bryok Fiachna?" I laughed through my heaving breaths. "Not one elder or chieftain at the Truth Telling Tree turned their back on me."

"West Tribe elders—"

"—Three were on their knees before me when I left! The others faced me!"

The prince looked to his right and I followed his gaze. Several elders and North Tribe's chieftain had apparently followed me here to validate the challenge I issued at the wedding ceremony. The chieftain dipped his head, confirming my words were true.

Fury contorted Bryok's face. Then, with a growl, he charged.

I was ready for the fecker.

Like an eejit, he lowered his shoulder to pommel me like I had him instead of keeping his fists up in defense. My swing was swift. His head shot to the side with the bruising hit to his jaw. The knuckles on two of my fingers split. But adrenaline numbed the pain.

He tilted toward the ground from the momentum.

I grabbed his hair with a hard yank and stopped his fall. Clawing at my hands, he tried twisting out of my grip instead of attacking my open side while, once more, leaving his body unprotected. The disgusting arse had never had to fight for a single damn thing in his entire entitled life until Filena and it showed.

I kneed him in the gut. Air punched from his lungs in a choked breath.

Tugging him close, I growled in his ear, "If you touched her—"

"We all did," he answered with a dark chuckle.

I detonated.

Grabbing his head, a guttural roar ripped from my chest. He thrashed in my hold. I squeezed. I wanted to crush his skull. I yearned to snap his neck. But I wouldn't. I needed him alive—

Bryok shifted into a raven and flew from my grasp with a loud caw.

"Fecking coward!" I shouted.

Power surged up from the earth into my shaking muscles. Wind whipped around me and fluttered my wing feathers. I stayed in place and tracked him with my eyes. That pompous arse blended into the shadows right as hands seized my arms and jerked me backward.

The tips of my wings flung his gang off me with little effort.

I knew this was a pack attack to distract me—which was against the rules. But so was shifting into a raven. I could call the challenge and the elders would declare me heir. But Bryok hadn't suffered enough.

Pivoting on my heel, I shot my palms out, like I had seen other elders do. It was stupid to turn my back on Bryok. Still, I focused all my energy on creating a large gust of wind, the best defense against Ravens. Air rushed around my body. The warm, solid magic of earth beneath my feet quaked with my building anger. Bryok's boys lunged at me again. The wind spinning around me raced down my arms and jetted out where my palms faced.

The bastards were blasted backward, knocking down attendees as they flew past.

I lowered my hands, too enraged to fully consider the power I had just wielded. Or that, when in my elven form instead of a raven, I had little issue commanding the elements.

But I felt the magic loss immediately.

My head floated in dizziness for a couple of seconds. I staggered forward a step only to abruptly halt. Bryok shifted in front of me. A gruesome smile was my only warning before he tossed an object at my face. Dozens of white-winged moths suddenly swarmed my head. I knew it was an illusion. Still, I reared back in reflex. Bryok's taunting grin widened as moths flew from his mouth.

I froze at the disturbing sight.

"Rhylen!" Sean called out nearby.

My head snapped back. Stars burst in my vision. Another hit—this one to my chest—knocked the gasping breath from my burning lungs.

I was an eejit and fell for his trick.

But not again.

Baring my canines, I balled my bleeding fingers into a fist and swung.

He burst into six different ravens, the five illusions and him flying in different directions. The birds swooped and dove at me. My instinct was to flinch and cover my head. But I didn't feel a single peck.

One bird, I noticed, flew out of range of my hands or wings. Bryok must have expected me to bat the illusioned birds away and, thus, stayed out of reach. My gaze locked onto his form flying circles around me. I knew it was him. The flying was too smooth, too calculated.

Clenching my jaw, I pulled at the wind with clawing fingers and threw a ball of air at him—and hit.

The gust knocked him into a rapid tumble. His wings flapped furiously to regain control. But the force had disoriented his balance too much. He shifted right as his body smacked into the invisible wards and bounced off. The cracking snap of bones rolled across the hushed, riveted crowd. Then his loud cry when his body hit the ground.

The field tilted in my vision. I needed to replenish my magic. But I wouldn't shift yet. I had declared a challenge against Bram and wouldn't give the elders a reason to disqualify me. Despite my lightheadedness, I strode over on solid footing, feeling the crowing victory with every step.

From my closing distance, I noted the blood gushing from Bryok's broken nose and split lip. His left arm laid in the grass at an unnatural angle. The lower part of his jaw was swelling, one eye nearly shut, and his hair was a tangled mess. He had shifted away his wings, though. A smart move. I would break them both if he had kept them out.

I should kill him. Oh how my blood screamed to spill more of his. It was within my right. But West Tribe needed two things going into winter: hardworking individuals and money. Bryok was lazy and, as a former heir, would fetch a hefty bag of coin from Seren—a fate worse than death for him. As the winner, I was allowed to sell the defeated in a gov challenge to protect me against retribution.

I slowed over his supine form, delighted by how his body

shook in pain.

"You are no longer heir—"

The shrill scream of a girl echoed from the woods. A fresh wave of terror pebbled down my skin. The crowd around me broke into cheers. The murmuring voices of those making wagers boiled my already scalding blood.

Bryok's greasy, bloody smile was slow. "Didn't sound like Fáiléanna's scream."

My head whipped toward the Hunt.

Was he suggesting . . . ?

The bruising breath in my lungs squeezed.

Another scream ripped over the charged crowd and bile coated my tightening throat.

Filena, Filena, Filena . . .

They sold her to The Wild Hunt?

How? Nobody here owned her.

Or was this another trick?

My gaze frantically darted around. A few top hats lifted their drink in salute. The ones who bet on me and won. Fury thundered hot down my trembling muscles.

My mate.

My beautiful wife.

A sob lodged in my throat. "Get her out!"

Bryok only laughed as he fought for consciousness.

My eyes locked with Sean's. My breaths were sharp and quick. Sweat dripped from my forehead. I couldn't think.

"My mate," I whispered, the horror painfully swelling inside me.

Sean moved toward me. "You have el—"

"Lonan." Bram spoke my name in an eerily calm tone. His son, West Tribe's former heir, lay broken at my feet, the elders and North Tribe's chieftain witnesses to my victory, and Bram had managed to sound utterly bored with just one word. "Let's make a bargain."

Chapter Forty-Four

RHYLEN LONAN

I spun toward the chieftain.

"Rhylen," Sean stressed behind me. "You can—"

"Cillian MacCullough is under arrest."

My gaze shot to where he pointed and my already weakening pulse stuttered. Men surrounded Cian, keeping him on his knees. My brother's hands were tied, his mouth gagged. Where was Owen? Did he fly back toward the wedding event in search of him?

"Cian Merrick is a free man," I snapped.

Roiling fear darkened Cian's eyes. I had never seen my brother so afraid. I started to move but Cian shook his head, a warning to do nothing rash. Then his gaze darted to the Hunt and my stomach lurched.

Filena, Filena, Filena . . .

"Cillian delivered the constable right to us too." Bram took a nonchalant sip of the whiskey in his hand. "Your former slave lied to West Tribe about being orphans and hid Fáiléanna Mac-

Cullough from her rightful owner."

I stormed toward him. "You can't sell him. Cian Merrick is *not* a slave."

Bram cocked his head. "He's willing to sell himself to Seren to save your sister from joining you in jail."

I closed my eyes for a furious second to gather myself before I went into a primal blackout rage. Bram could still win a case to sell Glenna to Seren in further restitution if Cian didn't bring him a sum large enough to pay back property losses.

Was selling Cian to Seren to compensate Hamish?

No, the mortal was under arrest and guarded. He had no legal rights now.

Who was demanding reparations?

Every muscle in my body stilled. I blew out a slow breath, trying to focus in my spiraling panic. But all I could hear were those screams from the forest replaying over and over again in my head.

My wife . . . was she safe? Had a fae marked her already?

Gods, my heart was breaking.

"Who sold my bonded mate to the Hunt?" I choked out. "That, too, is illegal."

"Here's my bargain, Rhylen Lonan. Sell yourself to Seren and all debts your clan owes for harboring runaways will be paid."

My gaze traveled back to Cian and he violently shook his head.

The lawmen watched me with sharp eyes. A couple readied cuffs of enchanted cold iron—the local village authorities I had asked Cian to bring to arrest Hamish. Another wave of guilt tightened the sob forming in my throat.

I had failed to protect him too.

I looked to the elders and chieftain of North Tribe, but they wouldn't interfere in a challenge.

And this was *still* a challenge.

Bram was a trickster. His family had held unchallenged legacy roles for centuries. He would lose to me in a physical fight now that I had elder magic. Challenging a gov didn't require physical domination, though. Tricks and cleverness to legally remove the sitting gov from the tribe would also count as a win—and why Bram had ordered banishment before I could officially challenge him.

Too much of this evening was premeditated. And Hamish MacCullough had no believable claim.

My back straightened. "Filena Merrick is *not* a slave," I gritted out. "How was she sold to the Hunt?"

"Brenna Meadows and Glenna Lonan are boarded up in their wagon," Bram added. "Agree to the bargain and they'll be released."

The fury was instant. "You made a bargain with me before West Tribe!"

"They're not physically harmed, being starved, freezing, or banished." Bram took another sip of his whiskey. "What bargain have I broken, Lonan?"

"You locked up an ancient? My sister who is innocent?" My voice rose and I practically screamed, "What the feck is wrong with you?!"

Gran would remain calm but Glenna would be terrified, and my gut twisted into painful knots as another wave of guilt hit me.

Bram's eyes darkened. "You nearly killed my son and—"

"In a fair fight!"

"—not the first attempt either. Your anger continually clouds your judgement and has become a liability to West Tribe. I don't want to lock up an ancient, but I need to protect West Tribe from your unhinged fire."

His words were like a sharp slap across my face. Gran had warned me to keep my fire under control. She knew the Fiachnas were baiting me. She also knew I would go to any lengths to protect those in my care.

I rolled my bottom lip into my mouth and tasted blood. My head was light from magic loss and fury. Pain bloomed along my jaw and where I was punched in the chest.

But *nothing* compared to the pain of failing my family.

My eyes flicked to the game field once more. Mist, illuminated by the Harvest Moon, swirled low to the ground. The shapes of our ancestors appeared and dissipated into the night's shadows. Were my da and mam among the spirits? Granda?

A scowl pinched my brows. I drew in a deep breath and exhaled slowly. Bram was playing with my emotions instead of answering the one burning question I had.

"Who sold my mate to The Wild Hunt?!"

Bram didn't even blink an eye. "Her mortal husband visited me earlier today. Did you know she was already married?"

Brady Sullivan, Hamish's voice slurred in my head. *Kill him.*

My whirling thoughts came to a skidded stop.

Her contracted husband was here? My gaze drifted to Bryok, who was being lifted onto a makeshift stretcher. I scanned the crowd, but so many men were of middle years and older. Even if this Brady fellow were her mortal husband, only a Traveler could sell their slave into the Hunt.

I focused my attention back onto Bram.

There was only one logical explanation.

The required mortal registrar from the Kingdom of Carran's constabulary was either tricked into believing the raven on File-na's wrist was a slave mark or he was paid off to ignore the truth. And the Fiachnas would trick first to profit most off my wife. Especially if they sold her for debts owed.

My sickening gut shouted that Bryok was listed as her master too.

Another scream ripped through the night sky and hot tears pricked the back of my eyes. The primal rage coiled tight in my belly hit my bloodstream.

Sean slid in front of me and gripped my arms before I exploded. "Don't fall for his trick," he rushed out in a whisper.

"Agree to my bargain, Lonan," Bram said, as if speaking to a spooked animal, "and I'll personally bring back Fáiléanna. Cillian will walk free and your nan and sister will be released."

"And if I don't?"

"Debts for your family's negligence have to be paid somehow."

My heart was violently pounding against my ribs.

I didn't know what to do.

I didn't want Filena marked and not because she was my wife. I would love her regardless. I would *always* want her by my side. To be marked in a Hunt was an abhorrent violation. Gods, I wanted to vomit just thinking about it. The Fiachnas had a plan to buy her back too; there's no way they'd part with her that easily. She was too great of an asset. Bryok didn't care about consent either. He would take what he wanted—like he had with Braelin.

To protect Filena from just one of those horrors, I would sacrifice myself a hundred times over.

That fecker would *not* sell my sister or Cian to Seren to pay for debts either.

"Rhylen," Sean gritted out, his eyes wild.

"I . . . I must . . . promise to care for her and Cian." I could bare-ly get the words out. My soul was shattering. I dragged in a sharp breath and grimaced against the pain. "Look after my family."

His fingers dug into my skin. "You asked me to step in if they were cheating." He leaned in close to my face and harshly whis-pered, "I've been trying to tell you, Rhy. You can pass through the wards. You have elder magic, aye?"

I reared back.

My head snapped to the game field.

Holy gods . . . I had forgotten. I had seen the gates pre-gala and built the chieftain's game tent but had never attended The Wild Hunt. Fellys weren't allowed. This event was explicitly for ladies and gents of higher ranks and classes.

Feck, Bram had dug so deep into my head I couldn't think straight in my primal state.

"You're a gov now, lad," Sean whispered. "Make them all at-tend *you*, heir of West Tribe."

Tears of gratitude blurred my vision for a moment. I grabbed Sean's face. "I owe you my life, friend." I kissed his forehead and stepped back, fluttering my wings until I alighted in the air.

Knowing Filena's safety was no longer held hostage to a bar-gain changed everything. Gran's, Glenna's, and Cian's too. I need-ed to secure Bram, though, to ensure he couldn't harm others while I hunted down my mate.

Cillian delivered the constable right to us too.

I counted the villagers around Cian—eight. Two were in the tent. There were far too many lawmen here for arresting one drunk mortal. And why did so many carry enchanted cold iron?

Authorities . . . not from Brady.

My mind stopped whirring for a full, throbbing second.

This Brady Sullivan mortal didn't bring legal representation to validate his claim? And Bram still bargained with him? My gaze wandered back to Cian and it hit me. Arresting Cian, holding Filena hostage against me, banishing me . . . they knew Brady was coming. Bram must have had the nearby village authorities in his pocket too.

But whatever he had planned with Brady must have backfired. He refused to answer my questions instead of flaunting the evidence before all.

Bram sipped his whiskey, ending with an apologetic dip of his head to the attendees around him. The arrogant bastard was a master at verbal sleight of hand and placating whatever emotion distracted others from seeing the trick.

"Who is asking for reparations?" Mountains were quaking in my voice.

Bram smirked to hide the growing fear in his darting eyes. Was he looking for Brady Sullivan? "Every second you stall, she—"

"I demand proof of the marriage!" I shouted for all to hear.

The chieftain laughed under his breath, a dark, slithering sound—a scared sound. "There's a contract, naturally. Mortals like everything in paper."

More deflection.

"What lawmen were present to validate the marriage contract? Who signed as witness to the reparation bargains?" When neither Bram nor any of the authorities spoke up, I turned toward the registrar and added, "I released my wife from legal indentured servitude before we exchanged vows. The raven on her wrist is our mate bond mark. Bryok Fiachna isn't her master."

At that, Bram's eyes widened slightly. So, I had guessed right. *Make them all attend you, heir of West Tribe.*

I pointed at the lawmen. "Contain Bram Fiachna until I return. He is *not* to be released to anyone but me, under any circumstances."

The lawmen didn't move.

But another tribe's elder did. Grabbing a cuff, the gov gritted his teeth through the pain and snapped it onto Bram's wrist to ensure the former chieftain couldn't shift and fly away. Bram fell to his knees in a soft cry. Before he could react with his elemental magic, a different elder stepped forward.

"Bram Fiachna, with the authority appointed by the gods, we revoke your elder magic until a trial determines your guilt or innocence."

"He married a mortal!" Bram said between gritted teeth. "He failed his bargain with West Tribe."

"A mortal is his True Mate," an elder said. "You believe yourself above the gods, Bram Fiachna? And if you illegally sold his True Mate to The Wild Hunt, you have broken both mortal and fae laws."

A different elder dipped his head. "We will contain him until your return."

The validation emboldened me and I continued. "Release Cian Merrick. There's no proof my family has committed any crimes, aye? And," I said, pausing a beat, "find a man named Brady Sullivan and hold him for questioning."

I may regret that decision. But I had a sinking feeling the contract wasn't valid or he would have brought the law to Bram's doorstep when he arrived. Why else would he sell Filena to The Wild Hunt under Bryok's name? He could get far more from court ordered reparations.

With a flap of my wings, I shot into the sky and sailed past the wards toward the woods, fear chilling my blood. Trees whipped past me; my vision blurred with the shifting shadows. Bile burned its way up my throat as panic settled deeper into my frantic pulse. When the woods thickened, I landed and ran, calling out her name. When the forest thinned, I alighted into the air again.

Filena, Filena, Filena . . .

I had failed to protect my mate this day, but the night wasn't over. I wouldn't fail her again.

Chapter Forty-Five

FILENA LONAN

My teeth chattered. The chill had seeped into my bones. I could no longer feel my feet and unbound hands. The numbness had dimmed the throbbing in my ankle, though, which made it easier to move at times, thank the wishless falling stars. I rubbed at my bare arms and frantically swept my gaze around the moonlit woods.

I had lost all track of time. Once yanked off the cart, we were given fifteen minutes to run, hide, or accept our fate before the hunters were released. I only knew the loud thudding of my heart in my ears and the fear that any shadow would reveal a monster. Every so often, a scream would pierce the air and fresh tears would clog my eyes.

Moving kept me hopeful, but it also made me a target.

The Blackthorn card vision showed that Rhylen would rescue me. But what if the gods changed their mind? What if he fell for Bram's and Bryok's trap? *Seeing* the future wasn't a guarantee of what was to come.

I needed to find shelter.

Limping as quietly as possible, I moved through the under-brush and ducked beneath low-hanging branches. Scratches lined my arms and face, but I couldn't feel anything but the cold's sting—

The sudden crunch of leaves startled my skin into goose-bumps. Biting back a whimper, I quickly crouched behind a tree trunk skirted by tall ferns. It could be another girl. I hoped it was just another girl.

I started to lose my balance and adjusted my weight. Stab-bing pain sliced across my ankle. I dared not move. A cold flush of clammy sweat beaded on my forehead from trying to hold still. My camisole and petticoats practically glowed beneath the full moon and I prayed the shadows were enough to hide me.

Magic trickled down my arms to my fingers. I could feel the lightness of words forming on my tongue. How this was possible, I didn't know. But I was grateful for even the smallest measure of protection.

Movement caught my eye.

Three yards away, a hunter crept by where I hid and stilled—a fire spirit from the mountains beyond Carran's borders. Shaggy red hair fell to the sharp point of his long ears. He tilted his head to lift one of those bladed ears to the wind. Moonlight bathed his tawny skin in brushes of silver. Unnaturally bright golden eyes roamed over the forest as his nose scented the air.

"A field of wildflowers . . ." The elf's gravelly voice scraped the silence and I flinched. The hunter scented the air again.

"Little half-fae," he growled low, taking a step closer, "let's bargain."

My eyes narrowed. He believed me part fae because I smelled

like wildflowers? Was this the scent of my magic? And bargain for what? No, I wouldn't fall for his trick.

His nostrils flared once more. Then his lips pressed into a look of disappointment.

Not keen on smelling like you either, pet.

Magic continued flowing down my arms and warmed the tips of my fingers. Stars, the heat felt good. But I feared I would pass out if I released the slightest drop of power. Where was this energy coming from? Was it normal to regenerate within twenty-four hours? And how was I growing resistant to the magic restraint on my good ankle?

Those gold eyes hunted closer to where I hid.

Don't see me, don't see me . . .

I held my breath.

Twigs snapped behind the fae male. He twisted to peer over his shoulder. A half-second later, he began stalking toward the sound. His movements were graceful and calculated—deadly.

Let it be a wild animal and not a girl.

A large stag to ram that bastard with its antlers would be especially delightful.

The words had barely left my mind when a doe leapt from the underbrush. My mouth dropped open. Was that a coincidence? I was thinking of deer when—*Merciful stars . . .* from the shadows, a stag moved into a wedge of moonlight.

How?

My mind couldn't make sense of what I was seeing.

The stag lowered his head with a loud grunt. And, the next flutter of my breath, he jumped into a sprint. Hissing in a language I didn't understand, the fire spirit spun and ran past me, too focused on the angry buck to see my cowering form in the ferns.

Strands of auburn hair blew across my face in his wake.

Air rushed from my tight lungs.

What . . . what had just happened?

Spooked, I searched for movement, too afraid to move but more afraid not to.

Satisfied I was now alone, I started to stand on shaking legs. A bolt of fire shot up from my ankle. A cry clawed up my throat but I clamped down my jaw. Move. I needed to move before that fae male tracked back to my scent. Gritting my teeth, I blindly reached out for a tree to grab onto when something wet licked my cheek.

I clapped a hand over my mouth and whipped toward the source, begging the gods, once more, that it was only a wild animal. And . . . a smile flitted across my trembling lips. Large brown doe eyes blinked back at me.

Gods. Stars. *Sweet moons above*, I was on the verge of fainting from relief. I had to stifle a tear-choked laugh.

The doe nudged my hand then gently leaned against my body, as if she wanted me to use her for support. Grateful, I placed my shaking fingers onto her back and pushed up, grimacing against the ache in my ankle. I would kick Cian when I saw him again, the dramatic arse. *If* I saw him again.

The doe licked my arm and my heart burst. I missed Barry's grumpy-but-squishy face so much. Tears gathered on my lashes. I craved snuggles with Sheila and laughter over Lloyd too. Would I see my familiars again?

I had to believe so. Rhylen's Blackthorn card vision was the *only* thing keeping me from completely falling apart right now.

But also, I really wanted to kick Cian's ankle followed by

both calves—who knew calves could tempt payback violence too?

Once steady on my feet, the doe began walking, encouraging me to hold onto her.

I felt like a fawn taking steps for the first time, my legs were so wobbly from pain, fatigue, from endless fear.

"Thank you, darlin'," I whispered.

Her ears flicked in reply and I blinked back more emotion. Falling suns, I was an unraveling mess. But I needed to keep my wits about me. Straightening my spine, lifting my chin, I took another determined step to survive this night unmarked by a male that wasn't my husband.

We moved downwind and kept to the shadows.

As we navigated deeper into Caledona Wood, a fluffle of bunnies appeared at my feet. One let me scoop her up to nuzzle against my cheek. Every few minutes, other animals joined my growing herd. A spotted owl swooped onto the doe's back. Two black forest cats wove playfully between the ferns.

My teeth continued to chatter. My skin burned from the night's chill. But my steps grew stronger and my lungs were breathing easier. I could feel more and more of my magic returning too.

A beautiful gray fox trotted up beside me from the underbrush. Then three ferrets happily scampered ahead of the doe. At my heel, waddled a mother skunk and her tiny brood of wee skunklets. They were so darling I almost scooped them up to hold in my arms too.

For a few stolen moments, I felt safe, as if I had awoken from a nightmare and fallen into a fantastical dream.

But this was real.

I was being hunted.

The animals who followed me would attract attention. My forest friends probably masked my scent, though. The sounds of their movements hid my very human ones to trained ears too—

A scream rent the air and my entire body locked up.

My vision blurred. I drew in a hiccuped breath. The forest around me grew deathly still.

Rhylen, my heart wept. *Rhylen* . . .

Closing my eyes, I imagined him wrapping his arms around me. I yearned to press my cheek to his strong chest and sigh at the sound of each fiery heartbeat. Smiling, he would then bury his face into my riot of hair and hum a hauntingly beautiful melody.

Our song.

And just like that night a week ago, while barefoot and in my underthings, my body would begin to sway with his in a slow dance beneath the trees. I ached for him. His deep, melodic voice, his laugh, his romance . . . My heart. Stars, my heart had fallen from the night sky and was still falling, forever falling for Rhylen Lonan.

My eyes fluttered open and I swallowed back the emptiness carving out my chest.

I had to believe he would find me.

If I let that spark of hope slip from my fingers, I would perish beneath the grief.

I brushed at a tear on my cheek and paused. The stag who had come to my rescue watched me from a shaft of moonlight filtering through the trees. My breath caught. White fur softly illuminated in the shadows, setting off the lovely golden hue of his large antlers. Stars, he was magnificent.

But how did he know I had needed help at that precise moment?

My brow furrowed and the corners of my lips dipped.

I was so relieved to escape that fire spirit hunter, to have the doe's assistance, to feel a soft bunny snuggling against my cheek, I had forgotten about how the stag suddenly appeared, as if summoned by my plea to the gods.

The very gods who allowed one of their own to be enslaved by mere fae and mortals?

I shoved Bryok's disgusting voice from my thoughts.

But I couldn't help but mentally stumble over his insinuation—*one of their own.*

Fae blood is in your veins.

Memories of the faerie lady in The Wilds flashed in my mind, of her rounded belly, her golden hair so much like Cian's and Mam's . . . her forest animals.

My heart hammered in my chest.

The Mother had sent her messenger squirrel to me, to ensure I married my True Mate while we had six full days before Samhain Eve.

And, if Bryok was to be believed, Gran spoke with—

Holy Mother of Stars!

Was I actually related to a Sisters Three?

As absurd as that sounded, and it really, really did, puzzle pieces began to furiously click into place. Was this why I often felt like two different people? Well, three, apparently.

I could *see* the future, like the Maiden.

And like the Crone, I could curse.

Then there was the Mother and I bit back a smile while burying my face into the darling wee bunny in my hands.

Even my beautiful, sweet, witty, chaotic brother had unapologetically identified with and manifested this powerful feminine magic inside of him too.

I didn't know if I wanted to laugh or cry over this revelation.

Midnight skies above, Cian and I were descendants of a faerie goddess.

And I felt like such an eejit. All the clues were there all along. But I couldn't *see* my own future—the price of my magic. I swore the gods found ways to keep those around me silent until I empowered my own sight too.

Rhylen knew I was a mortal demi-goddess and treated me no differently than before. He encouraged me to not fear myself nor my future, to see myself as the same girl I had always been—the one he loved.

But Bryok's obsession . . . it twisted and writhed inside of me.

All his cruelty these past two weeks was all to be in the possession of a goddess. To sire children who would carry the blood and magic of the gods. To dominate the descendent of a legendary, immortal creature of fae.

And I was done.

Lowering to the forest floor, I grabbed the ankle cuff with my frozen fingers.

No one would force me to be subservient to them again.

Clenching my teeth, I pulled; a molten forge of fury poured down my arms.

I didn't exist for their pleasure or profit. Nor would I be made to fear myself. I was strong, kind and unkind, loud, clever, fierce— powerful.

The cold iron clanked to the ground.

Magical.

I was *magic*.

Power rushed back into me in an equinox tumble of tree blossoms and autumn leaves—life, death, and rebirth.

The Mother, Maiden, and Crone.

Seer and witch.

Mortal and fae.

I peered up at the Harvest Moon, a Mother's moon that was full and bright, and I bowed my head.

Let every hunter in these woods fear me.

And if Rhylen didn't finish Bryok, that bastard would face my wrath next.

Chapter Forty-Six

FILENA LONAN

The trees groaned in a low gust of wind. My eyes tracked each moving shadow. Mist curled at my feet. The stag walked ahead of us, ears perked, his large antlers and white fur otherworldly in the moonlight.

Shapes formed in the low-moving fog before fading into the night's shadows. I pressed a hand to my heart to honor the ancestors who guarded this meandering corner of Caledona Wood.

"Protect the girls," I whispered.

I felt endless guilt that the others being hunted didn't have the same protections as me—not in magic, not in companions. I hadn't crossed paths with a sigil-marked boar yet either. Hopefully that meant most were hiding and hiding well.

The ferns danced in a midnight breeze and a shiver prickled my skin.

My body swayed—I was hungry, thirsty, and chilled to the point of burning. I felt like I was fevering. If I could heal myself, how would that affect my energy levels? The mortal side of me drained to the point of near-passing out with any large draw of magic. And I couldn't afford to be any weaker physically. Already, with how intensely my head floated in dizziness, I didn't know if I could take another step.

But I also didn't know how much time the hunters had left.

The doe guiding me down various trails slowed and glanced back at me. The corners of my mouth tilted in a tired smile. I could continue—*would* continue. However, I would give my last slice of cake to not feel a breeze ice my skin and dance through my rat's nest of hair. The camisole clinging to my frame was thin; my petticoats were equally threadbare.

The doe's ears flicked and then she nodded her head while peering back down the trail.

I followed her gaze and my tired smile fell.

I blinked.

An adorably fluffy raccoon stood in the middle of the trail and held up a wool sock.

"George?" I rasped in a breathy whisper.

He waved the sock for me to follow and I had to bite back a giggle.

If this were a fever dream, it was a welcome diversion.

The doe began walking again and I rested my hand on her back to steady my balance. We followed the trail around a large, sprawling oak covered in moss and lichen. George scampered ahead, pausing only long enough to ensure I still followed. The path wended through more trees and rambled by a hollowed-out log—and I froze.

I had seen this log in a vision.

A vision about my mam.

I sucked in a hopeful breath. Would I actually see my mam? My heart trilled but I quickly squashed the excitement. Emotionally, I was in a fragile place. It wouldn't take much for me to shatter right now. Surviving mark free until the end of the Hunt could be my only focus.

George climbed atop the log and made a chittering sound.

Grimacing, I lowered to my knees and peeked inside.

My jaw slackened.

Piles and piles of mismatched clothes were tossed inside: socks, shirts, coats, caps, suspenders.

"Moons and stars, how large is this thieving operation?" I asked him.

George gestured at the opening, hitting my face with the dew-sodden sock—*three times*. Cian would give up all his secrets to watch a raccoon playfully hit me with a wet sock. Barry too. Those two were not allowed to join forces, not even in my head. Skies, I suppressed a laugh and crawled inside.

A groan passed my lips. The relief was immediate and my wind-chapped skin could weep. George shuffled inside after me and began rummaging through clothes. His little paws handed me a lad's knit cap first. Amused, I put it on my head. Next, he selected two different colored woolen socks—one gray, the other tan. Excellent taste. A gent's navy blue silk smoking jacket was arranged around my shoulders last. My fingers rubbed at the soft material, trying not to laugh that the first time I wore silk was while sitting inside a log with a shifty raccoon. Satisfied that I was warm enough, the little fella climbed into my lap, circled to find the coziest position, and then settled in.

So tired was I, so overcome with wave after wave of heart-stomping emotion, that I barely registered the lick on my chin.

A pair of yellow eyes blinked at me.

"Barry?" I nearly squealed, quieting my volume at the last minute. George chittered a coo as I threw my arms around my fox's neck. "I missed you, Muffin Moo."

If he were here, that meant Gran and Glenna were released and a layer of stress sluffed off me.

I leaned back to squish his grumpy face and he licked my chin again, making me laugh under my breath. Then he glared at George, who still occupied my lap, before laying down at my side and peering out into the forest, on alert.

Across from the log, the doe curled into the ferns but the stag remained on his feet. He peered into the woods and I had the strangest notion he was waiting for instructions. Did I want him to stay or help others?

There was only one answer. I had magic. It wasn't much in my present state, but it was far more protection than the other sigil-marked boars possessed.

"Help other girls," I whispered. "Save as many as you can, aye?"

He dipped his head low, as if bowing to me, then trotted off into the shadows.

The doe lifted her head and the forest cats, ferrets, gray fox, and skunks moved in to settle around her while the owl flew to perch in a tree. The bunnies, however, hopped into the log, much to George's delight, who pulled them in close to him.

"You really do like cuddling, don't you, darlin'?"

George lifted a paw to my mouth. I was about to snort when I heard it—a voice. It was faint, but it sounded male and . . . frantic. My brows creased. I forced myself to breathe and pet George's soft fur. What if it was a hunter? But what if it was Rhylen? I leaned forward and angled my head to peer out into the darkness.

The cry came again. He was screaming a name. The voice wasn't close, though. The hoarse, strained quality muffled the shouted word. Tears pricked the back of my eyes. What if it was Rhylen and he flew over the log and didn't find me?

I started to move and my gut seized.

What if it was a trap? A sound illusion to lure out girls desperate to be saved?

The pounding in my ears was so loud, I feared I wouldn't be able to hear my own whisper.

"Filena!"

My heart came to an abrupt stop. But my body exploded into motion. *Rhylen.* Gingerly setting George and the bunnies aside, I crawled toward the log's opening—and halted. The shadows of trees shifted over the forest, the only movement around me. I was too physically weak to stand. I couldn't run away if a hunter found me.

But I was desperate to see my husband. And he couldn't see me if I remained hidden.

Fear prickled the back of my neck.

I moved anyway and crawled onto the trail.

The forest animals were on their feet. I was so focused on spotting Rhylen, I didn't notice the forest cats' hackles on full alert, or how Barry stood beside the gray fox and snarled. Not until a dark chuckle gripped the silence around us.

I twisted to peer over my shoulder with a faint gasp.

A hunter stood a few paces behind me on the trail.

Silvery hair fell to his chin, his skin pale in the moonlight. Pewter eyes roamed down my back. And, atop his head, were a sooty pair of horns. It was the Puck from the bordering kingdom who, on Áine's Day, tried to glamour my mind.

"On hands and knees like a good little boar," the male purred.

I gripped the log to turn myself to face him, too weak to pull myself up to stand.

But not too weak to curse his horned arse—I hoped.

"End your hunt," I warned, jaw clenched to hide my shaking as I knelt in the mossy ground. Magic heated the tips of my fingers, to my relief, and the words grew lighter on my tongue. "Or you'll blow away with the breeze—"

"Filena!" Rhylen screamed again. Closer this time.

My eyes shot to the sky. I opened my mouth to shout back, but my throat had closed. A sob pounded behind my ribs. He was here. He was truly here. It wasn't in my mind. It wasn't a trick.

And I had almost forgotten about the Puck.

My eyes slid back to him.

The horned arsehole grinned at me and his long, sharp fangs gleamed in the moonlight. "Pretty mortal, I was told to not touch you," he said with a lick of his lips. "But I claim you."

Then he lunged.

Grabbing my arm, he yanked me to my feet.

"Rhylen!" I screamed, thrashing in the Puck's hold. "Rhylen!"

The Puck's grip on me tightened. Not knowing what else to do, I bit the back of his hand until I tasted blood. The hand clasping my arm released and I immediately fell back. My arse hit the ground first; sharp, bright pain bolted across my head second. With a groan, I quickly rolled to my stomach and clawed at the ground to inch away.

"Rhylen!" I shouted again.

The Puck grasped my injured ankle and squeezed. A cry whimpered past my trembling lips. With a purring chuckle, he dragged me to him, delighted by my terror. My camisole caught on the rough ground and ripped along my lower belly.

And I exploded into a wild rage.

No, that animal would fear *me*.

"So be it."

The words rang in the air. Power surged through me, hot and hungry. It wanted to devour this Puck and spit out his cursed bones. Yet, despite the rage demanding blood, I couldn't stomach actual gore or dismemberment, I learned. Gnats like him could be dealt with in other ways, though.

"Earth you shall return, dead as leaves," I hissed out through my tears. The words soared from my tongue. "Wind, he is yours to play with as you please."

He tugged me harder. With a clenched scream, I kicked as furiously as I could.

A cold gust of autumn air whipped at my skirts and frenzied the swirling fog into a cauldron's stir. He dropped my leg and I rolled to push myself up to a seat. Cackling delight lodged in my knotted throat.

The Puck's eyes grew owlish.

Then he fell to the earth.

Dry, brittle leaves flew into a laughing wind and blew away in a tumble. The tinny, crinkling song of his remains was a victory dance in my ears and I grinned.

That was a type of curse I could live with.

What would happen if I turned the next arsehole into a cute animal? My gaze caught on the mama skunk and her wee brood peeking out from beneath a cover of fern fronds and I nearly giggled over the idea—

The forest tilted.

My stomach lurched.

Oh gods . . . magic drain was quickly becoming a thorn in my side.

I reached out for the log and propped myself up when a large pair of wings eclipsed the moon. My eyes lifted to the night sky. My heart was beating so fast, I swore it was flying beside his. I couldn't see his face in the shadows, but he had seen mine. A second later, Rhylen swooped down to the deer trail in a graceful landing and . . . our eyes locked.

The world stopped spinning.

Time no longer existed.

My husband, my True Mate moved toward me, his eyes wild. And, sweet goddess, his preternatural beauty stole every drop of air in my body. I could die at just the heady sight of him.

The gold lining his tattoos gleamed in the shifting shadows. A black wrap hung low on his hips. Around his bicep was a gold torc. Rings graced his fingers and hoops lined his ears. His silky black hair was swept up into a warrior's knot and decorated with a crown made of twigs, leaves, berries, and feathers. Moonlight caressed the mesmerizing contours of his sculpted body. Those crushed elderberry-hued eyes of his were lined heavy with ash that streaked toward his temple.

Otherworldly eyes that were filling with tears.

"A *stór*," he choked out as he fell onto his knees before me.

The other half of my soul, my eternal true love had found me, and all the pain, all the anger, and fear of these past few hours hit me full force. A sob loosened from my chest. A sob that mirrored his own.

Before I could say his name, he pulled my shaking, weeping body to his.

Chapter Forty-Seven

Rhylen Lonan

Nothing felt as right as holding Filena in my arms. Just the touch of her cheek pressed to the curves of my shoulder lightened the panic still raging in my bloodstream. My body shook with tears. I couldn't stop them.

Her terror had gripped me since standing beneath the Truth Telling Tree with Braelin. My mate, my wife, she had called out for me and I was powerless to protect her.

Didn't sound like Fáiléanna's scream . . .

Bryok's final attack while I crowed over him dug at me endlessly. Had he heard her scream before she was sold to the Hunt? What had he done to her? I wanted to ask Filena, but I was afraid of her answer and I needed to handle the Fiachnas in a way that would benefit the tribe—not me.

But as my wife quietly wept in my arms, grief's blade twisted in my gut. A slow, painful death of guilt.

"I am so sorry, *mo ghrá*," I whispered into her hair and sucked in a sharp breath, grimacing back the bleating ache. I had torn through the trees, not caring if the branches shredded my wings. I would have ripped open the night sky, bloodied, broken, while fighting for one more breath, just to find her. "Whatever you ask of me—"

"Mark me," she gasped between hiccuped sobs. "Please mark me."

Despite my grief, despite my disgust over The Wild Hunt, the primal animal side of my courting magic moaned at her plea.

Just two words—*mark me*—and I was suddenly drowning in sensation.

I swallowed thickly, trying to push away the territorial arousal. The Harvest Moon seduced my magic, the thinned veil weakened my restraints. And being separated so cruelly from my True Mate? I was salivating to mark her, to take her to my bed and make her sing my name, for every part of her to smell of me.

The magic didn't care what she had just endured, though. But I did. Enough males had tried to own her this night. Stars above, it was taking everything in me to not hunt down those pieces of shite and snap their necks. To not kill Bryok and Bram too for touching my wife in *any* way.

"I . . . I could feel your terror." My teeth clenched. "I don't want to remind you of those monsters you just escaped."

"You are *nothing* like them, Rhy." She kissed the tears along my jaw. "Let all three kingdoms know I belong *only* to you."

My eyes fluttered closed as another wave of magic heightened my primal instincts.

"Mark me," she pleaded again. "Make me yours again."

And I lost all control.

Cradling her in my arms, my lips dragged down her neck and I inhaled deeply. *Feck* . . . "Your scent intoxicates me," I groaned. At the soft scrape of my canine on her perfect skin, my wings curled around our bodies. Only she existed. Only her and me. My fingers combed into her hair at the back of her head.

"I love you, Filena Lonan," I murmured, pressing her hand to my chest.

Then my teeth sank into the space between her neck and shoulder.

A bonfire burst into flame in my pulse. The heat of her name entwined with mine in a scorching trail of kisses across our souls. I softly growled a husky moan against her throat. Her nails dug into my pectorals, where I still covered her hand with mine; her quickened breaths grew languid. *Gods* . . . this pleasure. Ecstasy consumed me until I was only ash and smoke. Until the seductive drumbeats of our dancing hearts finished branding one another in fire and song.

"You are *mine*." My tongue licked the bite. "No one will harm you again." I leaned back and cradled her face. "No one will ever separate us. I promise you this, *mo shíorghrá*."

The rough callous of my thumb brushed her cheek. A tear rolled down her flushing mouth. I tipped her face up while I lowered my mouth to hers and then sealed my oath on her lips.

Our kiss was slow, reverent. The salt on her lips mixed with mine and our breaths trembled. Her hand left my chest to wrap around the back of my neck, pulling me closer. But nothing separated us now. Our souls were eternally intertwined in a magic so ancient, so pure, it felt as if the heavens and earth collided inside of me.

"You are achingly beautiful," Filena murmured against my

mouth. "I could die at the barest sight of you." Her fingers trailed down my shoulder blades to my wings.

Feck.

Me.

I shuddered before she even stroked one feather. "Lena . . . mate . . . gods. Make me lose all control when your body heals, lass."

"*All* control?" she blurted. "Seven suns, Rhylen, *that* confession was supposed to dissuade me from touching you?"

"Mhmm . . ." I nibbled on her bottom lip and moved my wings back with a flirtatious smile. "Incentive to rest."

"Only if you promise to pretty up for me like this again"—her fingers brushed the crown nesting on my head, then my granda's gold band around my bicep.

I leaned onto my heels and met her gray eyes, trying to calm my breathing. I needed to move away before I caved. Plus, we needed to laugh. *She* needed to laugh.

Taking her hand, I pushed back the rage at seeing the rope burns on her wrist and kissed the raven mark instead. Then my lips slid to the boar sigil, a mischievous slant to my smile. Laughter bubbled up from her chest. I knew how to distract her—delicious morsels of gossip and scandalously dark humor. We were always playful together, she and I. It was how we had cared for one another over the years.

Behind the mischief, though, a fury, one different than my territorial anger for her, rippled off me in furious waves. Our night was far from over. I still needed to deal with Bram and claim West Tribe.

But this moment . . . it was ours.

I blinked innocently at her.

"Don't you dare." She mocked glared at the teasing tilt of my lips.

Holding her gaze, I kissed the palm of her hand next. "Swill." Followed by the other. "Bill."

"I hope you get a brush stuck in your hair before the next full moon."

I grinned. Her fake curses never ceased to amuse me.

A breeze fluttered by and Filena shivered, then tugged a navy blue silk robe tight around her chest. My brows pushed together, just now aware of her ensemble. What in the fiery skies was she wearing? My eyes tipped up to the boys' cap knocked almost completely off her head, then flicked back down to the gent's smoking jacket, lower, lower, cataloguing every inch of her to the mis-matched wool socks drooping on her small feet. The scowl between my brows deepened. Had she only been in her underthings when taken?

"George dressed me." She kept her face straight and drawled, "Fashion is his passion, it is."

"George?" My scowling brows shot up.

"Aye, pet."

As if waiting for this very cue, George shuffled from the log Lena leaned against, holding a lady's stocking.

A loud bark of laughter erupted from me at the sight.

Barry eyed George with a disgruntled chuff.

"Muffin Moo," Lena cooed. "He's your best forest friend, be nice."

Her fox lowered the lids of his eyes in a dismissive gesture that I knew was all bluster. So did George, who patted the side of Barry's snout as if a nan doting on their grandchild.

"Filly Lo," I sighed, peering at all the dozens of animals sleeping around us, "tell me these are not all our furry familiar bairns."

Barry shot me a take-that-back-look that made me sputter another laugh.

"You missed a beautiful white stag," she answered softly, as if growing too tired to talk. "He fought off a hunter for me."

My laughter died and blinding fury rushed back in. "The Lord of the Hunt guarded you? Did he kill that fae bastard?"

"The Horned God?" Her eyes widened. "You think the actual Horned God was protecting me?"

"Aye, he's the only white stag I know of in Caledona Wood." I smoothed out my features and added, "But I've never seen a god before, lass, so I can't say for sure."

Cian was a *demi*-god, unlike the white stag. So I wasn't lying.

Filena arched a playful brow. "Never?"

By the impish glint in her eyes, she knew. And she wanted to watch me riddle myself around the truth. This girl . . . she was going to be the death of me.

I bit my bottom lip, trying not to laugh. "I said god, not demi-goddess, *pet*."

Filena snorted, then opened her mouth to quip back and yawned instead.

She was startlingly, sickly pale. The skin beneath her eyes chafed red, her lips slightly cracked. The stress and magic drain fatigue was evident in her slower movements and sleepy blinks too. Filena also studied my face, taking in the forming bruise on my jaw and my swollen bottom lip. Aye, I had marked her, kissed her in my post-fight state. But I hadn't felt the slightest twinge, too consumed by my mate to notice anything *but* her.

"Is . . . the Hunt over?" she asked.

I nodded, understanding her real question. "I'll help those marked girls."

Her shoulders relaxed.

"I'm . . ." I drew in a breath and let it out slowly. "I'm now heir of West Tribe."

She angled her head to better see my eyes. "You killed Bryok?"

"He lives." All humor was gone between us now. "I plan to sell him to Seren."

"No," she gritted out. "Braelin and I deserve our vengeance first."

I didn't even hesitate. "Aye, his fate is in your hands, mate—"

My head whipped up.

Hurried footsteps traveled down the trail.

Before I could take in my next breath, I had covered Filena with my body, my wings out wide, my teeth bared. We didn't have to wait long. A woman pushed through the underbrush and slid to a stop, slapping a hand over her mouth to muffle her gasp. I immediately relaxed, not wanting her to think I was a hunter.

"Rhylen Lonan, new heir of West Tribe," I said calmly, moving away from Filena and lifting my hands in a surrendered gesture. The woman lowered her hand and studied me with wide, green eyes—an uncanny look, as if she had seen me before and not just in passing. Soft blonde curls had fallen from a loose knot and framed her face in flyaway wisps. A face that shockingly resembled Cian and a chill raced across my skin. "I mean you no harm, lass," I added. "Only protecting my mate."

Lena sucked in a quiet breath. "Mam?"

Chapter Forty-Eight

FILENA LONAN

y eyes blinked back the disbelief. Just a couple of days ago, the gods showed me a vision of my mam after not seeing her in over ten years. And now she stood before me in a tattered drab brown dress, hanging limply on her slender frame, and wearing old cloth shoes riddled with holes.

Familiar green eyes filled with tears as she studied my face. "My brave girl."

"Mam . . ." My chest heaved back the breaking sob. But the emotions slammed past before I could stop them.

Rhylen moved to give us space. Mam didn't step forward at first, though. Her eyes tracked Rhylen for several long beats, her body braced to run or cower, before quickly dashing to my side and gathering me to her.

"How I've missed ye, minnow."

I cried into her neck, burying myself deeper into her embrace. I had dreamed of this moment for so long. Her dirt-smudged fingers stroked my hair and I felt like a little girl again.

"How . . . how are you here?" I finally managed to ask, pulling back enough to see her face.

Stars, I had forgotten how beautiful she was. And how much Cian looked just like her. She was truly otherworldly for a mortal. Now that I knew, her elven heritage was obvious in her daintier features, the slight angle of her eyes, the faintest tip to her ears.

"Yer da sold me to South Tribe a week ago." Her thumb trailed the gentlest caress across my cheek to wipe away a tear. "It was how he learned where ye were."

That was how he had money for drink and readings. Unless he spent it right away on dice and cards. The tiniest tug pushed through the magic loss. Aye, it was Bryok's money he used and my stomach sickened. He sold my mam *and* gambled away the money within days, maybe that very night.

"Who is your master?" Rhylen quietly asked.

Mam flinched before twisting toward my husband, her muscles tight. "Clan Brannagh."

The chieftain's family.

Rhylen's eyes shot to mine. The way he was peering at me—brows pinched and hanging low over his storming eyes, the corners of his mouth pressed into a thin line—he had surmised, same as me, that Bryok discovered my da and mam through Doireann. Da's first visit to my divination wagon was no mere coincidence. It was staged for Bryok to trick us into a confession, one he didn't receive.

"They keep enchanted cold iron on me." Mam pointed to the cuff and my blood boiled in fury. Fading bruises mottled her arm. "But before yer da sold me, I *saw* a vision of ye." A smile trembled on her lips. "I snuck away from me owners and hid here in the woods before the wards were turned on. I had to see me wee girl."

Had Da sold Mam to find out where I was?

Was that the cost for information on me?

Bryok had to be involved. He knew I was related to the Sisters Three before the Autumn Night Market. Which meant, he knew my mam was also a seer, possibly more. Was she his fallback plan if I didn't produce him children?

Disgust wormed in my gut. The Fiachnas and Brannaghs were *not* allowed to touch my family. They would *not* possess and exploit our feminine magic either.

I curled my fingers around her wrist and gritted back the pain of feeling my magic dampened—again. Dark skies, I could sleep for a thousand years, I was so tired.

"Nae, minnow." She removed my hand. "Ye'll burn yerself out. I'm well fer now."

"But—"

"I only have the Sight," she said with another soft smile.

Rhylen scooted closer and pointed at the cuff. "May I touch you?"

She flinched again and he lowered his eyes to seem less aggressive. My mam still shrank back at his large presence. But Rhylen didn't move. Visibly swallowing, she eventually nodded and slowly held out her hand, as if at any moment he might strike. My heart broke into viciously sharp, furious pieces.

"When Filena was fourteen," Rhylen began, sliding me a glance, "she volunteered to help my younger sister Glenna bake berry oat cookies for a revel."

I groaned. "Rhylee Lo, you're telling her *this* story?"

"It's a fair warning, lass," Rhylen said quite seriously. "Everyone should know."

I lifted my chin with a huff. "George wants to dress you too."

Rhylen side-eyed the raccoon and winked. "She enjoys the view too much, lad. Pick out something special for Cian, though." George climbed over Barry, making my fox growl, and disappeared inside the log.

"Filly Lo"—Rhylen tossed out and touched the enchanted cold iron—"Mam doesn't know about your talent to make ducks disappear."

Mam.

He called her Mam. As if she were his too.

Tears edged my eyes. "Only ducks, pet?"

He lifted his head and smirked. "And appetites."

I snorted, the arsehole.

Mam looked between us, her eyes softening, her body uncoiling beneath Rhylen's gentle hold of her arm. Threads of green spilled from his fingers onto the iron.

Elder magic.

"Like most tales about our Filena, it begins with her march toward the confectionery wagon full of hope and returning hours later in a panic." The metal grew malleable as he spoke. "She was in charge of adding sugar to all the bowls and added salt instead." A corner of Mam's mouth lifted. "The bakers teased that the dessert line would disappear if they served salty cookies."

The cuff fell off my mam's wrist, but Rhylen kept talking, his fingers still on hers.

"She fed the bitter, sad cookies to the ducks, she did," he said with a playful lilt. "Then went for a walk."

I sighed. "And when I returned, all the ducks had disappeared."

My mam's eyes crinkled in the corners.

"She wept and bargained with the gods—"

"—bring the ducks back," I drolled, "and I'll never bake cookies again."

"They returned an hour later." Rhylen gently squeezed my mam's hand. "From their nesting spots in the woods."

I glared at him. "You and Cian didn't tell me."

He grinned. "It wasn't the first time you baked your delightful personality into a confection, Lena. We, too, care about the lives of pond ducks and . . . other unsuspecting victims." My jaw slackened, pretending to be insulted. Rhylen deliberately ignored me and slowly met Mam's eyes. "She's my best friend, my True Mate, and the saltier half of my magic." I tried not to laugh, but he wasn't wrong. Then he kissed my mam's hand and softly added, "It must have broken your heart to do so but thank you for sending Filena to me. I have loved your daughter since the day she arrived in West Tribe."

My mam's eyes filled with tears again. "I saw a vision of ye the day before I sent her packing. Ye, Filena, and a large brood of children beneath Seren. And . . . And . . ." her voice cracked. "She was so happy."

A *large* brood of children?

My mind slipped back to the tree a fortnight ago. When Rhylen asked if he and his mate would have children, a question he had asked me hundreds of times prior during our fake readings. A question I always answered humorously until then.

She craves your touch day and night. Aye, your marriage will be full of passion, the kind that would lead to many children.

As if reading my thoughts, Rhylen's eyes slid to mine beneath lowered lashes in a delighted look that said *wagons full*. And, stars help me, I had to keep from swooning. Images of my husband prettied up as a wild fae Raven king warrior, like now, while holding our wee babe to his bare chest, made me deliciously woozy with want.

To redirect the melting puddled path of my thoughts, I readjusted my position against the log and cleared my throat. "I *saw* a vision of you last night, when Hamish visited my divination wagon," I replied with a tired smile. "You stopped at this very log. But I didn't see why. I . . . I can't *see* my own future."

Mam tilted her head. "The Maiden's magic can riddle in a seer's future during another's vision, but only a clever *fáidhbhean* can change the view." Goosebumps raced down my arms and shivered across my torso. Was it the Maiden who whispered those words to me? Or the Mother's guidance? Mam's eyes searched mine, then she took in all the wild animals now curled around us in sleep. "Ye have Nan's magic too, it appears. The more familiars ye have, the less magic drain ye'll experience as a mortal."

Barry groaned and I had to bite back a snicker.

Instead, I replied, "I also have transmutation magic . . . like the Crone."

Her brows lifted at that. "A *cailleach*."

"Aye and why I barely have a thread of strength left in me."

"Most of these animals here are not faerie touched, just attracted to yer magic." Mam's thumb gently caressed the fingers she held. "The Sisters Three are ancient and strange to our mortal minds. Ye might meet yer great-nan again, ye might not. Ye might, one day, meet one of her sisters, too, or not at all."

My great-nan . . . the beautiful elf in The Wilds.

The Mother.

Then I nearly rolled my eyes. Of course, it was the Mother. The Maiden was untouched and the Crone was past her child-bearing days. George poked his head out of the log and I wrinkled my nose at him to stay quiet. I received enough grief from Barry. I didn't need it from his fluffy, adorable thieving partner too.

Mam's eyes narrowed onto George for a quick second. "Cian has a familiar?"

"George is his familiar?" I practically squealed in delight. I grinned at the raccoon. "Darlin', Cian needs more cuddles, aye? Mess up his hair to irritate Glenna too."

Rhylen laughed when George lifted a pair of lady's boots. "Is there a stash of clothes in that log?"

"It's a magic log, it is," I replied with a dramatic arch of my brow. "For faerie raccoons with excellent fashion sensibilities."

"Feck, Cian will use George to build him a wardrobe that will require its own wagon."

George chittered in agreement and both Rhylen and I burst into laughter.

"George," Rhylen said when his humor calmed, "find Mam a warm coat. The lass could use those boots too." Mam bunched her shoulders and winced when peering Rhylen's way. "No favor owed," he added with a kind smile, though I could see the fury in his eyes—for her, not at her. "You're with family now and I take care of my family, no bargains, tricks, or strings attached. And," he continued, "you won't be a slave for Clan Brannagh after tonight. You'll live with us. Gran will love your company."

"Hamish?" she asked in a small voice.

"I had him arrested earlier when I learned there was a bounty on his head. Not sure that will hold up in court, though. I need to verify Brady Sullivan's marriage contract first. But that vile man will *never* touch you again, Moira MacCullough. He already sold you and gave up his rights as your husband." He gentled his voice more. "I'm the heir of West Tribe. By sunrise, I will be chieftain. You're safe now, Mam. Be with your children and many, many grandchildren without fear."

My mam shyly smiled at Rhylen and, stars, the moon appeared to grow brighter at the otherworldly beauty of her happiness. How long had it been since a male treated her with kindness?

"Call me Moira Merrick." She nervously smoothed out her skirt. "Me mam's family name. I'm a MacCullough no more."

Merrick was my nan's maiden name? It meant "power" and "ruler" in the common fae tongue. A proper name for a halfling mortal goddess.

"Moira Merrick," Rhylen said with a dip of his head.

"Yer tribe needs ye," she said to Rhylen after a pause. "Yer family too. Ye best get back with Filena."

"We can't leave without you," I hurried out.

George shuffled over to Mam with a dark blue, heavy knitted shawl and a gray pair of men's trousers. Pointing at the log, he chittered, appearing to gesture for her to follow, then disappeared back inside.

"I'm where I need to be tonight," she said to me, but her eyes had stilled on a spot in the forest. I peered over my shoulder, above the log, and gasped. The white stag had returned. "The Horned God will stand guard until Cian finds me."

That really was the Horned God?

Wait.

A wrinkle formed between my brows.

Until Cian finds her? . . . oh. *Ohhh.*

I swore Barry rolled his eyes at me.

Well, if she had a vision, I couldn't protest.

Mam gathered me in her arms again and whispered in my ear, "Ye'll see me again, minnow."

My heart wasn't ready to say goodbye. My hand wasn't ready to release hers and my eyes weren't done recommitting her to memory. But Rhylen did need to return to crow his victory over Bram before sunrise.

And, so, for the second time in my life, I left Mam behind for a new future with West Tribe.

Chapter Forty-Nine

RHYLEN LONAN

Bram eyed me with building contempt. The flickering shadows of lantern light danced across the soon-to-be former chieftain's face and stretched along the red, purple, and gold stripes of the canvas tent wall behind him.

Elders from East, North, and South Tribes had placed a cuff of enchanted cold iron on his ankle, gagged him, and tied his hands behind his back. Beside him lay Bryok, still floating in and out of consciousness. Hamish sat beside Bryok, tied to a chair, too battered and drunk to remain awake long. And on Bram's other side, also gagged and tied to a chair, was Brady Sullivan, an older mortal with both a trickster's smile and sharp knives glinting in his eyes.

A man who bargained to own Filena as his child bride.

Had he set up Hamish to gamble away his daughter?

A wave of disgust slammed into me and quickly turned into an all-consuming fury for my wife.

While flying back to the game tent, Filena had shared all the details of her trials this evening, beginning with Bryok abducting her and ending with the moments leading up to my arrival with the Puck. And since I was no longer under the bargain, I confessed Gran's first encounter with the Sisters Three before Filena and Cian had arrived in West Tribe. Most of what Filena had shared confirmed what I had already suspected: Brady Sullivan's marriage contract was a trick and Bram's plan was to coerce Brady to sell Filena back to Bryok at little to no cost to West Tribe.

And then all their schemes went terribly wrong.

Filena and I had touched ground right before the hunters left with their marked prey and before the unmarked girls were returned to their original owners. Since I, nor the elders of each tribe present, could yet prove if the Fiachnas allowed and participated in other illegal transactions, I convinced the registrar that the Kingdom of Carran would be at fault for reparations for approving and recording mis-owned slaves.

As a result, the registrar released all the hunted slaves to West Tribe since we, technically, were their owners during the Hunt and revoked any marked claims. The hunters were quickly reimbursed with an additional payout to mollify their complaints. They were pissed but their hands were legally tied.

Then I released the girls from their debts.

All were now free.

Even the girls who remained unmarked.

Drawing in a tight breath, I swept my gaze over the tent and strode toward the opposite side. The registrar and constable sat at a tea table, hunched over a lantern and reviewing the marriage contract. Both lawmen had instruments to detect different types of illusions and spells.

I slowed my walk as I neared Filena, who was curled up on

Cian's lap half-asleep, with Sheila cuddled to her chest and Lloyd snoring in the folds of her petticoats. Filena's heavy eyes fluttered open when feeling my shadow. The silk jacket had slid down her arm. With a crooked smile, I tucked the hem back over her shoulder and pulled the fabric close around her. My eyes drifted to the welts on her wrists and white-hot fire restoked inside me. Several times now, I had to exercise an enormity of self-control.

Humor curved Cian's lips but he said nothing. He didn't need to. Aye, I was fussing over my mate like a nesting hen. But he felt protective too, insisting he hold her while I dealt with the problem behind me. Glenna gently played with Filena's hair in soothing caresses while Gran openly gazed at me with pride. Gods, I wanted to tear into the Fiachnas behind me again. Only a weak, cowardly fae would harm an ancient in a fight for power.

Behind my family stood Sean, Braelin, Owen, and Corbin. Out of habit, the lads' eyes were lowered and a muscle ticked along my jaw. "Fellas," I whispered and gestured for them to lift their chins. Braelin smiled at Sean and squeezed his hand—without an illusion to cover her scorn mark. And Sean gazed at her as if she were the very moon in the night sky. I owed Sean Byrnes my life for saving me from Bram's bargain. Tonight might have been far different had he not stepped in.

"Mr. Lonan," the registrar finally spoke and I spun on my heel. "Aye, sir?"

"The marriage contract is indeed fake. The Kingdom of Carran's seal too. Both are under layers of illusion spells." The mortal peered at me over his spectacles and my heart spurred into a gallop. "You have grounds to press charges, Mr. Lonan, on all parties involved. Or to seek justice among your kind, so long as it falls within the laws of Carran. I will sign as witness."

"Aye, I will too," the constable said.

I dipped my head. "Allow me a moment to consult with my wife."

A part of me wanted to laugh. Brady swindled Hamish out of his family and home. Hamish tried to swindle the Fiachnas into reparations after selling his own wife on a gamble and lost her too. And then the Fiachnas attempted to swindle Filena from both Hamish and Brady. The latter who then swindled the Fiachnas when the Fiachnas failed to swindle him.

A perfectly riddled tale of trickery and shite luck.

One that began with Filena being sold in marriage to pay off her da's gambling debts and ended with me sold into marriage to pay for the Fiachna's gamble to own Filena.

A fake marriage contract that led the Merricks to my clan and that had, ultimately, been part of Fate's direction in my journey toward becoming chieftain.

Or perhaps not Fate, but the Sisters Three.

Filena was a *cailleach* and I was chosen by the gods to protect her.

I knelt before my wife and brushed a strand of hair from her cheek. "Did you hear the registrar?"

She faintly nodded her head.

I gestured for Braelin to join us who lowered onto her knees beside me. "The poor lass," she said quietly.

"Filena asked for Bryok's fate to be in your and her hands, and I agreed." Braelin's brows lifted. "Whatever you both decide, I will honor."

Smiling at my mate, I pushed to my feet and walked away to

give Filena and Braelin space to talk without my angry hovering. I moved to where the elders and chieftain of North Tribe watched the proceedings, as well as Doireann Brannagh-Fiachna and Aidlena Fiachna, Bram's wife, who were summoned while I was in the woods.

"Do I have your support as West Tribe's chieftain?" I didn't ask if they declared me the challenge's winner. I seized my Fate while looking each gov present in the eyes.

"We need to consult the tribal leaders at the Truth Telling Tree," an elder from East Tribe answered.

I bowed my head. "Do I have your support to sell Bram Fiachna to Seren?"

His wife lifted her chin and ground her teeth. But not once had she shed a tear over seeing her husband and son bound and beaten. Doireann smiled coolly Bryok's way every so often too—until I asked this question. The immediate family were often sold or banished along with the guilty. I had no desire to punish innocents, but I also couldn't have potential vengeance seekers in my flock either.

"We spoke while you hunted down your mate," an elder from North Tribe said, "and it is indisputable that both Bram and Bryok conspired to own Filena Merrick by illegal means—"

"Lonan," I corrected.

The elder cleared his voice. "To own Filena Lonan, illegally sold your mate to The Wild Hunt, illegally claimed Bryok was your mate's owner, and harmed an ancient and innocent girl to trick you and your family into bargains."

There was so much more, but if the reasons they stated were enough, I wouldn't add another bone to the fire.

"Aye, prince," a different elder answered, "you have our permission to sell both Bram and Bryok Fiachna to Seren. His elder magic will be permanently revoked now."

Prince.

I had to blink back my surprise at being called a prince.

But I was now an heir, a title I had earned.

Bram's wife continued to glare at me down her nose and Doireann's gaze darted around the room.

"Bram and Bryok Fiachna's wives and extended family are not banished from the Caravan fae," I said to the elders, "but they're not welcome in West Tribe either. Will East, North, and South tribes welcome the Fiachnas into their flocks if Doireann Brannagh-Fiachna grants me a bargain for her and Aidlena Fiachna's freedom?"

Doireann stiffened.

The elders and chieftain exchanged looks, then nodded their heads in agreement.

I turned toward Bryok's wife who continued to regard me with a stiff bearing but also frightened eyes. Despite being a notch above slaves, fellys were far more socially clever than govs recognized, bargaining being a top skill. We had to bargain for most things in our lives. It was how das and husbands supported their families on so little for centuries.

As a female, Doireann couldn't hold a gov position. But, as a princess, she did have power over slave ownership in her family—though married to Bryok. They were still within their five day mate bond period, so doweries and bargains were not yet set. And I had leverage to bargain well.

"Did your family purchase a mortal this past week by the name of Moira MacCullough?"

Doireann blinked. "Aye."

"Trade Moira MacCullough to me for your and Aidlena's freedom. I'll not seek more from you, lass."

The princess's shoulders sagged in relief. "I agree to your
bargain, Rhylen Lonan. For my and Aidlena's freedom, I give you
immediate ownership over Clan Brannagh's mortal slave, Moira
MacCullough."

"Elders, you witnessed the bargain?" I asked.

"The bargain will stand," one answered.

I nodded. "Aidlena Fiachna and Doireann Brannagh-Fiachna,
you and your extended families are free. Aidlena, you may join any
tribe who will take you in. Doireann, you may return to your family in South Tribe." The princess smiled at me, tears of gratitude in
her eyes. "I'll send my brother, Cian, to fetch Moira MacCullough
by sunrise, no trouble to your family, aye?"

She nodded.

Aidlena Fiachna, however, continued to glare at me and, I realized, she refused to see me as anything other than a felly.

A made-up class by govs to feel powerful. A constructed illusion we all accepted.

Whatever she believed of me, I had beat both her son and husband fairly in a challenge witnessed by representatives from each
tribe.

"Constable," I said, walking back to the tea table. "I press
charges against Brady Sullivan on behalf of my wife."

The lawman's gaze roamed over me curiously. "He's committed hanging offenses. There will be a trial."

I locked eyes with the child bride trickster, but said to the constable, "Leave his body in a cage for the carrion." I flexed my wings

with a canined grin. "Let my crow and raven brethren of Caledona Wood eat his soul until his mortal bones are picked clean."

Brady's skin turned green, the first time he had shown any flicker of fear.

"What are my options with Hamish MacCullough?" I asked both the registrar and constable. I knew I had nothing now that the bounty would be voided. A man was allowed to beat his wife and children in Carran. They were his property, after all. He wasn't required to provide for his family either. In the law's eyes, Hamish hadn't committed any crimes. But now Filena had legally belonged to him—until we married, that is. Hamish was within his rights to seek reparations if he walked free today.

"He'll stay in jail until Carran settles Brady Sullivan's case," the constable answered. Then added, glancing briefly at Filena in understanding, "We will . . . check in with local gambling establishments to see if he attempted to dodge lost wagers too."

Good. But also not good enough. I strode over to Cian's and Filena's da. One of his eyes was nearly swollen shut. Blood had dried on parts of his face and shirt. He blinked at me bleary-eyed while breathing heavy from the pain.

"Hamish MacCullough," I gritted out, "I curse you with bad luck. May the gods never show you favor or kindness all the remaining days of your life." I turned to Cian. "Do you want to add anything, brother?"

He shook his head. "My da died when I was thirteen."

"Aye," I replied softly.

My gaze fell to my wife and she gently shook her head too. Braelin had already returned to stand beside Sean. "And Bryok Fiachna?"

"Give me two days to regain strength," Filena said with a weak smile. "Then Braelin and I will have a gift for our new chieftain." Her steel gray eyes flicked over to the elders. "The gods showed me a vision, pets."

There was a slight impish tilt to her lips, one to Braelin's as well.

I studied my wife a second longer, then turned back to the lawmen and asked, "Anything else needed of me this moment?"

"No, Mr. Lonan," the registrar answered.

"Then," I said to the govs present, "let us proceed at the Truth Telling Tree."

I scooped Filena from Cian's arms and gently kissed her, not caring if a room full of people witnessed my affection for my wife. "I need to fly to the next hearing."

"Aye." She nuzzled her face into my neck. "Let's go."

Attendees still milled around the Truth Telling Tree. When I arrived, many recognized me from my fight with Elder Connel and cheered. Several Caravan fae cheered too. But the crowds grew quiet when they saw Filena in my arms.

The elders and chieftain of North Tribe had flown behind me and were now joining their tribe's govs on the stage. My lads, Glenna, and Gran settled in front of the stage a minute or so later. Owen lowered Cian to the grass and clapped him on the back. Owen hadn't seen Cian in The Wild Hunt's gala area, I had learned, and so flew over the market in search of him. Bram had Cian blocked from sight until I arrived.

I helped Filena stand on the stage beside me. She was unsteady at first, but she quickly found balance while holding onto my arm. I kissed her forehead and whispered, "Ready, *a stór*?" She nodded and I straightened to face the govs from all four tribes.

"Brothers of the North, the South, East and West," I began, loud enough for those in the crowds to also hear. "Witnesses can confirm that I won both challenges against Bram and Bryok Fiachna and was declared heir." The elders and chieftain who were present nodded their heads. "Proclaim me Chieftain of West Tribe."

"This is your mortal True Mate?" An elder gestured to my wife.

"Aye," I answered. "Filena Moira Lonan, *fáidhbhean* of West Tribe."

"She was first your slave?" he asked next.

Instead of playing a roundhouse of questions I had already shared during the banishment, I divulged all the events leading up to this moment. I had nothing to hide nor would I let them look down on Filena for protecting herself from a man who purchased children to marry. I didn't share her relation to the Sisters Three, though. That was for her to share, when she was ready, if she ever decided to share at all. Though, depending on what she and Braelin had planned with Bryok, defending her as a *cailleach* might come sooner than later.

The elders leaned in to talk with one another when I finished.

Murmurs rippled through the crowd and grew louder the more we waited for the govs' edict. Several Raven Folk still acknowledged the banishment and had turned their back on me while others regarded my wife with open disgust.

"Rhylen Lonan," a commanding voice said and I pulled my gaze away from the crowd and settled it on the cluster of elders and chieftains, including Elder Connel and other govs from West Tribe. "The gods chose a mortal as your True Mate. But Raven Folk flock together. To marry outside of our kind dilutes our ancient magic from Lugh."

A quiet applause moved through the fae.

"We do not question the gods' choice in a mate for you," he continued. "But a chieftain must uphold the laws of our Caravan kind. And, therefore," the elder said, "the tribes have rejected your claim to West Tribe as chieftain and revoked your title as heir."

The gathering immediately erupted into disgruntled boos and approving cheers.

"I have elder magic," I shouted back. "You all witnessed it, as did they." I swept a hand toward the crowd. "Why would the gods give elder magic to me if not to govern West Tribe?"

"No chieftain in the history of Caravan fae has taken a mortal as their bonded mate," the elder reemphasized and I growled. "Or married a fae outside of our kind."

"I have elder magic," I also reemphasized. "Clearly the gods find favor in me regardless of the laws of Caravan Ravens."

"Aye," he said, but didn't say more.

My wings snapped out and the muscles down my body flexed.

"Rhylen," Filena whispered and I stilled, "*Your* tribe, remember?"

My eyes whipped to hers. "My tribe," I repeated under my breath.

"Not a *Caravan* tribe. You plan to rest our wagon wheels, aye?"

She once told me this on the night of Bryok's wedding. Her words hadn't fully registered, though—I could think of little else but challenging that bastard and protecting my mate. But she was right, I didn't want a Caravan tribe. I wanted something entirely new—a Night Market no longer run by the unkindness of Ravens.

Where people caravanned to us instead.

I eyed the elder who spoke for them all. "Am I still granted the right, as the challenge winner, to sentence Bram and Bryok Fiachna for their crimes against my family?"

"Aye, of course," the elder said. "That was fairly won and the former chieftain and heir are guilty."

I nodded, nervously licking my lips. The crowd was riveted and I . . . I was trying to keep my heart from beating out of my chest.

"I accept your judgement," I said next. "However, the gods do not gift elder magic on accident. I'm meant to be a chieftain. I am *not* meant to remain Caravan Folk, though."

The govs looked amongst each other. But the chieftain of North Tribe held my gaze and subtly dipped his head.

"What is your plan, lad?" he asked.

"West Tribe will break down our area of the Autumn Night Market tomorrow. But my family will not migrate to our former tribe's winter fields." I paused and peered into as many eyes as I could. "I plan to move west and settle beneath Seren, by the ferry docks. And, there, I will lead a new tribe."

The audience exploded into cheers and protests.

Caravan folk didn't accept change easily. We had traveled the same roads for so long, migrating a new course was unfathomable.

But not to me, a felly boy who became gov. To me anything

was possible.

I pulled Filena closer. "I will not allow slavery. Mortals and fae will work alongside each other equally to build a Night Market unlike any other. Children who choose to work will be compensated. They're not free labor. You will be allowed to marry your heart's choice without fear of banishment." I tilted my head at the elders and shouted, "There are no social classes. Govs are appointed by the gods to care for their flock. That is our *only* job, aye?" To the crowd, I said, "You will have a job too, one that is also important for the tribe's success. And our food will be communal. Aye, meals shared like family, regardless of your role in my Night Market."

Mortals and fae were still reacting—cheers, applause, arguments shouted at the stage, a few others turning their backs on me.

I drew in a large breath, blowing it out slowly.

"My family leaves in two nights. Any are welcome to join us."

Chapter Fifty

RHYLEN LONAN

Clucking, I encouraged the horses to trot forward. We were lining up our wagons with the rest of West Tribe before leaving the Autumn Night Market. There, Filena would announce her and Braelin's judgement over Bryok and where I would sell Bram to Seren. West Tribe would, then, depart for their winter grounds under the care of their elders until a new chieftain and heir were selected.

The past two days had passed in a blur. I still led the setup and break down crew as if nothing had changed. But everything had and, after this night, there would be no turning back.

My former tribe, as well as other Caravan fae, either ignored me, as if I were banished, or smiled at me as if I were a faerie tale come to life. Several asked me about my new tribe, how I planned to afford to build a stationary Night Market as a former felly with little belongings.

I didn't have full answers yet. But I knew bargaining would be involved. Perhaps I could make an arrangement with Ravenna Blackwing, the Corvus Rook of Seren. And I was selling Bram Fiachna too. As a former chieftain, one taken down by a felly, he would catch a very pretty price. Either way, the land east of the ferry dock and train station was open for development. Very few dared to build in the shadow of Seren. But they weren't Raven Folk.

My Seren cousins didn't scare me.

Wagons lined the field when we arrived. Families stood around their traveling home and horses before Bryok and Bram and the elders of West Tribe. I pulled on the reins and slowed near the back, then set the brake. Hopping off, I unhooked the stairs from the wagon's side and fastened them into place on the opposite end of the wagon, away from the horses. Filena opened the door and I . . . I nearly stopped breathing.

Glenna had styled Filena's auburn strands into a pile of curls, held together by whittled sticks. But it was the lavender ribbon in her hair that spread warmth across my chest. The only other time she had worn a ribbon outside of Beltane and Áine's Day, was when I broke my wing. Today, I would break away from the wing of Caravan fae I was born into, the only tribe my family had followed for centuries.

I offered my hand to Filena and helped her down the stairs before pulling her into my arms. "You are beautiful," I murmured against her mouth before stealing a kiss. Movement around my upper knees caught the corner of my eyes and I chuckled when Sheila poked her head out from Filena's skirt pocket. Gently scooping the hedgehog into my hands, I brought her to my face. Sheila waddled close until her nose touched mine. "You're very pretty today too, lass." I caressed the scrap of bow behind her ear.

"Nose kisses later, aye? I need my husband back, pet." Filena nestled Sheila back into her hands and quickly tucked her away. She then cocked her head, brow arched. A challenge glinted in her eyes.

Before Filena could chastise me, for what I didn't know, Glenna plunked down the stairs of my and Cian's wagon, hands on her hips, as she glared at my best friend. "Ask your thieving sidekick where he put my lace glove."

Cian flicked the ashes on a cigarette he stole at some point, a slow, impish slant to his mouth. "George," my brother drawled. "His name is George, darlin', and one does not question the thieving ways of a faerie raccoon. Some things in life should remain a mystery, Glennie Lo."

Glenna marched over and plucked the cigarette from Cian's mouth. "One does question unless that faerie raccoon wants to steal prettier things for me than you."

Cian gasped. "Take that back, darlin'. George is dedicated to my fashion needs first."

"Lady of Man," my sister cooed, winking at George, "bets."

"Gent of Fem," Cian cooed back, "bets."

Glenna dragged on Cian's cigarette before sticking it back in his mouth. With a crowing grin, she then reached into her pocket and pulled out a crumbled cookie. "Come on George, I have a list of fashion ideas."

The raccoon chittered and followed Glenna down the trail without a single look back at Cian's slack-jacked expression. I laughed under my breath, earning Cian's glare.

"Glennie Lo has us all trained on treats," I said with a grin.

"The minx," he mumbled back. But a tiny smile curved his lips.

Moira moved to the front of Gran's wagon, holding Gran's arms, and helped her down the steps. The Merricks' mam was a lovely lass, full of wit, quiet kindness, and stories of the Sisters Three. She disappeared into herself around males who showed her the slightest hint of attention—understandably so. But she was growing more and more comfortable around me by the minute.

After years of abuse and isolation from her family, it would take time to heal.

But she was the Mother's granddaughter. Her life would be long and the majority would be lived well in safety and happiness, surrounded by family who loved her.

Including the one who was currently looking at me with wide, impatient eyes.

"Rhy," Filena said with a tap on my nose.

My lips twitched and I arched a humored brow. "Filly Lo?"

"You promised me, remember?" She narrowed her eyes. "You have a history of breaking your bargains, pet."

"You can't curse me," I quipped back. "Not even with bad luck."

"No, but I can make your drawers suddenly woven from the quills of porcupines. One or seven or thirty-two might spontaneously wiggle from their weave to poke your feathered arse."

"Itchy drawers, porcupine quill drawers . . . you just want to undress me, lass," I said with a flirty grin. Then I leaned in, dragging my nose along her jaw to her ear and whispered,

"Undress me when we rest the horses. Make me lose all control, wife."

A soft moan left her and I smiled while nibbling on her earlobe before kissing her neck. Feck, her scent drove me wild.

"Not unless you keep your promise," she whispered back, breathless as I continued to kiss down to the hollow of her throat. "If you break your bargain . . . you'll only know porcupine quill drawers and making yourself lose all control, while alone, for the next week."

"Mam," Cian called out. "Tell me you *saw* a future where Filena and Rhylen never discuss their weird sex life in public again?"

"They have many bairns, love bug," Mam tossed back.

I barked a loud laugh then mouthed, "Love bug?" at Cian who shot me a rude gesture.

"Rhylee Lo," Filena scolded with a frustrated growl I found far too adorable. But I managed to school my face—barely.

"I promise you, Filena Lonan," I answered, repeating my words from earlier, "I will trust your decision and accept Bryok's fate at your and Braelin's hands without interference or I'll be forced to wear woven porcupine quill drawers as well as satisfy myself alone for the next week."

Glenna walked back, just as I finished that last line, and wrinkled her nose in gagging disgust. George shuffled behind her and I snorted at Cian's smug, waggish grin promising vengeance.

Tucking Filena's arm in mine, I gestured with my head for the rest to follow and then strode toward the field where the elders and several representatives from Seren awaited us.

I caught Sean's eyes and he nodded back, escorting Braelin to the field to join us. Not wanting to be left out, Owen and Corbin broke away from their families to meet up with us too, sidling up beside Cian when we slowed to a stop.

Over the wagon lines, the sun began to set, marking the beginning of a new day. The gold tinging the sky's horizon also gilded the strands in Bram's and Bryok's hair. I should have them both shorn. Well, Bram. I couldn't touch Bryok . . . yet.

Elder Connel dipped his head at me in greeting and I gritted my teeth.

The gov acted as if he hadn't tried to banish me on Bram's orders. Not my problem, though. West Tribe would have to sort out the elders they could still trust and whom they had ask the gods to reconsider as protectors.

Lowering my eyes, I quickly slid a calculating side-glance at my gang. *Make them mine*, I prayed. Filena angled her head my way slightly, her brows narrowed, but those granite eyes of hers were fastened onto my fellas. A smile teased the corners of my mouth.

"Lonan," Elder Connel said and gestured toward the Seren Ravens, "You requested an audience?"

"Aye," I said and stepped forward, Filena still on my arm.

I considered my distant wild fae cousins, the fine cut of their suits, the much shorter length of their hair. No ash around their eyes, either. But they did wear jewelry on their ears and fingers and around their necks. Among them was a female in a rich burgundy, bustled gown edged in black lace and feathers. A black top hat tilted on her loosely coifed hair.

"Rhylen Lonan," she said with a slight bow. "I'm Ravenna Blackwing."

My heart completely stopped in my chest.

Ravenna wanted to speak to . . . *me*? Without me first requesting an audience?

"My lady," I said and bent at the waist while Filena dropped into a curtsy.

Ravenna placed a finger beneath Filena's chin and tilted her face up. "You resemble her most," she spoke just barely above a whisper. "The Maiden is my friend. I served her for several years as a spy while under Ren Cormac's thrall."

The blood drained from Filena's face. "West Tribe doesn't know who I am."

The former Queen of the Raven Folk smiled, a look as beautiful as it was deadly. "They cannot hear us, pet. Not until I release the partial blinding curse."

I was too captivated by Ravenna to notice how the world around us was strangely quiet.

Filena's body deflated against mine. "Stars, I couldn't breathe." Blowing out a slow, measured breath, Filena squared her gaze back onto Ravenna. "The Maiden spoke of me to *you*?"

"Aye, her magic was stirred by the deep, unbreakable bond you share with your True Mate." She lowered her hand. "It was she who *set fire* to your destiny."

I sucked in a quiet gasp.

Was Ravenna riddling that it was the Maiden who started the fire two weeks ago?

I didn't know what to do with that information. Until this moment, I was convinced the Fiachnas had loosened the oil lamps to set the lottery into motion. But, had the Maiden not started that fire, I would still be pining for Filena. She would still be my slave, not my wife.

And I wouldn't be standing before Ravenna Blackwing as a gov with elder magic.

As if reading my thoughts, Ravenna's black eyes swept my way. "I have a message from the Mother for you."

I blinked back my nerves and straightened.

"Fire destroys those it claims," Ravenna said. "But fire refines *you*, Rhylen Lonan. Your iron-strong heart is now forged steel. A fire-made sword and shield for my great-granddaughter."

Tears pricked the back of my eyes. "I love her great-granddaughter and would walk through a thousand fires for her."

"Aye," Ravenna said. "The Maiden told her you would long before you were born."

Humility washed over me. I had so little, just a felly boy with rocks and buttons in his pocket. And, yet, the Sisters Three knew I would give Filena my heart, my soul, my body . . . my entire world.

"I have a message from the Crone for you."

I bit the inside of my cheek to calm the next rush of nerves.

"Trust your mate, pet," Ravenna intoned. Filena quietly snorted and I shot her a playful side-eyed glare. "I whispered into her ear the curse to use on the former heir of West Tribe. To break a bargain with her this night is to break a bargain with me."

At this, Filena's mouth fell open and I whispered, "Feck," under my breath.

"I have a message from the Maiden," Ravenna continued, ignoring both our reactions. "As a dowry for my niece . . ." Ravenna brushed her hand in an arc and sound crashed into my ears. The wind in trees. The whinny of impatient horses. The voices of West Tribe who watched us. "The City of Stars will grant you three bargains," Ravenna proclaimed loudly. "Three bargains for your tribe and Night Market, Rhylen and Filena Lonan."

Filena squeezed my hand and grinned up at me.

But, for a moment, all I could think of was that I had married a girl . . . *with a dowry*. Not only had I riddled around the bargain made among the elders, but I had also unwittingly obeyed the magic too.

A dowry that would save *my* tribe.

Stars, the gods were so cheeky sometimes.

"I don't know who will follow me," I spoke low so only those nearby could hear me. "Or what skills and amenities will be needed." What if no one followed us besides my lads? I cleared my throat, determined not to let my building anxiety tie my racing thoughts into knots. "If I make one bargain today, will Seren grant me two bargains at later times of my choosing?"

"Aye," Ravenna answered with a dip of head. "Request me when you are ready to use another bargain, Rhylen Lonan, even if that is a hundred years from now."

Filena tugged my shirt until I leaned down enough for her to whisper in my ear, "Bram owes you a Night Market, chieftain. Ask for one, not coin."

I studied Bram, whose dark eyes were obsidian daggers as they returned my inspection. My wife was right. I won our challenge and the elders denied me. But the Sisters Three granted me a second chance.

"For Bram Fiachna, the former chieftain of West Tribe," I began, "I ask for a fleet of twenty Caravan-made wagons and enough timber and canvas to build four small tents, five medium tents, and three large tents. I ask for a wrought iron entry gate with a sign that reads *The Night Market* in blue, purple, gold, and black. I ask for all of these items to be delivered beneath Seren, east of the ferry docks, no later than early spring. What you do with Bram is your choice." I lifted my chin and held my gaze steady. "Will Seren agree to my trade bargain?"

Ravenna tilted her head. "And will Seren lose money over your Night Market?"

"No, my lady. We are only open from sunset to sunrise. Our markets are not the same as yours. We will bring crowds who will also travel to Seren as a result."

"Chieftain Lonan," Ravenna announced, "Seren agrees to your trade bargain for Bram Fiachna." She then listed the items I requested as proof that no tricks were involved.

Relief flamed through me, an explosion of gratitude, disbelief, and awe as I grabbed Filena and kissed her. I couldn't stop smiling.

Holy Mother of Stars! . . . I had my own market.

The clans of West Tribe erupted into shocked conversations all at once.

But I kept kissing my mate. Let them reject our love. Tonight, we began anew. Tomorrow, our past would be far behind us.

Slowly, I pulled away and rested my forehead against hers. "Well, my wee feral swine wife," I teased, "I'm ready for the gift you and Braelin have for your new chieftain. Then let's leave, lass. I want you all to myself."

"Will you let me touch your wings later?"

I moaned. "Fecking stars, Lena, *please*."

She flashed me a wicked smile and heat pooled low in my belly. Gods, just one look from her and I could fall to my knees at her feet. She made me so weak.

Smiling, she pulled away and moved toward the Fiachnas, where Braelin joined her. Filena gestured for Glenna to join them as well and my sister gleefully dashed out and took Filena's and Braelin's hands.

The former prince's face darkened, his eyes glittering with contempt.

"My mate, Filena Lonan," I shouted, "and Braelin Byrnes will decide the fate of Bryok Fiachna."

Filena scooped up a handful of dirt from the field and slowly poured it in front of Bryok's face. "The gods showed me a vision, pet." The dust clouded in a breeze and blew away. The former prince growled while his eyes blinked wildly from the grit. "You are destined to become a curiosity, a cautionary tale of greed and woe for many generations. The stench of your vile nature will be captured to profit the very one you tried to profit from first."

Filena's gaze flicked to mine, a warning to behave.

"I declare you my reward, Bryok Fiachna. You will serve me and my family all the days of your life, days that will be determined entirely by me."

Rage detonated inside of me.

She wanted *what*?!

I would *not* have that fecker in my household or anywhere near my wife. A low growl left my heaving chest. My teeth bared; my fingers shifted into talons. But I promised I wouldn't interfere. And . . . that I would honor Filena's and Braelin's wishes.

But I wasn't sure I could once we were alone.

The moment Bryok was in my possession and no one was around, I would kill him.

Sean was in no better condition either. Braelin must have made him bargain to accept Bryok's fate too.

Filena picked up another fistful of dirt and released the particles to a breeze in front of Bryok's face. "You will eat the dust of the tribe you nearly destroyed. And, when the last wagon is no longer in sight, you will become my pet."

Bryok's eyes widened in growing horror. The color rapidly drained from his face when Filena grabbed Braelin's and Glenna's hand once more and cackled, a loud delighted laugh, my wife's eyes bright and wild in the encroaching twilight.

"Move him to the front of the wagon line," she said to the elders. Then to West Tribe, she shouted, "If you seek to join Rhylen Lonan's tribe, meet us at the river bridge to Seren. We have business to attend to first."

My brows shot up. But I didn't argue and just nodded.

The girls leaned into each other, talking rapidly while quietly laughing. I exchanged a look with Sean and he shrugged. Cian was grinning, however, his arm draped around his mam's shoulder, his other hand holding Gran's. He knew what those three were up to and I clenched my jaw. Had Moira *seen* something? Or had he figured out Filena's riddled curse? Or was he just amused by the girls' antics?

Yesterday, Filena had shared her and Cian's heredity with the fellas. She had apparently already shared with Braelin in the game tent while discussing their plan for Bryok.

One that was now being set into motion.

The elders moved Bryok to the front of the wagon line,

as directed. A candlemark later, West Tribe began moving northeast while those who chose to follow me moved northwest—two dozen wagons made up from Folk from all four tribes, mostly fellys. A felly market was more than grand, it was perfect. And stars, my heart. It was bursting with pride and crumbling with humility. Folk actually wanted to join my tribe.

Bryok coughed and thrashed in his chair despite his broken arm, his eyes watering from the dust and grit. The more he fought, the more the girls laughed.

Eventually the sound of wooden wheels on the forest ground quieted until only my family and my lads remained. Ravenna and her two representatives had returned to Seren shortly after the wagon train east and west began, Bram in their talons.

"Form a circle around me and Bryok," Filena asked us and my muscles tensed. But I complied and encouraged the others to do the same. "Forest friends, surround me." Barry and George leaned on her legs; Sheila poked her head out and Lloyd scampered up her body to rest on her shoulder. Her mam's familiar, a red cardinal named Enid, swooped down from a branch to Filena's other shoulder.

Bryok growled through the cloth gagging his mouth, his dust-reddened eyes narrowed to slits.

"I have wanted to curse you to fly until your wings molted to ash." His eyes bugged and then he began making pleading sounds. "I have wanted to curse every strand of hair on your body to fall to your feet. For your arse to drag across a field of jagged rocks until you begged me to shave your head in a plea for mercy. I have also wanted to curse you to beg the ground to bury you alive." She took a step toward him and he reared back. "My imagination craves violence." She smiled then, a smug, playful tilt to her lips that was all Filena. "But my reality pines for forest friends." She looked at Barry then and cooed, "Isn't that right, Muffin Moo?"

Her fox huffed a tired sigh. I would laugh, except I still didn't know what my wife was about to do.

"Braelin and Glenna also share a fondness for adorable forest animals."

"Aye," Braelin said with a grin, "especially adorable animals displayed for our market's bread and butter."

My jaw slackened.

I knew what Filena was about to do. What the Crone had whispered in her ear.

You are destined to become a curiosity, a cautionary tale of greed and woe . . .

Braelin and I will have a gift for our new chieftain . . .

Gods, that was my favorite display at the curiosity tables too. And my market wouldn't need to illusion an old toothbrush.

"Bryok Fiachna, for your deceit, your cruelty, you are hereby cursed to become a Crone's ornamental pet." She reached out a single finger toward him and Bryok started screaming. The moment she made contact with his head, Bryok's body froze, his eyes round with terror.

Filena began to sway and leaned on Glenna for support. A low, cackling laugh left her lips and whipped around our circle. Lifting her finger from Bryok's head, she intoned in a strange, magic-infused voice, "So be it."

Not one breath passed and Bryok disappeared from sight.

Nothing existed in the chair he was bound to save a pile of ropes.

The next intake of air, a skunk appeared.

A taxidermized-like-but-not-quite skunk wearing a red vest, with long black hair decorated in a couple beaded braids, and . . . a pair of raven wings.

Everyone was silent.

Then Filena, Braelin, and Glenna squealed.

"Now *that's* adorable," Glenna said.

"I don't know," Cian replied, the words slow, his brows pinched. "The fecker deserved far worse. My vote was on flying until his wings molted to ash."

Owen raised his hand. "I liked the hair loss curse, personally."

Corbin leaned forward. "I agree with Cian."

"To hear his screams after asking the earth to bury him alive, though, lads," Sean added with a soft shake of his head. "I'm confused."

"Aye," I agreed.

But it also made complete sense.

Filena had a humorously terrifying outward persona at times, but she was a thickly frosted slice of cake on the inside. Actually hurting another wasn't her nature despite her violent and at times disturbingly bizarre creative threats. Turning a piece of shite like Bryok into a dressed-up forest animal was exactly what my wife would do . . . *did* do.

Braelin pulled Filena and Glenna closer. "Imagine a curiosity display made entirely of skunked enemies."

"Ohhh," Glenna answered, her eyes big. "We can dress them like the villains from ancient faerie tales."

As I watched the girls, I couldn't help but laugh. I wasn't sure I had ever seen Braelin genuinely smile and so animated before. It was like she had transformed into an entirely different person. The soft way Sean's gaze lingered on her glowing happiness, he must not have seen this side of his wife yet either.

The girls were holding hands, hugging each other, laughing, and—

"I'm still confused," Sean said.

Gran chuckled. "My wee Filly girl used her magic to transform her pain and the pain of others into laughter. A beautiful gift, it is."

"She was both the Mother and the Crone in that moment," Moira added, her eyes darting nervously between the fellas. "It's confusing enough to be just one aspect, let alone two or even all three at once." Moira glanced at me. "The gathered touch of familiars prevented large magic loss, it seems."

"Aye," I said, grateful for this knowledge.

Gran smiled wistfully while watching the girls. "Sisters three, those girls are."

My wife's gaze met mine and I was thunderstruck by her power and beauty and the kind cleverness of her curse. Her brilliance too. He was still alive, despite his taxidermized-ish appearance . . . if tales about the Crone's cottage were true. That fecker would hear every disgusted word of horror at his sight. Every coo of delight too. And we would make more money on him as a witch's skunk ornament in the long run than any trade bargain with Seren.

But, to the lads, I angled in close with a conspiratorial smile and whispered, "I can still snap his neck when she's not looking."

Chapter Fifty-One

FILENA LONAN

*C*aledona Wood slept while Rhylen and I wove through the trees, hands laced together. There was little time to fully pretty himself up while on the road, but he still changed into the wrap he wore at the Fire Dance and as a groom on Samhain Eve. He had quickly tossed his hair up with a couple adornments he had saved too. A candlemark later, he led me into the forest.

We traveled most of the night and would travel part of the day too. By nightfall next, our wagon wheels would permanently rest beneath Seren. The excitement was palpable. Rhylen's Night Market would be magical in ways the Caravan fae could never achieve while constantly on the road. Our attendees would mostly comprise of pleasure travelers too. Mainlanders from the eastern cities carried more coins in their pocket than the average villager. Rhylen's workers would be well compensated.

Slowing, Rhylen paused beneath a large oak tree and . . .

Oh my stars!

I was so lost in my head, I hadn't noticed the oak tree while meandering down the path.

Ribbons wrapped around the trunk and hung from the lowest branches. A blanket was spread between the roots. Did Glenna, Braelin, and the lads throw this together while Rhylen changed?

Where had they found the ribbons?

"George and Barry." Rhylen grinned as he lit a lantern with a book of matches our family left for us.

"They stole the Truth Telling Tree ribbons?"

"Some of them," Rhylen answered with a soft laugh. "While we were sleeping earlier. Lloyd was deeply offended he wasn't included. I had never seen the lad speak so fast. I could barely read the paper before the next words appeared."

My burst of amusement scared an owl into flight, making me cackle harder. Grinning, Rhylen pulled me in close and kissed my happiness.

"I love your laugh," he murmured.

"It scares old superstitious Folk."

"And owls."

I sputtered another laugh and Rhylen's arms wrapped tighter around me. I melted into his warmth. I could stay forever this way, my cheek pressed to the smooth planes of his chest with his breath kissing my hair.

The tree ribbons fluttered around us and I bit back a smile. My mate's courting magic made my head float above the clouds.

But his voice? Rhylen started humming *our song* and gods . . . the rough, smoldering melody blushed across my tightening skin. Beneath our very own Truth Telling Tree, his body moved mine in a sensual slow dance. And heat began pooling low in my belly with every turn.

My hands drifted from his waist to the small of his back, then up the muscled lines of his spine. Soft feathers brushed along my knuckles and his breath caught mid-note. My hands continued their ascent up his biceps, his shoulders, to sink into the decorated strands of his hair. Mine, mine, mine . . . every inch of this male belonged to me. I couldn't mark him in the way he had me, but I would claim him in as many ways as possible.

Our mouths hovered close.

Our bodies, swaying, swaying . . .

The pad of his thumb caressed the underside of my corseted breast. "Make me lose my mind." Gripping my hip, he stroked the hardness of his body against mine and I gasped. "Unravel me," he whispered, "until my prayers only know your name."

The fingers first teasing my breast deftly slipped open a button on my bodice, followed by another, each loosened button a beloved courting gift from him.

"Make me lose *all* control, Filena Lon—"

I didn't let him finish.

Our lips collided in an ignited explosion of longing.

The fiery way his mouth moved against mine enflamed my roaring pulse. His hand left my hip to fist the back of my bodice. A wild part of me wanted him to rip off every article of clothing from my body.

Instead, he undressed me in a flurry of kisses and possessive touches across my heating skin. The satin tips of the lavender ribbon he gifted to me brushed along my neck. He noticed, fingering the edge, his purple eyes gazing into mine with such love, I thought my heart might shatter in bliss. My soul, next, when he lowered me to the blanket beside him.

Candlelight spilled across the curved contours of his muscles. As he leaned over me, wisps of obsidian hair fell from the decorated strands knotted atop his head. But it was his wings that made me sigh. Wings he spread and flexed explicitly for my pleasure. And falling stars, the sensual tilt to his lips drizzled the richest honey down my body to my curling toes.

He was so divinely, sinfully beautiful I could weep.

Pressing a kiss to my throat, his long fingers trailed down my torso, lower, lower, brushing over my sex and I sucked in a sharp breath. I bit down on my bottom lip, hoping, praying he used those fingers to send me to the Otherworld. Or I'd find creative ways to make him suffer too.

Rhylen kissed down my chest, his smile growing devilish as he peered at me over the swell of my soft curves, pleased by my reaction. Those dark purple eyes lingered on my swollen lips and then . . . he slid the tip of his finger down my slit and back up.

"So soft," he whispered.

The very moment he slipped a finger inside me, he sucked my breast into his mouth and . . . I became electric.

A pulsing heat that bucked my hips and tightened my core.

He pulled his finger back out and pumped it back in. His tongue swirled around my breast. My nails scraped over his shoulders as the rippling sensations in me swelled with more and more intensity. Rhylen slipped in a second finger and holy gods. The feel of his breathy laugh across my breast when my body arched was another mouthwatering slice of pleasure that trembled inside me. I was dying. The whimpers leaving me were growing louder in need.

Pushing up to my mouth, he moaned, "So fecking soft," across my lips.

And I officially died.

My body throbbed with molten moonlight. Whispering my name, his mouth crushed mine, claiming each night-drenched moan that thrummed free from my release. A possessive kiss that deepened into a heady slow dance of lips and tongues.

My fingers yearned to stroke the length of his wings while his body deliciously stroked the inside of mine.

But, I wanted to make him unravel in other ways first.

Gently pressing on his chest, I rolled him over to undress him. He shifted his wings away, to make it more comfortable for us both as I then crawled up his body, savoring every flexing inch of his masculine beauty.

At my touch, Rhylen's arms fell above his head. Then his eyes fluttered closed in a parted-mouth expression that somehow managed to be both the soft, flushed look of arousal and the barely contained stillness of a primal male on the verge of going feral.

His chest rose and fell in a deep, languid rhythm as my body slid up his, one kiss and lick at a time. My mouth mapped the shape of him, the defined lines of his pectorals, the V of his hips, each dip and rise of his abdominals, the flexing tendons of his neck, and the muscles of his jaw that were clenching in pleasure.

Finding his mouth, I gently nibbled on his bottom lip. But there was nothing gentle about his grip on my hips. His breathing was labored. Beads of sweat had dewed on his forehead. Releasing his lip, I sank down the hard length of him, slowly, inch by inch, delighted by the strangled cry of tortured relief that left him. The delicious feeling of fullness, of feeling his body joined with mine, was paradise.

His eyes slowly blinked open and his gaze devoured me whole. "My beautiful wife."

"My beautiful husband." I rocked against him and his lids lowered partway on a breathy gasp. "I want you like this always."

He grinned at that, a flirtatious smile while dragging my hips back and forth across his. "Not the sideshow our market needs, lass."

I rolled my eyes. "Not like *this*."

"Mmm . . ." he playfully moaned. "It wouldn't take much to convince me to be like *this* always."

I ground my hips harder and he swore through gritted teeth.

Stars, the power I had over him right now was addictive.

"I meant," I continued with a teasing smile, "I want you always prettied up for me."

"Aye, you do," he replied in a breathy whisper and I snorted. "Gods, Lena, the feel of you." His head tilted back and his eyes drifted close. "It's ecstasy."

"Not yet, pet."

I crawled off him with an impish look, but he was too desperate for me to play. With the athletic grace of a hunter, he rolled to his knees and snapped open his wings. The purple of his eyes darkened, a wild glint in his ravenous stare that shivered down me in excitement.

"Time to lose all control, husband."

His lips were on mine before I could blink.

Growling into our kiss, he slid deep inside me in one thunderous, hard thrust. Gods, his body . . . the powerful way he moved, over and over. Each obliterating swing of his hips flooded me with a singeing pleasure so hot, I became only breath and ash in his arms.

A week ago, when we made love for the first time, we hadn't almost lost each other. We didn't know the terror of losing everything. This ache, this longing, this desperation in the anguishing sweep of our lips and the yearning, grief-tinged rhythm of our bodies soothed lingering remnants of the anger and fear.

And I was quickly coming undone with the hungry way his lips trailed embers down my neck, the possessive way his hand cupped my breast. Sighing when the cool, silky strands of his hair began spilling loose from his knot to drape across my face.

Holy goddess, Rhylen was exquisite when feral for me.

The fingers I was digging into his shoulders relaxed and I lazily trailed my hands over the slope of his back to his glorious wings.

"Unravel for me," I whispered into his hair.

The tips of my fingers stroked down his silky feathers and Rhylen moaned in a full-body shudder. And dying stars, his sweet agony . . . it was one of the most erotic sounds I had ever heard. I stroked him again, mesmerized as my fingers glided along the ridges and velvety down of his wings.

"Feck . . ." His hips crashed into mine.

Candlelight limned the sensual dance of muscle down his arms, across his chest. The black strands of his long hair wildly fell around us. And his moans . . . gods, his moans were sensuous flames licking down my flushing body.

My fingers caressed the sensitive line of feathers once more.

And he broke.

But not in the way I expected.

The motion of his hips slowed to a tender rhythm. His breath quivered across my lips. And then I felt it. A tear slid from his cheek to mine. The wings I had been worshiping curled to cover us until only he surrounded me.

Cradling my cheek, his mouth reverently brushed across mine. He drew in another hiccuped breath as his nose slid along mine.

"Does my mate love me back?"

His voice cracked and so did my heart. Tears blurred my vision and I smiled against his mouth.

"She loves you with every breath in her body." My fingers traced the lines of his jaw. "She loves you more than every drop of water in the oceans, more than every leaf on every tree. She loves you endlessly, passionately."

The sensual arc of his hips was blissfully destroying me.

"Does she think me handsome?"

"You are so beautiful, Rhylen, she perishes at the barest sight of you."

His muscles trembled, his rhythm building faster, deeper, his breath hot on my skin.

"Will we marry?"

This was the question he had been asking me for years, hidden behind a different one. My eyes lifted to the Samhain ribbons fluttering above us and the moon-touched sky filled my veins with starlight.

Rhylen's romance was every love ballad ever written, every aching, poetic word bled onto the page.

And my heart sighed.

"I, Filena Moira Merrick Lonan," I spoke to him, to the Truth Telling Tree, "mate bind myself to you, Rhylen Lonan, my True Mate, for as long as my soul exists. I belong to you, husband, for now and for all eternity."

He gently wrapped a strand of my hair around his finger with a smile. "I, Rhylen Lonan, mate bind myself to you, Filena Moira Merrick Lonan, my True Mate, for as long as my soul exists. I put you above all others and will protect you with my life. I belong to you, wife, for now and for all eternity."

With a soft tug of my hair, his lips owned mine in a claiming so beautiful, so intimate, I fell apart to the soft beating of a thousand wings kissing my pulse.

And I was thirteen all over again, my pinkie curling around his in secret.

Fifteen and laughing with him over the frosting and crumbs stuck to Barry's whiskers.

Turning eighteen and shyly accepting a button he shyly gifted to me.

Halfway through twenty and risking everything to make Rhylen Lonan forever mine.

He was the purest magic, the pulse in my veins, the laughter in my soul.

My best friend.

My husband.

The one chosen by the gods to love me for all eternity. And falling stars, the way he loved me . . . no amount of cards or visions could ever predict a more perfect future than ours.

Epilogue
9 years, 5 months, 29 days later

FILENA LONAN

The cool night air kissed my flushing face. Stars, I could groan. The farther I walked away from the bonfire field, the less I felt like I had swallowed the sun. Beltane had begun an hour earlier. Our gates would open in thirty minutes for lovers to have first access to the courting rituals and fortune telling games.

Aye, an entire reveling night of moony-eyed girls, throwing apple blossom branches into fires, cups overflowing with sweet woodruff infused faerie wine, and weaving ribbons around a hawthorn pole in a courting dance . . . couples kissing everywhere one looked. Couples doing far more in whatever shadowed corner could be found.

With a full Flower Moon above and the veil the thinnest until Samhain, faeries grew drunk on fertility rituals this night and all the next day.

Goddess save me . . .

All I longed to do was hike my skirts up and eat my weight in cake while Rhylen massaged my feet. I placed a hand to my rounded belly and wrinkled my nose at Barry, who trotted at my side with his mate, Carry. I wanted to know what god giggled manically over the idea of sending Barry a Carry. And stars above, she was grumpier than him.

Which was why I adored her more.

Barry narrowed his yellow eyes my way. "Muffin Moo," I cooed in as syrupy a voice as my breathless state could muster, "you know no one compares to your squishy face, my fluffy red rain cloud."

He lifted his snout in a dismissive gesture and I cackled.

My divination tent finally came into view and I couldn't wait to sit and, well, sit.

Behind the black, blue, and purple striped tent was a wagon reserved for the children and anyone helping me throughout the night. And I needed the help.

Rhylen and I had four children with another on the way.

I swore, anytime my husband glanced my way, I was carrying his child again. He was just so pretty and I was just so ridiculously weak for him. His playful, boyish smile alone made me yearn for a hundred more of his bairns.

Our children were just as pretty as him too.

Outside in rocking chairs, Mam and Gran held our two-year-old twins, Ciana and Devlan. It was their first nap of the night and, like all baby birds, they preferred to rest under the wing of a caregiver.

I wistfully fingered the red curls of Devlan's hair. He was the only child of mine who had inherited my auburn tresses—only child *yet*. The wee one I carried still had another month before we met them.

Mam rubbed Dev's back with a soft smile and my heart sighed. Gran was quietly humming a lullaby to Ciana, who had fallen asleep with her sweet little face pressed into the crook of Gran's neck. Her soft blonde curls haloed around her head and fell around the tiny points of her ears.

"Ye should go sit down, minnow, before ye faint." Mam's smile was mischievous and I arched a brow. "Yer cheeks are flushed."

Mam was the *fáidhbhean* after each child was born and offered to be so this night as well. But it was Beltane, a fire festival for lovers. I couldn't ask my mam to endure hours and hours of matchmaking fortunes.

Gran's eyes twinkled. "There's a bit of moss in yer hair, Filly girl."

I placed a hand on my hip to hide my blush. "I added magic to the bonfires."

I really did. The embers would turn into softly glowing butterflies. But I also might have participated in *other* forms of Beltane magic too.

Burning suns, he really was so very pretty, I could weep.

Both Mam and Gran snickered and I rolled my eyes.

With a fluttering wave of my hand, I awkwardly spun on my heel—there was no graceful way to do anything in my condition, not even a dramatic exit.

I sighed.

The candles were already lit inside my tent when I slipped past the flowering hawthorn branches arching across the canvas opening—another Beltane tradition. Two plump, soft pillows had been placed to the back of my chair and I eagerly lowered to my seat, momentarily groaning in relief. Atop my table, beside dripping candles and sprigs of various herbs and flowers, were my mam's tree oracle cards and ogham rune staves and . . . my peony headdress and black veil.

Already I could feel that damn black bead falling in front of my eye. I should have tossed this costuming piece, but it was Rhylen's favorite. Glenna had replaced that bead and strand of beads a handful of times but it was possessed. Had I accidentally cursed it at some point?

Lloyd scampered up my leg and poked his head into my skirt pocket. Sheila rolled around and then squeezed past the smitten squirrel and waddled onto the few inches of leg still available. Alas, no lap these days. Lloyd climbed atop my belly to peer at Sheila with a little sigh, and his bushy gray tail tickled my face.

I scooped Lloyd up and placed him onto the floor, setting Sheila beside him. They'd hide beneath the tablecloth most of the night. My three other familiars, a badger and a mating pair of rabbits—*hilarious, gods*—rested beneath the wagon outside of my tent while Mam's familiar, a beautiful red cardinal, nested on top.

At the front of the tent, a little head of dark hair appeared before my eight-year-old son angled inside, balancing a girthy slice of cake. Farren Lonan concentrated on his task, his tongue peeking out at the side of his mouth as he strode toward my table. He looked so much like his da with dark purple eyes and chin-length, silky black hair.

Rhylen stood at the entry in a crisp linen shirt, the sleeves rolled to his elbows, a black and purple pinstriped vest fit snug against his muscled frame, with our four-year-old daughter in his arms. Well, four-and-a-half if you asked her. Brenlea was playing with one of Rhylen's beaded strands while singing to herself. He had placed a braid in her hair with matching beads yesterday and she had been gleefully showing everyone all evening. It was the pink satin bow in her black locks that made me smile, though. The ribbon he bought her soon after she was born.

Our eyes locked and my stomach swooped and dipped. A flirty smile tilted the corners of his mouth. Half an hour ago, those lips were worshiping me in the woods behind the bonfires. I could still feel his hands on my body, the starlight in my veins.

"You seek your fortune, Traveler?"

"Aye." Rhylen removed his silk top hat and walked in. "But I have no coins on me, *fáidhbhean*."

It was true. He rarely carried money on him.

"We have a slice of cake," Farren said and placed the confection topped with a hefty helping of berries on the table before me. I winked at him.

"Happy cake!" Brenlea added from Rhylen's arms.

"Sit, pets."

Rhylen lowered Brenlea after placing an object into her palm, then whispered in her ear. Our daughter dashed up to the table and opened her hand.

"Da found a button for me, Mammy."

Farren leaned over and whispered, "I offer you a button," and gestured with his head for her to repeat the correct words.

Brenlea's eyes rounded with delight. "I want that one." She pointed to a black button on Farren's blue vest.

Rhylen threw his head back with a loud laugh. Farren peered at me for help, then scrunched up his face and glared at his da. "She already took two buttons off my coat this week." Which only made Rhylen laugh more.

"Brennie Lo," I humorously drawled at our daughter, "you can't steal buttons off your brother's clothing." Brenlea played with the button in her fingers, her gray eyes bright in the way of Ravens when they collected a treasure. "Steal them off your da's clothing."

Rhylen tried to suppress his smile when the children peered at him and failed.

Farren lifted his chin. "Or Uncle Cian's."

"Oh aye," I said with a very serious nod of my head. "Steal all the buttons off Uncle Cian's clothing."

"But give a couple to George." Rhylen took Brenlea's hand and lifted the button to me. "So Uncle Cian suspects no mischief from you two."

I plucked Rhylen's gift to me from Brenlea's fingers and met his eyes . . . and nearly forgot the mechanics of breathing. Nineteen years I had known him and still he took my breath away.

"Two cards, pets," I said, forcing myself back into character. "One card for the cake and another for the button."

Rhylen lowered into the chair behind him, hanging his top hat off the back. "I will trade you a secret for a third card." Brenlea climbed into his lap and Farren scooted back onto his knee.

I leaned in, like I had hundreds of times with him. "I will trade."

"Glenna Merrick, have you heard of her?"

"The Raven Folk?"

"Aye, the very lass."

I shook my head. "Alas, I have not had the misfortune or pleasure, Traveler."

Brenlea and Farren giggled.

"Shame," he said with a twist of his lips. "Her brother is a fine looker, he is."

Dancing stars in a falling sky, that he was.

"Your secret, pet?"

Rhylen slid his gaze first to Farren and then to Brenlea, who was practically squealing in anticipation. "Auntie Glenna feeds George more cookies than Uncle Cian but tells Uncle Cian that he gets two times more cookies than George."

Brenlea gasped in genuine horror for Uncle Cian, who was her favorite person in the whole world. Farren, however, smirked, siding with Auntie Glenna, who was his favorite person in the whole world.

"My turn!" our daughter said with a wiggling grin.

In a melodramatically mysterious voice, I asked, "What question do you seek, pet?"

"Does a snail sneeze?"

Farren's brow furrowed, as if considering her question, then twisted toward his sister. "You want to know the future of a snail if they sneeze?" His lips pinched together. "You worry the snail might get hurt?"

Without missing a beat, Brenlea asked, "Mammy, do snails hurt their feelings?"

Rhylen was struggling to keep a straight face.

"Their own feelings?" Farren asked her, exasperated. "You want the fortune of a snail who might hurt their own feelings when sneezing?"

"Aye," she chirped.

The scowl between his dark brows deepened. Looking up at Rhylen, who quickly schooled his face, Farren mumbled, "Brennie

516

snuck another slice of happy cake when Auntie wasn't looking." Brenlea smiled waggishly at Rhylen, wrinkling her nose, and he lost it—again.

At this point, my husband was wiping away tears. "Well, *fáidhbhean*," he miraculously managed in his wheezing laughter, "tell us this snail's future."

I had to bite the inside of my cheek to keep myself in character. Our daughter was pure sunshine and chaos—like my brother. Locking eyes with Brenlea, I pulled a card and she clapped her hands, leaning forward when I flipped it.

Beith, the ogham rune for Birch.

The card of renewal and rejuvenation.

"I *see* a snail," I said in a dramatic voice. "Her shell is a dainty shade of butter yellow." Brenlea's eyes widened in excitement. "She loves flowers but, alas, she's allergic to pollen." Our daughter's smile fell. "When she sneezes, though? It blows the pollen onto the wings of butterflies so they can fly." Brenlea placed her little hand to her heart. "This makes the snail happy, it does." I paused a beat and smiled at her. "Aye, as happy as eating two slices of Auntie Glenna's happy cake."

Brenlea took Farren's hand in hers. "I love happy snail stories."

Farren curiously stared at his sister's still-sticky fingers in his, then me. "My turn."

"What question do you seek, pet?"

He tucked strands of black hair behind his ear and blinked, his brows still drawn together. "Will I marry one day?"

I wasn't expecting that question and caught myself before the surprise showed.

Embarrassed, he ducked his head and added, "I thought that

was the right question to ask tonight."

Rhylen pulled Farren close and kissed his head. "Aye, it's a perfect question on Beltane." My husband's eyes slowly met mine. *"Fáidhbhean, will Farren's mate love him back?"*

The adoring, melodic softness of Rhylen's voice, the familiar question he asked me stirred my magic.

Drawing in a slow breath, I flipped the next card.

Úr, the ogham rune for Heather.

The card of lovers.

My mind faded into the tent's shadow and the ferry docks beneath Seren appeared in my vision.

> *A girl around twenty or so with long, wavy, forest green hair, pale freckled skin, and dark, earthen brown eyes approaches a gent in a sharp suit and chin-length black hair falling gracefully around the points of his ears. She looks around at all the passengers loading the train to the eastern cities and the ferry to Seren. Nibbling on her lower lip, she bumps into the male and steals a locket from his pocket.*
>
> *The gent turns and they both freeze.*
>
> *His purple eyes roam over her face curiously. "Are you all right, miss?"*
>
> *"Aye," she says, a bit breathless, then quickly stashes the locket up her sleeve. "Just a bit wobbly in these new boots."*

"Dangerous things, new boots. Allow me." He holds out his arm. "The ferry . . . ?"

"The train." She accepts his arm and peers around the docks nervously. The arm he holds is the one concealing the locket. And she doesn't have a train ticket. With a forced smile, she bobs her head and says, "Kind of you, love."

"Farren Lonan." He smiles back and my heart twists. It is so much like Rhylen's smile. "And you are, miss?"

"Annie Ó Dair." His smile falters a moment but she ignores the strange reaction. They walk along the train in charged silence and she eventually points to a car. "This one."

He helps her up the steps, a mischievous glint in his eyes. "Hope we bump into each other again . . . Annie."

He steps backward and lifts the locket. Her heart stills. With a wink, he turns on his heel and fades into a puff of steam.

She waits a few seconds, her breath coming in quick, before stepping off the train and disappearing into the crowd. For a full candlemark, she searches for the faerie boy with the manners and clothing of an eastern

city gent but who steals like a common street thief—
and finds him.

He peers over his shoulder at her, a flirtatious half-
smile playing on his lips, tips his top hat, and then
strolls into The Night Market.

The tent pulled back into view and I blinked.

Oh she was adorable.

And clever trouble too.

Annie Ó Dair was perfect for our family and I couldn't wait to meet her one day.

Farren studied me with pinched brows. My son . . . stars, my beating heart. He grew into a fine, handsome lad. A spitting image of his da in many ways. I had never had a vision about one of my children, not until this moment. And Rhylen could tell. A muscle moved along his jaw and his black brows pushed together—like Farren's.

How much should I share with my son? This was new territory for me.

A knowing tug pulled in my gut and my muscles relaxed. There was a reason his smile had faltered and why he had baited her to follow him into The Night Market.

Lifting my eyes to Farren, I smiled. "Aye, one day you'll marry, Farlee Lo. To a girl named Annie Ó Dair. The day she steals a locket from your pocket, she'll also steal your heart."

"Annie?" His face twists up. Farren shrugged a second later, removing his hand from his sister's and tucking another lose strand of black hair behind his ear.

Romance wasn't usually a top priority for an eight-year-old boy. But he was also a Raven Folk male ruled by courting magic and it was Beltane. I didn't know when those first stirrings began.

"Da's turn!" Brenlea said with a little hop on his lap. A matching smile appeared on Farren's face. These two always looked forward to this moment.

Arching a brow at Rhylen, I asked, "What question do you seek, pet?"

Playfully narrowing his eyes, he held my gaze and, in a straight tone, asked, "Will I have children?"

Brenlea and Farren giggled.

Still holding his eyes, I melted into his warm gaze. He loved being a da, doted on his family endlessly, cherished their faerie child antics and their mortal complexities.

I wasn't surprised when I flipped over *Fearn*, the ogham rune for Alder.

The Alder card favored him most, always had.

The Tree of Ravens, the card that wept blood for sap and spontaneously burst into flame. The tree the wild fae had used for making their shields too.

Rhylen's fire heart would burn for his blood kin until his soul's dying breath. He was our sword and shield.

"Aye," I finally answered. "You have wagons full of children, but they're songbirds by day and feral frogs by night." Our son and daughter beamed. "They hop all over Caledona Wood, croaking cookie recipes to the stars who then whisper them to Glenna. Magical cookie recipes that make faerie raccoons snore bubbles in their sleep." My eyes slid to Barry, who had inched closer to my slice of cake when he thought I wasn't looking. "And make faerie foxes detest the taste of cake."

Barry chuffed and I swore he rolled his eyes at me.

Rhylen grinned. "*Feral* frogs?"

"Aye, if any see your children before sunrise, Rhylen Lonan, before they return to their songbird forms, they'll transform into a lily pad pond for your feral frog bairns to croak from the next night."

Brenlea croaked and Farren croaked back.

"My wee feral frogs," Rhylen said in a singsong voice, "time to croak at the stars beside Nan and Gran. The gates open in minutes."

The children leapt from Rhylen's lap and hopped to the tent opening, Barry and Carry right behind them. Muffin Moo watched our children like a wee fussy mam. He'd return once they were safely beside Gran.

Rhylen laughed quietly under his breath as he lazily stretched to a stand and walked around the table. We could hear Brenlea and Farren croaking the entire way to the wagon.

Kneeling at my feet, Rhylen cradled my belly and whispered, "A *stór*," to our wee one with a kiss. *My treasure*. "You kick like a feral frog too." The boyish tilt to his smile swooned in my thrumming pulse as he leaned up and kissed me next. "My wee feral swine wife."

His nose playfully caressed mine as we smiled. Then he captured my mouth in a sensual slow dance of lips. The magic of the Flower Moon still smoldered inside me, igniting into flame at his tender touch. Only an hour ago, he had lowered me to a bed of moss and quickly made love to me while the Beltane fires limned his wings in amber light. We had to sneak in hurried moments together these days.

But I wouldn't trade our life for anything.

Reluctantly, he pulled away and caressed the lavender ribbon I wore in my hair for Beltane. "I'm so in love with you, Filly Lo."

"I'm madly in love with you, Rhy."

He pressed a gentle kiss to the heated pulse in my neck, then stood. In a few steps, he fetched his top hat from the back of his chair and tilted the brim low on his forehead before striding toward the exit. He paused at the canvas opening and peered over his shoulder at me, our eyes locked for a single heady beat of my besotted heart. Then he shifted into a raven and flew into the moonlit night.

Gods, this faerie boy . . . he consumed me.

The End

But also not *not* the end.

(keep flipping, you'll see what I mean)

Thank You Reader

Thank you, my wee faerie reader, for adventuring across the pages with Rhylen and Filena. I will forever be your fangirl if you took a few seconds to leave a 1-2 sentence review. It doesn't have to be fancy. Just something to make the Amazon robots happy. Because when the Amazon robots are happy, I can write more books. Believe it or not, reviews keep an author in business.

Want more from the Bound by Ravens world? Of course you do!

Darlin'... Cian and Glenna will be getting their own bonus content novella this spring called, THE HEARTBREAK SHOW. You can bet it will be full of humor, wit, chaos, kissing competitions, raccoon mischief, and more. The ebook will be available for free to newsletter subscribers or available in paperback on my Etsy.

Also, if you've read the prequel short novel, BOUND BY RAVENS, then you'll be delighted to know that Kalen Kelly's book is up next, titled LAST GREENWOOD WILDS. And like the title suggests, Kalen will be adventuring into The Wilds to save the wild fae from Carran's military by bootlegging them across the border into a neighboring kingdom. Filena might have seen a vision about him. Just saying. <<whispers>> *Slender Bow of Rain* . . . Of course, no story about Kalen would be complete without his best mate, Finn Brannon, who will make an appearance or two or three. Or complete without a faerie cat and a stowaway tavern girl.

To get first peeks at these upcoming books, the character art, scene snippets, and more, be sure to join:

Newsletter

Jesikah's
Forest Faeries

MoonTree
Readers

The Night Market
Amazon

* Tips hat to you *

Glossary of all Things

PRONUNCIATIONS

Filena — fill-en-nuh (from Old Gaelic *filí*, which means "seer" and "ena" which means "little fire")

Cian — key-ahn (From Irish *Cían*, meaning "enduring one." Cian is a warrior god from Irish mythology, the son of the goddess Danu, who dressed as a woman to steal back his magical cow from an enemy king and fell in love with and married the daughter of said king while dressed as a woman. He is best known as the father of Lugh, the powerful sun god with two pet ravens, and grandfather of Cú Chulainn, one of the greatest warriors in Irish mythology. Cian was slain by the three sons of Tuireann while hiding in the form of a pig.

Rhylen — rye-lyn (from Irish Ríalann, a derivative of "Rían," which translates to "little king" and "lann" is Old Gaelic for "land." In Old English, "Rylan" means "rye fields")

Glenna — glen-uh (from Gaelic *gleann* and the name Gleanna, which means "glen")

Lonan — low-nun (from Irish *Lonán*, meaning "little blackbird")

Bryok — bree-yock (from Old Gaelic, meaning "prince")

Fiachna — fee-yah-ck-nah (from Irish, meaning "raven")

Fáiléanna — fail-een-ah (from Irish, "fáil" which means "destiny" and "éanna" which means "bird-like")

Cillian — kill-ee-ahn (from Irish, meaning "from the church" or "bright-headed")

Fáidhbhean — foy-van (from Irish, meaning "seer" or "wise woman")

Cailleach — kaul-yawk (from Irish, meaning "witch, crone")

Torc Triath — tork tree-at (Irish cognate of Twrch Trwyth, the Welsh boar of Arthurian Legend)

Áine — Awn-ya (Irish: Anne, she is the goddess of summer, light, love, as well as goddess of the faeries in Irish mythology)

A stór — ah-store (from Irish, meaning "treasure," an endearment that also means "darling" or "dear")

A stór mo chroí — ah-store muh-cree (from Irish, meaning "treasure of my heart")

Mo shíorghrá — muh-heer-grawh (from Irish, meaning "my eternal love")

MAGIC SYSTEMS

BOUND BY RAVENS — a bargain struck between two people in agreed upon ownership, either as mates or as master and indentured slave. The arrangement is bound by the oldest magic of the fae during a time when the fae couldn't lie (a magic traced back to the two wood ravens owned by the sun god Lugh). When the bargain is struck, a raven mark appears on the wrist as a seal. A maximum of two seals are present: one for a mate, one if an indentured slave or as the master of an indentured slave, regardless of how many one may own.

COERCION MAGIC — the ability to glamour a mortal mind, either to compel them into obedience or to trick with an illusion. Faeries can't compel each other, but they can fall for one another's illusion tricks.

CURSE — invoking bad luck on another in certain conditions that are honored by the gods (breaking bargains, harming ancients, committing certain acts of violence against an innocent). However, fae witches (a cailleach) can curse in every way imaginable and Raven Folk elders can curse with limited coercion magic over fellow Raven Folk.

ELDER MAGIC — magic that is gifted directly from the gods to Raven Folk top gov rank individuals, unlike fae magic which is a part of their being from conception. Elder magic is elemental at its base. But it also allows limited coercion over other faeries, such as glamouring the mind to not see or hear another person. This coercion bonus was effective magic during wars long ago when the Kingdom of Carran was run entirely by wild fae.

FAE MAGIC — depending on faerie race, it can include coercion, illusions, shifting into an animal form, or be entirely elemental.

FAE MARKED — an injection from a fae's canines into a mortal's neck that imparts a piece of their magic. This can allow the fae to enthrall the mortal to control or just simply to mark their territory with their magical signature. Either way, other fae can smell the magical signature on the marked mortal, making that mortal less appealing to them. A mortal can only be marked once while a fae can mark numerous mortals. When a fae injects a piece of their magic, though, they'll never get that magic back, making them less powerful than before. A fae can mark another's bonded mate.

SEER — an ability to see the future with or without divination instruments.

TRANSMUTATION MAGIC — the ability to alter an object into something entirely different. Such as turning lead into gold. Or like turning a trespassing mortal into a skunk ornament.

TRUE MATES — a match made by the gods in the Otherworld, the equivalent to soulmates.

SOCIAL CLASSES

FELLOE — lowest Caravan fae class. Called "felly" for short, they get last choice in food, wear hand-me-downs, and are not allowed to look those of a higher class in the eyes, unless challenging. The class name comes from a fellow, the inside of a wagon wheel's rim that the spokes fit into, a part that comes close to eating the dirt of the road. To the Caravan fae, the spokes represent the community.

MIDDLE RANK — the largest Caravan fae class. They receive the largest share of food, can afford new clothing, and often run the merchant tables and wagons.

GOVS — the royalty and elders of the Caravan tribe. The elders are made up of Raven Folk of all ages who are appointed by the gods to lead. The chieftain is an elder, but the heir is not. Elders receive elemental and coercion magic from the gods to help judge and protect the tribes.

Thank You Friends

No book is complete without a grooming tent of attendants. There's soooo much that goes into prettying up a book for a reader and THE NIGHT MARKET wouldn't be anywhere near as swoony without the help of my Raven brothers and sisters.

THE MOO CREW

Andra Prewett, Jessica Maass, Jill Bridgeman, Kelly Stepp, Kim Gerstenschlager, Lana Ringoot, Michelle Downing, Sarah Carner, Sarah Jordan, Tyffany Hackett, and Victoria Cascarelli . . . my forest friend familiars, thanks for making Rhylen's and Filena's story full of magic. Your protection wards and pockets full of happiness and courage helped me not only cross the finish line but also made this story sparkle and shine. <<gifts you each endless buttons and pretty rocks>>

Additional thanks to Sarah Jordan for naming our favorite grumpy, cake-stealing fox, Barry.

And a million thanks to my Dublin friend, Deirdre Reidy, for helping me with my *Gaeilge* (aka Irish). Any and all errors are mine.

AUTHOR BETA READERS

Robin D. Mahle, Tyffany Hackett, and Hanna Sandvig . . . thank you for taking my story under your wings and lending me your clever fae storytelling craft to make Rhylen's and Filena's romantic journey less of a faerie riddle and more of a faerie tale. <<gives you each girthy slices of comfort cake with extra handfuls of berries>>

TATER MCTOT

Kelly Stepp, my darlin' potato faerie assistant, thank you for your endless supply of memes, spicy pointy-eared lad art, and fun book chat. I have nothing but endless gratitude for how you care for my publishing company, branding, and . . . me. <<gives you pretty raven "angel" wings>>

KATE ANDERSON

You are the editing wind beneath my WIPs raven wings . . . thanks for ensuring the grammar in each sentence soars smoothly so the readers can fly through the pages with as few typo turbulence incidents as possible. Your memes and coloring pages feed my soul too. <<gives you elder magic to protect the faerie books>>

MOONTREE FAERIE QUEENS

Alisha Klapheke, Melanie Karsak, Elle Madison, and

Robin D. Mahle, your endless bookish support, laughs, encouragements, and guidance as we navigate the faerie markets of indie publishing together is everything. I adore you four to itty bitty pieces and couldn't ask for better book witch sisters. <<gives you each a cackle that frightens Amazon's superstitious algorithm from mischief>>

JESIKAH'S FAERIE ARC READERS

My magical faerie market tribe . . . reviews and social media recs are an author's bread and butter. I can't express my gratitude enough, not only for gifting me your precious time and energy to my story, but also making sure others hear about it too. <<gives you a fashionable outfit hand selected by George>>

MY READERS

You wee darlin's . . . this author is your forever fangirl. Thank you for celebrating my stories and characters. I am continually humbled and moved by your support. Your comments and shares and reviews and cards you send me are *everything*. There will never be enough words to share how grateful I am to you. <<gives you a bottomless plate of romantical forbidden cheese>>

And now, I'm off to write LAST GREENWOOD WILDS . . .

More Books

BY JESIKAH SUNDIN

THE BIODOME CHRONICLES

ECO-DYSOTOPIAN FAERIE TALE

She is locked inside an experimental world.
He has never met the girl who haunts his dreams.
A chilling secret forever binds their lives together.

 LEGACY
ELEMENTS
TRANSITIONS
GAMEMASTER

THE EALDSPELL CYCLE

EPIC FAERIE TALES WITH A HISTORICAL FANTASY TWIST

Dreams are dangerous . . .
Unless she unlocks the powers of her mind.
He fights his Otherworld shadow self.
And with only fae magic to re-spin their tales.

 OF DREAMS AND SHADOWS
OF HEART AND STONE
OF THORNS AND CURSES

A BOUND BY RAVENS NOVEL
NEW ADULT FAE FANTASY ROANCE

*A world of thieves, caravans, faerie markets, bootleggers
and mob bosses, all run by the Raven Folk.*

BOUND BY RAVENS
THE NIGHT MARKET
LAST GREENWOOD WILDS

THE KNIGHTS OF CAERLEON

AN ARTHURIAN LEGEND REVERSE HAREM FANTASY
Under J. Sundin

*Four cursed knights. One warrior princess.
A faerie sword that binds their lives together.*

THE FIFTH KNIGHT
THE THIRD CURSE
THE FIRST GWENEVERE

A HARTWOOD FALLS ROMANCE
CONTEMPORARY ROMANCES

Under Jae Dawson

MOONLIGHT AND BELLADONNA
HEARTBEATS AND ROSES SNOW-
FLAKES AND HOLLY

Etsy Shop
MOONTREE BOOKS

**A dash of moon magic. A pinch of tree laughter.
Stories whispered on the wind.**

Hello Etsy wayfarers! Welcome to my bookish shop.
When not slouched behind a computer, cursing the keyboard gods, you can find me frolicking through the woods
with a camera around my neck or on the Comic Con
circuit as MoonTree Books. Have fun poking around at
my wares.

BOOKISH WARES FOR SALE

- Signed Paperbacks
- Limited Edition hardbacks
- Book Swag
- Book Boxes
- Custom Character Candles

Scan the QR code to visit my store.

Have questions? Message me on Etsy and we'll figure out
your next fantasy adventure together.

JESIKAH SUNDIN is a multi-award winning Fae Romantasy, Dystopian Punk Lit, and Historical Fantasy writer, a mom of three nerdlets, a faeriecore and elfpunk geek, tree hugger, nature photographer, and a helpless romantic who married her insta-love high school sweetheart. In addition to her family, she shares her home in Seattle, Washington with a rambunctious husky-chi and a collection of Doc Martens boots. She is addicted to coffee, GIFs, memes, potatoes, cheese, kilts, mossy forests, eyeliner on men, and artsy indie alt rock.

www.jesikahsundin.com

Made in the USA
Middletown, DE
27 April 2024